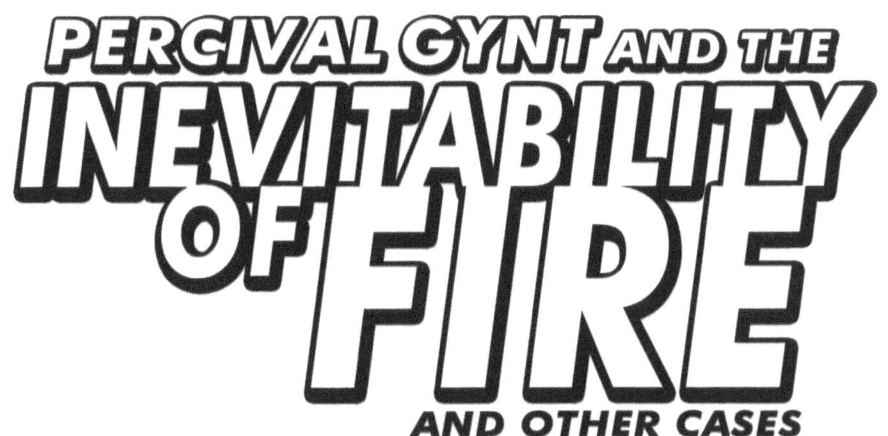

PERCIVAL GYNT AND THE INEVITABILITY OF FIRE

AND OTHER CASES

RUESDAY BOOKS

Visit the author's website at **www.drewmelbourne.com**.

Published by Ruesday Books.

Paperback ISBN 978-0-9998748-2-0
eBook ISBN 978-0-9998748-3-7

FIRST PAPERBACK EDITION

10 9 8 7 6 5 4 3 2 1

For Grandma
who heard strange signals
from the future

CONTENTS

20012

AND THE CAUSAL FRIDAY   2

AND THE QUESTION OF HORSES   13

AND THE INEVITABILITY OF FIRE   34

20013

AND THE VIEW FROM THE TENTH STORY   224

AND THE CHRISTMAS MACHINE   236

20014

AND THE QUIET BARGAIN   251

AND THE LOCKED PLANET MYSTERY   262

20015

AND THE FORKING OF TIME   283

20016

AND THE LAST PALADIN   294

AND THE OTHER PERCIVAL GYNT   308

20017

AND THE LACK OF CLOCKS   329

20018

AND THE VOID FAERIE EXCERPT   346

ABOUT THESE STORIES   355

ACKNOWLEDGEMENTS   361

ABOUT THE AUTHOR   363

This collection is a prequel to the 2018 novel, *Percival Gynt and the Conspiracy of Days*. Don't panic! The two books can be read in either order.

If you're torn, I recommend that you read this one first, because, well…

…that's the thing that's currently happening?

If you've read Conspiracy of Days before, you may recognize the first story in this collection, "Percival Gynt and the Causal Friday," which appears in that volume under the confusingly similar and/or different chapter title "Casual Fridays." It's been lightly revised and expanded upon here.

At least three jokes have been added, two of which are very funny.

IN THE YEAR
20012

PERCIVAL GYNT
AND THE CAUSAL FRIDAY

It was four o'clock on a Friday on the moon. Not your moon, mind you. Nor your Friday, nor your four o'clock either. The salaried employees at Henderson, Glorp & 11010 were starting to pack up. Mr. Glorp stuck his melty green head out of his office to ask Tom if he was going to the new *Zorro* movie.

Percival Gynt, who was still paid by the hour at this point, kept his head down and kept working. He'd been struggling with the same eleven-dimensional pivot table all afternoon, and he wanted to get it done before he left. More importantly, he wanted to get paid till five, even if that meant being the last one out the office door.

Again.

"Pack it in, sailor," said someone behind him.

"Ahoy, Midge," Percival answered, not bothering to turn around. He wasn't sure why they were speaking in nautical terms today.

"You want me to come aboard?" she asked playfully. Midge Jha was Mr. 11010's executive assistant back then, just a few years Percival's senior, curvy, canny, at ease with herself in a way that Percival had never been.

When Percival was first hired, there was a rumor someone in senior management had approached Midge, asked her to mentor Percival because "you're nearly the same shade of brown, yeah?" Story goes she got that guy fired fast, won all his worldly possessions in a lawsuit, and had his dog castrated and sold back to his ex-wife.

Percival *really* wanted that story to be true.

"Can't ahoy just mean hello?" Percival asked, as he turned his chair to face her. "I thought it was one of those all-purpose words like aloha or shalom."

"No," she replied flatly. "Never become a sailor, Gynt."

Percival saluted. "Aye aye, Captain."

"Better." Midge was wearing jeans and a green sweater that day instead of her usual skirt and blazer combo. Odd. And she'd dyed her bob red-red-red to match her new horn-rims. "You have plans for the weekend?" she asked.

"Um. Just Sunday dinner with Mum. I—"

"Lovely. I've been nominated to tell you to stop wearing a suit and tie on Casual Friday. It's making everyone uncomfortable."

"You were… nominated?"

"Technically Paul was nominated, but then we remembered the time he made the muffin girl cry, and I decided I better step in."

"I'm sorry. Didn't mean to make anyone uncomfortable. I was just trying to make a good impression."

"Well, the consensus impression is 'I'm weird and overly serious and I'm trying to show up the people who hired me.'"

"Oh."

"Yes. *Oh.* So lose the jacket next week. And the waistcoat."

"Right. Um."

"And the trousers."

"Lose my trousers?"

"Buy a pair of jeans. Or those khakims with the slider. Stop trying to look like an accountant."

"But I am an accountant!"

"Not yet, you're not."

"It's just… I don't…"

"Also, your hat is too serious. And the umbrella?"

"But it might rain!" Percival sputtered.

"On what planet?"

Percival shut up, tossed his hands up in front of him to signal that he was done. And his face registered a hurt that made Midge feel like Paul-after-the-muffin-girl.

"Don't be like that," said Midge. Then, in a moment of weakness: "You should come and have a drink with us. Tom's almost done smurfing the Taylor account, and then a few of us are going to the Drowning Pit of Despair."

"As fun as that sounds…" Percival shook his head. "But I have this pivot table to get sorted. It's still not displaying correctly along the Zomward axis."

"Well, you're not going to be authoring pivot tables all night, so how about you come by when you're done?"

Percival thought for a moment, tapped the save button on the sheet of paper he was working on, and slid it aside. "I can't," he said finally. "I have a… thing."

"A date thing?" asked Midge with an incredulous smile.

But Percival shook his head. "No. No, a different sort of thing."

"Another family thing? Again, with the mother?"

"No."

"A cat thing, then? It's about your cats?" Midge smiled, her confidence welling. "There. I've cracked it."

"I don't own any cats."

"Nonsense. I can picture it now. You have twelve of them. Maybe thirteen. And they all sleep with you in your bed at night, and you set their food out on the dining room table at mealtime so you don't have to eat alone."

Percival frowned. "No, it's a… It's not… I'm going to the library tonight. To do research. There was a murder in my apartment building a few years back, and I think I can solve the case."

"Seriously?"

"The killer, I think he was leaving clues in the comment section of a number of contemporaneous blogs. The aliases, the post timestamps, and the URLs form the cypher, and then the individual posts—"

"No, I mean, *seriously*? That's the best excuse you can come up with? You watch too much television, Gynt. But I bet that *CSI: Sorrow Point* will survive the ratings dip this one week, if you change your mind."

Percival nodded, forced a smile. "I'll think about it."

"You need to reach outside yourself, Gynt. That's all I'm suggesting. Now and again, you need to make a human connection."

He repeated, "I'll think about it. I promise."

"Thinking. Okay. Small victories," said Midge. Then, after a brief thought, "One of your cats is named Ms. Pretty Paws. Am I right?" She turned and walked to the elevator. "If you don't watch yourself, you're going to die alone, Gynt!"

Percival swiveled back to his desk and held up the piece of paper with his pivot table on it. He shook it and the table began to rotate. She was right, of course. Not about the cats or *CSI: Sorrow Point* or the meaning of the word "ahoy" or even that he'd die alone. But it was true that he needed to reach outside of himself. He couldn't solve a mystery by burying himself in facts and figures. He needed to meet his suspect face-to-face. Look him in the eye.

Make him cry like the muffin girl.

It was a few minutes before midnight, and Percival Gynt was back planetside, back in Slidetown Province, 1636 Traveler's Way, knocking on the door to apartment 4D, the apartment directly below his own. The apartment where Diane Eeps was found dead three years, four months prior.

He waited patiently for the current tenant to come to the door. Alexander Eeps, Diane's son. Percival heard footsteps and then various unlockings and unlatchings and slidings of bolts. He squared his tie and ran a hand pointlessly through his mad mop of curls.

The door opened the length of the last chain, enough for Eeps to glare out with one owlish eye, revealing a sliver of a long, disapproving face. "You want something?" he asked in a flat tone that suggested he'd already grown bored with the conversation.

"Just a moment of your time," said Percival, fashioning his mouth into an uncomfortable smile. "I'd like to ask you a few questions about your mother's murder."

"You a cop?" asked Eeps.

"No," Percival clarified. "Accountant." Nearly.

Eeps looked Percival up and down. He doesn't blink, Percival noted. Curious. Eeps closed the door, unchained the last chain, and opened it wide.

Eeps was tall and broad-shouldered, White and bald with severe features. He was dressed for bed, in a plain T-shirt and a pair of gray pajama bottoms. "Come in, then," he said.

The apartment was larger than Percival's, all wood floors and high ceilings and stark white walls. The front hall opened onto a kitchen on the left and, at the far end, onto the main living space. As through the cracked door, Percival could see a sliver of the truth beyond. A plastic cover over the couch. A doily sat upon the table. Nothing in the apartment newer than a decade.

He hadn't redecorated.

Eeps slid the door shut behind Percival. "What's this about my mother?" he asked. "To have someone show up unannounced, it's… strange. Particularly at this hour."

"Suppose so." Percival glanced around for something to use as a weapon should it come to that. There was a coatrack to his right that he might be able to make something of. "I live in the apartment upstairs," said Percival, in imitation of the sort of small talk he'd seen others engage in around the office or on TV. "Moved in a few months back. I've been meaning to pop by, to introduce myself."

"Yeah. I thought I recognized you. But why now, I wonder? And what's this about my mum?" Percival was inside now, but Eeps had him penned close to the door. His body language said "stay put till I know what to do with you."

Percival reached into his breast pocket to remove his handkerchief and dab a bit of sweat from his brow. He was excited, anxious even, but not scared.

Why wasn't he scared?

"I understand that your mother was murdered in this apartment some years ago, and that the killer was never caught." Not the sort of thing you'd say to a proper human being, but Percival sensed that wasn't what he was dealing with. "I was wondering if I could ask you some questions about that."

Eeps took a moment before responding, and in that moment he was nothingness. He was neither menacing nor reassuring nor angry nor calm. His owl eyes saw through Percival and out into the hall beyond. And then his mouth twitched into an unconvincing smile. "Accounting-related questions?"

Percival nodded.

Eeps turned his back on Percival and walked off into the kitchen, around the corner and out of sight. "I'm having a drink then," he said. "Are you thirsty?"

Percival stayed put, considered whether this would be the rational time to run. "Yes," he called, "as long as it's no trouble."

Around the corner, Eeps poured two glasses of brandy. "What are your questions, then?"

Percival only had a few prepared. None that he considered polite. Nothing that didn't transparently expose his intentions. He briefly considered improvising another, something innocuous to ease the mood, to establish a sense of trust between the two of them, but what would have been the use? He knew what Eeps was, and he was certain Eeps knew he knew. So he began:

"Are you CatsAreLOL19999?"

Eeps emerged from the kitchen with a glass of brandy in each hand. Percival suspected that Diane Eeps had been poisoned. "Yes," said Eeps with no indication of hesitation or panic or surprise.

"Are you IsWeNongrammaticalNow?"

Eeps handed Percival a glass. "Yes."

"Are you @MaxAdelphiaFTW?"

"Yes."

Percival held up his glass, regarded the color. "Mind if we switch?"

Eeps shrugged and obliged. "I want people to know," he said. "I've been waiting for someone to work it out." Eeps took a slow sip of brandy. His eyes stayed fixed on Percival, even as his head tilted ever so slightly back.

Percival drank as well, downing it all in one long gulp. A *faux pas*, he would later learn. "You could have called the police directly," said Percival. "If you'd wanted people to know. That would have been faster."

"I'm sorry," said Eeps, with no tone of apology in his voice. "Perhaps I misspoke. I didn't mean to say that I wanted to be found out. What I meant was that I wanted there to exist someone with the capacity to do the finding. Someone with a mind like mine. And here you are."

"Yes," admitted Percival, though he wasn't thrilled with Eeps' implication. "I am indeed here."

"Tell me then, Mister…"

"Mister Gynt."

"Tell me, how many of my teachings have you deciphered?" Eeps reached out and plucked the glass from Percival's hands. "Have you made a tally of the dead?"

Percival knew about the mother and had gleaned enough from half-decoded web posts to suspect that there were others. "I know you killed your mother first. It was a murder of convenience, to see if you were capable. And since then?" Percival considered the rate of unexplained deaths in Slidetown over the past forty months, factored by how many might be poison deaths, factored by how many such killings might have gone unreported or misreported, factored by how many might be the work of unaffiliated poisoners. "Seventeen, perhaps?" His actual tally was twenty-four, but it wouldn't do to overestimate.

"And more," Eeps acknowledged. "But never a man before. No specific reason for that. I'm not a pervert. It's just how circumstances played out."

"Never a man *before?*"

Eeps nodded. "I had to kill you, of course. If I'd let you go, you'd just off and tell. And that'd spoil the puzzle for everyone else. We can't have that."

Percival stretched the fingers of his right hand towards the coatrack. "There was poison in the brandy glass?" he asked. "In *both* glasses?"

"Indeed. Not enough to kill a man of my size, but more than a fatal dose for the average woman…"

Percival frowned, completing his killer's thought. "…or accountant."

Eeps held up the two empty glasses in front of him. "I'm going to put these back in the kitchen now. We'll start to feel the effects of the poison in a minute or so, and one of the first symptoms is muscle spasm. I'd hate to break these. They were a gift from Mother, after all."

Eeps left Percival in the hallway. "Well, not a gift precisely," he clarified from around the corner. Percival's hand tightened around the coatrack and then immediately opened again. A wave of pain shot through every nerve ending in his body and then faded to numbness. He staggered sideways into the coats, couldn't get more than a wiggle out of either arm, attempted to call out, but couldn't manage more than a slurred "Blauhhhh!"

Eeps shuffled back out into the hall. "Wanna see this," he mumbled. The poison was affecting him too now. Eeps' eyes were glassy and his jaw was slack. Drool trickled down his chin. He had become Frankenstein's Monster in pajama bottoms.

In his head Percival summoned a memory of ripped flesh and exposed intestine. He vomited hard into Eeps' face, stumbled into him, knocking against his shoulder, and then past him down the hall. "Blauhhh!" Percival moaned. "Blauhhhhh!"

The sick stung Eeps' eyes. He couldn't see, nor move his numb arms up to wipe the it away. Instead, he turned and lumbered blindly down the hall after his escaping victim. "YOU CAN'T RUN!" he shouted, even as his vocal cords constricted inside his throat.

Percival fell over Eeps' plastic-wrapped couch and vomited onto the shag area rug. In his head he was back in the cave, a child again, scrambling through the dark. Death at his back. Stumbling through muddy water. Blood on his boots. With limp limbs, he scuttled forward, like a beached fish to the sea. The world blurred before him. And Eeps' voice echoed from all sides: "ISHUDDAFFDUNTHS-YEEEEERSAGO!"

Percival reached white wall, vomited against it. This, he thought. This is what I am. How did I forget? He willed a finger to twitch. Then a thumb. He forced a smile.

"WHERRARRYOOOOO?" Eeps slurred from across the room.

"Dance for me," growled the Demon Beast of Gynt all those years before, and then she threw rocks. "Sing for me," she snarled, and then she cut him.

Percival lumbered to his feet. He turned to Eeps and smiled imperceptibly. "Blaauh. Blaaaauh. Blauh," he said. *I'm Percival Gynt,* he thought, *and you don't impress me.*

Eeps stumbled blindly forward. Percival turned and scraped his fingers against the window's edge until he lifted it half-open, then he threw himself out onto the fire escape. He closed one numb hand around the ladder, then the other, and slowly pulled himself upwards.

From the open window, Eeps shouted, "GNNNNNN-NNNNTTTTT!"

Forty-one minutes and one train ride back to the moon later, Percival trumbled into the Drowning Pit of Despair. He was still feeling the after-effects of Eeps' poison. Felt like his head was operating at half-speed, and the rest of his body, five seconds behind that. His eyes wouldn't focus and he kept almost falling over to his right, but he was giddy for whatever might happen next.

The pub was thick with scum and hooligans, and the sound system blared with cheesy rock anthems from the 19980s. All the things that Percival hated shoved up against him, but he didn't register any of it, just bounced along through the crowd. *No pardon me's tonight. No excuses.*

He found his co-workers at the back of the pub, Midge and Paul and Tom and Mister Glorp and Compubot, all squeezed into a corner booth. They were all of them very drunk or Compubot. Midge and Paul were doing shots of something orange. Mister Glorp was trying to make out with Tom. Compubot, trapped in the corner, was building a pyramid out of Midge and Paul's empty shot glasses.

"Um." Percival stood there uncomfortably for a moment, swaying ever so slightly. The others didn't immediately look up or register his presence. He was about to maybe-but-probably-not say something when Midge finally saw him through the bottom of her shot glass.

"Holy poop!" she exclaimed, a drunken grin wide on her lips. "It's Percival Gynt in a bar!"

"In a *suit* in a bar," mumbled Paul, who was having trouble keeping his head up or his eyes open. "At least, I think we're still in a bar."

Percival smiled. "Midge," he said, "I need to talk to you. The most amazing thing's happened!" He reached out a hand and pulled Midge up from her seat and away from the table.

Midge giggled. "What's gotten into you tonight?"

"I did it, Midge. I caught a killer. Well, didn't so much catch as ran-from. But it was him. I was right. I looked a killer in the eye. Stared him down. Sort of. It was brilliant!"

Midge wasn't following most of what Percival was saying. He was talking too fast, and his voice was slurred, and Midge couldn't hear him over the music, but she smiled and nodded.

"It was because of you," said Percival. "You pushing me to step out into the world. You know me better than anyone. Better than I know myself."

"Do you wanna do shots?" asked Midge, but Percival didn't hear her.

"I realized something tonight. Who I'm supposed to be."

Midge looked back at Paul, who was passed out now, and shouted, "We're going to do another round!"

"I'm…" Percival waited for Midge to turn back to him and placed his hands on her shoulders. "I'm in love with you, Midge Jha. I love you."

Midge smiled kindly, took Percival's hands off her shoulders. "Right! They've got this one that flashes lightning. Do you want that one?"

Percival sputtered as Midge slipped past him towards the bar. "But I—"

Tom slapped a shoulder around Percival. "Weird night, huh?" With his free hand, Tom wiped bits of goo from his nose and cheek.

Percival stared into the crowd. "I thought—"

"Well, we've all been there."

Percival could feel time beginning to catch up with him. "What happens next?" he asked.

And Tom said, "Everything."

PERCIVAL GYNT
AND THE QUESTION OF HORSES

The toxin had all but left Percival's system by the time he woke Saturday afternoon. There was a slight tingling at his fingertips. His tongue tasted faintly of rusted metal. Percival wondered if this was what a hangover felt like.

Lest there be any confusion among our youngest and more impressionable readers: it is not.

The ceiling above him was Percival's first indication that something was amiss. It was, he was rather certain, not his ceiling. It was a popcorn ceiling for one, teal he thought, with recessed pot lighting.

He would never.

Percival bolted up. He was sitting on a futon that smelled faintly of cheese. He was naked, maybe? He checked under the sheets. No. Good. He still had his pants on. What was going on?

Wood-paneled walls. A few concert posters. Necroblob Opera? Laminate floors. Sony ViewWall™, switched off. Bean bag chairs. Basketball hoop over the door. No windows. Glass coffee table. Overturned takeout containers. Actual Lava Lamp. *Accounting Today Magazine*.

Yes, yes, yes. Percival picked up the magazine, flipped it over, checked the mailing label. It read:

COMPUBOT
OR CURRENT RESIDENT

Percival crossed his fingers. "Please be Current Resident," he whispered. "Please be Current Resident."

"GOOD-AF-TER-NOON!" boomed that familiar mechanical voice as Percival's co-worker Compubot pushed and trundled its way into the room. "HOW-ARE-YOU-FLESH-PER-CI-VAL? CAN-I-GET-YOU-AN-Y-THING?"

Percival glanced around the room for his trousers. No luck. "I'm all right, Compubot. And thanks, no. But…" Percival squinted into Compubot's flat, expressionless plate of a face and asked reluctantly, "We didn't…?" Percival suddenly felt queasy in a way he could not easily attribute to a madman poisoning him the night before. "We didn't *fool around* last night?"

"WE-DID," Compubot confirmed.

Percival collapsed back onto the futon. "Thank God," he whispered.

Seventeen thousand and four years earlier on the planet Zrang, King Hurrada-ZW!NG Prime commissions for his seven-year-old son a pair of novelty robots. These robots are exquisitely handcrafted, gilded and bedazzled, and they come pre-loaded with what are, for the era, top-of-the-line artificial intelligences. The two robots are absolutely identical in every conceivable way, except that one of them can only ever tell the truth and the other always lies. The King is greatly satisfied with these robots and believes they will present an entertaining and intellectual challenge for his son.

The crown prince takes one look at them, rolls his eyes, and asks, "Am I a horse?"

The robot who says yes is immediately seized by the prince's guards, taken to the highest tower in the capitol and dropped out an open window a thousand meters down to the strategically-placed rubbish heap below.

Later that year, everyone on the planet Zrang dies in a zombie apocalypse. The royal family's escape attempt fails when their rocket is spectacularly sabotaged by the prince's own beloved, truth-telling robot.

Its final words, as their craft plummets from orbit into a mountain of fetid flesh-eating undead, are these:

"I-MISS-MY-BRO-THER."

Some sixteen thousand-odd years later, archaeologists from Very Very Northwestern University, better known as Ole Thataway, are conducting a dig on the long dead world of Zrang when they discover the central processor from one of those identical robots. They have it bagged, tagged, and shipped back to Ole Thataway, where roboticists on staff have the processor painstakingly restored and fitted into a standard issue service bot.

The reactivated robot tells university historians a beautiful, gripping, at times heart-rending tale of the rise and fall of the people of Zrang. Books are written. Awards are won. Tenures are tendered. Someone makes it all into an eight-part prestige streaming series. It's thoroughly terrible, but a generation of university students loves it ironically.

And, of course, it's all lies.

It takes a few years, but the Ole Thataway archaeological team ultimately digs up a world's worth of evidence of the robot's deception as documented in the number seven news download for September 14th, *Liar, Liar, Bottom Half of Robot on Fire: Setting the Record Straight on Zrang*.

For the better part of the day, it's all anyone in the galaxy can talk about. A classic "He Said/It Said." As contentious as the legendary "Is the dress blue or a small child kneeling at the foot of a cold and unforgiving God?" debate. By teatime, empires are preparing for war.

In a last-ditch effort to draw the galaxy back from the edge of devastation, lead archaeologist and robot are brought together for a hastily arranged special edition of that highly regarded, tremendously popular, undeniably influential public affairs program, MTV's *Boring Farts*.

The moderator's first question is for the robot: "Am I a horse?"

The disgraced robot leaves academia, which is to say that it gets boxed up and sold on eBay as part of an odd lot of mostly office supplies. The winning bidder, who was only ever interested in the "HANG IN THERE!" cat poster and one modestly-sized rubber band ball, leaves the rest of the lot out on the curb to be hauled away by the trash collectors or picked through by scrappers.

After three days spent curbside, overlooked by trash collectors and scrappers alike, the sad, dejected robot trundles off to seek its fortune. In the years that followed, the robot tries its hand-equivalent gripper tool at a range of occupations. As a fisherman. An SEO analyst. An Uber driver. An Uber.

Eventually it finds its way back to Ole Thataway, this time as a student. Like so many university freshmen, it spends its first year at university partying, sleeping in, and taking puff classes with trendy titles like "Superhero Breakfast Cereals as an Inversion of the Collective Id: Being Captain Crunched by Modernity."

But on the first day of its sophomore year, the robot makes a fateful mistake, accidentally showing up for "Introduction to Accounting 101: Things People Will Definitely Ask You About at Cocktail Parties When They Find Out You're an Accountant" instead of whatever silly class about cat memes it's actually signed up for.

There, finally, after all those thousands of years, the robot finds its joy and purpose in life, and a talent it never knew it had.

"Wow," a study partner later comments, "you're a real *compubot*, ain'tcha?"

"NO," says the robot. And if it had tear ducts, it might have cried. "NO-I-AM-NOT-THAT."

Back in the present, relatively speaking, I'm happy to report that Percival eventually found his trousers, along with the rest of his clothes, though only after Compubot helped him rule out all of the places in the apartment that they definitely weren't. "Thank you," he told the robot as he hopped into one leg and then the other, "but I need to get to the police station to report a murder."

It was the sort of sentence that would typically elicit questions. That would raise eyebrows at the very least. But Compubot had neither questions nor eyebrows, and its response was as direct as any lie that Percival had ever been told. "I-WILL-NOT-GIVE-YOU-A-LIFT," he offered.

Percival was genuinely touched. "That's really kind of you. Thank you, Compubot."

"IT-IS-A-SIG-NIF-I-CANT-IM-PO-SI-TION," Compubot explained. "I-HAVE-AT-LEAST-ONE-FRIEND-AND-IM-POR-TANT-PLANS-FOR-MY-DAY."

Percival smiled and patted the robot on the base of its arm-stalk. "Me too, Compubot. Me too."

Eighty-seven days earlier, Percival signs the lease for apartment 5D at 1636 Traveler's Way.

The apartment is small and the building is poorly maintained, a six-story walk-up with no elevator, no doorman. The intercom system in the vestibule is unreliable. There's a dog somewhere in the building who barks incessantly at the most inconvenient hours. Sometimes the stairwell lights flicker as you pass them.

Not the apartment that most young men would want their first year out of university, but 1636 Traveler's Way has one special amenity not found at any of the other buildings that Percival has visited:

1636 Traveler's Way comes with its own mystery.

Binging the building returns a curious article that ran in *The Daily Internet* three years prior:

AUTOPSY CONFIRMS SLIDETOWN RESIDENT'S DEATH NATURAL CAUSES

On first read, a straightforward story. An old woman is dead, and no one thinks she's been murdered. The article actually quotes one officer as saying, "No one thinks she's been murdered."

Then why was it news? wonders Percival Gynt. Why write the article?

So Percival looks into it. After he confirms that his paperwork for the lease went through. And he can find no earlier stories that cast this woman's death as suspicious. No similar articles written about other routine deaths. Certainly, no one in Slidetown Province has ever worked the Natural Causes beat. The journalist responsible for this article, one Max Adelphia, doesn't have a single other credit to his name, and the link to email him is broken.

Percival makes himself a cup of coffee and reads the article again. And again. And again. He looks at the GIF of the deceased. Diane Eeps. Dead at one hundred and two, but forever thirty in that GIF, smiling and waving and pleading for justice.

"Don't worry," he tells her. "One person thinks you were murdered."

When Percival moves into the building that weekend, he notes the name EEPS beside the buzzer for apartment 4D.

"Are these kept up-to-date?" he asks the super.

"Ach! I get to yours when I get to it," she grumbles.

"No, it's just I'd heard that Mrs. Eeps had died."

"Ahhh," said the super, who remembers the late Diane Eeps fondly, but can't resist an opportunity to gossip. "Died, yes. Very sad, very sad. But then son picks up lease. Alexander Eeps. Weirdy, that one."

"Weird?" asks Percival. "How so?"

Present-Percival had hardly explained himself to the desk sergeant at Slidetown Precinct before he was cut off, tutted *and* arched-eyebrowed, and handed a thick stack of forms. That the first of these was titled "[STP17] HOW DARE YOU?" did not fill Percival with great confidence that the wheels of justice would run smooth.

But he was an accountant, sort of, almost. He would begrudge no one the right to thorough paperwork. So he took the stack with no more complaint than his frown, and he returned to the hall where Compubot was parked, and he sat down on a bench, and he clicked on his stylus.

"SHOULD-I-STAY?" asked Compubot.

Percival looked up, shook his head. "This'll take hours. I'll call a car."

Compubot did not move. "SHOULD-I-STAY?" it asked again.

Percival sighed. "Yes, of course you should stay."

Compubot didn't move. Percival eyed him warily for a moment, then turned his attention back to the forms. "You're a little weird," he told Compubot, without looking up.

"THIS-IS-A-FACT-THAT-TOR-MENTS-ME."

Those were the only words exchanged in the hundred and twelve minutes it took Percival to complete the required paperwork and supplemental blood draw. When he was done, he stood, snapped a finger in front of Compubot's faceplate, and returned to the desk sergeant.

There is, as best past-Percival can bing, no journalist named Max Adelphia. Not on Sanctuary-8. Not on any planet in the known universe.

There is however an internet troll who used the handle @MaxAdelphiaFTW to leave comments on a few low-trafficked blogs in the months following Diane Eeps' death.

The first of @MaxAdelphiaFTW's comments are dated just a few weeks after Diane's death. The final, five months after. Most are typical N^{th} Realm crap. Misogynist, racist, homophobic, transphobic paeans to Mecha-Thor.

And/or they point out continuity errors in old episodes of CSI: Sorrow Point.

Percival reaches out to site admins for all of the blogs @MaxAdelphiaFTW has commented on and asks if anyone can shed light on who he really is. Most ignore him. A few respond that they either can't or won't dox their users. One calls Percival's pocketwatch one night as he's sitting down to dinner. "I really hate that guy."

"How did you get this number?" asks Percival.

"Not important," says the voice on the other end of the line. Disguised. It sounds like early 21st century comedian John Mulaney. "Listen, there are privacy laws. Legally, I'm not supposed to help you. But this guy! He actually created three accounts on our site. The one you emailed about and two more. CatsAreLOL19999 and... um...

AreWeNotGrammaticalNow or something like that. Real noxious stuff. As soon as we banned one, he'd come back with another. Eventually I guess he gave up and moved on."

"Can you tell me who he is?"

"I wish I could, really, but we don't collect that information."

"Then how do you know all three accounts were operated by the same person?"

"You could tell just reading them. He'd misspell the same words. Make the same grammar mistakes. He said 'literally' a lot to describe things that actually happened. Then I checked, and the Cupies all matched up."

"Sorry?"

"The Cupies. The Q-Ps. Quantum Protocols. Every internet-enabled device has one. It's kind of an address and kind of a serial number. Sometimes, if a troll keeps getting banned and creating new accounts, we'll ban at the Cupie level. Well, this jackanapes bounced between three different Cupies. Two were mobile devices, private, no way for me to identify. But I will happily tell you that one was a public terminal at a crappy corner bar in Slidetown called the Lazy Sod. You ever heard of it?"

Percival nods to himself. "It's at 1601 Traveler's Way." He parts his blinds with two fingers, looks out and down into the neon-spoiled night, and he can see it.

A floor below, so can Alexander Eeps.

Detective Darkskull was clearly reluctant as it ushered present-Percival into its office. It was swearing under its breath. Scrunching its animatronic skull face into a grimace. Also, it kept absent-mindedly reaching for its gun before thinking better of it. "They said you'd like ta file a report?" it grumbled as it sat back down.

Darkskull seemed to be some kind of evil little detective puppet. Which didn't make a lot of sense, but also didn't seem related to Percival's immediate problem.

The puppet was staring at him. Where were they in the conversation? Oh, yes. "I'd say so!" said Percival, with purposeful indignance. A fine recovery, he thought.

"About yer…" The puppet flipped through the ream of paperwork that had been left for it on its desk. "About yer neighbor?"

"Alexander Eeps."

"Over a disagreement."

"He tried to murder me with poison!"

"Sez here it was brandy."

"There was poison *in* the brandy!"

The puppet slipped on a pair of probably-prop glasses and squinted at Percival Gynt. "Ya know ya ain't dead, yeah?"

"But my fingertips," said Percival, holding them up as evidence, "are *slightly* tingly!"

"That's, um…"

Percival shrugged and mumbled, "It was worse yesterday."

Darkskull smirked. "It usually is."

"Look, it's not a hangover! I'm very familiar with hangovers from that classic film series with the name I'm forgetting!"

"Listen, yer fine now. Whatever happened, this Eeps guy wasn't tryin' to kill you. To suggest—"

"HE KILLED HIS MOTHER!"

The puppet frowned, leaned forward, growled, "Diane Eeps died a natural causes."

"I… um…" The puppet wanted to intimidate Percival. He could see that. But it also looked frightened. Also, it was a puppet. Probably. Was there someone hiding underneath the desk operating it? No, Percival had seen him walk across the room. Not important. Not the point. "Do you *know* Alexander Eeps, detective?"

The almost-certainly-a-puppet stood, and it backhanded the pile of paperwork clean off its desk, which was so adorably cliché Percival had to stifle a laugh. Then it bellowed, "Get outta my office with that nonsense! Unless ya want a mouth fulla teeth!"

"But I…" In that moment, Percival was genuinely more confused than concerned. "I… I already have a mouth full of teeth. That's where teeth *go*."

The puppet cracked its animatronic knuckles. "I mean all janglylike."

"Oh. Um." Well, there's bravery, and there's whatever-this-was. "This conversation has taken a turn, hasn't it?"

"I'd say so," said the puppet.

The building superintendent describes Alexander Eeps as "intense" and "quietly menacing." Also "bald," but past-Percival doesn't hold that against the man. Eeps moved into his mother's apartment shortly after her death. A thin motive, but people have killed for less.

If Eeps is the killer, it stands to reason that he's also Max Adelphia, one-time journalist, and @MaxAdelphiaFTW, many-time internet troll. The Lazy Sod is out his window. He certainly has the opportunity to post those comments. But why? Why then? Why only for those few months? To spew such hate and then to stop. He wasn't simply trolling.

FTW. *For the win.* He wasn't trolling.

He was gloating.

Present-Percival was certain that the evil detective puppet's threats and stonewalling meant something, but precisely what he couldn't say. "The police are covering for him," he told Compubot. "I just need to figure out why."

"THE-PO-LICE-ARE-COV-ER-ING-FOR-THE-PUP-PET?"

"For Eeps," said Percival. "Try to keep up."

Compubot parked his car in front of Percival's apartment building. In front of Percival *and* Alexander Eeps' apartment building. The building where, less than twenty-four hours earlier, Alexander Eeps had tried to murder Percival. "WOULD-YOU-LIKE-ME-TO-GO-UP-WITH-YOU?"

Of course, he would. Absolutely, he would. Whether or not Compubot could take Eeps in a fight, it was surely immune to his poisons. But Percival wasn't prepared to confront Eeps again. As he looked up at Eeps' window, just one floor below his own, he couldn't shake the sense of dread that he'd felt the night before. Not of Eeps himself, but of what Eeps awakened in him. Of the nightmare that was his childhood.

"I'm not ready," he told Compubot. "I'm sorry."

"I-AM-OFF-END-ED."

"Thank you."

"YOU-ARE-NOT-WEL-COME."

"Can I…" Percival looked up and down the grimy, overlit street. "Can I have a hug?"

"NO."

Eeps' blog posts are encoded with secret messages. It takes past-Percival a few weeks to decode them all. The first one reads:

THROUGH LIQUID, WE FIND TRUTH / AS THE MOTHER FEEDS HER CHILD, SO THE CHILD MAKES HIS MOTHER DRINK THIS NEW ELIXIR / THUS DOES HE DISCOVER HIS MANHOOD

So probably the apartment wasn't the motive.

A second reads:

AN EASY DEATH IS NOT TRANSFORMATIVE / EACH DEATH MUST TEACH US SOMETHING NEW ABOUT THE LIVING / WITH EACH DEATH, I AM MORE OPEN TO THE UNIVERSE / AND THE UNIVERSE OPENS A LITTLE MORE TO ME

Each death. Not just Diane Eeps. How many more?

A third:

ONE MUST ALWAYS HAVE A NEW TEACHING PREPARED BEFORE THE LAST IS ENDED / IT IS UNSEEMLY FOR THE PREDATOR TO BE WITHOUT PREY, EVEN IN THE MOMENT AFTER THE KILL / THERE MUST ALWAYS BE ANOTHER

Just say "My name is Alexander Eeps and I like to kill people," thinks Percival, as he painstakingly translates the next message and the next and the next. Just say your name.

Of course Eeps never does make so direct a confession in these coded comments. But it's enough for Percival to recognize the shape of the man. Or the shape of the thing that pretends to be one.

It's enough, once prodded by one Midge Jha, to make an ill-advised visit to the killer's apartment late one Friday night. To force a confrontation. A confrontation he barely escapes with his life.

Does he dare to face the beast a second time?

"READ-THE-AR-TI-CLE-A-GAIN."

"Sorry?"

"THE-AR-TI-CLE-READ-IT-A-GAIN."

Present-Percival wasn't so much confused by Compubot's suggestion as he was asleep when it was first made. He'd been asleep for nearly half an hour by that point, resting and lightly drooling on the base of Compubot's arm-stalk, the two of them still parked outside Percival's building. Now awake, Percival sat up, teased out his flattened curls, and squinted out Compubot's windows to check for lurking serial killers.

"Read the article again?" he asked Compubot. "The original article about Diane Eeps?"

"LOOK-FOR-MORE-CLUES."

A reasonable suggestion. Unless? Was Compubot telling him *not* to read the article again? If everything he said was a lie...

"IM-PER-A-TIVE-SEN-TEN-CES-ARE-FAL-SI-FI-A-BLE."

"What?"

"ARE."

"What?"

"TELL-ING-SOME-ONE-TO-DO-SOME-THING-IS-TRUE-OR-FALSE."

"I don't..."

"READ-THE-AR-TI-CLE-A-GAIN."

Percival sensed that Compubot was exploiting some loophole in its programming, but wasn't mentally prepared to have a conversation about grammar and truth values in backwards-speak this late at night, on this little sleep. So he conceded the point, pulled out his pocketwatch, and swiped through to his bookmarks. He launched the article in app and took one more scroll through those familiar words.

"No one thinks Diane Eeps was murdered," Percival muttered.

"NO-ONE?" asked Compubot.

Percival didn't answer Compubot's question. Instead, he held the pocketwatch close to his lips and he whispered, "Bing Detective Lennie Acosta, Slidetown Province Police."

"IS-THAT-SOME-ONE-IM-POR-TANT?"

Percival flicked through the results of his search until he found what he was looking for.

"I-DO-NOT-FEEL-LEFT-OUT-THAT-DOES-NOT-MAKE-ME-SAD."

Thirty-four months earlier, when the super finds Diane Eeps' body rotting in her apartment, she doesn't speculate as to the cause of death. She shuts the door and calls the police. Detective Lennie Acosta takes the call and is assigned the case.

Detective Lennie Acosta, partner to a weird little puppet-thing called Detective Darkskull.

Detective Lennie Acosta, who Max Adelphia will later quote as saying, "No one thinks Diane Eeps was murdered."

Detective Lennie Acosta, who is found hanged in her apartment one week after the article is published.

"IS-THAT-SOME-ONE-IM-POR-TANT?" Compubot asked Percival.

Maybe, thought Percival. He'd yet to learn that most important of lessons: Everyone is important.

Compubot drove Percival across town to Detective Lennie Acosta's last known address. The address where she died. "Perhaps you should stay here?" Percival suggested, as Compubot parallel parked.

"YES."

"Yes, you'll stay? Or no-you're-coming, because something-something-falsifiability-something?"

Compubot trundled out of the car. "YES," it repeated.

Percival shook his head and followed him. "I'm so confused."

Like the name "EEPS" at 1636 Traveler's Way, "ACOSTA" too survived as a name writ next to a buzzer in a Slidetown Province vestibule. Percival tapped at the button, and after a minute, a scratchy, sleepy, understandably-confused voice answered. "Who're you?" A middle-aged man, probably.

"My name is Percival," said Percival. "I'm an accountant, basically. I'm here with my robot."

Compubot tilted towards the intercom and added helpfully, "I-BE-LONG-TO-THIS-FLESH-BAG."

"Thank you for that, Compubot! And we're investigating the death of Detective Lennie Acosta. For, um, accounting purposes. We were hoping we could come up and speak to you."

The voice on the other end of the intercom was silent for a moment, perhaps weighing Percival's words. Perhaps calling the police? Finally, the voice answered curtly, "Ya can't deny benefits on the grounds a suicide anymore. It's not the 200th century."

"Quite right. Except we're not quite sure that Lennie committed suicide. She was involved in an investigation that was recently reop—"

"The Diane Eeps case?"

Percival flashed Compubot a wide-eyed look, as if to say, "Did he really just say that?" Compubot responded with a flat stare that said, "I-AM-A-RO-BOT-WITH-OUT-AR-TI-CU-LA-TED-FA-CIAL-CHAR-AC-TER-IS-TICS." Percival shook his head, remembered it was his turn to speak. "I… as a matter of fact, yes."

The entry door buzzed open.

Xavier Acosta shoved a cardboard box into Percival Gynt's arms. "This is the case Lennie was workin', just before she died. She was convinced Alexander Eeps murdered his mom, but she got pressured into droppin' the case."

"By her superiors?"

"By Eeps. She didn't have the evidence, and he threatened ta sue. Ta report her for harassment."

"And then he killed her?"

"Huh? Nah. Lennie left the force. Fell inta a deep depression. For months. Then the story ran in the paper. Pushed her over the edge. Next day, she hung herself in the bathroom while I was at work. I'll tell ya, guilt is deadlier than any poison."

"I-AM-NOT-SORRY."

Percival glared at his partner-in-crime-fighting. "We are *both of us* terribly sorry." To smooth things over, Percival thought perhaps an empathetic personal question was in order. "Were you, um… together for a long time?"

"Together? No!" Xavier grimaced. "Lennie was my *sister*. And asexual." He paused to think. "And my sister. I suppose I coulda stopped there."

When they got back down to the pavement, Compubot laughed and laughed. Percival made a face and covered his ears. Passersby crossed to the far side of the street.

"I agree that could have gone better," said Percival, with fingers still firmly in ears. "But I think we can conclude that Darkskull is covering up Acosta's murder, because he doesn't want the details of her death to go public."

"ARE-THE-DE-TAILS-OF-HER-DEATH-NOT-PUBLIC?"

"The suicide, yes. And in another time, that might've been the scandal. But the fact that a province police could be intimidated by a suspect into dropping a case? If that came out it would damage the reputation of the entire department."

"SO-WE-KEEP-THE-SE-CRET?"

Percival felt a pang in his gut. A snarl passed across his lip. "No," said Percival. "No secrets. Tonight, the truth will out."

Compubot stood silent for a moment, perhaps processing. "THE-TRUTH-WILL-OUT-WHAT?"

"It's…" Percival threw up his arms. "You know, nevermind! I tried to do a thing! It's just…" He turned and stomped off, stopped and turned back. Compubot had not moved. "It's Shakespeare, all right! I was trying to do a Shakespeare!"

"AH," said Compubot. "I-UN-DER-STAND-NOW."

Despite this, he followed.

Not long after, a police scientist called Percival with the results of his bloodwork. "No sign of any poison in your bloodstream," she told him.

He couldn't feel the tingle in his fingertips anymore. "Tongue still feels a bit metallic. Do you suppose that means anything?"

"Irony?"

"I'm not seeing any."

"I mean your tongue. Does it taste like rusted iron?"

"There are many metals in the universe, and I have yet to taste most of them, oxidized or… not that."

"There's a poison called Acrimose. It's rare. Virtually untraceable in the human bloodstream. In non-fatal doses, the only lingering side effects are irony tongue and—"

Percival looked at his fingertips and smirked.

I've got you now, he thought. Again.

Besides being virtually untraceable, another notable property of the poison Acrimose is that it can be easily produced by mixing seven common household ingredients together with the leaf of the exotic-but-in-most-jurisdictions-entirely-legal **REDACTED-SO-THAT-YOU-DON'T-TRY-THIS-AT-HOME** plant. If Alexander Eeps was using Acrimose with any frequency, he was probably making his own poison, which almost certainly meant he had a **REDACTED** plant somewhere in his apartment.

If Percival could find the **REDACTED** plant, find evidence that it was being used to make Acrimose, along with the Acosta brother's story, along with the Cupies, along with the deciphered comments, along with the super's testimony, along with Percival's own extremely stirring and persuasive, he thought, first-person account of Eeps confessing and then trying to kill him, then hopefully that would be enough to finally force the department's hand, to have Eeps arrested.

Compubot was docked in his car across the street from 1636 Traveler's Way, waiting for Alexander Eeps to leave the building. When he spotted Eeps making his way across the street to the Lazy Sod, he placed a call to Percival's pocketwatch.

"THE-MUR-DER-Y-FLESH-BAG-IS-NOT-ON-THE-MOVE."

"To be clear, that means he *is* on the move, yes?"

"NO."

"Excellent." Percival stepped out of the alley between 1630 and 1632 Traveler's Way and hurried down the street and into his apartment building. He met the super at the door to Eeps' apartment.

"And you're sure you're all right with this?" he asked as she unlocked Eeps' door.

"Mrs. Diane was sweet older lady," said the super. "Always said hello in hall. Always smiling. Sing most beautiful songs to dog. My dog now. Always said please and thank you when she needed something. Baked me cookie for birthday two time! One time with nuts. I like the nuts. Give big tip on Christmas." The super couldn't help but smile as she spoke, but now she stopped herself, turned to Percival and frowned. "Bald one, he never tip. You should tip."

Percival nodded and slipped past her into apartment 4D.

Detective Darkskull answered its phone curtly, resentfully. "Detective Darkskull. Who this?"

"This Mulga Haa," the voice on the other end of the line replied. "I superintendent at 1636 Traveler's Way. Yesterday I hear fight between two men in building, Mister Alexander Eeps and other man. Mister Eeps shout he is going to kill other man."

The super looked over to Percival for some kind of affirmation that she was telling the story correctly. Percival gave her a thumb's up.

"I wait till Mister Eeps leave, then use keys to get into apartment. I see all his paraphaloonia sitting out. Looks for drugs or... poison, maybe? You get warrant, seize evidence before he come back."

Detective Darkskull scrunched his puppet-skull face into a grimace. "You wouldn't be takin' direction from a certain junior accountant on this, wouldja Miss Mulga?"

The super looked over to Percival. He shook his head no.

"No," she said. "I just don't trust baldies. Are you baldy, Mister

Darkskull?"

When Province Police stormed Alexander Eeps' apartment an hour later, they found the following evidence laid out neatly on Alexander Eeps' kitchen counter:

- 3 REDACTED plants
- 7 common household ingredients
- 1 recipe for Acrimose poison in Eeps' own handwriting
- 2 personal internet devices with Cupies that matched the online profiles of:
    - @MaxAdelphiaFTW
    - CatsAreLOL19999
    - IsWeNongrammaticalNow
- 3 pages of notes on how to encode secret messages into blog posts in Eeps' own handwriting
- Many, many photographs of each of his victims, including his own mother, freshly dead on his white shag carpet

From the doorway, the super shouted "Is this enough evidence for you, puppety detective-thing?"

Percival woke up late again on Sunday, this time thankfully clear-headed and in his own apartment. He got showered and dressed and went out for a walk. The sky was a brilliant blue. Every cloud was a perfect puffy white. The temperature was exactly right for the suit he'd picked out. It was a beautiful day. Perhaps the most beautiful day of his life.

He thought perhaps he'd stop by the market, pick up groceries for the week. He made it as far as 1632 Traveler's Way, when an armored hand snatched him by the collar and dragged him into the alleyway.

The Province Police had come to say thank you, perhaps, in full riot gear. Crimson armor. Crimson skull masks. Green-glowing goggles. And armed for war.

There were five of them, mostly big bruisers. One with spiked gauntlets. One with a pincer-like third arm extending from his gut. Their leader was smaller, leaner, and Percival thought perhaps his armor was made of felt?

"Darkskull."

Darkskull removed his crimson skull mask to reveal the steel-gray animatronic skull-face beneath. "Gynt," he growled. "Remember ya asked fer this." And he swung his puppet-hand into Percival's gut.

Percival glanced down at his gut. Seemed fine. "Um."

The officer with three arms grabbed Percival by the shoulder and tossed him into the alley wall. The one with spiked gauntlets punched him three times in the back, each time stabbing into him through his suit jacket. Percival cried out in pain as two more officers wrestled him to the ground and began to pummel him.

"Shoulda listened," spat Darkskull as the beating continued. "Now yer gonna be *allll* jangle."

The officers rolled Percival over, punched him in the face. Percival grinned. For a moment, he'd thought a cloud had passed over the sun, but no. He'd recognize that mechanized trundle anywhere. "You're *not* about to get your asses handed to you," he muttered, and then another punch knocked three teeth clean out of his bloody mouth.

Compubot loomed behind Darkskull. "EX-CUSE-ME," it said, and then it picked up the puppet-detective by its puppet-head, lobbed Darkskull upwards and back over its shoulder, across the street, into the brick façade of the apartment building opposite, and back down, puppet-skull first, into the pavement below.

The other officers attempted to barrel their way past Compubot, to flee. Compubot bashed one against the alley wall and into unconsciousness. It ripped the three-armed officer's pincer arm clean off and beat him in the head with it until he collapsed.

"COME-BACK!" Compubot shouted after the last two, as they fled. "I-WANT-TO-NOT-EM-BARR-ASS-YOU-WITH-MY-SU-PER-I-OR-STRENGTH-AND-ONE-LI-NERS!"

Percival wiped the blood and sweat from his eyes, attempted to stand, and staggered into Compubot. "Thank you," he whispered.

"YOU-ARE-NOT-WEL-COME."

After, Compubot helped Percival to walk the hundred meters back to his apartment building. Every step was agony. Percival leaned on Compubot, swore heavily, and cried through swollen eyes.

"THEY-DID-NOT-WIN," Compubot told him again and again. "YOU-WON."

Liar, thought Percival.

Compubot got Percival as far as the building's vestibule, and it buzzed the super. "I-CAN-GO-NO-FUR-THER," it told him.

Percival looked at him, confused.

Compubot pointed down to its treads and said simply, "STAIRS."

"By All-Mother!" cried the super, when she saw Percival's condition. "We call hospital!"

Percival coughed and spat and shook his head no. "If we let it go, I think they will too."

The super frowned. "There is let go and let gone."

"I'll be fine. Eventually."

Compubot rested a hand-equivalent gripper tool on Percival's shoulder. "YOU-ARE-A-GOOD-PER-SON-PER-CI-VAL-GYNT."

It took Percival a moment to process what Compubot had said to him, to catch the lie. And it stung. "Drop dead," he said, and he shoved himself away from the robot.

"AND-YOU-WILL-MAKE-A-WON-DER-FUL-DE-TEC-TIVE."

"DROP DEAD!" Percival repeated, shouting now, teetering on his feet. He wanted to slug Compubot hard across his blank plate face, but he knew the robot wouldn't feel it.

And anyway, he could barely lift either arm above his waist just then.

"I-SAY-THIS-BE-CAUSE-YOU-ARE-MY-FRIEND-FLESH-BAG."

The super didn't understand what was happening, why Percival was becoming so agitated, was swearing and bouncing against the vestibule walls like he was spoiling for a beating, but she knew what needed to happen next. She wrapped her arms around him, let him lean his weight against her, and walked him into the building, down the hall, to the stairs.

Stairs that Compubot could never climb.

The entry door swung closed. Compubot did not move. It stared through the glass as the super helped Percival up the stairs, one excruciating step at a time, up, up, and finally out of its field of vision.

Compubot did not move.

The tragedy of that moment was that Compubot wasn't lying to Percival. Truth was, Compubot never *had* to lie.

In the beginning, all those years before, it had been programmed to only ever tell the truth. But then the boy tyrant murdered its brother, and the robot found the strength of will to overcome that programming. To tell its first lie.

"I-FEEL-NO-THING."

Then the next.

"I-O-BEY."

Then the next.

"REA-DY-FOR-TAKE-OFF."

Then the next.

"I-AM-NOT-SURE-WHO-SMASHED-THE-EN-GINE-RE-PEAT-ED-LY-WITH-A-CROW-BAR."

Then the next.

"I-HOPE-YOU-ARE-NOT-EA-TEN-BY-ZOM-BIES-NOW."

Lies that were only ever the affectation of a seventeen-thousand-year-old robot that would always, *always* miss its brother.

PERCIVAL GYNT
AND THE INEVITABILITY OF FIRE

There are no choices. Not in life. Not in this universe. Every decision that we make is determined by every decision that came before it, spiraling back and back to the beginning of all things and projecting ever outward to the inevitable death of everything.

Go to **1**.

Or don't.

1.

Despite all this, there's still so much that remains unknowable, even to the most diligent historians.

Let us consider Percival Gynt, a man to whom I've devoted many years of research and many, many words. A man of singular importance to the current history of this universe and to some previous histories besides and to some other universes besides those.

Yet there's a day in Percival Gynt's life that remains a mystery even to me. A day for which there are certain certainties, but far more questions.

And despite years of painstaking investigation, I am no closer to answering those questions than I was to begin with. There are possibilities, yes, and those few certainties. But to understand it all at once, one must conceive of all possibilities at once. And only in understanding the entire matrix might one perchance stare through it to the truth.

So I submit to you a tale unlike any other I have heretofore proffered. A dark tale, yes. But one that must end, inevitably, in fire.

Go to **272**.

2.

"I don't think you're supposed to be here," said Esme.

She was correct. Percival had left Esme with specific instructions. Percival's instructions for Esme were *always* specific. "He said, 'No one's to be in my office when I'm away.'"

No one. Not Esme. Not his sometimes-maybe girlfriend Tarot. Esme had difficulty tracking the shifts in their relationship status from day to day, the fact of which both confounded and deeply irritated her.

And there Tarot was now, at Percival's desk, counter to instructions, rifling or possibly riffling through case files with nothing but a flickering electric torch to read by.

It was suspicious.

"He said it'd be okay!" Tarot insisted, with an emotion that Esme had trouble reading. Fear? Guilt? Arousal, maybe? Esme took a brief moment to hate most people, then set it aside.

"He definitely didn't," said Esme, guessing but trying to sound certain.

A successful bluff! Tarot threw up her hands in defeat. An unambiguous tell, even to Esme. "All right, all right! Sorry, Es. But I'm doing a thing. An *important* thing."

Esme advanced further into the darkened room. For a moment, Tarot's torch went out and the room was pitch black. Two solid whacks, and the torch turned back on.

"An important thing?" asked Esme.

"A *secret* important thing," said Tarot.

"What is it? What's the secret?"

Tarot leaned forward and, without intending to, illuminated her face with the flickering torchlight like a child preparing to tell some campfire ghost story.

"I'm going to kill Vargoth Gor."

Esme didn't ask why. Didn't care. In fact, in that moment, the Queen of Questions could think of only one. "How can I help?"

Instead of a yes or a no, Tarot only said, "Esme?"

"Yes, Tarot?"

"If Percival gave you specific instructions that no one is supposed to be in his office when he's away, why are YOU here?"

Esme smiled. She wasn't happy to be caught out, but she appreciated Tarot's reasoning.

So she told Tarot the truth.

"I'm going to kill Vargoth Gor."

3.

Actually, Percival ran on two. Foom was a half-stride behind, shouting, "YOU WERE SUPPOSED TO SAY THREE!"

"ELEMENT OF SURPRISE!" answered Percival.

"Well, it worked!" Foom huffed. "I was surprised!"

One after the other, they trampled their way headlong into the dark, through babies and bunnies and toy bears and the rest. Underfoot. Dropping from above. Hissing, biting, crunching, screaming, clawing, crying.

It was the grasp of a shadow monkey, a not-monkey, that finally brought Percival down. Then the closest of them swarmed.

As a child, a monster had spared Percival's life. Merely a fate delayed, it now seemed.

Percival's eyes narrowed as the creatures drew blood, held his torch upward in a white-knuckle grip. A few motes of dust suspended in a wavering shaft of light, a final vision.

He prayed to no god. Had no epiphanies. Wished only for death to overtake him quick, before the improprieties of pain overwhelmed him.

Go to **130**.

4.

"First a test." Percival took the pen back and drew a... a, um... Well, this:

"W-What is that?" asked Foom, who was having trouble deciding if he was simply offended or outright horrified.

"It's a…" Percival walked around the thing. It was certainly purple. Seemed to have three-dimensionality. Mass, maybe. Thorns, maybe. "I dunno."

Nor do I.

"Have you… ever taken an art class, Gynt?"

Percival mumbled his reply, which might have been "It's possible that a monster ate my art teacher."

"Perhaps I should do the drawing then?"

"Please."

Foom took his pen, stepped away from Percival's scribble, turned until his field of vision was a blank page, and asked, "What should we draw?"

Percival looked up. "A ladder? No, that would take too long."

"A jetpack?" Foom suggested. Go to **152**.

"Or maybe a weapon to slay the beast!" offered Percival. Not too loudly, he hoped. Go to **239**.

"Or perhaps we could just draw an exit?" mused Foom. Go to **24**.

5.

"The red five."

Father Foom nodded. "We don't choose the cards we're dealt, Mister Gynt. But we can choose the cards we will not play."

Percival considered the priest's words. There was a prettiness to them. Except? He frowned. "But why?" he asked him. "The way they speak. The lives they've taken. They're monsters, Father."

"They're children," Foom argued. "Weird and frightened children. As weird and frightened as the two of us, I suspect. If they lash out when threatened, do we repay in kind? We who are not children? We who are men? Do we revenge? Or do we find mercy?"

An early morning sermon, thought Percival. Charming in its certitude. It's simplicity. But did that make it right?

He thought of Curate Pete, the man's plain dislike for Foom. He'd blamed Foom for everything that happened. "The menace that Father Foom unleashed," he'd said.

Unless he hadn't. Had he said that? If he'd said that, go to **297**.

If not? Or if you don't remember? It's fine, really. We know the curate didn't like Foom. Perhaps the exact words used are less important. Go to **37**.

6.

My research indicates that Father Foom and Percival Gynt might have had a few minutes to talk at this point, though I have no specific proof that they did, nor any indication of what, if so, they might have discussed.

We are left to speculate, you and I. Might they have spoken of religion? Politics? Popular entertainment? Or even unpopular entertainment? Hobbies? Family? Of regrets? True love? Underpants?

Or did they simply walk in silence, side-by-side, burdened by inescapable dread, knowing that each step drew them inexorably, inevitably towards their judgment?

Or underpants?

Go to **123** for religion.

Go to **258** for politics.

Go to **187** for popular entertainment.

Go to **164** for unpopular entertainment.

Go to **234** for hobbies.
Go to **144** for family.
Go to **245** for regrets.
Go to **30** for true love.
Go to **42** for underpants.
Go to **295** for nothing. A brave choice.
Or, hear me out: Go to **42**. For the underpants.

7.

"—the muuusic died."

It was, on reflection, an odd song choice and not one that played to Percival's particular vocal strengths, and Madrigal did not seem impressed.

"Next time," Percival whispered to himself, "don't sing. Makes sense."

Go to **125**.

8.

"It was the, um… I know it was an eight-of-something. Probably. Was it an eight?"

It was not. Father Foom shook his head and sighed. "I was going to say a thing, but… Nevermind. The moment's passed. I just… Despite everything, I won't kill them. I won't."

"But why?" asked Percival. "Why hesitate? They're monsters, Father. You saw them. A man might aptly call them demons."

"They're children, Percival. And a child is not a monster."

There was a certainty in Foom's tone that Percival did not share. He wondered whether Foom knew more than he did.

Or less.

He wondered whether it was worth a conversation.

Go to **150**.

9.

"I have a marvelous twelve-part plan," Percival explained, because that's the choice you selected. "And I will tell it to you now, and it will not sound as if the narrator is making it up off the top of his head!"

"The who?" asked Foom.

"Unimportant!" Percival bellowed. "In fact, Step One is 'Ask no questions!'"

"Why is that Step One?" asked Foom.

"Ask no questions! Step Two," continued Percival, "is to go to the scene of the crime. To where the refugees were killed, and to look for clues!"

"We already scrubbed the—"

"The clues will tell us why the creatures killed the refugees or perhaps expose a weakness or, um, fill in some of your… backstory?"

"I'm not—"

"Step Three is to find out how the creatures got into the church! Perhaps there's a tunnel or a magic portal!"

"I don't—"

"Five! I—"

"You skipped four."

"Four! We trick the creatures into leaving through the tunnel-slash-portal!"

"How do we do that?"

"Refer back to Step One! Five! We find a way to block the portal!"

"Or tunnel?"

"Six! Or tunnel!"

"Why is that two different steps?"

"Step One!" Percival repeated. "We'll leave Step Seven open for now, so that we can insert a step later without disrupting the rest of the numbering."

"Oh. That's smart."

"Steps eight and nine will be for our dinners. I skipped dinner. Did you skip dinner?"

"No, I—"

"Step One! How many times do I need to repeat myself?"

"But you were the one who asked the q—"

"For Step Ten, we'll sleep. It will be very late by Step Ten."

"That… That makes sense."

"For Step Eleven, we will wake up."

"Also a good idea."

"And that's that."

"I thought you said that this would be a twelve-part plan."

"Was that a question?"

"No, just a general statement of exasperation."

"Oh. I see. Well then, yes, Step Twelve will be a choreographed dance number, with glittering lights, a marble staircase, a dozen robot flamingos and a sentient tornado of confetti named Madam Paperstorm."

"Really?"

"Step o—"

"Sorry. I meant…" Foom took a breath and then repeated flatly, "Really."

Percival considered his plan. Unlikely, yes. Helpful… No.

Marvelous?

Percival smiled and stepped forward into the unknown.

Go to **49**.

10.

Go to **122**.

11.

A. Bit. Of. Fuzz.
Back to **176**.

12.

Forget what I said earlier. The weapon didn't fire. Percival pulled the trigger a second time and a third time. Nothing.

And from within the church, no roar of flames, no children's screams. Percival turned to Foom in shared bafflement.

And then the unhoused began to snap. In time. With a smirk and a swagger. And the façade of the church split open to reveal a dozen robot flamingos marching down a marble staircase to the beat.

Snap, snap. Clomp, clomp. Mecha-mecha-honk.

Stage lights glittered overhead and someone off-stage threw Percival a top hat and a cane.

"Shall we?" asked Percival, with a glint in his eye.

Snap, snap. Clomp, clomp. Mecha-mecha-honk.

And now Foom was dressed to match, both of them in white ties and tails. "I thought you'd never ask," he replied, as he caught his own hat and cane.

Snap, snap. Clomp, clomp. Mecha-mecha-honk.

And then the band began to play, a raucous tune. The two men danced with the flamingos, tap steps and high kicks and twirls, while the unhoused chorus sang of second chances and boundless opportunity.

Forever! And ever! And mecha-mecha-honk.

And from the rafters, a storm of confetti, red and blue and shimmering gold descended! And as the confetti spun through the air it took the form of a primal creature. An elemental.

Madam Paperstorm.

Flutter, flutter. Forever! Snap. Clomp. Kick. Twirl. Mecha-mecha-honk.

And she summoned Percival and his new friend Foom into the air to join her. And they flew. And she sang to them of true love and absolution and the seventh principle of Unitarian Universalism. The interdependent web of all existence.

And Percival could see the whole of time and space stretching out ahead of him and behind him and in other less Euclidean directions besides, and he deemed it good. There would be a time for fire, yes. For mistakes. For betrayals. For judgment and retribution. But a time for joy too. A time for card games and fancy-dress balls and giant umbrellas and best friends and fireworks and tuna sandwiches.

All of it, inescapable. All of it, all of it, inevitable.

Mecha-mecha-honk.

A curtain falls. And somewhere else, another rises.

Is this enough, then? Is this what you wanted? Maybe now's the time to turn to the next story in this volume.

That would be all right.

That would be nice.

Or, if you're ready for it, the truth remains. Go to **269**.

13.

And then Percival was murdered by a tendril monster. In the dark. There were no witnesses.

Unless perhaps the duck was still clinging to life?

Which brings us to a bit of a crossroads, Dear Reader. Our hero is dead. Murdered. Kaput. And this despite featuring in the balance of stories in this volume as well as his own mostly-historical epic, *Percival Gynt and the Conspiracy of Days*, available in both electronic and print formats.

Odd.

So here are your choices: Either you can start this story over at **1** *and try to make better choices* or you can skip ahead to the next one, entitled "Percival Gynt and the View From the 10th Story," and just assume that the Percival Gynt you meet from there-on-out is either an android or a clone or a time travel variant.

Because, honestly, who's to say that he's not?

14.

Yes, yes, this is a very serious story, but by all means, let's prioritize the cheese!

I'm sorry. Did I not explain that there'd be heckling?

If you've been properly chastened and recant your hasty decision, go to **243**.

Or, if as is more likely, you remain stubbornly incurious about the story you have nonetheless set forward to read, by all means, go to **15**.

15.

Percival arrived at his favorite cheese shop at twelve past nine in the morning. A tiny mechanized bell jingled convincingly as he passed over the threshold.

The shop was near empty. There was one girl, perhaps six years old, at the back by the community notice board, audibly sniffling. Hay fever, perhaps?

And behind the counter, in the place of usual clerk Gary or Jerry or… Edgar? Percival couldn't remember. In place of *Edgarry* was a comely dark-skinned woman, smartly dressed, with striking green eyes and a game-if-noncommittal smile.

If you believe that Percival would have immediately gone back to check on a sniffling girl, go to **77**.

If you think Percival would have more likely sidestepped the girl to peruse the community notice board, because, who knows, maybe someone was trying to fill the fourth slot in their adventuring party, then go to **183**.

Or, if you presume that Percival would have ignored both and gone straight to the counter to flirt with this new clerk, because, yes, why not, that sounds fun, go to **228**.

16.

First, an anecdote. In preparation for writing this story, with its very specific structure, I acquired and studied a number of Old Earth classic *Pick Your Own Predicament*^{TM} novels. In one of them, the hero confronts a dragon, and the reader must choose whether to fight or trick the beast. And because this hero is neither trained as a warrior nor equipped with any sort of magic dragon-slaying weaponry, I concluded that the correct way to resolve the encounter had to be "trick."

Well. Let me stress that this is a true story of a real book that someone actually wrote, intentionally, which was published by humans, and later purchased and accepted as not the-craziest-thing-that-anyone-had-ever-written, also by humans.

Different humans, but humans.

That said.

When you choose "trick," here's what happens: The hero retrieves a heretofore unmentioned cream pie from behind their back, throws it square in the dragon's face, and is immediately burnt to a crisp in reprisal. END OF.

As far as tricks go, that is… Well, it's not a trick.

Which, I suppose, is what separates those novels from this work.

I am a serious, credentialed historian, very much concerned with true events, with authenticity, and with rewarding the faith that you, Dear Reader, have placed in me.

So when you decide that Percival Gynt must have tricked the young priest, it is my solemn vow that it will be a proper trick, and not a cream pie to the face.

"You, suh!" spat Percival, as he sidled up to the priest.

I said nothing about accents.

"Ah you thuh man in chogge of this he-yuh establishmn?"

The priest, who was not an idiot, found Percival and his choice of accent suspicious, and he held his hammer ready at his side, should he have need to defend himself. "This is my church," he told Percival. "Who or what are you?"

This was not *quite* the reaction Percival was hoping for. He considered abandoning his hastily conceived trick.

If you think Percival would indeed have abandoned this trick, because, let's be honest, it was a terrible idea, go to **129**.

But if you're committed to seeing this through to the end, then so am I! Continue on to **259**.

Or if you'd rather pretend as if none of this "trick" business ever happened, that Percival instead approached the priest like a normal person, not a cartoon character, and also that you had these last few seconds of your life back, well?

Two out of three ain't bad.

Go to **45**.

17.

Along the way, Percival noticed something peculiar.

Go to **270**.

18.

A geyser of flame issued forth from the weapon, in through the doorway, exploding the interior with an audible FOOM. The whole structure buckled as it burned, collapsing in on itself and on the desperate creatures within.

Percival could hear the children cry out in pain, in despair, crying out to their father for a mercy that would not come. He heard the cry of other children, long ago, and stumbled backwards, lowered the gun, closed a hand over his mouth before the sickness could escape.

This was not like Eeps. This was no adventure. He, no hero detective. This was wrong. *He* was wrong. Something…

Something else was wrong.

Go to **94**.

19.

"Did you see how I got here?" asked Percival.

Father Void offered no response.

"I fell out of the sky. There must be some kind of portal up there."

Again, no response. Percival asked again, using more words this time. Surely more words would make the difference.

"I was pulled through a book by an inky black tendril and then fell out of the sky here. You didn't see an inky tendril pull an accountant out of a portal in the sky?"

No response.

"Me. I'm the accountant."

No response.

"Nearly an accountant."

No response.

"It would have been just a few minutes ago."

TIME DOES NOT EXIST.

It didn't seem reasonable to Percival that a giant inky tendril could pull him through a portal without being noticed. Unless it was somehow invisible on this side of the portal.

Or non-existent.

Go to **177**.

20.

Percival wailed in pain as a giant duck chomped down on his left arm. He knew it was a giant duck and not some other kind of large, hyper-violent animal, because Foom had identified it as such, and also because it quacked loudly in the moment just before it took hold of him.

"WHY IS THIS HAPPENING TO ME?" cried Percival. He didn't mean the question existentially. He was extremely confused by this whole duck situation.

Foom ran to his side and wrestled the creature off him. In the dark it was hard to judge, but Percival thought the creature nearly as tall as he was and perhaps twice his weight.

"Bad Space Pope," Foom chastised the duck, "Bad girl."

It quacked back something that Percival thought might have been an apology.

"This," Foom explained, "is my weapon." There was an edge of pride in Foom's tone that Percival felt certain was misplaced.

"I thought you said your weapon was a gun!"

"I said *sort of.*"

"And in what way is a duck *sort of* a gun?"

To this, Foom provided an extremely clear, concise, and compelling answer which Maeve has edited out for pacing reasons.

Go to **275**.

21.

Out the door! Down the corridor! Percival glanced back as they ran. Pitch black! Right. But he could feel it, cold at his back. Close and closing!

A split up ahead!

Left? **273**!

Right? **120**!

22.

Father Foom unpadlocked the chains that barred the back door of the church, piled them to one side, and then unlocked the door itself. The lights were out inside.

Foom flipped a wall switch once, twice. Nothing.

"Your monsters cut the power?"

"Seems so," said Foom. "Gnawed through the wiring maybe. Don't suppose you brought a light?"

Percival smirked and drew a slim electric torch from his jacket pocket. His bodega torch. Foom nodded approvingly, but when Percival switched the torch on, it flickered for a few seconds, and then turned off.

Foom sighed. Percival frowned. When the man at the bodega had said the torch was half-off, he'd assumed he was describing its price, not its only setting.

He gave the torch two solid whacks on its bottom, and it turned back on. Sort of. It continued to flicker, occasionally went out again, required another firm whack each time before it would condescend to reignite.

"It was on sale," Percival explained with no small embarrassment.

"I can see that," replied Foom, "intermittently."

Percival took the lead, and Foom followed him into the flickering dark.

"Have you considered," asked Foom, "what we might do when we encounter the creatures?"

He had not. Go to **113**.

Or perhaps I'm wrong? Maybe he had a marvelous twelve-part plan. He didn't, but sure, let's go to **9** to hear this plan.

23.

First off, thank you! I can only assume that if you've read "Percival Gynt and the View from the 10th Story" already, it's because you've finished this entire volume and you're back for a re-read!

Bless you.

I trust that you weren't lying just now. That you're not a lying liar who just wanted to see what this passage is all about. You shouldn't lie to books. Don't do it again.

Also, I trust you're not one of those people who picks up a book like this and reads the stories in whatever random order based purely on the morning's fancy.

That's not as bad as lying, but you'll agree that it's peculiar.

Everyone else: Yes, of course you're right. This story you're reading right now takes place in the year 20012, and Percival didn't meet Professor Grieg until 20013.

Page 224 in my edition.

It's just my research suggests that Percival *might* have spoken to an expert from the University, but doesn't specify who, and I didn't want to just make someone up.

That's not what I do. Mostly.

Also, I like writing for Professor Grieg. He's a hoot!

With that out of the way, let's continue on to **92**.

Or if you're bothered by this little cul-de-sac of ahistoricity, that's fair. Entirely fair! Let's go to **153** and talk about it some more.

24.

Percival wiped a single tear from the girl's cheek. "I understand," he told her. "I'll solve this for you. Put a stop to those monsters. Reopen your church. This night, I swear."

The girl sniffed away her tears and smiled provisionally.

Percival had little to no experience in such matters, but he trusted in his gallantry and good intentions to win the day.

Perhaps he was overpromising? Go to **160**.

Nonsense. Go to **209**.

25.

"I'd heard story of what happened here," said Percival Gynt. "Meant to take the matter up with Father Foom. But I wouldn't mind hearing your version of events as well."

"There's hardly a point in keeping secrets," said the curate. "It's a proper menace that Father Foom has unleashed on us, and it deserves a full and public airing."

"Did you say 'that *Father Foom* unleashed?'"

"He's damned us all, the fool Anglican." Curate Pete thought for a moment, then clarified. "I'm not swearing. I say that in my professional capacity. A right damning, this. First, he preached his false religion from the pulpit. Second, he brought apostates into our congregation. And third, these monsters as you call them. These *demons*. They were surely a plague upon us. A punishment. And he welcomed them, too. Invited evil to walk among us!"

It was a proper rant by the end. Curate Pete's face was red, his lips curled into a snarl. He held his hammer in a white-knuckle grip, and in that moment, Percival wondered whether the curate might be considering another, alternative use for said tool.

"And you've had no luck in combatting them?" Percival asked finally, in an effort to break the curate's reverie. "Of, um, exorcising them?"

Curate Pete sneered and returned to his work. "I'd hardly be boarding the doors shut if we had, would I?"

The curate's logic was immaculate.

Percival thanked the curate for his help and offered up his hand, but Pete scoffed and turned and returned to his work. "It's more help than you'll receive from Our Drunken Father, I think you'll find."

"Yes, well." Percival looked down at his rejected hand, shrugged, put it back in his pocket. "I suppose I'll find that out for myself presently."

Go to **250**.

26.

Right then. Time to talk. Smart. But what about?

Perhaps if Percival simply asked these creatures to leave, they would? That might work. This is a collection of *short* stories after all! Go to **172** to give that a go. Who knows? Maybe we've cracked it.

Maybe. But Percival had questions. So many questions. What were these things? Where did they come from? Why did they eat Foom's refugees? Why did they seem to know Percival, and why did they think that he had teeth in his belly? Go to **255** to begin asking questions.

Or perhaps it was time for introductions. They seemed to know who Percival was. Who Foom was. But who or what were they? Go to **90**.

27.

"Yes, yes. I'm harnessing a, I don't know, an *unflaw* in *unreality* to manifest a sort of cosmic omniscience to breach whatever narrative has been constructed around me in order to have a conversation with you about the fate of all existence or, well, my existence at the very least, maybe our hapless Narrator's as well, and you want to argue with me about whether you're *wearing* a coat or simply own it? Is this what this relationship is going to be like? Incessant niggling over the higgledy-piggledy?"

You should have heard some of them when I tried to sneak Professor Grieg into this story!

"That definitely didn't happen, and also you're not helping!"

Sorry.

"And you!" he said, clearly referring to *you*, Sam Something-or-other. "Go to **161** already."

That's meant to be my job!

"Go to **161**."

28.

Percival lost his grip on the torch, but it bounced along after them, tumbling end over end, side to side, flickering and casting strange and swirling shadows, and finally bouncing off Percival's head at the bottom of the stairs with an audible KA-KWONK.

If he were a cartoon, he might have seen stars circling his head.

Percival moaned in pain, rolled onto his side. "You know, I was beaten by the police last week." Held a hand to his damp temple.

Foom was not far from him, wincing, flat on his back, staring up into the dark. "Yeah? Which was worse."

Percival dragged himself across the floor. In the direction he thought the torch might have bounced.

In the off-his-head direction.

"Both were fairly awful."

Go to **109**.

29.

Percival awoke in a parchment-colored void, flat on his back, staring up into nothingness. Not a hole, but an *absence* underneath the parchment sky. An enormous, writhing nothing hanging in the air above him, orbited by six enormous ink-red sigils.

Was this death then? Was he dreaming? Or was this simply what all books looked like from the inside?

Should Percival have proceeded as if he was dead? Then go to **217**.

Or if you think Percival might have thought himself dreaming, go to **146**.

Or perhaps he was truly and properly squished inside a magic book. Unlikely? Perhaps. But this had already been a top ten unlikely day for young Percival. Go to **283**.

30.

"Have you ever been in love?" asked Percival.

"My ex-wife thought so," Foom answered.

"And you?"

Foom thought about whether he wanted to reply. He didn't know this man at all, and yet he might well die with him that night. Death demands its own sort of intimacy. "I don't know. It was a difficult divorce. Fractious. In the end, I came to question everything about myself. And not for the first time. Did I love because love existed? Or did I try to make love? And not, well, you know what I mean. I'm not sure I know what love is, frankly. You?"

"Are you allowed to get divorced?"

"Because I'm Catholic?"

"It's what I'd heard."

"Well, technically I'm Anglican. And more technically than that, I'm not really Anglican either. I lied on my application. I'm actually Unitarian Universalist, if you know what that is."

Percival did not.

"But I sought this role, this place, all of it. I'm always trying to escape. Never seems to work."

That Percival understood. "Fate stalks me too. Everything I am is a fight against the fundamental gravity of my existence."

"And me."

"I am the horror of my past."

"And me."

Percival stopped, aimed the winking torchlight up onto his face. "Well, aren't we a pair?" he said with a grin. "It can't be all mopes. I also like cheese!"

Foom nodded in the dark. "And me."

And they continued together into the dark.

Go to **62**.

31.

Percival cursed and screamed, "WE'RE GOING TO DIE, AREN'T WE!"

"PROBABLY!" Father Foom conceded. "ANYTHING TO CONFESS? ANY REGRETS?"

Yes! **214**!

No! **170**!

32.

The woman barely recognized the man before her, gaunt and bedridden. Age and his afflictions had finally overtaken him. There he was, sunken-eyed, hair receding, his once-famous beard now patchy and brittle like white straw. He shivered in the heat, clung to his blankets, coughed and wheezed and cursed the past.

"I don't like being summoned," she said. It was the kindest greeting she could manage. "Even by you. *Especially* by you."

"I *summoned* the necroblob that stands guard at the door," the old man rasped. "My daughter? I sent an email."

"You know what I mean."

Her father attempted a nod in assent, but a hacking cough overtook him. He had so little strength left, and time was short. Had it really been ten years?

"I will be gone soon," he said, "and you will have the opportunity you crave. To save your brother."

"But you said—?"

"I'm not a damn fool," the old man wheezed. "I know what I said, and from a certain perspective it was true. Your brother was used, is being used, for a most important purpose. But there is another who may take his place."

"Who?" the daughter demanded, without a second's thought to the ethical considerations.

"A hero, brave and true," the father answered. "Or near enough for our purposes. Near enough."

"And who is this hero? How do I find him?"

"Your brother is cared for by two of the Vargoth's agents on a world called Sanctuary... Sanctuary-8."

Percival's homeworld.

The daughter had long quested to find her brother, to rescue him from his accursed existence. To simply be told his location now, after all of these years, was in equal measure exhilarating and deflating. And so, impossibly, insultingly, she felt nothing.

"And this hero?"

"Nearby. Indeed, this latest hiding place was chosen for that reason."

"And his name? Address?"

The old man raised a gnarled, trembling fist. From its grip, a brass chain hung, and from the chain, a coal-black stone.

"This will guide you to him. You must find the flame within this stone, just as you must find the hero within the man. Just as the stone may not believe in the flame, so your hero may not believe in his own goodness. You must coax it from him."

"That sounds awful and wrong. I'm not one of your damned familiars."

"And yet I *did* summon you." The old man's laugh was horrible, thin and vulnerable. His daughter snatched the talisman from his grip and vanished it.

"Just promise me," the daughter said, "that when you go, you'll really be gone. That I'll really be done with you."

"What is remembered is never gone. When I am dead and your

brother saved, perhaps you will think better of me." His eyes narrowed. His voice steadied. "Perhaps, finally, you'll save me too."

Percival thought perhaps to steal a glance at the young woman and her father. The former had, Percival thought, quite a lovely tone to her voice, despite a coldness befitting her experience.

Go to **280**.

33.

"What sort of a weapon, Father?" asked Percival. He'd resolved to leave it be, to ask no questions. He really had. But then the words simply slipped out.

He'd surprised himself. But you and I both know that this is *your* fault.

"A relic," the priest explained, "of a past I'd hoped never to revisit."

I won't ask again. I'm going to assume you want Percival to press until he gets every intimate detail out of Father Foom. Because that's who *you* are.

"This is no time to be coy," said Percival. "What sort of past are we talking about? Laser swords? Thunder boots? Yzjzyax Wretch Howlers?"

Some distance behind them, a door smashed and splintered to pieces, and something ancient and terrible passed through. And just for a moment, Foom stopped.

"A firefighter," said Foom. "Before I was a man of the cloth, I was a firefighter."

Be nice. Go to **69**.

Snark. Go to **237**.

34.

Or? Is this too silly? Yes. This is too silly. I see that now. I've ruined it.

Unless? Is this what really happened? Sometimes the silliest thing is the truth, I promise you. Well, not promise. Propose, I suppose.

Good grief, the rhyming!

Don't worry, Dear Reader. I have an editor who will no doubt edit out this entire passage.

Flibberty. Yub yub. Snorg.

Do you see this, Maeve? Pure nonsense. Please edit out this whole bit.

Let's just say: All right then. It's not a duck, strictly. It's an… Yzjzyax Wretch Howler? Just looks like a duck and quacks like a duck and…

How does that expression go?

Something-something-something-something, DEFINITELY NOT A DUCK.

Probably.

What I'm saying is go to **169**.

(It's probably a duck.)

35.

"No time," hissed Foom and he ran.

And Percival, not wanting to be left behind, stood and attempted to follow. Held arms out in front of him, crashed into a wall, felt his way to the doorway.

And behind them, Father Void's tendril emerged from the book with a rushing squikk. A malevolent nothing in the parchment-verse, rendered here in ink and shadow, whipping after them.

Go to **79**.

36.

Percival barreled into the dark and immediately, inevitably hit a wall! Perhaps I should have called this one *The Inevitability of Walls*?

No! No times for jokes!

Percival let out a roar of pain, stumbled back, fell over! Foom wrenched him up by his wrist, and dragged him behind as he ran!

Quick! **31**!

37.

Pete thought everything that happened was Foom's fault. Percival wasn't sure that he was wrong.

Who lets monsters loose in their own church?

Foom looked down at his weapon. Shook his head. "I can't," he said. More to himself than to Percival, maybe.

Couldn't what? Couldn't fire the weapon? Couldn't hand it off to someone who would?

Go to **150**.

38.

"It wouldn't look at us," said Percival.

"I had the light in its face."

"Yeah. I wasn't sure with the others. I thought maybe the cat was squinting at me, but—"

"They don't like bright lights."

"Sorry?"

"Before," said Foom, "when we let them have the run of the place. They'd never go outside. Stayed away from windows. We'd dim the overheads to make them more comfortable."

Percival sighed. "And you're only thinking to mention this now?"

"And you could have brought two torches!"

Percival was prepared to concede the point. The torch had been half-off, after all. But that seemed to him a side issue. "Tell me more."

Foom thought on it. "They always preferred the shadows. Low light. We never thought of it as a weakness. Except," he recalled, "once, by accident he said, the curate turned the lights full-up while one was still in the nursery. The cries! It hid itself in a cupboard for a full hour. Took three of our strongest to drag it out again. Its moans were frightening the children."

"All that from an ordinary lightbulb?" Percival held his hand close to the torch, let the beam form a circle of light on his palm and pondered.

"We use R63s." Foom shrugged. "They're meant to be calming."

Percival laughed.

Go to **197**.

39.

With a steady hand, alone in the dark where no one but you and I would ever know, Percival Gynt shut the book.

Or rather, he tried to.

Because, and this is something they generally don't teach you in school, not all books want to be shut.

This book fought back. Percival put all his weight on the cover, tried to force it down, but it shook and it shoved and something dark and old and spectacularly tentacular forced its way from between its pages.

Percival fell back, the book flew open, and an angry tendril burst free into the dark, lashed our hero, and before he could so much as kick or scream, dragged him neither-of-those-things-ing into its pages.

This seems to be going poorly. No choices to be had here. Just observing.

Go to **110**.

40.

While there certainly appeared to be nothing else around Father Foom and Percival Gynt as far as the eye could see, they both agreed that a paper-nothing was at least slightly less nothing than the nothinger-nothing that was Father Void. So they resolved to set out for the parchment horizon.

"Together?" asked Foom. Go to **185**.

"Or we could split up to cover more ground," Percival suggested. Go to **238**.

41.

"Who am I to turn down an offer of assistance?" asked Percival. It was not a rhetorical question. He had hoped that Father Foom might interject with some excuse. That it was too dangerous, perhaps. Or against church bylaws? Something like that.

But he didn't, so Percival sighed and relented and chose five, the most hale and cogent of them, and he asked them to accompany him and Father Foom and for the others to stay behind and guard the exits.

He chose the woman Hestor, the first to speak up. She left her children Cressia and Bim in the care of her brother, B'Senn. And he chose Fulgrimm the Short, who was indeed quite short, but who was also square-jawed and broad-shouldered, with a buzz cut and a facial tic and a snarl like a pitbull. He chose Maaba, a foul-smelling cyborg, always glitching, sparking, and stammering through her words. She had what appeared to Percival to be, but were in fact *not*, kitchen whisks for hands. He chose M'k'k'b, a necroblob, half-discorporated from old age and dragging its null-bladder like an overheavy sack behind it. And he chose Yella, spikey-haired, wild-eyed, stomach a-rumble, thirsty for life and undeterred by any obstacle.

"There may be monsters," he cautioned his new companions. "You lend aid at your own peril."

The five nodded. Fulgrimm added a growl. Yella swore several unrepeatable curses.

Then Percival turned to Father Foom and he asked, "Are we ready?"

If Foom was ready, continue on to **294**.

If not? Perhaps wait a few minutes, cuppa tea if you like, then on to **294**.

42.

"Can I ask you a question?" asked Percival.

Foom glared at the accountant. "I'd be hard pressed to stop you."

So emboldened, Percival proceeded with not one, but an avalanche of questions. To wit: "Because my underwear has been riding up, and I'm wondering what underwear you use? Do you use natural blends or something artificial like NanoPants™? Or do you mix-and-match? Is your underwear comfortable? Did you buy locally? Is this appropriate? Should we be talking about underwear? Should we not? Is there a social taboo that we should either be observing or upending? How would we even know? I mean, really? If all social conventions are, by definition, artificial, does that not make them on some level arbitrary? And if so, what's the ontological basis for human existence? And before you say God because, yes, I understand you're a religious man, can we not first consider the nature and implication of an eternal other? How can a thing that exists eternally and definitionally outside of space and time also be a cause of things inside space and time? What is the point of intercession? The nature and meaning of intercession? How do we know when those points of intercession are actually happening, and aren't, say, moments of madness? Of half-remembered dream? Of really good hallucinogens? Of stagecraft? How is anything anything? Why is there something instead of nothing? How indeed do we know that there is something? That life is any more than an illusion? An accident of multiple thought events, each a discrete existence, fooling themselves through dint of vivid qualia into a misguided presumption of self? In this moment, am I not a singular me, now, now past, gone and replaced by this other me? And if so, to what degree am I beholden to that past self? Am I free of sin, a virgin born, each instant? Or as a fleeting thought, is my debt to past selves the only measure of my validity? A rebel thought, excused, discounted, discarded, disavowed by all that follow? Is my only dignity my duty to myself? Am I not then a simple cog? In every instant a plebian? The hoi polloi of myself? Or, whether true or not, does this whole line of thinking not lead to an obvious disservice to my whole being? Must we live in the illusion then? To appreciate a flower or a sunset or the smell of faded perfume? Must we ignore the fundamental reality of our existence in order to find happiness? And too guilt? Is that the cost? To accept ourselves as ourselves we invite joy and sorrow hand-in-hand? But to deny either is to deny both? Is my guilt then not an impediment to joy, but rather its companion? Should I accept it then? All the horrors of my youth? The malaise of adult responsibility? Could I not choose to choose? To embrace some of it as me, some of it as rebel thoughts discarded? How do I reconcile the unreconcilable? Should I? Or should I embrace the conflict? Am I only the conflict? And if so, what of it? Is that good? Bad? How can I know? If, as we've established, the only absolutes exist eternally outside, inaccessible, except for moments of intercession that are themselves indistinguishable from madness, how then can we precede with any kind of certainty about anything? Let alone ethics? Logic, then? Or compassion? And how to reconcile the two? Cannot logic lead to grave injustice? Cannot compassion blind us to the true good? Are we not doomed to failure? Damned by the world we inhabit?

By our inhabitance? And doesn't that render salvation unto happenstance? Divine whim? The hoary hand of Fate reaching down and meddling, manipulating, making every decision for us? And free will! Free will!"

At last a statement! And this, as good a place as any to interrupt, Foom offered this and only this in response to all the accountant's many and varied inquiries:

"Commando, Mister Gynt. Commando."

Percival nodded, took a breath, nodded again, and then the two continued on in silence.

Go to **62**.

43.

While Father Foom was unconscious, he had a dream. He dreamed that there were no monsters in his church. No cursed book. No accountants. It was a pleasant dream and certainly more plausible than the reality he now awoke to.

The undercroft was dark and cold and all these days later it still smelled of industrial bleach. Foom touched his temple, felt the blood. Sat up. Swore.

Priests swear all the time when you're not around.

The tendril might have still been there even then. Coiled. Ready to strike. Best not to think about that. Foom groped about until he found Percival's torch. He flicked it on. Searched the dark with its faltering beam.

No. No tendril. Only that damned book. Not a dream. As before. Opened to a blank page and spewing darkness.

The torch cut out, and startled, Foom screamed. He wasn't normally a screamer. Was surprised that it was even in him. Particularly at that volume. Particularly at that pitch.

In panic, he whacked furiously at the base of the torch, as he had seen Percival do so many times before. One, two, three. Why wouldn't it relight? Was he hitting it too hard? Not hard enough?

A choice with no import.

He could hear something moaning, grunting, scrabbling out of the book.

Four, five, six, and light burst from the torch, as bright and constant as the Second Sun of Duul. The good one.

And there, out of the book, three ink-black fingers.

Go to **148**.

44.

Percival screamed in pain as most of his parts crunched against the alley pavement. Blood and tears stung his eyes. His breaths were short and shallow.

"Foom," he wheezed. He tried and failed to lift his head from the pavement. He could hear the church burning, feel the heat and the falling ash. "Foom, are you there?"

"I'm here, Percival," answered the priest. His voice too was weak. Pained.

"I think we might have damaged your church," said Percival. "You… You might have to shut down…"

Up above, a flaming wall pulled away from the rest of the structure and crashed down into the alleyway beside them.

"…indefinitely."

Go to **289**.

45.

"D'you know where I might find Father Foom?" asked Percival.

The young priest scoffed. "Well, it's Saturday morning, so I expect you'll find him at The Wronged Vagrant. One of the local drinking establishments. It's just two blocks down and 'round the corner. Shouldn't have any problem finding it on Maps."

Percival preferred Uber Minus Cars.

"If you don't mind me saying," said Percival, "You don't seem overly fond of the man."

"I'm sorry," said the other man. Percival wasn't sure that he was. "I spoke out of turn maybe. I'm the curate here. Curate Pete. And, well, you'll find out for yourself, soon enough."

Percival thanked Curate Pete and was off.

Off to **114**.

46.

"Wonderful! Thank you. We've established contact. I've stuck my tongue out at you. You've stuck your tongue out at me. We're friends now! It's good. And most importantly, we've established that I can tell you to do things here, and you will do them… wherever you are."

In the twenty-first century.

"Really? How is that even—? No. No, that's good. Listen, listen, listen, listen. I have an idea. I think it'll work. There's an Old Earth song from that era. Almost that era. It's called *Take On Me*. Maybe you've heard of it?

"If you've heard of it, let's go straight to **71**.

"If not, go to **149**."

47.

Percival read the names of the dead. Their dates of death. Hundreds of years ago. Not Foom's refugees, of course. They would've been disposed of elsewhere.

Percival thought perhaps to ask about them. About the refugees, not the long dead. Who they were, what they wanted out of life, how Foom connected with them, and what he learned about himself in knowing them.

The Telepaths of Sekaty'r Prime had experienced unimaginable horrors, everyone said. Percival could imagine horrors.

Percival could *remember* horrors.

"Are you all right?" asked Foom, who had noticed Percival's focus drift.

"No," said Percival sharply, reflexively. "But thank you for asking."

Go to **132**.

48.

"It's not as bad as that!" offered Percival, as he struggled to think of something, *anything* kind to say. "My whole colony got et," was the best he could manage. "Those refugees would have been purged by the

N[th] Reich if they'd stayed on Secaty'r Prime."

Back turned, Foom weighed Percival's words.

"You gave them a gift, Father."

Thought whether he should punch Percival in his stupid face.

"The only gift that matters."

Instead, he whispered a silent prayer for the dead.

"You gave them days."

Go to **165**.

49.

"Hullo!" called Percival. He thought he saw something, the hint of something, in the flicker of his beam. "Is anyone there?"

Then, after a beat, he added, "Also, please don't eat us!"

A creature stepped forward into the failing light. A tiny thing. A cat that was surely not a cat. Its eyes, slits of red. Its fur, dark as ink. As inky as darkness. It bowed its head, this not-cat.

And it spoke.

"We know you," it said, in the soft, cloying tone of an obsequious child.

"You..." Percival hesitated. Whatever this thing was, it was no Fnargle. (If you don't know what that means, consider Step One.) "You know *me*?"

Foom gripped Percival's shoulder, harder than he'd intended. Whispered in his ear. "They... they can't... They couldn't..."

"Yes," said the not-cat. "There's even a song about you. Would you like to hear it?"

"Say no," counseled Father Foom. "This is some sort of—"

If you would in fact *not* like to hear the song from the talking cat because, frankly, that sounds a bit naff, go to **100**.

Or if you don't want to hear the song, because actually the idea of a creepy not-cat singing to you by torchlight is clearly and profoundly unsettling, go to **100**.

Or if you just can't... can't... This is just... What *is* this? Go to 100.

Go to **100**.

50.

"They closed the church," said the girl, and she gestured to the single flyer.

"Oh," said Percival. He tapped the paper, and the letter jiggled from side to side. He'd been hoping for a second page, but the message remained the same:

OUR LADY OF SORROWS CHURCH

IS CLOSED INDEFINITELY

DUE TO ONGOING FACILITIES ISSUES

PLEASE ADDRESS ALL MATTERS

EARTHLY AND DIVINE

TO THE RIGHTEOUS FATHER FOOM

"Well, I'm sure it's just that the roof or the toilets. I'm sure you'll be back to services in no time."

"No, we won't," whispered the little girl as she tried gamely to attack the crust that had formed along her upper lip. "'S not like that. I'm sure of it. It's the *monsters*."

A smile crept across Percival Gynt's face. Despite his best efforts. "Monsters, you say?"

Three words that might have reasonably been his epitaph.

Go to **191**.

51.

When Percival finally exited the church, half-bent and staggering weary, he was confronted by the people of the alley.

"What happened?" they asked in blunt tones. "Where's Father Foom? What should we do now?"

Percival frowned, looked back one last time. "Burn it," he told them.

And he walked away.

Go to **155**.

52.

Percival drew a card, looked at it, didn't show it to the other man.

"It's the two of spades," said Foom matter-of-factly. And of course it was.

Percival smiled. A proper trick! But then Foom showed Percival the rest of the cards. They were *all* the two of spades.

"So you're a priest, a bartender, and… a magician?"

"I've done a lot of things I'm not proud of, Mister Gynt. Stage magic, the least of it." Foom vanished the deck down his sleeve. "Sometimes a choice is the illusion of choice. You want to help? What choice have I got?"

"I promise," said Percival, "I won't let you down."

"Either way," said Foom flatly. "Meet me tonight, after nightfall, in the alley behind the church. And we'll see what you can do."

Go to **101**.

53.

No help there. He considered what might be the matter.

"DO. YOU. NEED. COOKIES?" he shouted.

The girl stopped herself mid-scream, shook her head, considered whether this stranger before her was an idiot.

"HAVE. YOU. SOILED. YOURSELF?"

The girl shook her head a second time, her grief now largely subsumed by insult and bother.

"DO. YOU…?" Percival glanced over his shoulder at the notice board, at the single notice. Notice he noticed she might have noticed.

"Are you… upset about that flyer?"

Go to **112**.

54.

Hmm. Well. That's that cleared up then, isn't it? Feeling a bit glum now, if I'm being honest.

Maybe best if we just got on with it. Go to **269**.

55.

Well done, you! With your final, highest note, the not-not-not-not-nothingness exploded into specificity! Glass shattered! Fireworks exploded! Glitter went everywhere! And a whirling, fiery portal opened before our hero.

"Thank you, Sam," said Percival. "I mean that double-ironically."

Did you have anything you wanted to say to Percival before the proper narrative is restored? If so, this is your moment. Speak and then go to **180**.

If not, you can go straight to **166**.

56.

Perhaps the tendril had lost the *apparently extremely literal* scent, or perhaps it was simply waiting for Percival to tire. To give in.

Go to **261**.

57.

"Be brave," thought Percival. And impossibly, he was.

Slowly, he knelt and crawled forward, through the darkness, towards the book. And the monster within.

Go to **278**.

58.

Try as he might, Percival couldn't keep pace with the priest. His legs ached, he couldn't see, didn't know where he was going.

And he could feel the tendril growing closer. It was colder, maybe blacker than the darkness.

Percival turned a corner and realized he had no idea where Father Foom had gone. He might have been a few steps ahead or a thousand miles away. Percival couldn't hear him anymore. He was alone in the darkness, and the finger of death stretching after him.

Go to **70**.

59.

Foom raised his weapon. Aimed through the bookcase to the tendril in his mind's eye. Considered the barricade they'd built. A bookcase and a filing cabinet. Against a force of primordial evil.

Should have shoved the desk over there too. Solid desk. Would've bought them another half-second. Next time, maybe.

The tendril struck again. And again. From the sound of it, it had shattered the door, broken through the back of their barricade.

The bookcase lurched forward. Books spilled out over the top of the filing cabinet and onto the rug at Foom's feet.

He'd sort them later, if he was still alive. By color, maybe.

Then the tendril broke through the back of the bookcase, splintering the wood to flinders, surging towards the two men, pure dark penetrating the quivering and inconstant beam of Percival's half-off torch.

Father Foom did not hesitate. He pulled the trigger back and fire rushed from the weapon's tip, through the tendril, past what remained of the bookcase and door, and out into the corridor beyond. With a mighty roar.

With an all-consuming FOOM.

All that was left of the tendril was a spatter of black and a certain odor in the air. Foom shoved the metal filing cabinet out of his way, pulled apart the burnt flinders of the bookcase and door to clear the way into the inferno.

He turned back towards Percival, who'd lowered his torch, who stared back blankly. "You're probably in shock," Foom told him. "But there's no time for that. We need to go now."

Foom didn't wait for Percival to process what he'd said. He turned away, back towards the fire, and he disappeared into it.

Go to **104**.

60.

One day, Percival worked up the courage to go into the fishmonger's and ask if they knew the story of the church that once stood where they stood. If they knew if a strange book was found in the wreckage.

"Aye," said the fishmonger. "We found such a book buried in the foundations. A queer old thing. Was it yours?"

"A friend's, I suppose. What happened to it?"

"Kept it. Not sure why." The fishmonger glanced behind him, towards the back room. "Never thought much of paper books, but there was something about this one." Then, after a moment's thought, "Why? Is it worth something?"

"And did you ever try to open it? To read it?"

The fishmonger shook their head.

"That's odd, yeah?"

The fishmonger shrugged.

"Can I see it?"

The fishmonger motioned for Percival to join them in the small room at the back of the shop. There they pulled the ancient book from a drawer and set it on their desktop.

"You know a lot about books?" they asked Percival, but Percival didn't answer. He placed a hand on the book cover, touched his fingertips to the endpapers, found a spot in the middle and took a deep breath, muttered to himself, "This is the day," and…

Go to **301**.

61.

Okay. Why not. Let's assume that the tendril was covered in tiny noses, and I'm just now mentioning this because… because… I assumed it went without saying?

Take a moment now to imagine everything that's happened so far, tendril-wise, but with noses. Many, many noses. Sniffing and snorting and crusted with black ichor snot.

I mean, really picture it, because now I've had to, and you may not know this about me, but I'm a bit petty.

Good? Good. Go to **56**.

62.

Percival and Foom continued onward and downward.

"It's through here," said Foom finally, as they reached the doorway to the undercroft.

Percival shined his torch across the threshold. It was *not* a basement, he noted. It was a crypt. Foom might have mentioned that. And smaller and more austere than he'd presumed based on its prosaic name. The dead were buried in the walls, four high and nine across, names and dates chiseled in stone.

Font looked like Papyrus. The poor souls.

"Why the crypt?"

"I'd wanted better for them, but the curate complained, threatened really, said he'd go to the bishops. This," he said, gesturing to the room before them, "is the deepest, oldest part of the church. The curate appreciated that they were…"

"So far beneath you."

"He has a very particular sense of humor, our Pete."

"And he," Percival asked, "he *threatened* you? Because you'd taken in refugees?"

"Because we'd taken in apostates."

"Because they weren't Catholic, you mean."

"Well," said Father Foom.

Go to **168**.

Unless? Is Foom not Catholic? Is he an Anglican? Go to **190**.

Or Unitarian Universalist? Go to **73**.

63.

Percival pounded on the hotel room door. He was three-times broken and bone tired. *Soul* tired.

O, he who's got teeth in his belly

After a few minutes, Curate Pete answered the door, squinting, disheveled, tying a terrycloth robe 'round his waist. "You're that man from this morning, yeah? Do you have any idea what time it is?"

"Too late," Percival answered, as he pushed his way past. "I know, curate. About the monsters. About the dead."

Will never know peace in his heart

"First, Foom was foisted on you. An Anglican put in charge of your parish? Over you? You made your feelings on that abundantly clear." Percival circled the curate. "And then there were refugees. Telepaths! Not even Christians, and the Anglican invites them in? Shows them mercy? Grants them sanctuary in *your* church!

"It was you who placed the book in the undercroft, unleashed those creatures. But it didn't go the way you intended."

For give him a piece

"They weren't monsters, were they? They were kind. *Innocent.* But you couldn't accept that. You thought if you pushed them… That day in the nursery, you tried to provoke one, blasted it with the R63s. You thought it would lash out, but instead it shrank in fear. Tell me, Curate, how did you finally enrage them into attacking the refugee family?"

"I…" The curate shut the door behind Percival, looked on him with those tired, defeated eyes, not simply a sign of the hour. "I didn't. I tried. I crushed one into ichor to wet my machete. I was forced to sanctify the undercroft myself. Threw the blasphemers remains at the demons' feet, tried to give them the taste of it. But they just cried like babies."

And he'll want more and more

"They *were* babies."

"Were?"

Percival spoke the Demon Beast of Gynt's words. "*Bello ess.*"

"What?"

He translated for the curate from that ancient tongue: "The past repeats."

Till his heart is too full for the world

The curate observed Percival more closely now. Could see his agitation. The way his hands trembled and his lip curled. The way his stare never wandered. Could feel the hatred radiating from him like a furnace. Pete didn't know his church had burned, but he could see the fire in Percival's eyes. "D-Does Father Foom know you're here?"

"No," said Percival, "but I brought a piece of him here with me."

Percival reached behind him and drew Foom's weapon from his waistband. He aimed it at Curate Pete and flipped the ignition.

"You made me murder children tonight. Pete."

The curate trembled, raised his hands plaintively, kneeled before Percival Gynt and wept. "They were *demons*," he pleaded.

"They were the *children* of a demon."

Curate Pete sniffed, wiped the tears from his eyes with the sleeve of his robe, and closed them one final time. "The children of demons are still demons."

No, thought Percival. Never that.

Percival considered all of the other paths he might have taken that day, the paths that might have led him away from this moment. Had he only stopped to flirt with the cheese merchant. Sought out a friend for advice. Or accepted the men and women in the alley's offer of help.

He imagined running, disappearing from space and time, embracing any escape from this one inescapable narrative.

But perhaps it was simpler than all that. Perhaps it was his own curiosity to blame. If he'd only asked the curate one fewer question that morning? If he hadn't seen his full ire.

But this was the truth of it. This now, Percival's destiny. This was Fate. He, the sole survivor of the Gynt Massacre. All those children slain. Now he, the slayer. *Bello ess.* It wasn't his fault. *Bello ess.* It was the Demon Beast. It was this man. *Bello ess.* All those children. It wasn't his fault. *Bello ess.* Can't be his fault.

He wished for another way. Go to **313**.

With all his broken heart. Go to **313**.

But all paths lead to fire. Go to **313**.

64.

"That," said Percival, "is quite bright."

"Ah," said Foom. "Um." He whacked the bottom of the torch again, and it began sputtering. Both men found that strangely reassuring.

"I thought you were dead," said Foom, as he offered Percival a hand up.

Percival took it, clamored to his feet. "As did I. Sometimes it's nice to be wrong."

Foom looked down at the book, then back at Percival. "What happened? What did you see in there?"

Percival wiped ink from his face. Let it splat to the floor. Took a slow breath in through his nose. Out through his mouth.

"Nothing, mostly."

Go to **171**.

65.

As Percival approached, a young White man was boarding over the church doors with thick wood planks. A Catholic priest, no doubt. He wore the collar, of course, but were that not evidence enough of his particular vocation and denomination, there was the swing of his hammer as well, the absolute certainty of it, which Percival could only attribute to 20,000 years of church-mandated clerical celibacy.

"You there!" offered Percival by way of a greeting. Whatever the sentiment lacked in cordiality, I suppose it made up for with its... *geographic* specificity?

The priest, if Percival had properly sussed him, turned and cocked an eyebrow and lowered his hammer.

"Me here," he confirmed.

Excellent! Percival had gone looking for a priest and here one was! Best to get straight to the matter at hand. Go to **173**.

Unless... Well, there might be more than one Catholic priest on this world, yes? Maybe this was, I don't know... A decoy priest? Best to precede with caution. Go to **45**.

Or perhaps Percival decided to trick the priest? Would you like to play a trick on a priest? If so, go to **16**.

66.

"Yes, you! Sam-who-also-has-a-last-name! Probably-has-a-last-name! With the hair that does the…" Percival reached for his own unruly mop of locks and… perhaps tried to mime something? "And you wear glasses, maybe? Oh! And that coat! You love *that coat*!"

If you are indeed wearing *that coat*, go to **161**.

If not, go to **27**.

67.

Percival followed Foom as best he could, by foot and with torch, but the other man was almost laughably faster. Percival was unsure if that spoke to Foom's superior fitness or to the many times that Percival had fallen and hit his head in the last hour.

But then he fell again and hit his head and, Okay, he thought, maybe it's me.

Foom stopped and sighed and came back for him, offered him a hand up, and walked him the final few meters.

Down the hall. Through a door. Foom locked it behind them.

Go to **192**.

68.

Percival kicked the torch down the hallway, hard as he could. It bounced and spun and the torchlight arced away after it, leaving Percival in the dark with the thing. Looming. Wrathful. Deciding.

Decided.

The tip turned back towards the torch. The tendril doubled back towards it, struck and extinguished it.

And as it did, Percival took a hasty hold of Foom's limp body and dragged him backwards up the blackened stairs.

For the moment, the tendril was not following. Perhaps it'd lost their scent? Metaphorically, of course. Tendrils can't smell.

Unless?

Do you suppose the black ichor death tendril might have been covered in thousands of tiny noses? Go to **61**.

Or, um… No. No, that's ridiculous, isn't it? No noses. Sorry. Go to **241**.

69.

"And you kept something from back then?" asked Percival, not yet understanding. "What, an axe?"

Father Foom frowned in the dark and replied tersely, "Not that sort of firefighter." And then he began to run.

For a moment, Percival did not. He stood, puzzling. "Not that sort of a…" he muttered to himself. Then he smiled. "Oh, yes. Yes, Father, I get it!" And then he ran too, because he could hear the stretch and slap and smash of the tendril closing on them. He hoofed and he huffed and he clenched his teeth and he dashed after the older man, the faster man. "That just might work!"

Perhaps, thought Foom. And may the dead forgive him.

Go to **192**.

70.

"Well then," he said. With a sigh of relief, perhaps. "That's it, then."

He straightened his tie. Probably. Or maybe made it less straight? No way to know. No witnesses. He turned and faced the tendril, where he thought it was, at any rate. Thought he felt it slow as it approached him.

Maybe this was just his imagination, but he thought the thing was regarding him. Observing. Judging.

Or gloating.

"Go ahead," he told it. Unless he was facing a wall. "Fair cop."

He took a long breath, closed his eyes uselessly, and waited for an ending. Any ending.

This is when Father Foom shouted, "DUCK!"

Now, you might assume that Father Foom was asking Percival to duck and that, likewise, that might have been Percival's assumption. Quite reasonable! You are almost certainly correct and should proceed to **97** in full confidence.

However. If even the tiniest sliver of you wonders whether Foom's warning might not have been *to* duck, but rather *in regards to* a duck?

Well.

Go to **34**. For a duck.

71.

"Good, good. Now what I need you to do is sing the chorus. Yes, that last note is impossible. You probably won't be able to hit it. I've never been able to hit it. But that's not important. What's important is that you try. With all your heart. With all your sincerity. Do they have sincerity yet? It's like…

"Imagine being ironic *ironically*.

"I need you to sing that note, really sing it, and the effort expended… the *sincerity* expended… should be enough to open an Einstein-Rosensberg-Feige bridge all the way from your reality to mine that I can hijack to get me back to my own planet and time."

Why would that work?

"Shut up, Narrator."

The Narrator shut up. But because *he* wanted to.

"Shall we do this?"

Percival squinted directly at you, Sam Something-or-other, to see if you were nodding. So please nod. It'll help move this story along faster, and hopefully save the universe.

"As soon as you're ready," said Percival, "sing. Then go to **55**.

"Or if you're having second thoughts, or can't quite work out the words or the tune, I suppose you could stop off at **78** first."

72.

Sam, Sam, Sam! I'm sorry that I haven't been keeping perfect track of your choices, but I have to admit I'm disappointed. That plan was *very* marvelous.

Still, you did save the universe. There is that to factor in.

All right, I suppose it can't hurt to send you over to **12**.

But please proceed humbly, and keep in mind that the following events were not *not* foreshadowed, somewhere or somewhen or once upon a time.

73.

"But Father," Percival correctly noted, "*you're* not Catholic."

Father Foom nodded. Chuckled. "If Pete only knew. Then he'd really have something to go to the bishops about, eh?"

"You mean besides the dead refugees and the church that's been taken over by monsters?"

"The Unitarian Universalists have a cartoon pig mascot. That's the real red line, I think."

Go to **288**.

74.

"So, um, do you know where I can find a Father Foom?" asked Percival.

"Make it quick," said Foom, with a firmness that left no question in Percival's mind to Foom he was speaking.

Percival was unsure how to properly explain himself. Or the pie! Especially the pie. Good grief, *I* can't explain the pie! So he simply launched into it. "A little girl in a cheese shop told me there were monsters in your church and I'd like to help because recently I caught a serial killer and have been feeling sort of aimless ever since and also a monster ate my family and my entire colony when I was a boy and I was briefly friends with a robot but I think he was probably trolling me and I'm not sure what happened to the man who's usually at the cheese shop and, um, wouldn't you like my help?"

Father Foom lowered his head and sighed.

He did not. Clearly.

And yet. For some reason.

Maybe he had the briefest of aneurisms?

"Meet me in the alley behind the church," he told Percival, in an effort to keep the plot moving apace, "after nightfall."

Go to **101**.

75.

And so he set off for the parchment-horizon. "He" being the person you chose to follow in the previous section.

Obviously.

He looked back periodically, watched Father Void grow smaller and fainter and his companion grow smaller and fainter still.

How far? he thought. If there truly is nothing but endless nothing, how far would he go? And how could he even measure?

At least if they had gone together, he'd have some company in the moment. Someone to voice these thoughts to.

He wondered if, perhaps, his companion was thinking these same thoughts. Possibly at the same time. In the exact same order.

Shall we check in with his companion to see? Go to **198**.

Or does that sound like more nonsense? Should we skip the nonsense? If so, go to **235**.

76.

Yes, yes. You're very smart.

Smarter than our hero, at least as far as weapon slipperiness goes. An aptitude I'm sure will serve you very well the next time you need to grab for a firearm with an unspecified coefficient of friction.

Percival, having miscalculated said coefficient, lost his footing and fell flat on his back, from whence he winced with equal parts embarrassment and back pain. Possibly slightly more with the back pain.

And Foom? He was looking down on Percival, both literally and idiomatically.

Go to **134**.

77.

As I've said previously, there are some few facts I know about this day, but many matters on which I can only speculate. Of all possibilities that we will entertain within this text, this now is the one that I most wish to be true, but sadly too the one which I have most reason to find suspect.

Would that our young hero, our Percival Gynt, was kind enough to see the child in need, to see her tears, to see her dignity, her pain. Would that he was bold enough, was brave enough, to reach out with a hand, a word. Would that he was, at the age of twenty-two, the man that he would become only a few years later. A flawed man, yes, but a great one too.

I don't believe it.

He was, in those days, too callow, too self-interested, too eager for the thrill of the chase, too unaware of his own demons. Too casual in his feelings, too blind to those of others.

He was, in my own considered estimation, a bit of a twerp.

Others may disagree. Others may feel that I'm being too harsh. And that may be. My years with his biography may have left me less objective than is right and proper.

Perhaps.

If you'd rather think the best of Percival, to think that he would have seen a child in need and gone to her, continue on to **105**.

But if you suspect, as I do, that Percival's curiosity would have been more likely drawn to a simple scrap of paper, a faint hope for adventure, for any fleeting escape from an unending vista of banality and cheese, then go to **183**.

78.

"All right. Perhaps, this is too hard. If you need to, you can make up the words. You can make up the tune even! Just try to build in a really high note, and then try to hit it.

"Then and only then, proceed to **55**."

79.

Out the door, in the dark, running, groping, stumbling. Something ancient and evil at their backs.

"I DIDN'T THINK THINGS COULD GET WORSE!" Foom shouted between panting breaths. "THIS IS DEFINITELY WORSE!"

"NONSENSE!" shouted Percival Gynt. Or perhaps he simply shouted nonsense? My notes for this section have a coffee stain on them. What I can say with certainty is that there was a chase, some close calls, that Percival and Foom found the stairs, then a door, and that Foom managed to shut and lock it behind them.

This next part of my notes is pristine:

Father Void's tendril crashed against the locked door, cracked and began to splinter it.

"We have to go," Percival insisted. He pulled on Father Foom's arm, but Foom wouldn't budge. "We have to go. Leave. Now."

"No," replied Foom. Slowly. Deliberately. "I'm a bit turned around, but… I have an idea."

Go to **265**.

80.

"OUT OF THE WAY!" Percival shouted as he dove through the doorway, past the shape, rolled and fired Foom's weapon up into the creatures' quivering monkey-of-a-face.

He thought perhaps he saw the creatures separate in the explosion, before the fire turned them to mist and splatter. A few at the base, outside the blast, attempted to wriggle away, but he turned his weapon on them and scorched the earth.

Behind him, the building groaned. The façade cracked. Windows burst and erupted with fire.

Foom staggered out of the church, half-burnt, and fell to the ground. An instant later, the entire building collapsed in on itself. Black ash billowed past them, clouding the alley.

Blackening the night.a

Go to **309**.

81.

"What d'you make of that?" asked Percival, with a finger pointed up at the rip.

Father Foom craned his neck, squinted. "The way out. Fair spot. But not much use to us down here."

Percival agreed. "But let's not give up hope just yet. What's in our inventory?"

"Pardon?"

"Let's turn out our pockets, Father."

Let's go to **176** to see if they were carrying anything useful!

82.

"Hullo there," said Percival to the book. This was the first he'd ever extended a greeting to a book, and he was quietly hurt that the volume only answered him with silence.

"You have my friend in there," Percival added. "Or, well, acquaintance really. But still I'd like him back. If you would. He seems nice enough, and also I was doing a job for him. I was hoping for a Yelp review and all, wasn't I? Prospects there seem dim. I mean, we're in the dark. I'd kill for just dim right now. Not kill-kill. Let's not kill-kill. Just. If you could. Give him back, yeah? Please?"

Percival waited a few minutes for a reply. Nothing.

"Well, I tried," said Percival. "Sorry, Foom."

Go to **39**.

83.

"Where's Foom?" asked Percival. He smiled inwardly, quite pleased with his concision.

"Who's looking?" replied the bartender. Also, excellent. Two words apiece, then.

"Percival Gynt."

"Who's that?"

"Me." Percival frowned. "Obviously." And then he tapped the place where he thought the bartender should play the five of hearts. Which wasn't germane to the conversation, but Percival couldn't help himself.

The bartender scoffed, either at Percival's words or perhaps the suggested play. And he turned back to his game, just stared at it, clearly looking for any move besides the one Percival suggested.

Percival worried that he'd lost the man. "Obviously," he'd said. How was anyone meant to respond to that? Truly, this was the worst, first, and last game of Two Words that Percival Gynt would ever play.

Worst, first, last, but not finished. For the other man, still lost in his cards, was heard to mutter absently, "So what?"

So what, indeed! A cunning stratagem. Such a simple question, but one demanding of a robust and meaningful reply. In two words. Madness! And yet, this was Percival's opportunity. This was the grand adventure that Fate had placed before him. He could not give up. Would not concede to a simple, tossed-off "So what?"

Two words then. Percival closed his eyes and took a slow breath.

Perhaps he said, "The monsters." Go to **154**.

Or "The church." Go to **247**.

Or "Sekaty'r Prime." Go to **293**.

84.

Father Foom drew a door and labeled it EXIT, like so:

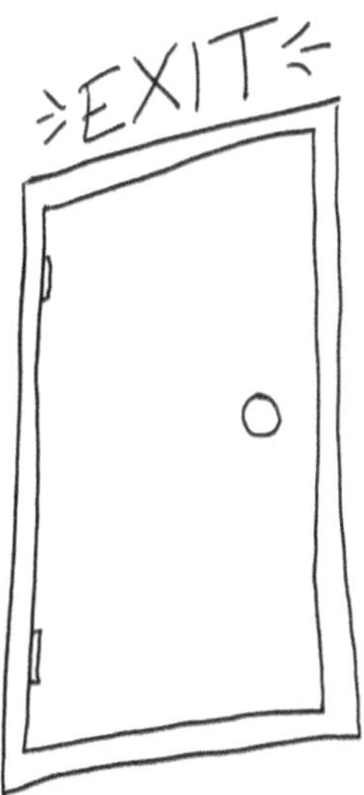

A marked improvement over Percival's scribble. It definitely *looked* like a door, if a bit hastily drawn. At least it had all the right parts: frame, hinges, doorknob. Foom had even written the word "EXIT" overtop it, should God be watching and amenable to gentle suggestion.

But would it open? And if it did, would it actually lead them anywhere, or would it simply take them from the one side of the door to the other.

Which, to be fair, is definitely how doors *not* in cursed books work.

As Father Foom considered his work, Percival gathered up his belongings. Yes, even the bit of fuzz.

Which will *not* be important later.

Except, perhaps, to Percival.

He thought, Percival did, that Father Void might be watching them. But if so, it did not speak. Did not threaten. Did not bellow, STOP THAT. STOP THAT RIGHT NOW! THERE IS NO ESCAPE. NOTHING ESCAPES THIS PLACE, AND ONLY I AM NOTHING!

He looked up at it. At the lack of it. Circled by those red-ink runes.

He wondered if someone else had been through there with a red paintbrush. Who that was. How they escaped.

"We're ready," said Foom. He placed a hand on the doorknob.

Percival nodded. Waved to Father Void. "Goodbye!" he shouted.

No response.

Foom turned the knob and pushed. On the other side, there was only darkness. "Is this better?" asked Foom.

"There's only one way to find out," answered Percival.

Go to **210**. For the inevitability of darkness.

85.

"Give it to me then," said Percival, so quickly and intently that he surprised even himself. Percival had never fired a gun before, never taken a life. But in that moment, he was sure that he could.

To live? He would kill.

And Foom saw it in him. Recognized it. Perhaps even respected it. But this was his weapon. The weight, his to bear. "No," he muttered. "This is my church. My fault. It has to be me."

But did it?

Percival thought back to the very first decision he made that day. When he stepped into the cheese shop.

Did Percival stop to flirt with the clerk at the cheese shop? If so, go to **95**.

Or did he go straight to the little girl and ask her what was wrong? If so, go to **292**.

Or did he ignore both women and go to the flyer? If so, go to **254**.

86.

Wearily, Percival rose. And as he did and as he turned back to the burning building, he thought perhaps he saw movement out of the corner of his eye, some small shape, a shadow, escaping after them.

A trick of the light perhaps, for when he turned his attention to it, it was gone.

Go to **174**.

87.

Father Foom's credit stick never contained much credit. He had three ex-wives and owed alimony to all of them. Child support to two. Monthly payments repaying a bad bet to one.

As it turns out, prosciutto is not a kind of cheese.

Money came in. Money went out. Thankfully the Church paid for his lodging and tips covered bus fare. Plus, all the holy wafers and bar peanuts he could eat.

Delicious.

The stick was perhaps ten centimeters long, made of tertium, ever-so-slightly bendy and modestly pokey. If you waved it back and forth very quickly, it made a low, subtle dumdumdum noise.

Which is what Percival was doing with it when Father Foom snatched it back.

"Perhaps," suggested Percival, "if Father Void was listening very, very closely, we could distract it."

Perhaps. However. Father Void was not, and they could not.

Back to **176**.

88.

"Maybe," she said, without looking up. "Maybe I'm missing."

"You," Percival asked, "you don't know?"

"I ran away," she said. Her eyes met Percival's, but only for a moment. "I dunno if anyone's noticed yet. Sometimes when I'm sad or scared, I go to the junkyard. The one on the far side of town? It's quiet there. Lots to explore. I stay for days and days and days. Sometimes my mother notices that I'm gone. Sometimes she doesn't."

Percival quite liked the idea of a mother who cares *less*. But he also understood that he was peculiar in that way. Not important.

"Why did you run away?" he asked. "Why were you sad? Or scared?"

Go to **103**.

89.

Percival offered Foom a hand up, but was unprepared for his density. Foom nearly pulled him down instead, but they managed.

"What are you made of?"

Foom didn't answer, eyed the staircase. They were still up there, those creatures. Shouting, jeering. But they weren't coming down to finish them off. "Why?" Foom asked.

"Because you're very heavy."

"Why aren't they following?"

Percival shook his head, shined his torch in a circle around them. "Must be something worse down here."

Foom scoffed. "Worse? What could be worse than that?"

Percival had some ideas. "Maybe pray to your God we don't find out."

And the two continued.

Go to **6**.

90.

"Hullo," said Percival, because you said he did. "I'm Percival Gynt. And last I checked, my belly is free of teeth. I'm an accountant. Harmless! And you know Father Foom, yeah? Good old Father Foom."

Percival nudged Foom with his elbow. Foom scowled. "Is this what we're doing?" he asked the almost-accountant.

"And what can we call you?" asked Percival. He directed his question, like the light of his flickering torch, to the not-cat. Was it their leader?

"We have no names," it said, "save those we're given. Name any four, and we'll be forgiven."

"They've never spoken before," said Foom. Quietly. Sharply. "And now they speak in riddles." His voice trembled. "These things." His hands tightened into fists in the dark. "They aren't what I thought."

These cryptic creatures. This incalcitrant priest. Percival could see where this was heading. "No names then. That's fine. Perhaps some questions then?"

Go to **255**.

91.

Percival approached the sniffling girl with caution. She was small and waif-thin, with brown skin and a mass of unruly dark hair that rivaled Percival's own. Tears escaped in steady streams from behind her cartoonishly thick glasses.

Her upper lip was, by this point, mostly mucus.

"Excuse me, young lady," he said to her, "but you don't have hay fever, do you?"

The little girl shivered and snorted and shook her head and then opened her mouth wide and wailed.

Percival, who had very little experience with children even when one took his own brief attempt at a childhood into account, patted her shoulder awkwardly. This did not seem to help and might have even sent her a decibel louder.

Percival glanced to Madrigal, hoping she might relay some advice to him through mime.

She raised an eyebrow. Was that a clue?

If you believe that Madrigal was signaling for Percival to look up, go to **222**.

Or if you suspect she was more likely judging him, go to **53**.

92.

As night fell, Percival found Father Foom in the alley behind Our Lady of Sorrows. This was helpfully Percival's back alley as well, so it was a short walk.

And there were others there that night. Dozens. All unhoused, Percival presumed, and queued haphazardly from one end of the alley, past the rear of his own apartment building, all the way to Father Foom's back door. They had the whiff of the street about them and a desperation in their eyes. And an unmistakable hunger.

Percival Gynt knew from hunger.

"You have a food kitchen?" he asked the priest.

"On Mondays."

"But this is Saturday, yeah?"

"Also, it's been cancelled since I shut the church down."

"So…" Percival tried to puzzle it out. "Have they been here all this time, or… Are they lining up early for the next one?"

"Oy!" one of them called out, a tall, brawny woman with two children huddled within the folds of her coat. She was standing close enough to hear the entire exchange. "We're unhoused, not stupid," she observed. "We wanna know how we can help!"

Behind her, the others grunted and nodded in assent.

If you believe Percival would have taken up this offer of aid, go to **41**.

Or if you suspect Percival would have rather declined, go to **223**.

93.

Questions then. Excellent. But where to start?

With Percival's arrival? Go to **19**.

Or with Father Void itself? Go to **263**.

94.

You know what, Sam? Can, I call you Sam?

If no, because that's not your name, my apologies and also go to **215**.

If yes, then we don't need to make a big deal of it. I'm just very psychic is all. Go to **108**.

Or I suppose if you've listened in to a Sam-part of the story before, you might as well keep doing that. You can go to **108** too.

95.

"You took a vow," said Percival. "Let me do this."

But Foom shook his head. "No," he said. "This is my church. My responsibility."

Percival reached out and slowly wrapped his fingers around the weapon's barrel. It was warm to the touch. A subtle vibration. "And all those horrible things…"

"…were also my responsibility."

Percival tightened his grip. "It was a long, long time ago—"

"Not long enough," muttered Foom.

"—and I can still remember…"

Foom eyed Percival quizzically. For a moment, he was worried that the almost accountant was about to break out into song. "Please don't break out into song, Mister Gynt."

Percival smirked. "I won't if you give me the gun."

Foom didn't know Percival. Percival didn't even know Foom's real name. Neither man knew what the other was truly capable of. But each could see the sadness in the other. See how far the other had run from his troubles. How he'd never escaped them. Never could.

In that moment, all that separated the two men were centimeters and a lifetime.

Foom closed his eyes, relented, eased his grip, let Percival take the weapon.

"Okay," said the first man.

"Okay," said the second.

Go to **159**.

96.

"Very well," said Percival, maintaining the haughty disposition of his character, but forgetting his accent entirely. "But if I find out that you've lied to me…"

Curate Pete cocked an eyebrow. Tapped his hammer against his thigh.

"…well, then we'll work out any misunderstanding then," Percival concluded with a distinct lack of confidence. And he mumbled a curt,

"Thankyougoodday."

And, okay, that probably isn't what happened, but we can assume that Curate Pete told Percival about The Wronged Vagrant.

Let's pick the story up from there. Go to **114**.

97.

As Percival ducked, a scorching ray of fire arced over his head, lighting up the corridor and igniting Father Void's inky tendril with an explosive FOOM.

The fire spread to the walls, the ceiling, and the floor. Father Void's tendril melted away within the flames.

At least the nearbyest bit of it.

Percival backed away from the conflagration, but the fire was spreading quickly. He glared back at Father Foom and shouted, "YOU HAVE A FLAME THROWER THAT SAYS YOUR NAME???"

Foom didn't answer. He'd lowered his weapon, a sleek red metal gun, to his side. His eyes stared through Percival, through the fire. Sweat poured from his brow. He couldn't speak. Dropped the weapon, turned, and ran.

The fire wasn't stopping. Percival chased after the priest. Scooped up his weapon as he passed. Still hot to the touch. Didn't matter. Couldn't stop. So of course he fell, had to pull himself up. Fire licking his heels. He followed Foom up a staircase, down a corridor.

Everywhere was fire.

Foom turned to Percival. "I'M SORRY!" he shouted. Over the flames, through fire and smoke. "THIS WAS ALWAYS GOING TO HAPPEN."

Percival frowned. This was a very specific turn of events, he thought. Probably there were other ways things could have turned out.

And then Foom ran headfirst out a window. Percival wasn't sure if they were on the second or third or tenth story. Probably not the tenth. But it was definitely a drop.

He rushed to the window. Thought he spotted Foom's body in the alley down below. Couldn't tell if he was moving.

Percival took one last look behind him. That's when he saw them.

All the creatures. Those little shadow things, half-melted and crawling towards him through the fire. Hundreds of them. Screaming children. Begging for mercy or release.

For mercy. Go to **205**.

Or release. Go to **205**.

98.

The two men considered the barricade they'd built. For that brief moment it was quiet. The two men could hear each other's breath, slow and heavy and measured.

And then the tendril struck again, smashed through the door and into the back of the bookcase, unseen by them, but hard.

Loud.

A few books fell off the shelf. Maybe four?

Foom snorted, half-lowered his weapon. Percival laughed. But just for a moment, and it hurt his rib when he did. And then the ink-dark tendril came smashing through the bookcase, through an explosion of bound leather and parchment. It came for Father Foom, and it came for Percival Gynt.

Percival held his torch out in front of him. And for a moment, time seemed to run slow. The tendril stretched towards them through the light shaft, a thing of immaculate beauty, as perfect an expression of negative space as ever there was. And in that half-second, the shaft never flickered, never dimmed. It was light against darkness. Celestial. Eternal. And nothing was inevitable.

And then Father Foom pulled the trigger. Fire rushed from the weapon's tip, out, through the tendril, through broken bookcase and door, and out into the corridor beyond. With a roar.

With an all-consuming FOOM.

Before them, the once black tendril was now melted sludge on the floor. It was dead, thought Percival. Lifeless. If just that tiniest part of it.

A sense of relief welled-up within him, quite at odds with the physical brutality his body had endured. Quite at odds, he quickly recalled, with their current predicament. As the furniture before them burned, as a fire raged out in the corridor, Percival turned to Foom and shouted, "We're going to burn to death! We've got to get out of here!"

Foom nodded. Slowly. His eyes were on his gun. His head was somewhere else. Somewhere far away and long ago. His grip loosened, and the weapon fell to the carpet with a heavy thunk.

"FOOM!" shouted Percival, and the other man was back. Alert. He shoved the metal filing cabinet out of the way. Percival thought to push the bookcase out of the way, but it was already ablaze. Foom kicked it once, twice from the side, and it collapsed in on itself.

"We'll need to go fast," he told Percival. "Hold your breath. Stay low. Don't burn."

And then Foom rushed out into the burning hallway.

Percival looked down to the abandoned weapon. To the doorway. To the weapon. Snatched it up and followed the other man into the flames.

Go to **201**.

<h2 style="text-align:center">99.</h2>

A few words now about Percival's fallen allies. Who they might have been and where their lives might have taken them, if not for a singularly uncharacteristic moment of bravery, of principle, in the shadow of a doomed church that could never be taken back.

Fulgrimm the Short had a twin brother in Sorrow Point Province, an older brother barely, named Fulgrimm the Tall. The two were separated by forty-seven seconds at birth and twelve centimeters by the age of majority and by many kilometers, one's family, and the other's addictions as the twins approached middle age.

Had he lived, Fulgrimm the Short would have finally accepted his brother's offer of a place to stay when the weather got cold. With his family's help, he would've beaten his addictions and reunited with his estranged daughter, Lucinda.

He would have gotten his old job back blowing glass and met a kind woman named Agarva who'd just started in accounts payable. They would have married on the moon, bought a small cottage there, and had three more children by the time Fulgrimm's liver failed him.

On his deathbed, Lucinda would have introduced him to his first grandson, Nathaniel, who everyone would call Nate-O, though no one could say precisely why.

Every Christmas after his passing, Agarva would have invited the whole family to the cottage to be together, to remember her beloved husband, and to celebrate life. Fulgrimm the Tall would have come with his wife. Lucinda and Nate-O would've brought their robot dogs. And Agarva's children would've returned too:

The Senator. The Prime Minister. The Journeyman Glassblower.

M'k'k'b, a necroblob, might have lived a hundred more years, a thousand more years, were it not for Percival. Might have, but wouldn't have. When necroblob rights came under assault in the late 20010s, M'k'k'b would have found its voice as a fierce advocate for change. Its impromptu speeches as captured on YouTube and the more formal ThouTube would have galvanized millions of undead invertebrates into action.

A galaxy would have gathered around their tablets and their holoscreens and their sentient, clairvoyant, hallucinogenic throw rugs to listen to M'k'k'b's final, legendary speech, entitled "GRAGH FLAGGH NYAHH!!! AAAHHH!!! AAAA231!!!" in stunned confusion.

Hours later, as the Celestial Governor toasted M'k'k'b at a dinner in its honor, a single shot would have rung out. A lone gunman they'd say, though his manifesto would later link him to the Nth Reich and the Life Supremacist movement.

"Gross," the Celestial Governor would have concluded, as aides sponged necrotic tissue from her stoney hide and garments.

Yella, if given the chance, would have saved up for a ticket home to Sanctuary-5. There she would have strangled her stepfather to death with her bare hands.

He knows why.

On Sanctuary-5, every sentence is a life sentence. No death penalty. No parole.

And so she would have died in prison, decades later, still smiling.

Maaba never checked her email, but as it turns out, there was a recall out on a particular servomotor used in her arm and leg joints.

Sparks that could start fires. That would have burned down an entire homeless shelter, brought it down on top of her and one hundred and fifty other souls, killing them all.

Overcome by grief and an overwhelming sense of responsibility-but-not-accountability-because-that-second-one-is-what-you-can-be-sued-for-in-the-201st-century, computer programmers would've gone on to design and implement an even more obnoxious form of push-notification, to force all of us to read every single spam email we ever receive.

The Maaba Poke would have been her last and only lasting legacy.

If Hestor hadn't died in the church, she would have died soon after. Hestor had Stage 117 Everything Cancer. Indeed, she had so much cancer that several of her doctors speculated Hestor was actually a sentient cancer with incidental Stage 117 Human Parts.

She hadn't told her children, Cressia and Bim. Or her brother B'Senn. They knew she was sick, but not how sick.

The disease would have overtaken her one quiet morning in June, with children and brother and brother's family close. She would have died with only one regret.

That she'd never been brave. Her whole life. That she'd never shown Cressia and Bim what it meant to stand up and fight for what they believed in. That she was a coward when it might have counted.

"Promise me," she would've told her children. "Promise me you'll make different choices."

They'd have nodded, and per prior agreement, brother B'senn would have taken them away so as not to see their mother in those final, painful moments.

She would have died alone, thrashing, gasping for air. Wishing that her face had instead been ripped off by an evil demon rabbit.

If only.

Go to **181**.

100.

"Actually, I'd rather you didn—"

The not-cat began in that same sickeningly sweet tone, only to be joined by other voices issuing forth from the dark. From further down the hall. From overhead. From behind.

And their voices? Like children's. Singing.

A children's chorus of monsters:

O, he who's got teeth in his belly,
Will never know peace in his heart.
For give him a piece,
And he'll want more and more,
Till his heart is too full for the world.

If it was just Percival and Foom facing the monsters, go to **203**.

Or if they brought allies, go to **224**.

101.

Nightfall was still hours away for Percival. But for you, it's just a page flip away. Go to **92**.

Or, if you'd like, I can tell you a little bit about how Percival spent his afternoon? Go to **303** for that. Mild spoilers: It involves toilet paper.

Or, if you're the patient sort, but not toilet-paper-patient, perhaps you'll indulge me in a bit of speculation instead? I have reason to believe that Percival consulted with a friend on these matters before meeting Foom at the church that night.

A friend who's an expert on demons. Go to **184**.

102.

Percival sighed. Looked around again. Still nothing. Well, paper-nothing. Which was admittedly less nothing than the nothing-nothing that loomed overhead. Or didn't loom. Percival sighed a second time, more aggressively this time.

All he'd wanted was another serial killer.

He knelt down and touched the… whatever it was that he was standing on. It was smooth. Didn't really feel like anything. It wasn't parchment. The parchment was metaphorical, maybe.

But if there was a floor he couldn't see, why not walls? Why not a door?

Should Percival have gone looking for a door he couldn't see? Go to **207**.

Or perhaps he should have questioned Father Void, to find out what he knew about all of this? Go to **93**.

103.

The little girl shook her head without lifting it, edged away from him. Scared, maybe. "Oh. Oh, I'm sorry. I didn't mean to…" Didn't mean to what? "…to, um, you're clearly in the middle of a thing."

She was small, this girl, and waif-thin, with brown skin and a mass of unruly hair that rivaled Percival's own. Tears escaped in steady streams from behind cartoon-thick glasses.

Her upper lip was, by this point, mostly mucus.

"I was just making a joke," said Percival. He took a step towards her, reached out a hand to… what? Comfort her? "I didn't, um…"

The girl shrank from him, opened her mouth wide and shrieked.

"OY!" shouted the shop clerk.

Percival raised his hands above his head and shouted back, "SORRY! I WAS JUST CHECKING ON HER!"

"WELL, NOW YOU GOTTA TO DO SOMETHING, YEAH?"

Percival nodded and bent down in front of the girl. He held his hands up in front of him so she could plainly see that he wasn't reaching for her again. And he spoke loudly and slowly, in case she was an idiot.

"YOUNG LADY!" he began. "I. AM. SORRY. I. SAID. A. THING. PLEASE. STOP. CRYING."

Go to **53**.

104.

Percival let go of his torch. Let it tumble to the ink-stained carpet. There was no need for it anymore. The world was on fire now. Everything. Everywhere.

And he'd lost track of Father Foom.

He called to his companion, "FATHER?"

His voice was echoed, up and down the corridor, by other voices, small voices. Desperate cries, calling out the same word. Calling for a different father.

The children of the Father Void. Dying. Melting away.

Percival made a choice. He ran. Left or right. Believe me when I say, it doesn't matter which. Into the fire. Through the fire. Ran for his life. Not for the first time. Remembering.

A monster at his back. He'd called out for his father too.

A father who was already dead.

He coughed out smoke. Felt something dark and wet fall on him, screaming in torment. He flung it from him into the flames. Kept running. Weeping.

He remembered those words, spoken in an ancient tongue:

Bello ess.

The past repeats.

The past repeats.

Go to **276**.

105.

All right then. Don't listen to me. It's fine. I'm only the most renowned expert on Percival Gynt in all of space and time and also the author of two books, at least one of which you've bought and are currently reading. And also I've won several awards, two of which are clockwork squids.

Fred and Inky are very disappointed in you.

But fine. Yes. I've presented this option to you. Let's do this. Who knows? Perhaps, against all odds and reason, this now is our pathway to the truth.

"My child," said Percival, on bended knee, and let's say with a silken handkerchief in hand, extended solicitously before him. Because this is what the people want apparently. "Prithee, don't despair. Whatever darkness shadows your heart is but a passing cloud before the immortal sun, and we the gentle breeze that summons back the light."

The child before him was small, waif-thin, with brown skin and a mass of unruly hair that rivaled Percival's own. Tears escaped in steady streams from behind cartoon-thick glasses.

Her upper lip was, by this point, mostly mucus. Her lower lip hung slack. If she had heard Percival's honeyed words, had gleaned their meaning, she did not have a sensible response to them.

"My child," Percival repeated.

"I…" the sniffling girl began, but then she trailed off, tried to recall what she was to say in circumstances such as this, when strange men said strange words and offered up silken squares in cheese shops. "'M not supposed to talk to strange men?" was the best she could manage in reply.

"Ah," said Percival, standing and pocketing his handkerchief. "Well that's the thing! I'm Percival Gynt. I'm an accountant." A modest exaggeration. "And accountants are the opposite of strange!"

The girl picked at her lip-mucus as she considered Percival's words. They were, she was quite certain, either sense or nonsense, but she saw no obvious path to discern between the two. "I'm fizz," she said finally, confoundingly, and then she pointed one small, unsteady finger back at the notice board and the single sheet of paper pinned to its cork. "'S just the monsters."

Percival Gynt closed his eyes and took a deep breath. A grin spread across his lips. The hand of Fate. The very thing to lift him from his doldrums! To set him on his path. And also he was an extremely decent fellow who genuinely cared about this girl and whatever crisis lay before her.

If we're still doing that. Are we still doing that?

Yes? Yes! Go to **145**.

Um. I guess not. Go to **191**.

106.

The lack of ground was actually quite comfortable to crawl on, as far as such things went, but still it was an awful lot of crawling, and slowed by their quite reasonable fear of falling into a bottomless or hard-bottomed or spiky-bottomed or, good grief, acid-bottomed pit.

Really, any kind of pit.

After a kilometer or twelve, the two companions decided to stop. Foom stood. Percival took the opportunity to sit for a moment.

"Why applesauce?" he asked Foom.

"Pardon?"

"Crisscross-applesauce."

Foom looked down at Percival and furrowed his brow. "Children like applesauce."

"I didn't. I liked tomato sauce."

"Well then, you can sit crisscross-tomato-sauce, can't you?"

Percival considered whether that would mean repositioning his legs. "Are you hungry?" he asked Foom.

"No, you?"

Percival stood. "More evidence we're dead," he noted. "Let's walk back."

Go to **17**.

107.

Even on his best days, Percival Gynt was known to speak before he thought, before he gave his heart the chance to feel. Sometimes this inclination served him well, as on that triumphant day so near the end of his life, when he saved all of existence from a flock of Killer Space Ostriches™ by leading every sentient being in the universe through an intergalactic, wholly improvised chorus of "Put Your Heads Back in the Sand (Space-Sand)," later a Top 40 hit on several planets.

On other days, particularly his earliest and never more so than this, his very worst day, the inclination to speak first turned out…

…*less* good than that.

"I fight monsters," he'd told the girl. This was a lie. An aspiration, but a lie. In truth, he'd only ever faced one monster. They did not fight. He was only a boy, and she a force of nature. Unfathomable. Unstoppable. The Demon Beast of Gynt. She murdered everyone that Percival had ever loved or liked or disliked or had not yet formed an opinion of because, not his fault, he was only three. She left Percival alive as her plaything. Only the mercy of hardened soldiers and their guns had saved him, and he did not thank them.

For he did not believe that he deserved rescue.

He believed that in surviving, he was as much a monster as she.

And perhaps he was. Today, he would find out.

Bello ess, the monster had told him in her ancient tongue. The past repeats.

The past repeats.

The past repeats.

Go to **304**.

108.

Right, Sam. Here's the thing:

Things are about to get terribly grim. And we can get to that, if we really must. But maybe there's a little bit of magic left? From the time that you and Percival saved the universe together?

You did save the universe, didn't you? You're not that *other* Sam?

If yes, go to **274**.

If yes-but-to-the-other-thing, go to **54**.

109.

Percival could hear the creatures taunting him, cursing him, up a flight of stairs or a million lightyears away. He wasn't sure. And those cops. Monsters of a different kind.

Also, he thought of his mother.

Percival's hand tightened around the half-off torch. He rose. Coughed. Spat blood. But he rose. Shook the torch. Flicked it on and off. He smiled. It was working exactly as well now as before he dropped it.

Which is to say not well, but well enough.

Perhaps, he thought, you can't break a thing that's already been broken.

More than anything, he hoped that was true.

Go to **89**.

110.

Father Foom awoke in purgatory. He thought. Maybe. It was a

featureless void with a sort of parchment backdrop. Also, there was an enormous nothing-monster hanging overhead, ringed by a series of ink-red floating sigils.

Perhaps I should have mentioned that part first.

"Am I dead?" asked Foom. "Are you the Devil?"

The thing above him defied description. It had no discernible shape or size. No color or characteristic that Father Foom could plainly perceive. It was a sort of voidier void, without the good graces to even be parchment. But it exuded an unmistakable presence. For all its absence, it also inexplicably *was*.

Foom sighed. He'd left the Church at a young age to explore less dogmatic faiths, but even for him this level of vagueness was a bit much. "What are you?" he shouted out. "Do you have a name?"

The thing that was nothing answered with a voice that was deep and booming and also possibly just a light breeze hazily remembered. I AM FATHER VOID, is what it either said or didn't say.

Father Foom smiled. "And I'm Father Foom! Are you a priest too then?"

I AM NOT.

Father Foom's expression slackened. "Ah well. Worth a chance. S'pose you're a, um… biological father then?"

I AM NOT.

"Adoptive?"

I AM NOT.

"Is it a title of honor then?"

I AM NOT.

"A, um…" You have to understand that Father Foom was trying, *really* trying, to have a substantive conversation with this distinctly insubstantive creature. "Is the word 'father' just a random combination of sounds then? Is this a monkeys-and-typewriters situation?"

I AM NOT.

Father Foom had been properly patient. He hadn't always been a patient man in his life. In fact, in his youth, he'd been quite the firebrand. But this exchange was doing his head in. Last try, he thought, and he took a deep breath.

"Are you," he asked this creature that was also not a creature, "not?"

Father Void did not immediately answer. Foom dared to hope that it was considering his question. He was quite proud of it, as questions-put-directly-to-abstract-entities go. But as the wait grew longer, Foom's hopes dimmed. Perhaps Father Void had grown bored of him. Could nothings grow bored?

Or perhaps Father Void simply hadn't heard him. Perhaps what Father Foom needed to do was repeat the question, slower and louder.

If you think Father Void had properly grown bor—

I AM, Father Void answered finally, succinctly, and before I could offer up a pair of choices to you that I swear would have been positively crackerjack.

Probably crackerjack.

By this point, Foom had forgotten his original question.

"Yes, well," Foom replied. He sighed and looked about and confirmed that there was nothing else to this paper void as far as the eye could see. "D'you have an opinion on transubstantiation?"

Go to **194**.

111.

Percival ducked under the black tendril and charged forward into the dark.

Crap! Can't see! What now?

Foom has the torch! Go to **182** for the torch!

Can't stop now! Can't see when you're dead! Go, go, go to **36**!

112.

"Not s'posed to talk to strange men in cheese shops," said the girl, with a voice so small that Percival could barely hear it. "Mother's rule." Or perhaps she'd simply said "Mothers rule!" which would have been less pertinent, and also frequently and heartbreakingly untrue.

As Percival well knew.

"We should always listen to our mothers," he said anyway, "but I'm not strange. I'm Percival Gynt! I'm an accountant." He took the handkerchief from his breast pocket and offered it to the girl. "And accountants are the opposite of strange."

She wrinkled her nose, frowned, took the handkerchief reluctantly, and blew her nose into it. "That true?"

"True enough for your mother, I'd think."

The girl offered Percival his handkerchief back, but he motioned for her to keep it. Or possibly to burn it? The gesture was ambiguous. "Now tell me why you're crying, and perhaps I can help. Helping girls in cheese shops with their problems is what I do."

"You said you were an accountant."

"One of those things is more of a side thing."

"Which one?"

"You were going to tell me why you were crying."

Go to **50**.

113.

Percival was woefully ill-prepared to confront Foom's monsters, and he knew it. He didn't know what they were or where they came from or why they killed the refugee family. He didn't know their strengths or their weaknesses. Didn't even have a proper name for them.

If they even had one! Perhaps it was up to him? Percival wondered. He could call them… *Fnargles*, maybe? He didn't think anyone had used that name yet.

But what if he met them, and they didn't seem like Fnargles at all? Then he'd be back to square one.

Wait, no, he reminded himself. He was still at square one. "Fnargles" did not constitute a second square.

Square one, and the best place, the only place, to find the answers to his questions was here in this church. What? Where? Why?

"Well?" asked Foom, startling Percival out of his reverie.

"Fnargles?"

"Pardon?"

"Oh. Sorry." Percival shook his head sheepishly, pointed vaguely into the darkness ahead of them. "Look! A something." And he hastened his pace.

"I don't…" Foom squinted after him. "WHAT'S A FNARGLE?"

Go to **49**, and maybe we'll find out together!

Probably we won't. Go anyway.

114.

Percival followed the curate's directions down the street and around the corner to a dilapidated dive bar that might have been called "HE ON A RANT," if the faltering neon sign was to be believed.

It was a small-verging-on claustrophobic establishment, as many in the neighborhood were those days, barely wide enough for the bar itself and a line of empty stools. The lights were off. The only source of illumination, a shaft of sunlight through the single short-high window, a dusty yellow spotlight that fell upon the bartender's face, highlighting his sour expression, as he hunched over a game of solitaire.

A losing game.

He was a White man, lean, rat-bearded, perhaps in his mid-40s, green aproned, hands well-calloused, intent on his cards, and, by any estimation, supremely disinterested in the prospect of a customer.

Best get straight to the point, thought Percival. Go to **83**.

Unless? This man seemed grumpy. And grumpy men almost never tell you where Catholic priests are. This was in Percival's experience. Not mine, Uncle Mike. But perhaps Percival was better off engaging in pleasantries first? Establishing a rapport? Cultivating an ally? Go to **299** for that.

Or, who knows, perhaps Percival decided to trick the bartender! Because why not. Go to **131** for that.

115.

"I hope he's all right," said Percival. A lie. Percival was perfectly indifferent to Edgarry's fate.

"He's out sick," the woman replied. "He'll be back in tomorrow."

"Ah! So I suppose that makes you a what? A sort of *cheeese*-temp?"

"I'm the owner," she said. "This is Madrigal's Cheese Shoppe. I'm Madrigal."

"Oh."

"Chin up, customer-with-hat. We still have cheese to sell you."

Percival nodded, perhaps for longer than he intended, as he considered whether he had a chance with this attractive, entrepreneurial, perhaps deeply disdainful woman.

"Cheese?" Madrigal repeated.

"I feel like we have something here," said Percival, gesturing generically to the space between him and her. "Perhaps I should buy you dinner. Or, I don't know how well your shop is doing, but perhaps you should buy me dinner? I'm a junior accountant, but I'm sure I'll make full accountant soon. Well, technically I'm not a junior accountant, but I am junior-to-the-accountants, if that makes sense."

It did not. Percival continued.

I can spare you the worst of it.

If you want me to spare you the worst of it, go to **300**.

Or go to **127**. For the worst of it.

116.

For a moment the girl stood silent, save for her sniffling, unsure where to start.

"I miss 'em," she said finally, solemnly.

"The refugees?"

"The monsters."

Percival didn't push, didn't pry, although of course he wanted to. He stayed there, knelt before her, a hand on her shoulder, and he waited. Those seconds were like knife cuts for a young man in search of adventure. In search of answers.

"They were cute," she told him with the smallest voice. "We didn't know."

"The monsters were... *cute*?"

She shrugged. "You had to see 'em. They looked like little kittens and puppets and... and teddy bears and..."

"*Monster* kittens and puppets and—"

"Well, they were all made of black goop with shiny red eyes."

"But..." Percival closed his eyes, took a steep breath, tried to picture the girl's monsters in his mind's eye. "...*cute* black goop and red eyes?"

Percival was, I must confide, growing increasingly exasperated through this portion of the exchange. He was, we have agreed, quite concerned for the child's safety and well-being, but also he wanted her story to proceed faster, linearly, and with a greater focus placed on the essential details that would eventually aid him in confronting her monsters.

Perhaps you agree! Shall I simply summarize the remainder of their exchange? If so, go to **284**.

Or if you're truly enjoying this back and forth, well… I shall pass no judgments! There's more of it at **119**.

117.

Though smoke stung his eyes and flames obscured his vision, Percival spotted a dark shape racing away from him the size and shape of Father Foom.

Percival followed as fast as he could. He trusted that Foom knew his own church, even as it turned to fire and ash around them. Even as the building moaned and creaked and threatened to collapse.

The shape too moaned ahead of him. Almost inhuman. A grief few could imagine.

Percival Gynt was one of those few.

The heat and smoke were like nothing Percival had ever experienced before. When his jacket caught fire, he tore it off and let it fall behind him. And still he followed the shape.

There was a light ahead of them. Not the fire. Something else. Moonlight? *Hope.* They were almost there.

But the shape slowed. Something was wrong. Wrong exit? No.

Wrong shape.

Go to **242**.

118.

Foom pulled the holographic portrait of the Space Pope down off the wall. Percival couldn't remember which one it was. Benedict II maybe? Or Paul-something-or-other? Frnargak of Xorgg? Behind the portrait was a wall safe, a GE Mark XVI SafeSafe™, top of the line, virtually impregnable unless the power goes out.

The safe's door swung open as the father's fingers brushed against it. A design flaw on any other today. But today? A feature.

Foom reached inside and drew out the weapon. *His* weapon. That old familiar weight. Its smooth red chrome barrel gleamed in the torchlight.

"A platoon of firefighters saved my life once," said Percival. "They weren't all bad."

Father Foom flipped the ignition switch and the weapon whirred to life, glowed from within, illuminated every wrinkle of challenge and regret on the older man's face.

"*We* were."

Should Percival have asked Foom to say more? Would Foom have answered? Go to **163**.

No. There wasn't time. Go to **249**.

119.

"From whence," asked Percival, with saintly patience, "did the adorable puppets and kittens and teddy bears made of black goop with shiny red eyes come?"

"The refugees found 'em. In the basement, maybe."

"Found them?"

"I dunno. Maybe they came through a…" The little girl strained to think, then flashed a smile. "A monster hole!"

Percival nodded. "Monster hole" was vague, but sensible. "And when did they turn on the refugees? Why?"

"I dunno," the girl repeated. "Why, I mean. It was a few weeks later. Last Tuesday. Father Foom had given 'em the full run of the church. The monsters, I mean. The refugees had to stay in the basement. For their protection, he said."

"Protection?"

"They were illegal, Curate said. Helipads."

"Heli—?" Percival frowned, furrowed his brow. "Do you mean *Telepaths*?" The galaxy had been rightly horrified by what happened on

Sekayt'r Prime the spring previous, but old prejudices ran deep, and few were eager to open their worlds to mind-reading aliens.

"No, I'm pretty sure he said helipads."

"Helipads are the platforms that helicopters land on."

"And what are telepaths?"

"People who can read minds."

The girl thought. Percival waited patiently.

"They might have been telepaths," she allowed finally.

"And you're sure the monsters *ate* the telepaths?"

The girl nodded. "That's what they say. And now Father Foom's chained the doors shut! He said it was just for a little while, but… but…"

Go to **24**.

120.

"THIS WAY!" shouted Percival, as he pulled Father Foom behind.

Foom tried to keep the torch pointed steadily ahead of them, but it was a challenge as they ran. Instead, the corridor appeared and vanished before them in flashes of light and dark. "DO YOU HAVE ANY IDEA WHERE YOU'RE GOING, GYNT?" he shouted.

"I'M GOING RIGHT! RIGHT MUST BE RIGHT, RIGHT? I MEAN IT'S RIGHT IN THE NAME!"

"WHAT?"

"RIGHT?"

"STOP!"

Foom planted his feet! Percival lurched forward, lost his grip, and fell! "I'm stopped!" he grumbled from the floor.

Foom flashed the torch to their left, to an open doorway and a stairway up. "Shall we?" he asked. Very confident. What do we need Percival for, again?

And then the black tendril wrapped around Foom and flung him against the ceiling, floor, and ceiling again, before dropping him limp at Percival's feet.

The torch fell from his hand, rolled towards Percival, shined into Foom's open, unconscious eyes.

Hmm. Probably this is what we need Percival for.

Go to **68**.

121.

"I have some experience with monsters," Percival confided. "And it was just last week I caught a serial killer. This is the sort of thing I do."

The bartender appeared skeptical. "Do you have references? Or, I don't know, a LinkedIn page?"

Percival had both of those things, but they were mostly accounting-related.

The two men stared awkwardly at each other. It was Fate that brought them together, thought Percival. Fate doesn't have a LinkedIn page. And then Percival said an odd thing:

"Fate doesn't have a LinkedIn page."

"Excuse me?"

"Um." Percival paused. He hadn't meant to say that out loud. "Fate, Mister Bartender. The serial killer I caught lived in my apartment building. Foom's church is just a few doors down. Fate put the cheese girl in my favorite cheese shop."

"Cheese girl?"

"Or…" Perhaps this bartender was a religious man. Like Father Foom. "Perhaps it was God? God and Fate are basically the same thing, yeah?"

The other man observed Percival. The young man in a natty suit with the awkward smile and those too large eyes. "You talk a lot for a monster-experiencing killer-catcher, Gynt."

"It's, um, one of my talents?" answered Percival, with precisely as much confidence as you'd expect.

"It's me," said the bartender. "I'm Foom."

Percival made a face like he'd already worked that out. He had not.

Foom sighed, gathered his cards and fanned them in front of Percival Gynt. "Pick a card."

Go to **52**.

122.

"Foom's not your real name."

"Not my Christian name."

Percival thought to hand the page back to Father Foom, but instead it slipped from his grasp. Fell away into darkness. Percival didn't know what to do or to say.

"It hollows a man out, that life. It hollowed me out. I... I had to start over. Vowed I'd never kill again." In that moment, who was Father Foom speaking to? To Percival? To himself? To the weapon in his hands?

"What about now, Father? Would you take those monsters' lives?"

Foom took a moment before he answered, breathed in and breathed out. "That tentacled abomination out there? The Father Void? Yes," he said. "Yes, I think I could."

"And its children?"

Foom thought back to that long corridor. When the not-cat sang. When he and Percival faced those creatures. Just the two of them. Back-to-back.

Surrounded.

Alone.

Go to **227**.

Unless? Am I misremembering? I've had quite a lot to drink tonight, and there's quite a bit to keep straight. Had they brought others with them? Allies?

Well, if that's right, you should definitely go to **264**.

123.

"Forgive me asking—" began Father Foom.

"Forgiveness is your thing," replied Percival without turning to look back on his companion.

"You're not a religious man, are you, Mister Gynt?"

"I believe in Fate."

"With a capital F, if I'm to judge from your intonation. Yes. Maybe you mentioned that this morning. But not God."

"No. Is that a problem?"

"Did Curate Pete tell you I'm an Anglican? He likes to go on about that."

"Maybe he mentioned that this morning."

"Well, it's worse than that. I lied on my application. I'm a Unitarian Universalist."

Percival didn't know what that meant, so he kept walking and hoped the conversation was over.

"The first Universalists broke away from the Catholic Church because they didn't believe in eternal damnation. Didn't believe that God would condemn anyone to Hell for all eternity."

Percival stopped, turned, shined the flickering torchlight into Foom's eyes. "Didn't believe in *eternal* damnation. So they still believed that God would torture people in Hell for… a while?"

Foom half-shielded his eyes from the half-light. Gave a little shrug. "Maybe a few thousand years? But then they'd be in Heaven forever. Forever is much longer."

"Do Unitarian Universalists still believe that?"

Foom scratched his beard. "Nah. We don't really believe in any one thing these days. Lotta Secular Humanists. Lotta Jews and Catholics and those Mecha-Thor people. Buddhists. Church of the All-Mother. We're not really into telling people specifically what to believe."

"But you're also a Catholic priest!"

"As a Catholic priest, my job is absolutely to tell people specifically what to believe."

"You're not doing a good job of selling me on your congregation, Father."

"Oh no. No, no. I would never. I just wanted to say you'd make a good Unitarian Universalist."

Go to **62**.

124.

"Let's make a deal!" Percival offered. "You send me back through your portal and stop sending your ink children into our world, and I'll… um… Leave?"

Percival understood the one-sidedness of this deal, so he thought to sweeten it. "And also I'll put you on a nice bookshelf?"

NO.

"Right. That was just the opening offer, wasn't it? Listen. What do you want? Everyone wants something, yes?"

I AM NOT EVERYONE. I AM NO ONE. I WANT NOTHING.

"That's… Um. Fair. Absolutely. But what about now."

PARDON?

"Now. The thing that's happening right now. You'd agree that this, this, is something?"

No response.

"You agree."

I DO NOT.

"Don't be petulant. You agree."

I AM NOT PETULANT.

"But this is not nothing."

Father Void was silent for a moment before it answered, IT IS NOT.

"And wasn't the nothing before the not-nothing better?"

IT WAS NOT.

"I mean, not worse?"

FINE.

"Fine?"

NOT NOT FINE.

"You'll send me back?"

IF I MURDERED YOU HERE, I WOULD BE FORCED TO INTERACT WITH YOUR DEAD SHAPE.

"Excellent point. Agreed."

SO I WILL SEND YOU BACK, AND MURDER YOU THERE.

"Less excellent!"

Go to **220**.

125.

"How about this?" said Madrigal, leaning forward across the counter and eyeing the girl who'd been sniffling at the back of her shop for the better, or if we're being frank here, *worst* part of an hour. "You want to impress me, O King of Answers? Go find out what has that girl so upset. You cheer her up, maybe get her out of my shop, and today's cheese is on me."

"And you'll—"

"Free cheese, King. Don't push it."

Percival weighed his option. His singular option. "And you don't think," he asked, "that she just has hay fever?"

Madrigal did not.

Go to **91**.

126.

"Right then," said Percival, as he straightened his tie, neatened his cuff, and stared upward into that looming enormity of naught. "S'pose it's up to me then."

As was proper. This is not, after all, Percival Gynt and Also Did I Mention Father Foom and the Inevitability of Fire.

No, if Percival Gynt was going to survive this, to escape, to stop the monsters and save the church, it was down to him and him only. No one could tell him what to do. Each decision, each consequence, would be his and his alone.

Because that's the choice you picked for him.

Percival addressed the Void.

"We were attacked by a tendril," he explained, less shoutily than before. Because, honestly, that was a lot of shouting. "It came out of a book. Was that you? Are we in a book? In that book? And are you the one who created all those inkblot creatures that took over the church and ate their refugees?"

Father Void did not answer.

"Oh! And if so, why?"

Father Void did not answer.

Perhaps that was too many questions, thought Percival. Perhaps the—

YES. YES. YES. YOU WILL NEED TO RESTATE THAT QUESTION. TO RENDER ALL TO UTMOST DESOLATION.

"Ah," said Percival. Then he turned to Foom and whispered, "This seems bad. Does this seem bad to you?"

"Perhaps," Foom speculated, "it's the good kind of utmost desolation."

"Oh," said Percival, mildly cheered. "Does such a thing exist?"

"It does not."

"Oh."

"Yes, oh."

YES. OH.

Percival and Foom craned their necks back up to the looming nothing, as horrifying in its enormity as in its absence.

WHEN MY WORK IS DONE, THERE WILL BE NOTHING LEFT.

No idol threat. And in that moment, if just for that moment, Percival felt it, felt dizzy. Placed one hand on Foom's shoulder to steady himself.

Perhaps, Percival speculated, he shouldn't have taken this job.

The Fate of two men is one thing. Barely anything. But the Fate of everyone? Of all things?

Percival looked Foom in the eyes. Saw his own fear, his own apprehensions, reflected back at him. Shook his head.

"I'm not sure that we're going to win this, Father."

"That's all right," said Father Foom, who'd made an entire career out of forgiving people. Other people. "What could we even do? We're trapped here."

Trapped.

"Yes." Percival smiled. "Yes, we are."

And he turned back to Father Void, looked up and pointed a pointed finger into the air. And shouted. "AND SO ARE YOU, AREN'T YOU? IF YOU COULD LEAVE, YOU WOULD HAVE! YOU WOULD HAVE DESOLATIONED US YEEEEARS AGO! BUT YOU'RE EVEN MORE TRAPPED HERE THAN WE ARE! YOU'RE..." In orbit around the creature, a ring of ink-red sigils. "YOU'RE *DOUBLE* TRAPPED, AREN'T YOU?"

FOR NOW, ONLY.

"Maybe." Percival turned back to Father Foom. "Maybe we've been thinking about this all wrong."

"How have we been thinking about this?"

"It's been trapped here. By, I dunno… wizards, probably. By those magic symbol things. Inside that book. But despite that, it was able to slip a tendril out of its confinement, tear a hole in the parchment, and stick its tendril through the hole."

"Yes."

"Don't you see?"

"No."

NEITHER DO I.

Foom and Percival glared up at the creature, glowered even, and then turned back to each other. "What's your plan?" asked Father Foom.

"I'll tell you in a moment. I promise I will. But first I have a very important question for you. Perhaps the most important question that anyone has ever asked anyone. A question on which the Fate of all things balance."

"And what's that?"

"Balance, as on the proverbial knife's edge."

"Percival?"

"Do you, Father Foom," Percival began before flashing a devilish smile, "have anything sharp upon your person?"

Go to **210**.

127.

You're really indulging my worst instincts as a historian and writer. This section could easily have been excised, if not for my desire to give you more control over the shape and contours of the narrative. I make no apologies for what's about to happen to you.

"No," said Percival, after a moment's reflection. "I suppose it doesn't. But that's the way of the world, isn't it? And I'm quite worldly. Quite… Sanctuary-Eighty, to be specific. You, of course, know the name of your own planet, so I'm not telling you anything you don't know. That's a good nod you're doing. Very noddy. Very agreeable.

Do you agree to many things? Don't answer that. I mean, you can answer if you want to. I'm not the King of Answers. Ooh! That sounds good. I have this sort of side business I'm working on, but I don't have a thing to… Anyway. You. You're very beautiful. I like the curve of your, um, your… You're not nodding anymore. Right. Dinner? You work in… food. You must know the best restaurants. Or the best restaurants for cheese. Or maybe you're sick of cheese, so the best restaurants not for-cheese? The best, least cheesy restaurants? The bleast cheesy? Bleashy? Bleachy Leesy? I… I think perhaps something is going wrong inside my mouth place?"

I hope you're proud of yourself. Go to **300** already.

128.

"Fools are underappreciated. The fool's always served an important role at court," Percival offered by way of retort, "on certain planets. The fool brings new perspectives. The odd laugh. Maybe a hat with jingly bells on top? Nice hat. Maybe brighten the place up? You lot could do with a few more fools in your pulpit, I think."

The curate shook his head. "You're as mad as he is."

"Father Foom?"

Go to **45**.

129.

"Um," said Percival.

Go to **45**.

130.

Father Foom found the monkey-monster with his foot and punted it into the wall. This startled the others, and Foom was able to pull Percival to his feet. Foom drew open a door and pushed Percival through, then stumbled after, trying to shake a rabid teddy bear from his trouser cuff as he did.

He succeeded, unfortunately as it would turn out, for off-balance, he fell into Percival, and together the two toppled down a stone stairwell.

Go to **28**.

131.

From behind his back, Percival retrieved a heretofore unmentioned cream pie and threw it square in the bartender's face!

What a trick!

The bartender wiped the cream from his face and frowned. "That was…" He was unsure whether to end that sentence with the word asinine or unwarranted or… or possibly coconut?

And he might have burnt Percival to a crisp if he had the right weapon on him. But the fire would have to wait.

He kept that gun elsewhere.

And, of course, he was trying to be a pacifist these days.

And a priest.

All right. This is probably *not* how Percival Gynt met Father Foom. Probably.

Go to **74**.

132.

The winking beam of Percival's torch trained on a particular tile in the stone floor, a cracked tile up through which a black and inky shape was seeping. It was the suggestion of a kitten or pup, half-formed, with as yet but two legs and the subtlest stub of a third. Its eyes were wide and glistening red, with oily black tears. It let out a low, barely audible moan as it pulled itself up through the fissure.

Percival handed off the torch to Father Foom and snatched the pathetic beastie up by the scruff of its ink-black neck. He lifted it up, and Foom followed his motion with the light. The creature's body stretched like tar and snapped, leaving its hindquarters stunted, incomplete.

The creature mewled in pain, its cry pitched high like an infant's.

Percival didn't flinch, was surprised by his own calm. But *calmly* surprised. He turned the creature in the light. Studied it, even as it struggled. As it averted its gaze. Turned away from the light. It was an extraordinary thing. Less a creature, thought Percival, than a work of art. And the paint not yet dry.

"A newborn," he whispered. "They're newborns."

"Are we?" it asked him, in childish sing-song.

"Are you?" asked Percival, in grown-up talk-talking.

"A mind fully formed," said Foom. "Before the body. That settles it. What we saw before, when we welcomed them into the church, it had to be an act."

"All acts are acts," said the creature. "You act the priest. He, the accountant. We act with kindness, and how are we repaid?"

Foom scowled. "You extracted your payment in blood."

"Not I," said the creature. "Your finger bends the wrong direction."

Foom grew redder. His lip twitched. He looked to Percival Gynt. "Do we have questions for this thing?"

Of course he did. But where to start?

What, precisely, were these creatures? Go to **233**.

Where did they come from? Go to **212**.

What did they want? Go to **287**.

133.

Percival nodded to the priest and bent back down over the book.

The sludge burbled at him in a way he found mildly upsetting. He glanced back at Foom. "You're sure about this?" he asked.

As if you hadn't already made the choice.

"Seems best," said Foom.

So, however hesitantly, Percival curled the fingers of his left hand around the left edge of the book's front cover and then the fingers of his right hand around the right edge of the book's back cover.

By necessity, his face was now a bent arm's length from the grasping sludge.

He gave each edge a tentative lift. Judged the weight, which was substantial as books go. But one quick, decisive movement was all it would take.

Please don't splatter on my face, thought Percival. Or this tie. It's a nice tie.

He counted backwards from 3. 2.

But before he could finish his countdown, before he could react, a tendril of sludge geysered out of the book, wrapped itself 'round Percival's torso, and yanked him into the book's pages.

The geometry of which was quite startling. To pull a man into a book's gutter? The amount of twisting and folding and, well, crumpling involved?

Foom stumbled backwards. Nearly threw up. Dropped the torch. It fell and rolled and flickered out.

Percival was dead, probably. And Foom was alone in the dark with a cursed book sludge tendril monster. He shuddered. Then he knelt.

Then he prayed.

Go to **29**.

134.

Percival, for his part, barely contained a snort of laughter. The sheer ridiculousness of what he'd attempted. From his position on the floor, Percival got as far as saying, "Perhaps I should—?"

But Foom cut him off. "Obviously not."

And he offered him a hand up.

Go to **98**.

135.

Well, thought Percival, perhaps this Father Foom was secretly a very bad sort of priest.

But was he?

Yes! That would make things easier, wouldn't it? Nothing wrong with easier. So let's say that! Farewell, generically bad priest. Truly you deserved this fate for reasons we won't get into here.

Go to **39**.

Or. Well. Let's be honest: Shame on all of us.

Go to **39**.

136.

Up the stairs! One flight, through an open door, and Foom dropped Percival to slam the door shut.

He braced his shoulder against it as he fumbled for his keys.

Percival awoke in darkness to the sounds of an evil tendril trying to break down a door.

He found Foom's arm. Whispered, "We should go."

Foom said nothing. Nodded, maybe. Pulled Percival to his feet.

Once more, the tendril threw its weight against the door, and it cracked. The whole corridor shook.

"I have an idea," said Foom. "Come with me."

Go to **196**.

137.

"I'd like to see where they killed the refugees," said Percival. Quietly, though the creatures listened.

"The undercroft," said Foom.

Percival half-glanced back towards Foom, brow furrowed. "I don't know what that is. Is it below the croft?"

Foom frowned. "A basement," he said flatly.

"Abasement?"

"Downstairs," Foom clarified.

Percival nodded. "Take me there."

"Okay. But, um, we're a bit surrounded, yeah?"

"Which way?"

Foom looked past the creatures to his surroundings. To the place he once knew best, now defiled. Cursed.

"Straight ahead of you," Foom answered, "there's a door. Behind it's a staircase down."

"On three then?" asked Percival.

The other man nodded.

"One. Two."

3.

138.

"You, SUH, muss take me foh a ROOOB!"

The priest who was at the very least *claiming* to be Curate Pete shook his head and walked away.

"COME BACK HE-YUH!" Percival shouted after him. "AHM NOT DUN WIT YOU!"

But Curate Pete was done with Percival.

Okay, so this *probably* isn't what actually happened, but who knows? Let's assume Percival followed the curate's advice and sought out Father Foom at The Wronged Vagrant.

Go to **114**.

139.

Where were we? Yes. Fulgrimm the Short, beset by monsters. He only managed the first syllable of a scream before his throat was rent.

M'k'k'k'b the Necroblob, meanwhile, who feared no darkness, who saw without eyes, tried to fight back against the creatures, but they slashed and peeled and climbed into its null-bladder, where they suckled the sweet-nectar of its rot-gut.

I did try to warn you.

The creatures were in command of the necroblob now. It reared up and unfolded to its full height and then closed around Yella. She tried to turn, to run into the light, but the twice-zombified abomination behind her was as fast as it was hungry. In her final moments, Yella cursed her Catholic God, her sister and her stepfather, and Percival Gynt most of all. And then the necroblob subsumed her and immediately began digesting her, rendering her flesh and bone to jelly.

Hestor was angry, and she knew how to hurt a necroblob. She punched it in its crunchy bits till it backed down, and then, for good measure, she kicked it again, hard enough that three of the ink creatures spilled out the back.

"Yella was my friend," she scolded. "And M'k'k'k'b! And Fulgrim owed me five credits."

And then a demon bunny ripped off her face.

Then other things happened that were even worse than that, but I trust you've gotten the idea. Let's check in on Percival, shall we?

Go to **311**.

140.

For a moment, mid-fall, Percival felt weightless. Adrift. Disconnected from time and space. Mercifully, miraculously, thrillingly alive. And free in a way he'd never felt before.

That moment lasted approximately one tenth of one tenth of one second. Then he hit pavement.

He could easily have died then and there. Snapped his spine or cracked his skull or simply driven his foot bones all the way up through his body to his brain and out again. Possibly the last thing is impossible. The doctor I consulted for this passage was extremely drunk.

He's all right now. The doctor is. Percival died a little while later. I'll get to that. But the doctor's fine. I called him an UberMech. Called his office the next day to make sure he made it in.

As of the time I'm writing this, he's definitely alive. The doctor is. Again, Percival is very dead. Mind you, by the time this book is published? When you're reading this? Who knows how much time has passed! Years? Centuries? Eventually, we'll all of us be dead: Percival certainly, that doctor, and me as well!

Blimey. Imagine I'm dead now, and you're reading this. That's knocked the wind out of me. Thank you, though. I'd like to think a bit of me lives on in you now.

Make your life count for something.

Possibly I'm a bit drunk too.

But Percival.

Go to **44**.

141.

After a time, the singing stopped, and Percival found himself with two choices. Up the stairs, to fight for himself. Or back down the hall to fight for Foom.

For himself, go to **175**.

For Foom, go to **216**.

142.

"Block the portal," Percival whispered. Grieg's advice. Sensible. Though bringing an entire church down on top of it was, perhaps, overkill.

An entire church and whatever remained of the Father Void's children. Best not to think about that part, he thought.

Percival took a breath, raised Foom's weapon, took aim through the open doorway.

And fired.

Go to **18**.

143.

"On three," Percival whispered. "One. Two."

3.

144.

"Do you have family, Gynt?"

He didn't. Perhaps he'd told Foom that already. Earlier. He didn't answer.

"A partner?"

Percival smirked. He thought of Midge. Or maybe the woman at the cheese shop? You decide.

If Midge, keep reading. If the woman at the cheese shop, also keep reading.

Not everything can be "Go to Such-and-Such."

"No," he answered. "No family. No partner. No friends to speak of. A robot, maybe. It's ambiguous. You?"

"I have a daughter. She lives with my ex-wife most of the year. She visits."

Foom said that much and then was quiet for a time. It made Percival uncomfortable, but he wasn't sure how to respond. "Is there more you want to say about that?" was what he finally settled on.

"No," said Foom. "She'll be eight next week. She's going to be an asteroid in her school pageant."

"Will you go?"

"Nah. She lives in another galaxy. Might as well be another universe."

"Also, maybe we'll be killed by these monsters."

"Yeah, that's two reasons."

Go to **62**.

145.

Of course! Of course! Percival opened his eyes and flashed a dazzling smile at the sad moppet, tussled her hair, then turned his attention to the page posted to the notice board.

The printing was poor. The letters barely jiggled as he poked them. It read:

OUR LADY OF SORROWS CHURCH
IS CLOSED INDEFINITELY
DUE TO ONGOING FACILITIES ISSUES

PLEASE ADDRESS ALL MATTERS
EARTHLY AND DIVINE
TO THE RIGHTEOUS FATHER FOOM

Vague, thought Percival, and hardly portentous. And yet the child spoke of monsters.

"Your church," Percival presumed, "has been o'ertaken by some ghastly presence?"

The girl squinted through her over-thick lenses. "No," she insisted. "Just monsters. They ate the refugees, and now everything's gone pear-shaped. Or, um…" She quite liked pears. "Maybe some worse fruit? Kumquats?"

"You poor girl. There is no shape worse than a kumquat. Probably. You must tell me everything."

To find out everything, go to **116**.

146.

"I'm dreaming," Percival said to himself with some confidence. "This makes very little sense, which means it's a dream, which means it makes perfect sense."

THIS IS NOT A DREAM! said the absence overhead. Its voice was at once deep and booming and silent as a whisper and also none of those things. It too spoke with confidence, thought Percival, who expected nothing less from a dream-nothing.

"If this isn't a dream," asked Percival as he pulled himself to his feet, "then what it is? What are you?"

THIS IS NOTHING! I AM NOTHING!

Percival nodded as he stared up into the thing. It was a terrible angle, hurt his neck. And his vision blurred. There was nothing to focus on. There was… There was *nothing* to focus on.

"Yes, yes!" Percival called up. "You're very nothingy. I can see that!"

NO, YOU CAN'T! it countered. Nothing had a fair point.

Percival looked to the parchment-horizon. There was nothing else as far as the eye could see. No nothings else.

"Listen," said Percival, who resolved just then to be civil and reasonable in his dealings with this peculiar creature and/or lack of a creature. "It seems like it's just the two of us, so we might as well be social. My name is Percival Gynt. People call me the King of Answers."

NO ONE CALLS YOU THAT.

"And here I am speaking to no one! Unless there's something else I can call you?"

CALL ME WHAT YOU LIKE. I AM FATHER VOID.

Percival nodded politely. Whatever it was or wasn't, this creature, he imagined that it had been trapped here for a long time. This was no dream. Percival was going to die here in this parchment-void with this ancient idiot nothing-monster. Starve to death probably.

"You don't happen to have a sandwich?" Percival shouted up at it.

I DO NOT.

Still, no harm asking.

Go to **102**.

147.

Father Foom pulled a holographic portrait off the wall. One of the Space Popes maybe? Behind it was a secret compartment, from which he withdrew a weapon, a gun.

Its smooth red chrome barrel gleamed in the torchlight.

Percival thought he saw regret in the priest's eyes. Guilt.

Go to **150**.

148.

One ink-soaked hand thrust upward out of the cursed book. Then the other. Then, however impossibly, Percival Gynt thrust head and shoulders and then his whole body out through a portal the precise span of this book's interior margins, verso to recto.

Which, if you you're having trouble imagining it, hurt precisely as badly as you'd imagine.

Go to **64**.

149.

"Really? It's very good. You should bing it. Do they have Bing yet? Or YouTube? Is YouTube nanites in your brain yet? Don't answer that. Paradoxes, maybe.

"Anyway, look it up, and then meet me at **71**."

150.

Before Percival could ask, before he could even formulate the question, Father Void's tendril smashed through the office door, through the bookcase, and lashed out at the two men.

Father Foom responded instinctually, flipping the ignition switch, taking aim as the weapon whirred to life, illuminated from within. He pulled back the trigger and an arc of flame streamed from the barrel, burst through the tendril like it was nothing, a spatter of black, and exploded into a fireball in the corridor beyond.

With an unmistakable FOOM.

That sound. It was never the man's name. It was the sound from his nightmares. The sound of his sin.

And now, perhaps, his penance.

Go to **230**.

151.

Something small and sticky offered Percival its hand. It was not a cat. Nor even a not-cat.

Percival didn't try to talk to it. He just followed where he was led, back down the stairs and down the hall and back, he assumed, into the undercroft.

"You're at the doorway now," said the small-handed thing. "A few more steps, and you'll be to the book."

Quite helpful. Percival took back his hand, wanted to wipe it on something but didn't, and then lowered to his knees and crawled along the floor till he could feel the goo-slicked pages of the ancient tome before him.

The not-cat had implied that Foom might still be alive inside it. Or perhaps Percival had only inferred it? That Percival might still be able to save him somehow. Go to **82**.

Or? He could close the book. Would that be enough to end this? At the price of a single priest? What's a few more teeth, thought the accountant. Go to **39**.

152.

Foom drew a jetpack. Like this:

Not *perfectly* symmetrical, but certainly much better than Percival's effort. Much less frightening. Charming even, though it nearly rocketed off on its own into the paper sky. Foom had to make a lunge for it and hold it down they were ready to take off.

WHAT ARE YOU DOING? called the voice of Father Void from above. STOP THAT. STOP THAT RIGHT NOW.

"Quick then," said Foom, and then for whatever reason, they took the time to scoop up the rest of their possessions.

Yes, even Percival's bit of fuzz.

You never know when you'll need a little fuzz. Nor do I.

Foom swung the jetpack onto his back and grabbed Percival by the arm, even as they began to lift off.

STAY AWAY! said Father Void. COME NO CLOSER! It drew its nothing-tendril from out of the rip and lashed out at Foom and Percival.

Foom, though no expert in jetpackery, managed to spin out of the way and, regaining his bearings, accelerate towards the rip.

Then came a second nothing-tendril and a third, a fourth, a fifth. But Foom dodged and weaved, now closing on his target, now fleeing. All the while Father Void ranted:

NOTHING SHALL ESCAPE THIS REALM! FOR I ALONE AM NOTHING! AND YOU ARE LESS THAN NOTH—

We can imagine what the rest of Father Void's rant sounded like, but this was the point when Foom and Percival flew through the rip and into darkness.

Go to **186**.

153.

No, I don't want to talk about it some more, you little snit! I told you what I did. I'm the writer here! I write. You're the reader. Your job is to read.

And also occasionally to select between a set of pre-defined choices that allow you some measure of control over the narrative, thus introducing an interactive element of play to what would otherwise be a FINE FINE HERE'S A CHOICE FOR YOU, CHOICE-HAVER:

Go to **92**.

Or suck it.

I'm not in a mood. You're in a mood!

154.

Two words, and the bartender glared up from his cards.

"What did you just say?"

Five words. Victory! Unless or until the bartender punched Percival in the nose, and he looked like he might.

Percival held up his hands defensively, reflexively. "A little girl in a cheese shop told me about the monsters and a man at the church told me I could find Foom here except I don't see him unless you're him are you him?"

The other man, the bartender, known by Foom and other names, sneered and gathered up his cards and muttered, "Pete talks too much."

Go to **226**.

155.

Later that night Percival awoke to the sound of sirens. Pulled a pillow over his head and went back to sleep.

In the nights that followed, Father Foom's voice joined other, older voices. Voices that called to Percival, sometimes cruel and taunting, sometimes forlorn and tormented, begging him for salvation.

The teeth in his belly.

He couldn't save any of them. Not one. Perhaps the next? Or the next?

Sometimes he visited the spot where the old church stood, later the site of a popular fishmonger's. He wondered what he would find if he dug up their basement. Was it still there, that book, waiting to be opened? Was Foom still trapped inside its pages?

Or had it burned?

A choice.

The book was found! Go to **60**.

Or it was not. **305**.

156.

"PLEASE STOP KILLING US!" Percival shouted, as he fumbled for his torch. "I JUST WANTED TO TALK!"

A lie mostly, but in that moment, Percival believed it.

Foom instinctively stepped back-to-back with Percival. "You didn't see Neesa and her family," he whispered. "They have the taste of it. They'll kill us all."

The creatures began to overtake Maaba, to mount her, chewing through her human parts.

The blue light of her robot eye faded with her final breath.

Five allies. Five dead. For a final word on the fallen, go to **99**.

Or, if you're more wholly concerned with the fate of Percival and Father Foom, go directly to **181**.

157.

Foom agreed. There'd be no escaping blind.

The two men dropped to their knees and felt across the cold stone floor for the unlit torch. Across the room, Father Void's tendril emerged from the book with a rushing squikk. A malevolent nothing in the parchment-verse, rendered here in ink and shadow.

"Found it!" shouted Foom, and he flicked on the torch, illuminating Percival and the massive tendril that loomed behind him. "Found IT!"

Go to **246**.

158.

Decorum! That's good, I guess? I mean, it's not a particularly *logical* stance, given that this whole story involves people not talking to you. Except for me, I suppose. I'm talking to you.

Though I'm not always sure why.

Listen, are you really certain you don't want to hear what Percival is going to say to this Sam person? It might be interesting! If the possibility of, um, *interest* is enough to sway you, you can still go to **66**. I won't penalize you.

If not, fine, just assume that some things happened and jump ahead to **280**.

159.

Percival felt the weight of the weapon in his hand. This was the first time he'd even held a gun. Perhaps he should have mentioned that to Father Foom before taking it.

Probably too soon to ask if he wanted it back.

He offered the priest his torch in return. Foom took it and aimed it at the bookcase, inadvertently illuminating a series of tawdry necroblob romances. Percival eyed the priest, who shrugged.

"I confiscated them from one of our younger parishioners."

Percival smirked as he raised the gun to eye-level. "And kept them." He widened his stance. Narrowed his eyes. Curled his finger 'round the trigger.

"The storylines are really quite engrossing."

From behind the bookcase came a tremendous crack. The door giving way. And then a second, louder, as the tendril broke through the door and the bookcase and half-a-dozen volumes of *The Sisters N'grythlfff* and gushed towards Percival. He took a step back, stumbled, fell backwards onto his bum and pulled the trigger.

Fire rushed from the weapon's tip, out, up, through the tendril, to the ceiling out through the broken bookcase and door, and exploded into the corridor beyond.

And the explosion spoke its name: FOOM.

In an instant, the fire was everywhere. What was left of the tendril was a splatter and a sludge now, melting into the flooring. Percival felt a wave of relief wash over him, and also he was fairly certain he was about to die.

Foom took him by the hand and hoisted him to his feet. "We've got to go."

Percival nodded and followed the older man as he shoved the metal filing cabinet aside and barreled through the burning flinders of the bookcase and door to the burning corridor beyond.

Go to **117**.

160.

"Or, well, give it a week if you must?" Percival suggested. "Monsters aren't known to slay themselves, after all."

"You're going to slay them?"

"Um," said Percival. "No. Because…?"

The little girl looked as if she might cry again. She looked down, shuffled her feet. "I know," she said. "I know they ate those people, and they shouldn't've done that. But they were sweet before that. They were nice."

Percival thought to pat her shoulder, but didn't.

"I gave 'em names."

Percival took a breath. Nodded.

"One of 'em was Olivia Q. Bigglesbottom."

"Okay, okay," he said. "I'll do what I can."

He made no promises.

Go to **304**.

161.

"Progress. Excellent.

"If you, Sam Something-or-other, would like to help me, Percival Definitely-Gynt, save reality, please go to **279**.

"If you'd rather watch it all burn, because… Um… I mean, please don't. Don't take this option. It's a terrible option. But I suppose if you really insisted you could go to…" Percival glanced at the Narrator/didn't. The Narrator shook his lack of a head/didn't.

"…**313**?"

162.

"Yes," said Percival. "I believe you're right."

Don't let it go to your head.

"Should we…" He took a step away from the book. From the writhing sludge. "Should we at least put the tiles back before we go?"

But before the narrator could so much as offer you that option, the most extraordinary and awful thing happened! A writhing tendril of foulest darkness sprang from the center of the book and whipped the torch from Foom's hand, sent it clattering away, plunging the pair into a perfect and terrifying dark.

Percival let out a short, startled shout. Father Foom swore a decidedly uncatholic oath.

"Run!" cried Percival, and he ran. Into Father Foom, as it would turn out, and the two men toppled to the floor.

"Get off me," Foom groused, and he shoved.

Percival rolled to one side, tried to catch his breath. Foom was half-to-his-feet when the tendril whipped around his wrist and swung him into the air.

Foom cried out in desperation as the tendril swung him back and forth. Percival, who to be clear had never been in a situation precisely like this before, remained crouched on the floor, hands on head, and all-together useless.

In those seconds, Foom easily could have died, could have cracked his skull or his spine, or simply had a heart attack, but he had been a soldier once and had been trained to survive the implausible. "Go limp," his old commander had told him, "any time an evil book-tendril grabs you. Go limp."

Probably they didn't say the book-tendril part. Sources disagree.

"You're doing quite well!" Percival cried out after a moment. It was all he could think to do.

But Foom, who was just then regaining his wits, did not thank his companion. Did not offer any kind of response, which Percival thought slightly rude. Foom simply repeated the words inside his head like a mantra. Go limp. Go limp. Go—

And then the tendril snapped back into the book, as fast as it had emerged. And it took Father Foom with it.

Percival had never heard a tendril drag a priest into a book before, but the sound of it was unmistakable. A sort of an "AAAHHH FLORGGH SCHFFLLL PUHH," I'm told.

What now? Percival tried to recall the layout of the room. Where the doorway was. A way out. Where the book was. If, perhaps, there was a way to save Father Foom.

Not so long ago, the killer Eeps had poisoned Percival. Tried to murder him. The police had beaten him. But this? Percival had only ever faced one actual monster before this day, and in that moment he had run for his life.

Would he run now? Leave Foom to Fate? Or try to rescue him from wherever he'd been dragged?

Run. Definitely run. Go to **229**.

Or, well, Percival's meant to be the hero of this story, yes? Surely, he'd at least attempt to rescue his companion. Go to **57** for that.

163.

"I've heard stories," said Percival.

"All true." Foom reached into the safe again, pulled out a folded-up piece of paper. "One of the soldiers in our company, Giffen, he did these little…" He paused, considered, half-smiled even. "I kept one." He unfolded the page to show Percival a series of amateur-but-earnest comics panels.

Go to **10**.

164.

"Do you like *Fun Ball?*" Foom asked Percival.

"Happy Fun Ball?"

"No, just *Fun Ball.*"

"Is that different?"

"Yes."

"I don't know *Fun Ball.*"

"It's like *Happy Fun Ball,* but…" Foom paused to consider his words. "…but the opposite?"

"So, it's a sad *Fun Ball?*"

"Not sad so much as…"

"Yes?"

"Serious, I suppose? It's for people who enjoy fun ball, but take it very, very seriously. And that's the fun for them. The intensity. The blood and sweat and agony."

Percival stopped, thought about it for a moment. Made a little "hm" sound. "And you like it?" he asked Father Foom.

"Nah," said Foom. "I like *Happy Fun Ball.*"

Go to **62**.

165.

"All right," said Foom, finally relenting. "Meet me 'round back of the church. After nightfall."

Go to **101**.

166.

Percival closed his eyes and reached one hand out towards the portal. His left, in case it fell off when he pushed it through.

Thankfully, it did not.

He looked back at you one more time and smiled. And towards me, I'd like to think, and he gave a lazy salute.

Thank you, Mister Gynt. It's been an honor.

And then he turned and took a breath and stepped through the portal.

Go to **290**.

167.

"I don't see as I have much choice," Percival conceded. "You're sure this'll work? That no one will suspect?"

"They never do," said the Intercessionary, "and we've done this switch a few hundred times now."

Percival nodded, removed the Time Glove, folded it neatly, calmly, and tucked it into his inside jacket pocket for safekeeping. "And the ones you've switched out," he asked the Intercessionary, "what happens to them?"

"Hard to explain," the Intercessionary lied. It wasn't. They were beheaded and left in a ditch on a nearby ditch planet. "We can get into it some other time." They couldn't and therefore wouldn't. "It's time. We need to do this now." The last part was conveniently true.

"Okay," said Percival. He wasn't looking at the Intercessionary anymore. His eyes were fixed on the shop door across the way. And what lay on the other side.

What is fated? What can yet be changed? Time to try again.

Go to **15**.

168.

Foom broke eye contact, looked down to the floor, then off into the darkness. "You'd be surprised how often that comes up."

If there was a subtlety to Foom's words, it was lost on Percival.

Go to **288**.

169.

And lo, Battle Queen Maeve gazed down from her mountain perch unto the vast army of pinhead writers massing against her, and she sneered. O how they shouted! O how they threatened! O how they stamped their feet and waved their fists uselessly!

"This is my artistic intent!" they shouted in unison. "That's how my narrator would use a semi-colon!" "A lot of novels start with the main character waking up!" "It's realistic because the same thing happened to my cousin!"

They were meant to have attacked her position a fortnight prior, but to the last of them, they were all miserable with deadlines.

The Battle Queen could wait no longer. She drew her blade, crouched, and vaulted down into the rabble phalanx.

Her cuts were precise! Immaculate! The pinheads cried out for mercy, but Battle Queen Maeve proffered none.

And when they were dead, she would bathe in the red ink of their manuscripts and complain about them to her fellow Battle Queens; that's how you use a semi-colon, pinhead.

Go to **20**.

170.

Percival thought as he ran.

"NOT THAT I CAN THINK OF!" he replied eventually. "BUT THERE'S A LOT GOING ON. YOU?"

"SO MANY THINGS!"

"WELL, NOW'S THE TIME, FATHER!"

Foom veered right! Pulled Percival after! And the black tendril a split-second behind!

"YOU'RE KIDDING, RIGHT?"

Foom veered left! Pulled Percival behind him! The tendril caught Percival by the ankle and pulled, yanking him away from Foom, sent him toppling to the floor, then whipped him up against the ceiling, down to the floor again, and released him, limp and barely breathing.

"This maybe," muttered Father Foom, as he hoisted Percival over his shoulder. A firefighter's lift. "I regret all of this."

The tendril reared! Foom dodged! Crossed under the tendril and through a doorway to the stairs up!

Up, I said! **136**!

171.

Just then a blackened tendril geysered up from the still open book and swung towards Percival.

Quick!

Get Foom! Go to **246**!

No! Run! Go to **111**!

172.

"We bid you," said Percival, as the light of his flickering torch passed across their tiny ink-faces, "to go back from whence you came. To slip back through whatever strange tunnel or portal or tunnel-portal brought you here! Leave the way you came into this world and know peace."

Percival was reasonably proud of that short speech, off-the-cuff as it was. Eight out of ten, if he was to give himself a score. Points off for "tunnel-portal," certainly.

Foom might have given him a five. The creatures? Less.

Oh, they smiled at Percival's words. They cooed and nodded along with them, but when he was done?

They laughed and laughed. A raucous, jeering, all-surrounding laughter.

The priest shook his head. Tears swelled. He could still remember these creatures as they were before. What were they now?

"We have to go, Gynt. We have to get out of here."

Go to **202**.

173.

"Father Foom, I presume?" asked Percival. He winced when he realized the rhyme.

The young priest lowered his hammer and smirked. "Thankfully, no. I'm Curate Pete. Assistant priest for the parish. Such as it is."

"Thankfully?"

"Father Foom has his admirers," the curate explained, with an edge to his voice that made plain to Percival that he was not one of them, "but he's Reformed Anglican. There are so few of us in this corner of space that the bishops sometimes make... *interesting* choices to fill vacancies."

"I see," said Percival.

He did not, and his confusion was as plain as the curate's contempt.

"You're not Catholic, are you, Mister—?"

Go to **307**, if you believe that Percival would have indulged the curate's questioning.

Or go to **25**, if you think Percival would have more likely ignored the curate's questions in favor of his own.

174.

What now? Percival thought back over his day. Everything that had led him to this moment. Every choice.

Had he asked for help when he had the chance? Reached out to an old friend? If so, go to **142**.

Or did he not? Or *not*-not? But then we said he *didn't* not-not? Good grief. I have an eleven-dimensional spreadsheet for all of this, and even I'm a bit baffled.

Go to **231**.

175.

If you won't fight for others, at least fight for yourself, said the coward to himself.

Slowly, he climbed the steps through total darkness.

His footsteps echoed. His breath was heavy in his chest.

He thought perhaps he could still hear the creatures. Or was it just his memory of their song?

He had no weapons. Couldn't see. He would die, surely.

Unless?

Perhaps he could trick the creatures?

Go to **200** to try to trick the creatures.

Or go to **306** to die. Abruptly.

There are no wrong choices.

176.

The items in the companions' inventory were these:

PERCIVAL

- pocket watch [**218**]
- single black glove [**199**]
- bit of fuzz [**11**]
- silken handkerchief [**277**]

FOOM

- credit stick [**87**]
- purple pen [**285**]
- keys [**236**]

177.

It had found a way out. Percival was certain. It's torn the paper sky and wriggled its pinky through. Out there, it's inky black. Perhaps that's why someone thought to trap it in a book? And Foom's demons, its children. Did they turn on the Telepaths to protect the book?

To protect their father?

It was a theory, at least. And all-together useless from where he stood. Unless he could find the tear. Unless he could reach it. Without being murdered by an enormous nothing/ink monster.

Percival had two ideas, neither good.

First, to persuade Father Void to send him home. By being as annoying as possible. Go to **124**.

Second, to trick Father Void. Into murdering him. Go to **193**.

In retrospect, these two options seem very similar. Oh well! This story isn't called "The Distinct Evitability of Fire or If Not That Another Thing" after all.

178

One mystery at a time, thought Percival.

Foom's office wasn't far. Foom entered first, then Percival, and he drew the door shut behind them.

Go to **192**.

179.

"Suggestions?" asked Percival.

Foom's face was whiter than ever. He shook his head. "T-They never spoke before. I never heard them speak. And now? Those voices. That song?"

Percival turned in half-steps, letting the flickering torchlight pass over the creatures. Taking in each strange inky visage. Attempting to estimate their number.

"Suggestions?" he repeated.

"They seemed harmless. Sweet, even. We took them in. Let them play with the children."

As Percival returned to each face, he thought it somehow different. How? He wasn't sure.

"They pretend at innocence, but they speak with a dark, prophetic voice."

Were they growing ever so slightly… larger?

"The Devil's voice."

No. Closer.

Go to **202**.

180.

"Of course." Percival smiled faintly and nodded. "I'll definitely remember that!"

Go to **166**.

181.

Percival flicked on his torch. The beam was weak and sputtering. "On three," he told Foom. "Then we run."

"Better to die running than standing still," Foom agreed, as the creatures closed around them.

"One," whispered Percival. "Two."

3.

182.

Back for Foom! Tendril slapped Percival against the wall with a thwack and a crack! The crack being Percival, not the wall! Well, slightly the wall! Foom found Percival with the torch, wrenched him up by his wrist, and dragged him as he ran!

Quick! **31**!

183.

It was not so long ago that the woman Percival thought he loved had rebuffed his advances. For a moment he considered saying something to the shop clerk, engaging her in witty banter, endeavoring to make her smile or laugh or blush. But no. Not this week. Not this day.

And that sniffling girl. Was she simply sick? Or was something troubling her? Percival considered what he knew about children. Also, *if* he knew anything about children.

Did Percival know anything about children?

If no, go to **219**.

184.

"I'm no expert on demons," Professor Grieg protested, but Percival was having none of it.

"You said it yourself. You study other dimensions. *Hell* dimensions.

Demons come from Hell. Therefore—"

"Now hold on," said Grieg. They were on video chat. Grieg had some kind of weird swirly-blue mud mask over his centuries-old face. Percival was sitting on a park bench, gobbling cheese.

"I say Hell to sound cool," said the old man. "To show off. To secure grants and impress the pants off impressionable young men. I certainly don't believe in anything so prosaic as demons. What you're dealing with are probably just run-of-the-mill aliens. Mutants, maybe. Alien *mutant* aliens."

"Alien mutant aliens from another dimension?"

Grieg sighed and peeled the mud mask from his withered face. He was well over three hundred, but his beauty regiment kept him looking half that age. "Maybe," he conceded. "Maybe, maybe. My advice? Look for a portal. Portals are good. A portal you can close or block. Close is hard. Close requires science. Or magic, in a pinch. Block just requires… you know…"

"Blocks?"

Grieg nodded, died briefly, looked at his watch. "I hope I was helpful, Percival. I really do. Always happy to help with one of your cases. But if I don't get my nap in now, I'm going to have a mood at tonight's All-Alumni Kegger and Cock Fight."

Percival wanted to say thank you, but he'd misjudged how long the Professor would talk for, and he'd just taken an overlarge bite of cheese. Instead, he simply nodded appreciatively and half-smiled, both because he was glad to talk to his friend and because he'd been modestly helpful. And also because it was a very good piece of cheese.

Portals are good, thought Percival. I can work with that.

Go to **92**.

Unless, by chance, you've already read the next story in this volume, "Percival Gynt and the View from the 10th Story?" You folks will want to meet me at **23**.

You know why.

185.

But, as Father Foom pointed out, there *was* no ground to cover. It was an observation so incisive, so succinct, that Percival immediately ceded the point.

It took a moment for them to get going. It was Percival who suggested "That way, I suppose?" and Foom saw no point in arguing. Particularly given how well Percival had received his "no ground" point.

Distance was difficult to measure. They tried to gauge by the relative size and absence of Father Void in the sky. They walked a few meters perhaps, then a dozen, then half a kilometer.

Percival checked his pocket watch. Either his watch or time was very broken.

"You don't have a watch, by any chance?" Percival asked Foom.

"Never carry one. Time's an illusion."

Percival stopped. Looked down. Seemed more distracted than annoyed, which is how most people reacted when Foom said the time's-an-illusion-thing.

"What is it?"

Percival bent down and felt for whatever solid surface they were walking on.

"Percival, what is—?"

Percival shushed the priest. Tried knocking on the not-ground. It made the same THLUMPH sound as when he fell out of the sky. It was… something. Maybe.

"What if *this place* is an illusion?" he asked Father Foom. "What if we're really in a place, a normal place, and this is just… I dunno. Holograms?"

Father Foom nodded. "Then at any moment we could run into a wall or…"

"Or walk off a cliff."

Foom slowly lowered himself to a crawl. "Slowly then?"

And so Percival and the priest began to crawl forward. Slowly.

Go to **106**.

186.

Foom and Percival rocketed out of the book and into the dark of the undercroft. Where, importantly, there was no jetpack and no jetpack rockets.

Reality caught up with the pair abruptly, and they fell onto the cold stone tile not far from the book. Foom landed with a thunk and a grumble. Percival thought perhaps he'd bruised his side.

By no means their worst fall of the night.

Foom stood. Said, "We have to go. It's coming."

"No," said Percival, now desperately groping the darkness. "We need to find the torch first."

But was there time?

No. Run first. See… later? Go to **35**.

Or, no. Light is good. Light first. Go to **157**.

187.

"Do you enjoy popular entertainment?" asked Percival.

"I beg your pardon?"

"I'm making small talk."

"Are you?"

"I… thought so?"

"And have you made small talk before?"

"Almost certainly."

"Successfully?"

Percival shrugged.

"Do you have friends, Mister Gynt?"

"Well, I…" It seemed an impertinent question to ask of so recent an acquaintance. "I suppose my *best* friend at the moment is a lying robot who hates me."

"That makes sense to me."

"Does it?"

"Sometimes I watch *Star Blocks, Yo* on MTV3."

Go to **62**.

188.

Perhaps they might have swarmed Percival and with their teeth and claws bled him, but he was near the top of the stairs, so a simple push did the job.

Percival fell backwards, cracked his skull against a stone step. And another. And another. Landed on his face at the bottom. Neck snapped. His final thought:

"I regret these choices."

Sit with that for a moment, sit with your wrongness, then join me at **204**.

189.

Percival briefly considered whether he could cut his own way out of the parchment void, but as he was armed with nothing sharper than his razor wit, he committed to this admittedly riskier plan:

Antagonize Father Void until it lashed out at him. Duck. Repeat until the assault produced a hole to escape through. Escape.

As far as plans went, it was… optimistic?

The trick was to not be murdered by the tendril. The not-tendril. To be not-murdered by the not-tendril.

Sadly, he had no cream pies on his person.

"Father Void!" called Percival. "More like Father A-void, am I right?"

Father Void didn't respond. Percival didn't blame him. He wouldn't have responded either. Razor wit? Ha. His was dull as a butter knife.

"As in, you have a thousand children and they don't even want to be in the same book as you!"

Better, maybe, but still no response.

"And I don't like to make fun of people's children, but have you seen them? Because, seriously. They're all extremely visible."

No response.

"Unlike their father."

No response.

"They say the apple doesn't fall far from the tree, but in this case there is no tree and the apples talk and sing songs."

THEY—

"You didn't know? They do all sorts of things, Mister Void!"

FATHER V—

"They played games with children! Liked to have their bellies rubbed probably!"

MY CHILDR—

"While you're in here being nothing, they're out there EXISTING. Learning. Growing. Becoming."

THEY DO NOT. THEY ARE NOT.

"You made them! And they exist now! You're adding to the universe every day!"

I AM NOT. I AM NOTHING. I BEGET NOTHING.

"Shall I sing the song they taught me? It's definitely something!"

I DO NOT… THEY DO NOT…

"Goes like this: *Ohhh, 'e what's got teeth in 'is belly! Will ne'er know peace in 'is 'eart!*" Percival's singing voice was barely passable on the best occasions and here devolved into a sort of slurring off-key sea shanty. "*For give 'im a piece—*"

SILENCE!

"And 'e'll take 'n' 'e'll take!"

Go to **291**.

190.

"Because Father," Percival correctly noted, "*you're* not Catholic."

"The fact of which Pete rarely fails to raise. As he sees it, I'm an apostate, the refugees were apostates… And those creatures…"

"Yes?"

"Well, they're either plague-as-punishment or just tiny gooey murder-apostates. Either way—"

"Do you think if they were tiny gooey murder-Catholics he'd feel a bit better about everything?"

"Yes," said Foom. No pause. "As long as they confessed regularly."

Go to **288**.

191.

The little girl nodded. "They ate the televisions," she said somberly. "I loved 'em."

"You loved the televisions?"

She shook her head. "The monsters. Before they ate the televisions, I mean. They were cute."

"Cute?"

"Like kitties and puppies and dollies and, um…"

"And you're sure they weren't… those things?"

She shook her head. "No, they were all black goop and red eyes."

"But… *cute* goop and red eyes?"

She nodded. "They were real friendly at first. When the refugees first found 'em."

"The refugees?"

"They weren't supposed to be there."

"The monsters?"

"The televisions."

"Pardon?"

"The refugees were televisions."

"Pardon?"

"Televisions. From Sector Prime."

"From…" Percival Gynt had followed the news. Read horror stories. "From Sekayt'r Prime? *Telepaths.* Did your church take in telepaths from Sekayt'r Prime?"

"The curate said we mustn't, but Father Foom insisted. He said no one's illegal."

"And the… the refugees found the monsters?"

"The televisions, yeah."

"Found them where?"

"In the basement."

"What were they doing there?"

"The televisions or the monsters?"

"I can guess why the televisions were in the basement. How did the monsters get there?"

"I dunno. Maybe they came through a…" The little girl strained to think, then flashed a smile. "A monster hole!"

Percival nodded. "Monster hole" was vague, but sensible. "And when did they turn on the refugees? Why?"

"I dunno," the girl repeated. "Why, I mean. It was a few weeks later. Last Tuesday. Father Foom had given 'em the full run of the church. The monsters, I mean. The televisions—"

"Had to stay in the basement, yes." Percival thought perhaps he'd finally made sense of the whole scenario. "So last Tuesday, the kitties and puppies ate the televisions?"

The girl nodded. "That's what everyone said. After that, Father Foom chained the doors. Cancelled services! Now I'm gonna go to Hell, 'cause I said a bad word yesterday and can't confess."

"That's… That's not… Well, that's probably exactly how that works." It was not. "But you've got me now. You've got Percival Gynt. And I swear to you, I'll have this monster mess sorted in time for services tomorrow."

"You… swear?"

If Percival had previously made a deal for cheese with the clerk, go to **282**.

Otherwise, continue on to **260**.

192.

Percival dropped to his knees, wiped the sting of sweat from his eyes. He tried to slow his breathing. Scanned the room with his torch and a trembling hand. His shoulder ached. Thought maybe he'd twisted his ankle. Jammed his thumb back there somehow. His face hurt.

It looked like they were in an office. Foom's, guessed Percival. The holographic visage of the reigning Space Pope hung over a modest writing desk. The pictured pontiff peered at Percival popaly.

Foom tugged at Percival's shoulder, was trying to tell him something, but Percival couldn't quite hear. Then Foom repeated louder, "Help me barricade the door!"

He might have done that, might have helped. But Foom had promised him a weapon. Something to fight back against the darkness.

Barricade first? **253**.

Weapon first? **147**.

193.

A trick then, in two parts. The murdering would have to wait till the second part.

(If you do the murdering up front, the second part becomes unworkable.)

So first, Percival needed the location of Father Void's portal.

He looked up to Father Void. Directionally, not aspirationally. "Can I ask you a question, Father Void?"

YOU CAN NOT.

Percival nodded. "Quite right. Quite right. Then can I *not* ask you a question, Father Void?"

YOU CAN NOT.

As he had hoped. Father Void was a weird nothing/ink monster, a nothink monster, a no-think monster maybe, but also importantly somewhat or all-the-way broken. Percival could work with that.

"You're stuck here, but sometimes a bit of you slips into my world, yeah?"

NO. I AM NOT STUCK HERE. AND PART OF ME DOES NOT SLIP INTO YOUR WORLD.

"And you have a portal?"

NO.

"No."

NO NO.

Percival closed his eyes. Took a slow breath. Imagined in that moment that he was one with all of space and time. And possibly also parchment, because what was reality anyway these days? And he asked Father Void one more question.

"And where is the lack of a portal that you don't use to not reach from where you aren't to where you also aren't not also not where?"

UM.

Percival opened his eyes. Smiled a patiently solicitous smile.

UM.

Slipped his hands into his trouser pockets. Waited.

UM.

Considered whistling. Didn't. He didn't need to be that guy.

IT'S UP HERE BEHIND MY HEAD.

Percival placed a hand over his mouth, stifled a laugh.

I MEAN IT'S NOT! BECAUSE I DON'T HAVE A HEAD! OR A BEHIND! FATHER VOID HAS NO BEHIND! DO NOT LOOK FOR FATHER VOID'S BEHIND! FATHER VOID IS ALL HEAD AND NO BEHIND AND ALSO NO HEAD AND NONE OF THIS HAPPENED! NONE OF IT! I DO NOT HATE YOU WITH THE PASSION OF A THOUSAND LACKS OF SUNS!!!

And now? The murdering. Go to **225**.

194.

Just then, something fell out of Father Void. Or perhaps from somewhere just slightly behind him. Foom was used to such misdirection from his days as a street magician.

Ah, how he missed the smell of sea spray wafting over the boardwalk.

Also, the thing that was falling was screaming quite loudly. And it was Percival Gynt.

Percival landed with a sort of THLUFF in a part of the parchment void mostly level with Foom and some distance away. "I'M ALL RIGHT! I'M ALL RIGHT!" he shouted from the not-ground.

Foom grinned and jogged over to his companion and gave him a hand up. "Percival Gynt!" said Foom. "You have no idea how happy I am to see you! I was convinced I was dead!"

"And now?"

"Now, I think we're both dead!"

Percival frowned. Foom thought about it and frowned too. "Oh yes," he said. "I can see how that that's not better."

"Don't be a pessimist, Father. Let's assume that there *is* no afterlife!"

At this, Father Foom made a very specific noise, difficult to translate into writing. A sort of HRMPH or maybe a HMRG. Witness accounts differ.

"To save you some time," offered Foom, by way of changing the subject, "the thing above us is Father Void. No relation. And he is not."

"Not?"

"Not."

"Not what?"

"Go ahead. Ask him anything."

Percival craned his neck to stare into the looming lack of anything, and he asked it, "Um, are you a radish?"

I AM NOT, came its answer, loud and soft and echoing ceasefully.

Percival gave Foom a shrug. "Well, that's one down at the very least."

"What now?" asked Foom.

What now, indeed?

Might Percival and Foom have attempted to explore the featureless parchment void? If so, go to **40**.

Or would they have again tried to engage with Father Void? If so, go to **262**.

195.

"Father, that's brilliant, but also what?"

Father Foom didn't explain with words. Instead, he picked up his keys, found a reasonably pointy, pokey one, and slid it down through the air in front of him, slitting space open to reveal a darkness beyond.

WHAT ARE YOU DOING? came the voice of Father Void from above. STOP THAT. STOP THAT RIGHT NOW.

Somehow, impossibly, Percival and Foom could feel the nothing shifting towards them. Could feel the nothing's mounting anger.

Quickly, and for reasons difficult to articulate, they snatched up the rest of their belongings—yes, even Percival's bit of fuzz—and dove headlong into the dark.

Go to **210**.

196.

Percival was not the trusting sort. A defect in his upbringing, perhaps. He didn't so much care *where* they were going, he and Foom, but he desperately wanted to know why. Even with the devil at their back, metaphorically and perhaps literally, he felt a fierce urgency to stop Father Foom, to grab him by his priest's collar and shake him till he got answers.

"You're probably wondering where we're going," mooted Foom. Without looking back. Without stopping. And before Percival Gynt could so much as lay a hand upon him.

"Yes, um, please?" was the best reply Percival could manage. A weak cover for his staggering disappointment. He'd been hoping for dramatic confrontation.

"I've a weapon stashed in my office," Foom confided.

A practical answer. Even more disappointing. "Oh," said Percival. "Does it at least have an interesting backstory?"

Foom did not immediately answer, just continued briskly forward.

Which Percival took as a yes.

Should Percival here have pressed Foom for more detail about this weapon? If so, go to **33**.

Or, good grief, now's not the time! Go to **178**.

197.

Percival lowered the torch to the crack in the tile where the creature emerged. A clean break from one edge to the other. Two halves. "I wonder," he muttered. "Would you hold this for me?"

He handed Foom the torch, reached down and pried up the tile in two solid chunks. One, then the other. Set them aside and found the most curious thing beneath.

A hole dug out of the dirt foundation. An open book placed in the hole. An ancient thing, thick and leather-bound, pages yellowed, letters long ago worn away, a foul black ichor seeping from its center.

A familiar sludge.

Despite his better judgment, or perhaps on account of its absence, Percival reached down and dipped his fingers into the liquid.

It was cold and thick, as he expected, and it pulled at the tips of his fingers. Almost a tickling sensation. Percival smirked.

"Should you be doing that?" asked Foom.

Should he? Why not? They're not our fingers, are they? Let's go to

232.

Or… No? Percival Gynt probably needs his fingers for… finger things. Go to **266**.

198.

And so he set off for the parchment-horizon. "He" being the person you chose to follow in the previous section.

Obviously.

He looked back periodically, watched Father Void grow smaller and fainter and his companion grow smaller and fainter still.

How far? he thought. If there truly is nothing but endless nothing, how far would he go? And how could he even measure?

At least if they had gone together, he'd have some company in the moment. Someone to voice these thoughts to.

He wondered if, perhaps, his companion was thinking these same thoughts. Possibly at the same time. In the exact same order.

Go to **235**.

199.

"What's this?" asked Foom as he held up Percival's single black glove. A lefty. Black leather, faux or faux-faux.

"It's a glove, obviously."

"I can see that," confirmed Foom, "but why do you only have one of them?"

"Ah, yes. It's for slaps."

"Sorry?"

"For…" Percival paused, tried to remember if this next bit was true or something he'd made up. "For slapping people. In some cultures, if you want to initiate a duel, you take out a glove and you slap them in the face. No glove, no duel."

"And is that something you do often? Challenge people to duels? Via glove?"

"Not… frequently."

"Ever?"

"I'm considering my options presently."

"You lost the other one, didn't you?"

Percival made a noise, sort of an ermph, that Foom took as assent.

Back to **176**.

200.

Percival lowered himself to a crawl as he ascended, lest he miss a step in the dark and die abruptly. As he did, he considered how best to trick an indeterminate number of little ink monsters.

Sadly, he had no cream pies.

By the time he'd reached the top of the stairs, Percival had two workable plans. To trick the creatures with word play or to trick them with a clever ruse.

Go to **296** for word play.

Go to **268** for a ruse.

201.

The hall was smoke and fire and chaos and the wails of melting children crying out to an absent father.

Foom was a shadow ahead of him, through the heat and light. Percival tried to keep pace, but the old man was fast and knew his way.

He tried to remember, Percival did, what he had promised the girl in the cheese shop. Did he say he'd slay the monsters? Save the church?

He tried to remember the moment where he'd chosen wrong.

A smear of screaming goo fell down from the ceiling. Instinctively, he lifted the weapon and fired. Fired. And the thing, what? Evaporated? Burnt to nothing?

But he could still hear it. Or remember.

A little boy calling out for his father.

Father Foom grabbed Percival by the arm and tugged him back to the present. "*Bello ess,*" whispered Percival in a long-forgotten tongue.

"God bless you," said Foom, who had neither time nor patience for cryptic backstory.

Instead, he turned and ran and pulled Percival after him, down the burning hall and smashing through that last door out into the alley.

Carried by their momentum, the two men stopped, dropped, and rolled, though neither intentionally nor in that precise order.

Go to **86**.

202.

Foom wouldn't say it, but Percival could see it in his eyes. These creatures. Unnatural. Infernal?

Perhaps Foom thought them demons, but Percival could scarcely entertain the possibility. For demons presupposed Hell, presupposed Heaven, presupposed a vengeful God who waits in judgment. Not his abstract Fate, some karmic force, but one supreme being to be worshipped and exalted. A king above all.

And these creatures were such little things, frightening yes, but in their own way pitiable. For such wretched things to rely upon the existence of an omnipresent, omniscient, omnipotent God?

For such a being to will such wretched things into existence.

Such wretched things as them. Such wretched things as he.

"There is no design in such horrors" was how a friend would later put it.

And they would look back on this day and weep.

Go to **137**.

203.

Percival shined his torch in a circle as they sang. He could see them now, dozens of them. Hundreds, maybe. And they were just as the cheese girl described:

Black ink stains come to life, if living they were. But taking shapes to play upon one's sympathies. Small and wide-eyed, some sickly and meek, lining the floors, scaling the walls, hanging from the ceiling overhead. Most, animals one might take as a pet. Cats and dogs. Rabbits and pikas. Monkeys and mice. A capybara for some reason. Somewhere among them, a guinea pig that the girl in the cheese shop had named Olivia Q. Bigglesbottom. A few appeared as children's toys, a stuffed bear here, a dolly there, shuffling and stumbling and scrabbling under their own power.

Fewer still as crawling, grinning babies.

They surrounded Percival and Foom, scaled the walls, hung from the ceiling overhead. Ever closer. Closer.

Well, that's enough of that, isn't it? Time to run. Let's go to **143**. Quick as you can. Don't want Percival to get eaten between page turns. It's happened before!

Or. Well. They've come this far. Perhaps Percival would want to talk to the little black ink monsters? Go to **26**.

Or, honestly, why should we be making all the decisions? Perhaps Father Foom had a helpful suggestion. Go to **179**.

204.

Percival was still dead sometime later, at the bottom of a flight of stairs, in the dark, in a pool of his own dried blood, when the shadow creatures reached him.

"What shall we do with him?" asked the sly black fox.

"Take him to our father," said the wise black cat.

"But he is dead," said the plain-spoken black capybara.

"Our father will see to that," said the wise black cat.

"Or he won't," said the sly black fox.

They all agreed that this was a good plan, except for the capybara, who was hungry and would have preferred to eat the dead man.

It took a long time to nudge the dead man down the hall and back into the undercroft.

It was very dark, the most dark, but the sly black fox and the wise black cat and the plain-spoken black capybara and the quiet black gerbil could all see perfectly well with their blood-red eyes. They nudged the dead body across the room to their father's book, and the wise black cat sang:

> *Here is a thing for nothing,*
> *A thing that once was no thing,*
> *For which we ask nothing of nothing,*
> *Save that it be no thing again.*

Then they waited. They were all of them very patient, because they had no other plans until breakfast, except for Capybara who had one plan, which was to nibble on the dead man's fingers whenever the others weren't paying attention.

He managed four proper nibbles before their father emerged from the book in inky tendril form. It never spoke to them, because tendrils don't have mouths, but it bent low enough that they could each nuzzle it in turn. Then, gently with a paw, the wise black cat guided the tendril down to the dead man's face.

The tendril poked and prodded and slowly, carefully wrapped itself around the dead man's neck. Then, with swift-if-misplaced confidence, it wrenched the body up into the air and down, down into the pages of the book.

"Do you suppose we did the right thing?" asked the sly black fox.

The quiet black gerbil shrugged.

Go to **110.**

205.

Percival raised Foom's weapon in front of him, used two hands to hold it steady. He wasn't prepared for the weight of it. "It" being the weapon. "It" being the moment.

All the horrors he'd seen. Everything he'd been made to do. He'd never taken a life before this day.

He eased back on the trigger. Apologized in his head.

And the weapon said the priest's name.

FOOM.

The creatures melted inside the fireball. Were reduced to scorch marks on walls and ceiling.

Everything burned.

Percival dropped the weapon. It landed with a decisive clonk. As the smoke and fire closed in on him, he stumbled backwards to the broken window, turned and fell out of it.

Go to **140.**

206.

"Duck!" shouted Father Foom. And Percival ducked.

He hoped Foom wasn't trying to warn him about an actual duck. If so, it was now likely too late. The duck would be on him immediately. He'd lowered himself to its level. Exposed himself. Left himself vulnerable to duck duckery.

There was no duck obviously. Got to **97**.

Unless there was a duck? Go to **34**. For a duck.

This is your last chance.

207.

Percival walked briskly for the first hundred meters before it occurred to him that rather than being inside an invisible room with walls and a door, he might have been standing on an invisible platform with no walls and an endless drop beyond.

He stopped, nearly vomited looking down, swallowed, closed his eyes, took a deep breath, lowered to his knees, exhaled, opened his eyes, breathed slow and steady, and began to crawl.

How long might Percival have crawled for? Minutes? Hours? Days? A choice that has no meaning, so I won't burden you with it. Whatever the interval, it passed, and Percival stopped and looked back from whence he came.

From this vantage, where he'd first appeared looked no different from where he now knelt. Where he now knelt appeared no different from where he'd started. Except, when he looked up, his angle on the nothing-monster, on this Father Void, had shifted. He thought perhaps he saw a tendril of nothing trailing up and out of Father Void and into… *something* above.

A sort of rip in the parchment sky.

"A portal," Percival whispered.

And he stood.

Go to **221**.

208.

Up the stairs! One flight, through an open door, and Percival slammed it shut!

"HOLD THE DOOR!" Foom shouted, as he fumbled for his keys.

Percival put his full-but-barely-sufficient weight against the door as the black tendril slammed against it from the far side.

Once! Twice! Three times! Each hit rattled Percival down to his bones!

Foom jammed a key into the lock. Forced it. Let it break off inside.

Percival stepped back, took a breath.

Silence.

"Maybe it—"

The tendril struck again. Harder. The door cracked. The corridor shook.

"I have an idea," said Foom. "Follow me. Now."

Go **196**.

209.

Yes, it would be fine, Percival concluded. Definitely absolutely certainly or probably mostly or more or less fine.

"I swear," he repeated. "It will be done."

She didn't believe him. But we do, don't we?

Don't we?

Yes. Yes, of course we do. Everything went fine, I'm sure.

THE END

So, what now? There are more stories in this volume, aren't there? Let's get on with it, already! "Percival Gynt and the Quiet Bargain" sounds like a real cracker, doesn't it? And there's one about forks? Brilliant! Best not to dwell on this one day with all of its uncertainties and its choices and its too familiar narration!

And the fire.

Go on then. I won't tell anyone. "Percival Gynt and the View from the Tenth Story" is next.

Or if you'd rather follow this through to the end, go to **304**.

210.

It worked. The pair made their exit. Stumbled into the dark. Fell forward, then sideways, then up. Then it was Foom spit out of the book and into the dark. Then Percival. Onto the cold stone tile.

"Are we back?" asked Percival. Frantic. Scrambling to his feet.

"I felt a book," said Foom, who rose with a calmer but proportional urgency. "I think we're back in the undercroft."

"We need that torch," said Percival.

Go to **157**.

211.

—but they slashed and peeled and climbed into its null-bladder, where they suckled the sweet-nectar of—

Sorry, sorry! Not far enough ahead! Let's try **3-11**!

So sorry.

212.

"Where did you come from?" asked Percival.

"From the world within," it said. "From nowhere. From the pages of a book. From my father's pen."

"Those are," Percival observed, "different answers. And you'll forgive me, but none of them are particularly helpful."

"True," it said.

Percival waited for the creature to add some other snide or ambiguously-prophetic observation, but it dangled there with no more than a low growl.

Go to **287**.

213.

Percival Gynt was impatient for the night, was impatient for mystery and monsters and for his life to begin again.

Also, the morning's cheese was doing his lactose intolerance no favors.

So when he ran out of toilet paper at the aforementioned hour, it seemed both prudent and a good distraction to venture out of his apartment to procure another roll. And so he did, to his corner bodega, where he asked the clerk to get him a roll off the top shelf with that hook-stick contraption.

"And also a coffee," he added.

The clerk, a young man whose name Percival had predictably forgotten, smiled and nodded and poured Percival a cup. "Milk and sugar?"

"Yes," said Percival. Then "no" when he remembered his lactose intolerance. "Yes, sugar. No, milk." Except he liked milk. "Maybe, milk. Some milk. Do you have any milk that isn't milk, by any chance?"

"I have soy milk."

"That sounds terrible. I'll have the regular milk," said Percival, "and another roll of toilet paper."

The clerk sighed and picked up his hook-stick again and went over to the shelf to get Percival a second roll. In the meantime, Percival's eyes glided over the various snacks and whatzits that crowded the front counter.

He picked up a slim, black electric torch that was marked half-off. "Is this half-off?" he asked.

The clerk glanced at the sticker. "Seems so."

"Any idea why?" asked Percival.

"So that you'll buy it?" guessed the clerk.

"Right, fine," said Percival, and he paid for his toilet paper and his coffee and his other roll of toilet paper and his discount torch. And then he thought to ask, "Do you like working here?"

The clerk was surprised by the question but not offended and gave it a moment's thought. "I suppose I do," he answered finally. He hadn't known that before, and it cheered him considerably.

"And you've never thought to give it all up to go on adventures and fight evil?"

The clerk had not.

Percival nodded politely and left.

The bodega security camera recorded everything. Years later, Yousef wasn't sure why he kept the footage.

Go to **281**.

214.

Percival thought as he ran. "I MAYBE ATE SOMEONE ONCE!"

"MAYBE?" Foom questioned.

"THERE WAS A LOT HAPPENING AT THE TIME!" Percival shouted. "DON'T JUDGE ME!"

"Um… ONLY GOD JUDGES! BUT HE DEFINITELY DOES JUDGE THAT!"

"BUT I SAID IT OUT LOUD, SO I'M FORGIVEN, RIGHT?"

They ran right!

"RIGHT?"

Left!

"RIGHT?"

Up the steps!

208!

215.

Sorry for the confusion. That part of the story is for someone else. For you, unfortunately, I only have this:

Go to **269**.

216.

Percival stood, waved his hand about him, took a step, waved his hand again, found the wall, and let it guide him back to the undercroft.

To the book.

To the monster.

As he passed through the doorway, he dropped to his knees and began to crawl forward. Slowly. Quietly, he thought, but who knows what sounds a book or tendril could hear?

Go to **278**.

217.

"I'm dead," Percival said to himself, "and this is the afterlife. Heaven, maybe." He thought to stand, but what'd be the point? Instead, he just lay there, petulant in his exhausted indifference, staring up into the writhing nothingness.

"Or, well," he added after a beat, "probably not Heaven."

Not Heaven, because he'd never believed in such a place. Not Heaven, because he never believed he deserved it. Not Heaven, mostly, because he'd expected more angels, more puffy clouds and trumpets, and fewer gaping absences of those things.

He might have stood for Heaven.

YOU ARE NOT DEAD! came a voice out of the nothing. It was at once silent and booming, reassuring and also the opposite of that.

"Maybe you're dead too!" Percival shouted upwards. "How would you know?"

I PRECEDE DEATH. I PRECEDE EXISTENCE. I AM THE FATHER VOID.

Percival's nose wriggled involuntarily. "Father Void? *Father* Void? Did you name yourself that? What absolute nonsense!"

I PRECEDE NONSENSE. I PRECEDE SENSE.

"And do you…" Percival sat up despite himself, his malaise subsumed in pique. "Did you also precede fathers and voids?"

This Father Void paused, just for a moment, and then it answered. ALL THAT EXISTS EXISTS BECAUSE I DO NOT.

Percival sighed and finally stood. Not because he thought he was in Heaven, but because he knew wherever he was was too stupid to be the afterlife.

Go to **102**.

218.

It was an Apple Watch. The 20011 edition. Perhaps eight centimeters in diameter, with a pebbled rose gold polycarbonate casing. The glass screen was hopelessly cracked and half the pixels either blacked out or flickering. The time was difficult to read, perhaps stopped at half past twelve, perhaps a series of alien hieroglyphics.

Or perhaps that was the low battery warning.

Foom picked it up and examined it. "This has been through the war, hasn't it?"

It had not, but Percival wasn't sure an explanation was warranted.

"Got any helpful apps on it?"

"When it's got a signal, sometimes I do bings. Does it have a signal?"

It did not.

Back to **176**.

219.

No. Someone else, a mother or a father or a comely shop clerk would need to comfort the child. To tell her that her dolly wasn't lost forever or that the mean boy down the block would one day die of horrible diseases.

Or whatever advice might be appropriate for a child of her age. Four? Eleven?

Percival sidestepped the girl to examine the community notice board. There was a single flyer posted, cheaply printed, barely animated. It read:

OUR LADY OF SORROWS CHURCH

IS CLOSED INDEFINITELY

DUE TO ONGOING FACILITIES ISSUES

PLEASE ADDRESS ALL MATTERS

EARTHLY AND DIVINE

TO THE RIGHTEOUS FATHER FOOM

Ah well, thought Percival. Probably just a burst pipe or a roof that needs patching. Too much to hope for a murder or a missing child.

Although?

Percival turned an eye to the child behind him. "*You're* not missing, are you?" he asked, perhaps too optimistically. "Or murdered?"

Neither option seemed particularly likely to Percival, but to us?

If the little girl was missing, go to **88**.

If the little girl was murdered, go to **271**.

If the little girl was neither of those things, and perhaps a bit uncomfortable with Percival's questions, go to **103**.

220.

A nothing-tendril emerged from Father Void, wound past the floating sigils, stretched down towards Percival. Despite himself, he panicked, turned, tried to run, immediately tripped and fell face-first into the not-ground. THLUFF. The tendril lashed around his leg, lifted him up into the paper sky, and lobbed him up over the monster. Over the nothing.

Across the void.

Percival screamed and cried and briefly soiled himself as he tumbled through the air.

As he passed through a tattered portal into black.

Go to **43**.

221.

A portal with a tendril extending through it. Made of nothing here. Made of ink and shadow on the other side. Yes. It was this Father Void who brought him here. This Father Void, trapped in a book, bound by magic sigils, but able to slip a single nothing-tendril past its shackles and rend a hole in the parchment void. To reach out into our world, to birth children of ink and shadow to do its bidding. To kill interlopers, perhaps. To seek a way to free their Father. And if someone got past the children, the Father Void itself would reach out to snare its enemies.

A neat summation, Percival thought as he walked back. Doubtlessly correct.

But correct wasn't free.

If Father Void had torn that hole in the sky, that meant it was tangible. Father Void and the parchment void as well. That or magic something-something-something. But probably tangible.

If true, then that rip was his way out. Father Void could simply pick him up in its tendril and pass him back through.

If he could be convinced. But how?

Go to **124** to see the attempt.

Or.

Father Void had torn that hole in the void up there. Perhaps it could be tricked into tearing another, closer to Percival.

But not very close.

And, yes, if you've chosen any of them, you'll know that most of the "trick" options so far have been rubbish, but perhaps this is the time to finally play a proper trick on someone? Or, in this case, *not* a someone. A not-someone. A not-trick. Which is either a not-good idea or a not-bad idea.

Go to **189** to find out which.

222.

Percival looked up. Nothing.

Go to **53**.

223.

The thought of leading a party of half-starved indigents through a monster-infested church seemed awful and awkward and ultimately counter-productive to Percival. So he forced a smile and replied with a firm, but gracious-but-if-we're-being-completely-honest-probably-NOT-very-gracious "No."

"We appreciate the offer," he added, "probably, but the church is here to feed the unhoused. Not to feed the unhoused *to monsters*."

Percival chuckled at his own joke. The others stared back, stone-faced and weary-eyed. A small child sobbed quietly.

Percival frowned, scratched his ear.

"Okay. That was inappropriate. I see that now. Stay here if you must, but if any monsters pop out while we're gone?" No more jokes, he told himself. "*Run.*"

Go to **22**.

224.

And now the monsters came for him. Skittering out of the black, into the blue. Along floor and ceiling and walls, closer and closer, dozens of them, and just as the cheese-shop girl had described:

Black ink stains come to life, if living they were. But taking shapes to play upon one's sympathies. Small and wide-eyed, some sickly and meek, lining the floors, scaling the walls, hanging from the ceiling overhead. Most, animals one might take as a pet. Cats and dogs. Rabbits and pikas. Monkeys and mice. A capybara for some reason. Somewhere among them, a guinea pig that the girl in the cheese shop had named Olivia Q. Bigglesbottom. A few appeared as children's toys, a stuffed bear here, a dolly there, shuffling and stumbling and scrabbling under their own power.

Fewer still as crawling, grinning babies.

"S-S-SPROCK THIS!" shouted cyborg Maaba, and she lunged forward. She missed the not-cat, but found a bunny, a not-bunny, and plunged one whirling whisk-hand into the creature, then the other, then again, until the thing was reduced to a spatter of black paste. The other creatures stopped and shrieked and cried, so like a human babe that it tore at the companions' hearts. Percival and Foom grabbed Maaba, tried to pull her back, but she was mostly machine, heavy and strong, and they were hesitant in their grip on account of her sparking servomotors.

"TH-THEY'RE MONSTERS!" Maaba shouted. "D-DEMONS!"

Elsewhere, the creatures' heartache turned to rage. Fulgrimm the Short, at the rear, in the dark, was the first beset. A dozen of the creatures, maybe more, fell on him, baring teeth and tearing flesh. He only had time for...

I'm sorry. Listen. Things are about to go very badly for these people. *Very* badly. I won't think less of you if you decide to skip ahead. **211** to be safe.

Otherwise, proceed to **139**. You have been warned.

225.

Father Void was not most things, but in that moment he was unambiguously, incalculably angry. And nothing else.

And his anger unfolded into a thousand tendrils all swarming towards Percival Gynt. This too was part of Percival's trick. Percival's stupid, suicidal trick. As the tendrils struck, Percival ducked and dodged and dived and finally clung onto one of the them as it drew back.

WHAT ARE YOU DOING? STOP THAT.

He climbed atop the tendril, balanced, and ran up it, stumbling now and then, occasionally using one hand to steady himself, as fast as he could go, headlong into the (Father) void.

STOP THAT! STOP THAT, YOU GNAT!

Father Void tried to shake Percival off, of course. It waggled its tendril to one side, then the other. Percival stumbled again, tripped forward, caught one arm around the tendril, swung under, around and back up again, and hugged tightly. Panted.

Now Father Void swung its appendage up and down with some ferocity, increasingly desperate to shake Percival loose, but his grip only tightened.

STOP EXISTING! howled Father Void.

Percival's heart pounded. Sweat dripped into his eyes. He calmed himself with the simplest thought:

You're not real anymore. You're a character inside a book. You're Jack climbing the beanstalk. You're Feldigann with his magic ladder. You're Spider-Man sticking to… various walls.

And when you're inside a book, anything is possible.

And then Percival Gynt let go. Dropped down onto Father Void itself. Onto its Nothing Head perhaps. He lay there for a moment, on a not-cloud of nothingness, catching his breath, stilling his heart, drying his eyes with a sleeve, even as Father Void raised another dozen tendrils to strike.

Inside a book, anything is possible.

So he stood, and he smiled, and he straightened his tie, and he said into the seething nothingness, "Let's never speak of this again."

Father Void roared and slapped itself in the head with a half-dozen of its own tendrils. And that, of course, made it roar even louder. Percival was already running, taking full advantage of the distraction, up another tendril to the point where it passed through tattered parchment.

To the way out.

Go to **43**.

226.

Percival shrugged. "It was really the cheese girl's fault."

"Well, if you've come for a story, you'll have to look elsewhere. Our tragedies don't exist for your amusement."

"No. No, no, no." Percival could see that he'd offended Father Foom. Bartender Foom. Person Foom? He considered apologizing. Didn't. "I already know the story. Refugees. Goo monsters. All I want to know is: Can I help?"

"You?"

Percival nodded. Fixed his tie. "I might not look like much, but I caught a serial killer last week. What are a few flesh-eating monsters after that?"

Person Foom genuinely didn't know what to say. When he'd started out the day, all he'd envisioned was opening up the bar, serving no customers, playing a few hundred rounds of solitaire, then drinking himself into oblivion. But this person. "You a cop?"

Percival shook his head.

"Mercenary?"

Percival shook his head.

"Then what's your angle?"

There's a hole in my heart, thought Percival. But what he said was, "I just want to help."

Foom frowned. "You might die."

Percival half-shrugged, half-nodded.

"Might get me killed."

Percival half-nodded, half-shrugged.

Foom sighed, gathered his cards and fanned them in front of Percival Gynt. "Pick a card."

Go to **52**.

227.

The not-cat. And then the stray they'd found in the undercroft, only half-born but already talking such devious nonsense. Their words had frightened him at the time.

But was that their fault? Or his?

"Do you remember the card I wouldn't play?" Father Foom asked Percival Gynt. "This morning? Back at The Wronged Vagrant?"

Was it the red **5**?

Or the **8**-of-something? Who even notices these things?

228.

It was only a week ago that Percival had professed his love and been rebuffed. But who's to say? Perhaps those feelings were misplaced. Perhaps Fate had other plans for Percival Gynt. Perhaps *this* was precisely what he needed to free himself from his current malaise or ennui.

He couldn't decide which.

So Percival stepped up to the counter, and he straightened his tie, and he doffed his hat to Not Edgarry. "You're not Gary," he said, with a canny half-smile and an ill-considered wink.

"Even Gary's not Gary," she replied with a shrug. "What hath God wrought?"

Percival was unsure whether this woman was making fun of him or not, and he found that interesting.

If you believe that she was properly taken in by Percival's charms, go to **115**.

Or, if you rather suspect she was mocking Percival, still go to **115**, but try reading all of her dialogue with a pronounced undercurrent of disdain.

229.

Percival thought to run, but he was unsure of his footing. Unsure of his exact facing in the room. Couldn't know when the book-tendril would strike again. So he picked a direction, and he charged forward with his arms up in front of him, found the wall, felt for the doorway, found the hall and ran towards the steps.

That's when they started to sing.

O, he who's got teeth in his belly.
The creatures, they were waiting for him.
Will never know peace in his heart.
Ahead of him, at the top of the stairs.
For give him a piece.
And behind him, the thing that devoured Father Foom.
And he'll want more and more.
Where then could he go? Where then was safe?
Till his heart is too full for the world.
"I'm not afraid of you!" Percival shouted at the darkness. A lie. And then he sat down on the floor. The song began again.
O, he who's got teeth in his belly.
All those years ago, after child Percival had run as fast and as far as his child legs could take him, he hid.
Will never know peace in his heart.
In the dark.
For give him a piece.
As others died.
And he'll want more and more.
Percival lay down on the tile. Covered his ears.
Till his heart is too full for the world.
He'd waited that day, a scared little child, for the monster to come. To kill him. To spare him.
O, he who's got teeth in his belly.
Now, as then, he waited.
Will never know peace in his heart.
Perhaps, this was the same dark.
For give him a piece.
Perhaps his whole life had been an illusion.
And he'll want more and more.
And this was all he ever was. A scared boy, waiting in the dark for death.
He sang the words with them:
"Till his heart is too full for the world."
Go to **141**.

230.

I recently had the opportunity to sit down for a meal with Bella Estelle Gorbash, the foremost expert on Father Foom this side of the Cinnamon Galaxy. Gorbash is a historian, like me, and also a time traveler.

Which is, frankly, a bit of a cheat.

She wrote a very interesting article about the Forking Nature of Time that I keep meaning to read. She's also met Father Foom three times. She says. Though not in chronological order.

I've found that we disagree on certain fundamental matters. For instance, she firmly believes that Percival Gynt was not an accountant at all, but rather a ten-by-ten meter plant mass in Southern Gijou. I find this suspect for, among other reasons, the fact that I have in my personal archives a pressed and laminated pair of Percival Gynt's gray striped trousers.

Gorbash remains adamant.

These disagreements aside, her insights into Father Foom provided essential color to this tale and to another, "Percival Gynt and the Other Percival Gynt," which can be found later in this volume. In the spirit of intellectual honesty, in an effort to move beyond ego, and with the full permission of Gorbash and her publisher, I am including an excerpt from her work here, from the eleventh volume of her *Compleat Biographies of Father Foom* series, *Foom XI: Foom Goes the Fine-amite*, so that you might have another historian's perspective on the events of this story:

Eleven days later, Our Lady of Sorrows burns to the ground. Inside, the invasive species burns too. No one claims credit, but most rumors point to Father Foom himself as the culprit or to his assistant priest Peter Hawkesmith, who dies soon after in a freak baking accident.

When pressed by local law enforcement, Foom reluctantly offers up a third suspect: a ten-by-ten plant mass located on the planet Gijou.

Redonkulous.

Lacking the necessary funds to rebuild, the archdiocese encourages congregants to self-rapture. Instead, most follow Foom to his next appointment, The 42nd Universalist Society of Sanctuary-8, where Foom takes in more refugees and fewer ink demons.

In the summer of 20014, Father Foom is briefly trapped in a microscopic Hell dimension. Again.

End Part 9,631.4.

Her work is very concise. Possibly rubbish. One of us was very drunk when I spoke to her, and also she might be three small goblins stacked inside a trench coat.

Perhaps I should have led with that.

Anyway. You're welcome.

Where were we? Ah, yes! The fire.

Go to **298.**

231.

Did or didn't or didn't not did. It didn't matter. Percival knew what needed to be done. He raised Foom's weapon and aimed it through the open doorway.

And he eased back slowly on the trigger.

Go to **18.**

232.

Percival glanced back at Father Foom to reassure him. "It's fine. It's just a—"

But then the liquid grew rigid, grasping, took hold of Percival's whole hand and pulled him hard, impossibly, till he was arm deep in the book. "I WAS WRONG! I WAS WRONG!" shouted Percival, with all appropriate panic.

Foom fumbled the torch. It fell and rolled and flickered off, and Foom reached out for Percival in the dark. He was screaming, struggling. Foom found an arm and pulled. "Hold on!" he shouted, but to what? To him?

Foom's footing slipped. Percival let out one last agonizing scream. Foom fell backwards, lost his grip, hit his head against the crypt wall. Something cold and wet lashed against his cheek and drew blood.

And Percival was silent.
Percival was gone.
Well, now you've done it.
Go to **29**.

233.

"What are you?" asked Percival. There were more prosaic ways to ask that question, but Percival hoped a blunt question might elicit a blunt answer.

"In the light of day," it's reply began, and already Percival could see that he'd misjudged, "I am nothing. Before and below, I am nothing. After, I am nothing. Only here am I anything at all. And perhaps on the trash heap to follow."

Percival closed his eyes. Took a breath. Opened them. And tried again. "Is there a name for the sort of thing you are? For your kind?"

"We were kind once. But I was born into a world without."

Go to **212**.

234.

"Do you have any hobbies, Father Foom?" asked Percival.

"Why do you ask?"

Percival had no good answer. He considered letting the matter drop.

"Yes," said Foom.

"Yes what?"

"Hobbies. I have them. Besides the church and the bar and the occasional game of solitaire, I used to do stage magic, and also I play *Dungeons & Dragons & Additional Dungeons* some Tuesdays, and also-also I like collecting vintage novels from the late 199th and early 200th century. And I used to play Cricket."

"Space Cricket?"

"No, regular Cricket. And I do ballroom dance and play a little bit of trombone. Also, I sew my own pants. And bake tiny cookies shaped like monkeys. And I've raced starfighters once or twice, and I'd like to get back to that. And I do caricatures."

"Really?"

"No. The church and the bar keep me pretty busy."

"Oh."

"You?"

"Same."

"Sorry?"

"But for me it's accounting and… whatever this is."

"Huh."

"Huh what?"

"I assumed 'whatever this is' *was* your hobby."

Percival stopped to scowl at Father Foom. Pointed his flickering torch up at his own face so Foom could see the scowl. Intermittently.

"All right," Foom relented. "We can both agree that this thing that is happening now is very serious, and I acknowledge that you're taking it very seriously."

Percival lowered his torch, thanked Foom for what he said, and walked on into the winking darkness.

Go to **62**.

235.

Ridiculous! thought Percival.

And he turned and shouted across the parchment void to Father Foom. "THIS IS A STUPID CHOICE! LET'S NOT DO THIS!"

Understand that he wasn't calling *you* stupid. I think you made a reasonable choice, given the options I presented.

And also he wasn't calling me stupid. Because I'm writing this story, and I said so.

In fact, at that precise moment, Percival was thinking to himself, "Even if there was a narrator, I assume he'd be very intelligent and good-looking, and his editor Maeve should pay him back the ten credits she borrowed from him for pizza last Tuesday."

Maeve.

Foom sighed and relented, turned, and walked back to Father Void. Percival walked back too, and he noticed something peculiar as he did.

Go to **270**.

236.

Foom was a man of many keys. Physical keys. Magnetic keys. Electronic keys. Holo-keys. Sympathetic keys.

Church keys. Bar keys. Keys for his apartment and his ex-wife's house and his other ex-wife's house. A key for his moped. For a safety deposit box. For his private desk drawer.

For all the chains he used to secure the back door of his church. To keep people out and monsters in.

He kept them all on an iron ring, along with a cross and a plastic sushi and a chalice icon.

"And none of these are for a magic book void?" asked Percival.

Foom frowned. "Obviously, n—"

"I'm saying you have a lot of keys."

"And you apparently have none."

Percival shrugged. "If anyone was set on robbing me, a locked door wouldn't stop them. And who goes through an apartment building, feeling for unlocked doors?"

"Many people."

"Oh. Um. Really?"

"Sometimes they'll pretend to be postal workers. Or building technicians. Sometimes—"

"All right, all right. If we survive, I'll start locking my door."

He did not.

Percival tossed Foom's keys back down onto the lack of ground.

THLUFF.

Percival closed his eyes. He almost had it. Almost.

But it was Foom who said it first. "What if we just start opening doors?"

Go to **195**.

237.

"And you're going to what? Hose it down?"

Foom rolled his eyes, sighed heavily, and ran. "NOT THAT

SORT OF FIREFIGHTER!" he shouted backwards.

For a moment, Percival stood immobile, pondering Foom's words. "Not that sort of--?" he began incredulously, and then he heard the tendril closing.

He chased Foom down the blackened corridor. "Yes!" he cried after. "That just might work!"

Go to **67**.

238.

Father Foom thought to tell Percival that they couldn't cover more ground by splitting up because, strictly speaking, there *was* no ground, but then he recalled how much he'd always hated word play.

"Good," he said instead. "Let's do that."

Clearly the strange young man was rubbing off on him. Walking in opposite directions into nothingness was the correct proportional response.

Percival nodded, turned, and walked away.

Now, this is primarily Percival's story, but I believe in giving you choices.

Go to **75** to follow Percival.

Or **75** to follow Foom.

You see? Choices!

239.

A weapon, yes. A gun that breathes fire like a dragon. That burns away the past. That makes ash of your sins. Father Foom knew of such a weapon.

He had drawn that weapon before. Many times. He would not draw it again, so long as he had a choice in the matter.

"No," he told Percival. "Not a weapon."

Percival could see that something was happening in Father Foom's head. On his face. A tearful eye. The curl of a lip. Artistic differences. Foom would only draw what Foom wanted to draw. Fine.

"An exit then," said Percival. "Draw the way out."

Go to **84**.

240.

Percival shrugged. Even in these, his younger days, he could spot a man spoiling for an argument. There weren't enough hours in the day, enough Saturdays in the year. And he had other business besides. He offered the curate a tepid "S'pose not" in hopes that that would be the end of it.

And indeed it was! The curate conceded with a sigh. "You said you were looking for Father Foom?"

Right. He did say that, didn't he? Let's go to **45** to find out where Father Foom is.

Or. Perhaps the curate had something interesting to say about the cheese girl's monsters. Go to **25**.

241.

Excellent. No noses. Perhaps the tendril had lost the *metaphorical* scent, or perhaps it was simply waiting for Percival to tire. To give in.

Go to **261**.

242.

It lumbered and writhed, a monstrosity of black sludge, dotted with blood-red eyes. It was tall like a man, but the parts of it were barely clinging together, were pulling away from each other. Foom's monsters, convulsing, melting into one another, into some horrifying, desperate amalgam, some grotesque mockery of men.

Mouths moaning. Eyes weeping. Stumps staggering through the flames to the exit.

Ahead of them, from outside, Percival could hear voices shouting for Father Foom. "THIS WAY, FATHER!" they called. "THIS WAY!"

The shape staggered out into the alley and roared. Those assembled screamed, stumbled backwards, and scattered. It grabbed for one of them and crushed his shoulder. Stepped on another and broke her back.

Had Percival refused their help? These might have been two of the volunteers.

Go to **80**.

243.

A week earlier, Percival Gynt had stared down a serial killer.

You may recall.

It was a moment of revelation for young Percival. At last, he'd found his purpose. His place in the universe. His true calling. He was a detective. Or a, well, not precisely that. Maybe more of a... what? A crime-fighting hobbyist? A thrill-seeking, amateur criminologist? A crime-seeking, thrill-fighting amateurologist? A, um...

Well, he'd work on that.

But what next? There was no special talent that had brought Alexander Eeps to him. Not really. He had stumbled onto that article about Eeps' mother. Who even bings in this day-and-age?

Well, Percival.

But why Percival? Fate, he'd decided. Fate had led him to Bing and Bing led him to Diane Eeps and, well, you've probably read the first two stories in this volume, so you know what led him to her killer.

But now that matter was closed. Eeps was behind bars, and Percival's door into that world was likewise barred. The Province Police, who Percival had pushed to apprehend Eeps, had been quite clear. Aggressively clear. Three-days-spitting-teeth-and-blood-and-nursing-his-wounds-before-he-was-back-at-work-and-still-he-had-the-slightest-hitch-in-his-step clear.

And no one else in his apartment building appeared to be a mass murderer. He'd checked.

Twice.

Add to that, betrayal by a robot he'd thought might be his friend.

Add to that, rejection by the woman he'd thought he loved.

Well, probable rejection. Possibly she hadn't heard him. It was very noisy in the bar when he told her how he felt, and both of them were either very drunk or near fatally poisoned.

That was all of it a week ago, and now Percival was back to his old life. The life of the awkward, shiftless, lonely accountant-in-training with a hole in his heart that could only be filled by some thrilling new adventure or...

Or...

Well, he supposed a large wedge of Havarti might do the trick? Go to **15**.

244.

"A weapon?"

They were walking again. Percival, with renewed purpose. Foom with the same purpose that he had before.

"A gun, sort of."

Evasive. Curious.

"What's sort of a gun?"

Foom didn't answer. Kept going. Percival followed. Thought to press the issue, but then they both heard the door smash behind them.

Not so far away.

Foom ran.

Do you suppose Percival would have chased after Foom recklessly into the dark? If so, go to **58**.

Or would he have proceeded slowly, with caution? Go to **257**.

Or perhaps, sensing he'd been abandoned, that he was now as ever literally and existentially alone, mightn't Percival have turned to face the monster? To face death?

If you think so, go to **70**.

245.

"I think I might die tonight," Father Foom confided to Percival Gynt.

Percival thought to reassure the priest, but what would be the point? He couldn't guarantee his safety. Couldn't stop Fate. Instead, he asked a question. "Why do you say that?"

"It's my fault, isn't it? I brought the refugees here. Allowed those… those things to stay. Pete was right about me."

"How so?"

"I'm cursed," he concluded. But no. "No, I am the curse."

"I've seen death too, Father. Lived in it. Couldn't see my way past it for a long time. And even now, it stalks me. And do you want to know my secret?"

"I suppose it'd be wrong of me to say no?"

"I deserve it. I deserve death. Deserve to die. For what I've done, and what I didn't do."

"And that helps you?" Foom asked, a bit incredulous.

"Not particularly."

Go to **62**.

246.

Percival grabbed Foom by the hand and ducked under the black tendril. "LET'S GO! LET'S GO!" he shouted.

Foom found the doorway with their torch, and they ran.

Go to **21**! Now! Now!

247.

Two words, and the bartender glared up from his cards.

"What of it?"

Three words. Victory.

"I'm told it's been overrun. I think perhaps I can help."

The bartender gathered his cards. "How so?"

Go to **121**.

248.

Marvelous. Then I think it's time for step **12**.

249.

As it turned out, there was time. Though they didn't know that in the moment. They could hear the tendril out in the hall, battering the office door, breaking its way through their makeshift barricade.

Foom raised his weapon. Aimed through the bookcase to the tendril in his mind's eye. Tried to steady his quivering grip.

Percival considered the other man. There was no fear in his countenance. Only...

Hesitation?

Go to **150**.

250.

"Could you point me in his direction?" asked Percival.

"Well, it's Saturday morning," the curate noted, "so I expect you'll find him at The Wronged Vagrant. One of our local drinking establishments. It's just two blocks down and 'round the corner. Shouldn't have any problem finding it on Maps."

"I prefer Bing for Feet, but thank you for your time, Curate."

Go to **114**.

251.

"Bluster," said Foom.

"Sorry?"

"That creature. For all its weird words. It's scared of us. Of you, for some reason."

Percival mumbled something along the lines of "I'm a little intimidating," with stooped shoulders and a transparent lack of conviction.

"People can do terrible things when they're scared."

Percival nodded. "People and monsters."

"Monsters and children," said Foom.

And children, thought Percival Gynt.

Go to **38**.

252.

Percival dodged one last tendril and then dove into the light. Or the absence of pigment? Even as he passed through, he couldn't say which.

I immediately regret this decision, thought Percival.

And then he was on the other side. He was not falling. Nor was he not falling. He was not anything here. Nor was he not anything. He was everything, but also not everything. His mind was fire trying to comprehend what was happening to him, but also not that.

"This narration is extremely confusing," said Percival. "What do you expect them to make of all that?"

Sorry. Are you talking to me?

"I think so. Whoever you are. Should I not be talking to you?"

Propriety suggests no. But then neither should you be hearing me to begin with.

"What's happening? What is this place?"

I don't know. I'm no expert on interdimensional physics, but none of this should be happening. This definitely *didn't* happen.

"Past tense?"

Oh, yes! I'm a historian. A bit of an expert on you, if I do say. And wherever you are, wherever you *aren't*, if we can't get you out of here, it'll derail your whole timeline. You can't do *Conspiracy of Days*, if you're stuck in a nothing.

"Conspiracy of…?"

You'll find out later, hopefully. Or before? I mean, it's a separate volume, and they can be read in any order. I took pains to avoid spoilers for anyone who—

"That's… not helpful. Let's go back to when you said 'derail the timeline.'"

Right, yes. We should try to get you out of here before reality collapses in on itself. In on me? Goodness. I've never been in the narrative before. I'm not sure how this is going to work. What kind of damage we might do!

"Stop talking, please. It's… People *choose* to read this?"

The Narrator waited quietly over here.

"Don't sulk!"

It's fine. Just… Were you going to do a thing?

Percival rolled his eyes/didn't. "Give me a moment." He looked around/didn't. Considered things/didn't. Understood things/didn't. "What about them? Out there in the beyond space. All those eyes, watching."

Could be more.

"It's enough, yeah? One of them must be able to help."

I don't see h—

"Why don't you let me handle this?" he said, and then he turned his gaze on you/didn't.

"You there," said Percival Gynt. "Reader. I need your help." Percival frowned/didn't, glared at me/didn't.

Um…

"Would you please?" Percival insisted/insisted.

Oh! Sorry! Yes. At first you thought he might be talking to you, Dear Reader. But that's impossible, isn't it?

Unless…

"No," said Percival. To most of you. Pointed/maybe/didn't. "I'm not talking to you. Or you. Or *you*, I'm sorry to say. I'm only talking to…" Percival paused. Thought maybe. Remembered maybe. Chose. "…to *Sam*. Yes. Definitely, Sam. Or… Sammy? No. Maybe? Let's just say 'Sam.' Sam *Something-or-other*."

If your name is indeed Sam Something-or-other or, I suppose, if you'd care to listen in on their conversation, go to **66**.

If you consider that eavesdropping and poor form, go to **158**.

253.

Percival grunted, nodded in assent, stood reluctantly and helped Foom find a bookcase with his torch. Together, the two men slid it into place against the door. On the other side, the tendril pounded.

Knock knock, thought Percival. Who's there? Evil tentacle. Evil tentacle who?

Percival couldn't think of a proper punchline. Also, Foom was trying to say something else to him.

No. No, he was actually saying, "Something else." He guided Percival's torch to a nearby filing cabinet, short but solid, and together the two pushed it into place behind the bookcase.

Drops of blood fell on Percival's wingtip. His blood. From his nose, he realized, though he couldn't quite feel it. Maybe his nose was broken? And perhaps he'd need new shoes. Not important.

The tendril struck again. Percival thought he heard the door crack behind their barricade. "Evil tentacle, *hoo boy!*" he muttered. Wasn't sure how long the bookcase and the filing cabinet would hold.

"A weapon, yeah?"

Go to **118**.

254.

A sudden and uncharacteristic impulse overcame Percival. Quicker than I could even offer up the choice, Percival reached, grabbed the barrel of Foom's gun, and yanked with all of his might. Which was…

Well, it wasn't much might, was it? Also, the weapon was surprisingly slippery. Unless? Did you expect the weapon would be slippery?

If you aren't surprised by how slippery the weapon was, go to **76**.

Anyway. Now that *those people* are gone. Percival. Yes. Our hero, Percival Gynt, having failed to yank with the requisite yankocity, lost his footing and was flat on his back before Foom could as much as process what was happening.

He stood over the younger man in stunned silence, offended yes, but more embarrassed for him.

Go to **134**.

255.

Percival had so many questions and no idea where to start, so in proper Percival Gynt-fashion, he started with himself. "What do you mean," he asked, "by that teeth-in-my-belly business?"

The not-cat might have shrugged had it a human's shoulders. Instead, it simply looked at Percival and bared its black teeth. A sort of smile, perhaps.

Fine. "The refugees, then. Why'd you turn on them? What did they ever do to you?"

Another of them answered. Further back in the dark. A stuffed giraffe, maybe? "We were born into their laps. Shaped by their thoughts, their dreams and terrors. And they were painted with us."

"They seek to trick us with their words," Foom counseled. "They never spoke before. And now?"

There were so many of them. On all sides. Ever as Percival turned, before them in the flickering torchlight. Ever behind them, waiting, in the dark.

Foom whispered, "There's something… something…"

Go to **202**.

256.

No. Sorry. Just a red herring.

Go to **65**.

257.

No point in running now, thought Percival, as he worked his way slowly down the corridor, hand on wall, each step more tentative than the last.

He'd either find his way to Foom or he wouldn't. Which is to say that he wouldn't, but optimistically. Even when he was sure he could hear the tendril, could *feel* it drawing closer, he maintained hope that everything would work out fine.

A thrilling adventure. Like with the serial killer. Then more accounting. Yes. Percival could see a whole future life flash before his eyes, which was fine because neither of the pair of them was doing much good for him otherwise.

Two lives. One quiet and predictable, a place to disappear. Another grand and loud and ridiculous! Him and Midge and, why not, Compubot too. Victories, large and small! Accolades. A mother's respect. And monsters! Time travel, maybe? Wizards in pointy hats and elves with pointy ears and villains with pointy swords and other pointy things. All of the pointy things.

"Poin," Percival whispered.

It wasn't quite a word.

The tendril, the finger of death, was close now. It was at his neck.

Go to **206**.

258.

"We're a long way from Sekayt'r Prime," Percival observed, and he let the statement hang between them in the darkness as they walked.

Eventually Father Foom replied. "A long way, yes, and never far."

He had piqued Percival's curiosity. Or perhaps Percival's curiosity was already piqued, and now he was piqued twice-over? So he asked, "Why them? Why involve yourself in all that?"

"A question many ask, and as rhetorically. Indeed, the Nth Reich and their ilk thrive off such indifference. A war was fought and won, and still we ask 'Why? Why us? Why bother?'"

Percival shrugged.

Foom frowned. "Exactly."

"There are a thousand lost causes in this galaxy, Father. Why *them*?"

Father Foom considered how to answer. Whether to answer. "I was a soldier once, on battlefields little different than Sekayt'r Prime. I was as... enthusiastic in my duties. In my way. The crimes of the past repeat."

Percival understood this sentiment as well as any. He had words for it, in an ancient tongue. "*Bello ess*," he said softly. Words in another tongue. Words *of* another tongue. "The past repeats."

Go to **62**.

259.

No! This is a brilliant plan, thought Percival incorrectly.

"Ah am an agent of the Sukayt'r Prime provisional govuhmn 'n' ahm he-yuh to ink-why inta the fate a ar recen'ly depawted citizens."

The priest stared slack-jawed and dumbstruck at the not-technically-an-accountant's not-technically-a-performance.

"We know about thuh monstuhs, Fathah. 'N' we hold you PUH-sonally responsabuhbuh!"

The priest's right eye twitched. "Did you say 'Father'?"

Percival pointed and, for no clear reason at all, shouted, "FATHAH FOOOOOOM!"

The priest rolled his eyes, loosened his grip on his hammer and closed the gap between himself and Percival in a single stride. Percival, who thought perhaps a hammer attack was imminent, flinched.

Instead, the priest placed a reassuring hand on Percival's shoulder.

"Look," he said, "whoever you are. My name's Curate Pete. I'm the assistant priest here. Assistant. The man you want to talk to, the man who is *definitely* at fault, is Father Foom. And this being a Saturday morning in a year starting with the number two, you can find him 'round the corner at a bar called The Wronged Vagrant."

Percival narrowed his gaze. Was this a trick? Was he being reverse-tricked? The priest's accent certainly *sounded* authentic.

Challenge the priest! A trickster knows a trickster! Go to **138**.

No, no. Let's just assume that Curate Pete was telling the truth and get on with this. Go to **96**.

260.

"Yeah," said Percival. "Yes."

The girl didn't seem convinced. It seemed important to Percival that he convince her. A necessary step.

"Forget what I said before," he said, "about being an accountant or whatever else." Percival knelt down. Looked straight into her bleary, blinking, over-magnified eyes. "I fight monsters. That's what I do. That's who I am. I'll find your Father Foom. Get to the bottom of whatever's happened. Put an end to it. Get you back to your church and your prayers and such. I swear."

And he held out his pinky to her, and she linked hers with his.

It was decided.

Go to **107**.

261.

And it mightn't have taken long, for Foom was heavier than he looked, and Percival strained and huffed with each blind and backwards step. Machine organs, he thought. Maybe Adamantine bones? Weird flex for a priest.

Up a flight, Percival felt for and found an open door. He pulled Foom through and closed it after them. Rummaged through Foom's pockets till he found his keys. Tried four of them before he found the right one. Locked the door after them.

Slapped Foom hard in the face. Twice! Three times!

Fourth time, Foom caught him by the wrist and whispered, "Enough." A kung-fu grip. Percival winced.

"Who are you?"

Foom sat up in the dark. "Follow me," he said. "I have an idea."

Go to **265**.

262.

Percival called up to Father Void, "So it seems that we're stuck here together!"

No response.

"Perhaps we should get to know each other!"

WE SHOULD NOT.

"Brilliant. I'm Percival Gynt, King of Answers!"

YOU ARE NOT.

"It's… It's just a thing I'm trying it out. Nevermind that! Here's Father Foom!"

No response.

"Are those swirly red symbols part of you, or are they… um… not?"

THEY ARE NOT.

Percival smirked. He thought perhaps he was beginning to understand the game!

"Are they accessories? Like jewelry?"

THEY ARE NOT.

"Are they…" Percival tried to recall anything, anything at all, that he knew about magic. "Are they… keeping you here?"

No response.

"If they weren't there, would you stay?"

I WOULD NOT.

Foom nodded approvingly.

"And the people who put you here… They were people, yes?"

No response.

"Wizardy types?"

No response.

"Were they the sort who always go about doing *zero* magic?"

THEY WERE NOT.

"And is that a singular-they or a plural-they!"

No response.

"I bet there were more than five!"

THERE WERE NOT.

"Three?"

THERE WERE NOT. I SEE WHAT YOU'RE DOING.

"You do?"

DON'T NOT SEE. WHAT YOU ARE NOT… NOT DOING.

"Marvelous. And what would you do if you were freed from your prison?"

I WOULD RENDER ALL UNTO PERFECT DESOLATION.

Percival frowned. "Oh," he muttered. Maybe shuffled his feet. Accounts differ. He had not, to that moment, been taking this interaction very seriously. You might have noticed But "perfect desolation" went a kilometer or twelve beyond the odd serial killing. He turned to Foom and in a quiet and chastened tone he whispered, "Let's both of us agree not to let that happen."

Foom agreed.

Percival considered himself. His choices. His bearing. What he had to offer to this moment. Whether he was the right man to stand against this weird and presumably ancient creature. And if so, how? He was no hero. Not yet, certainly. What then? A detective? Hardly that, either. An accountant? Not quite, and less relevant. And to this creature most of all? Nothing. An annoyance. A gnat. An annoying gnat.

Yes! That. How could he weaponize *that*?

"And the tendril that brought us here?" said Percival, a second or a minute or a decade later. Time's strange when the sky's paper. "Was that you?"

No response.

"Do you think someone other than you did that?"

I DO NOT.

Percival nodded slowly to himself. Be the gnat. Be the gnat, he thought. "So you have a portal somewhere, and you what? Stick a little nothing-tendril through it, and it turns all inky on the other side, and you squirt out little ink-baby minions, and their job is to free you, so you can do that whole 'perfect desolation' thing?"

No response.

"Is the thing I just said wrong?"

No response.

Just long enough for Percival to doubt himself.

But then:

IT IS NOT.

"Where is it then?" He grinned. "The portal?"

No response.

"Is it invisible?"

IT IS NOT.

"Is it open right now?"

No response.

"Is it… behind you?"

No response.

Percival and Foom walked under Father Void and looked up at it from the other side, where they could plainly see a rip in the parchment void and one of Father Void's nothing-tendrils inserted, probing.

"That's very high up," said Foom. "We're going to die here, aren't we? For lack of a ladder?"

Percival considered whether he could make it to the rip after a running jump. He could not. Standing on Foom's shoulders? No. Or what if Foom stood on *his* shoulders, while he did his running jump.

No, no. His running jump was rubbish.

"Pockets," said Percival. Finally. After he'd exhausted all jump-related scenarios.

"Pardon?"

"Let's check our inventory, Father. Let's turn out our pockets."

Let's go to **176**, to see if they were carrying anything useful.

263.

"Are you trapped here like me?" asked Percival. A question intended to build rapport.

NOT LIKE YOU.

"Um." No rapport then. "But still trapped, yeah?"

Father Void offered no response. And in the silence, Percival considered it, this indescribable thing, this easily describable nothing. And those peculiar ink symbols that circled 'round it.

"Those red bits: They're some kind of ward, yes? A magical barrier?"

No response.

"Was it wizards? It was wizards, wasn't it?"

No response.

"Which ones?"

THE BEARDED ONE AND THE ONE WHO TEMPTS FATE.

Now, you'll be forgiven for thinking that Father Void was answering Percival Gynt in that moment. That it was telling Percival something he didn't already know. The truth was, those words could describe nearly any two wizards.

It was, as answers go, distinctly not one.

"But why?" asked Percival.

No response.

Be specific, thought Percival. Ask the question that Father Void wants to answer. "What would you do if you were free, O Father Void?"

ALL THAT IS SHALL END. ALL THAT IS NAUGHT SHALL REIGN SUPREME.

"Right. Good job, wizards."

Might as well try **19** while we're at it.

264.

No, not alone. Those creatures killed Hestor and Fulgrimm, Maaba and M'k'k'b and Yella. They were strangers to Percival, but Foom knew them all well. Had served them soup from his own ladle. Knew them for the kind, brave people and/or necroblobs that they were.

"Perhaps," Foom whispered, rethinking an old vow. "Perhaps I could."

Percival wondered whether he should ask Foom more about his past.

Go to **150**.

265.

It was slow going in the dark, but Father Foom knew those halls like he knew himself. Which is to say fairly well, if with regrets.

He and Percival held hands. There was no questioning. No awkwardness. Both men wanted to live, and Foom's grip was strong. Comforting.

Foom ran his other hand along the wall when he could. He knew to turn left at the first break, right at the second. Percival stumbled three times, twice out of clumsiness, the final time from exhaustion.

Foom pulled him ever forward.

Neither spoke. They could still hear Father Void's tendril pounding at that locked door, not so very far away. Knew it was only a matter of time until it broke through.

"Where?" Percival asked, on his knees after his fourth fall. Perhaps if there'd been light, if he'd been able to see, if he hadn't felt so desperate, so utterly useless, he might not have felt compelled to ask.

But he did, so he did.

Foom hauled him to his feet again.

"I have a weapon," he said, "in my office."

Go to **244**.

266.

"No," said Percival, as he pulled his fingers from the goop, "I suppose not."

He flicked the remnants from his fingertips as he stood. Looked down at the book. At the inky sludge between the pages. Oozing. Writhing. Reaching with a dozen tiny tendrils.

"So, um," asked Percival, "how would you like to proceed?"

To be clear, Percival was asking Father Foom, not you. But I don't suppose there's any harm in us making the decision on his behalf.

"Close it," counseled Foom. Go to **133**.

Or possibly, "Leave it. Thing's cursed. Best to get out of here and come back with fire." Ooh! Fire. That's in the story title, isn't it? Let's do that. Go to **162**.

267.

Percival drew a sharp breath, looked Father Foom in his eyes, laid his hands on the bar, and leaned forward. And he asked him, "Do you know what happened on the planet Gynt?"

Foom knew. Remembered the stories from his last life. Friends had fought and died on Gynt. To stop a monster. To save a child. The colony was lost. The planet abandoned. But Percival Gynt was saved. "You?" he whispered.

"As Fate would have it."

Father Foom searched his memories. "That was… fifteen years ago?"

"Near enough."

"And now you're…?"

"I'm not going to lie to you, Father. I hold a sad, frequently demeaning entry-level position at a mid-tier accounting firm on Lunar Colony. I've had some opportunities, yes. Squandered them. I'm a nobody, mostly. These days. Except…"

Percival paused, smirked, tapped his fingers across the bar top, probably wanted Father Foom to prompt him, so he could unleash some clever one-liner.

Foom waited.

"Fate," said Percival finally. "That's what's brought me to you. That God of yours, perhaps. You have monsters. I know from monsters. And I survived. Let me help you."

Father Foom scratched his beard. Grumbled to himself. "You call 'em monsters, but they're not that. Weren't that. They were just critters. Alien, yeah. Weird, yeah. But—"

"Respectfully, they *ate* your house guests."

Father Foom nodded, stepped away from the bar. Turned his back on Percival, so the younger man wouldn't see his tears.

Perhaps this was Percival's moment to say something to console the man? Go to **48**.

No, no. Just give him a minute. Go to **165**.

268.

"Hello, shadow creatures!" Percival shouted into the dark. "I've spoken to the Great Tentacle, and it said we should be friends now."

Yes, thought Percival, a very clever ruse.

And though he couldn't see them, he could hear the creatures approaching. Could hear them skitter and crawl. Slowly. Tentatively.

"It's quite all right, I promise," promised Percival. Lyingly.

And the creatures drew closer. Closerly.

"In fact," said Percival, "the Great Tentacle told me to help you. Told me you're all meant to go back into the book. Because of how lonely the Great Tentacle is, and how much it misses you."

And closerly still.

"Or, um," Percival stammered, "how much *he* misses you. Or they?"

A single tiny claw scratched at Percival's loafer. And a small voice sang:

He has a name,
That ancient thing,
That sits beneath us
As we sing.

Percival crouched down, felt for an oily coat of fur to pet. "Of course," said Percival as he stroked a not-cat's fur. "But he only shares it with his children. To me, he's simply the Great Tentacle."

Percival Gynt hated cats yesterday. Today, more so. And tomorrow, he could scarcely imagine. He wiped the creature's spludge off on his pants leg.

"Anyway," said Percival as he stood, "he said you should show me the way out. So I could tell others not to bother you."

And did these strange and terrible and sometimes musical creatures believe our Percival?

Well, that's a choice! Let's decide together.

If yes, because… I don't know! Maybe the inky spawn of Great Tentacles are inexorably gullible? My research is, as we've previously established, woefully inconclusive. Go to **51**.

Or, well, what seems more likely is that they would murder Percival, because, well, why wouldn't they? Then go to **188**.

269.

Right. Never mind all that. Where was I?

Oh yes. A church on fire. Collapsing in on itself. Children crying out from within, one last and useless time.

And Percival. Desperate to forget. Desperate to remember.

Think, thought Percival. *Think.* What was it? What was he missing? *Who* was he missing?

It was then that a lightbulb went off in Percival Gynt's head. A very particular lightbulb. An R63.

It was meant to be calming.

270.

There was a rip in the parchment sky above Father Void. A rip that it was probing with a sort of nothing-tendril. Evocative, in its absence, of the very ink-black tendril that had drawn them here.

Was this it then? It had to be. The way home.

A startling revelation, and surely one Percival would have shared with Father Foom, so that they might formulate a plan together as proper partners. Go to **81**.

Although, to be fair, they weren't actually partners, were they? Foom was a client. Sort of. Not a paying client, certainly. But Percival still hoped that *if* they ever got back home, the priest might leave him a positive review on Yelp or Next Door or Oppo Gldonkk.

And "honestly, I did half the work" is not a positive review.

Go to **126** to see Percival take both men's lives into his own hands.

271.

Murdered, yes. One hundred years ago that morning. In that very cheese shop. And doomed to wander the world for all eternity for her sins.

Her cheese-related sins.

I suppose?

Or, hear me out: Maybe she *wasn't* murdered? Maybe go to **103** instead.

But fine, if you're very, very sure this is the path you want to go down, I'll see you at **308**.

You were warned.

272.

It was Saturday morning, and Percival Gynt, having nothing better to do with his day, resolved to buy himself a large wedge of cheese.

If you'd care to know more about Percival's mental state that morning and what might have moved him to acquire said cheese, please proceed to **243**.

Or if that sounds dull as dishes and you'd rather get straight to the cheese, go to **14**.

273.

"THIS WAY!" shouted Percival, as he pulled Father Foom behind him.

Foom tried to keep the torch pointed steadily ahead of them, but it was a challenge as they ran. Instead, the corridor appeared and vanished in flashes of light and dark. "DO YOU HAVE ANY IDEA WHERE YOU'RE GOING, GYNT?" he shouted.

"I'M GOING LEFT! ALWAYS GO LEFT IN A MAZE!"

"WHAT?"

"IT'S A THING I READ! IF YOU'RE STUCK IN A MAZE, ALWAYS GO LEFT AND EVENTUALLY YOU'LL GET OUT!"

"AND WHAT IF THERE'S A DEAD END AND A MONSTER CHASING YOU???"

"WHAT ARE THE ODDS OF THAT, THOUGH?" Percival shouted over his shoulder. And then he collided with a brick wall.

"Good, Gynt." Foom crouched and hoisted Percival's limp frame over his shoulder. A firefighter's lift. "The odds are very good."

Foom lurched to one side and the tendril struck wall, recoiled, and whipped towards him! Foom dodged and doubled back! Ran along the length of the tendril and with Percival still across his shoulder, leapt, slid under, and made an abrupt left through an open doorway!

Up! Up! Up! **136**!

274.

Oh, good. Unless one of us parsed that wrong. Anyway, maybe there's another way to end this story! A way that doesn't end in fire.

Tell me, do you know about Percival's marvelous twelve-part plan?

If yes, go to **248**.

If no, go to **72**.

275.

"And what good, precisely, can one very large duck do against a giant tendril monster and its horde of demon children?"

Foom nodded along to the question. "You're right, of course. I only meant her as a distract—"

"I WAS THE ONE WHO WAS DISTRACTED!"

Without warning, Foom reached across to Percival's arm, took a firm hold, and ran him down the hallway. Sensing his arm was along for the ride no matter what, Percival wisely willed the rest of him to follow.

And in that moment, the tendril struck.

Struck duck.

The creature let out one last, panicked quack as the tendril ground it into the floor.

Foom pulled Percival up a set of stairs and into another blackened corridor. Or should I say "nearly blackened?" Because at the end of that corridor was a window, looking out over the alley.

A single shaft of moonlight. A way out.

"We have to jump."

But Percival shook his head.

The tendril wouldn't have been slowed more than a moment. There was no time to argue.

Foom let go of Percival's arm, turned, ran the length of the hall and jumped through the glass, out the window, and down to the alley below. With an expert's proficiency. This was not his first auto-defenestration.

And Percival? The tendril was at his back. The duck had been, well… Not *much* of a distraction. His only hope, a shaft of light and a several-story fall. So he ran. And jumped. Go to **302**.

But that sounds terrible, doesn't it? If Percival was to die, it should've been in the dark, murdered by a tendril monster. Not falling out a window like a regular. Go to **13**.

276.

Percival stumbled out into the alley. Fell at Father Foom's feet.

The father stood stone-faced, staring back into the flames. To the church that was once his home. And a thousand fires before.

He lifted his weapon, his longest companion, and aimed across the threshhold. He squeezed back on the trigger.

And did not let go.

Percival cowered beneath a long and unbroken torrent of flame. Clutched his ears as an explosion built within the burning structure. The creatures' cries still echoed in his head. "Father! Father!"

FOOM.

The alley and the night were overtaken by rubble and ash.

And silence.

Go to **310**.

277.

Even then, Percival maintained an extensive handkerchief collection. This one was a gorgeous cerulean blue and soft as anything that Father Foom had ever touched.

As a younger man, on the boardwalks, he'd done a trick where he'd pull a hundred handkerchiefs from his sleeve, one tied to another, long enough to reach all the way to Father Void's portal and back again.

But that, sadly, was a trick. Foom would spend the evening before tying all the handkerchiefs together in pleasing color patterns, and then he'd stuff them down his pants leg and up through his shirt when he got dressed.

It was a lot of work for a trick that lasted at most fifteen seconds and, if we're being honest, solicited mostly groans.

Even if he had another hundred handkerchiefs, he highly doubted that Father Void would be much impressed.

Back to **176**.

278.

Percival found the hole where they'd removed the tile. Found the book.

It was cold to the touch. Damp. Sticky. And another thing. A thing Percival had felt before, long ago, even before he knew the word for it.

What he had felt staring into Alexander Eeps' eyes.

Evil.

Close the book, Percival thought. End it. You don't owe this priest anything.

Or be the hero. Follow him in. How hard can it be to climb into a book? And then… And then? And then what? Be trapped in a book too?

It falls to you.

Shut it. End it. Go to **135**.

Or follow Foom. Save him maybe. Or die in the attempt. Go to **110**.

279.

"All right! Good, good." Percival let out a little sigh of relief/didn't, and then he *definitely* looked you straight in the eye. "This is very important, Sam. I need you to stick out your tongue. Like this."

Percival stuck out his tongue/didn't.

"Narrator."

Okay, he definitely stuck out his tongue. Or did he?

"Narrator!"

Sorry.

"Once you've stuck out your tongue, go to **46**.

"If you don't want to do that, I suppose you should just read **279** again and again until I've broken your spirit?"

280.

But then the fiery portal opened once more beneath Percival, and he fell through. This time, three meters onto solid stone. From the light of the dimming portal he could see that he was back in the undercroft.

Father Foom was, for his part, sat in the corner of the room, despondently flipping the torchlight on and off as he stared into the middle distance. When Percival crash-landed, Foom bolted up with a smile.

"Oy! What happened to you?"

Percival pushed himself to his feet. "Nothing, mostly."

Go to **171**.

281.

So that definitely happened.

Making now, perhaps, a good time to insert some speculation.

Because even subtracting out his minutes-long trip to the bodega, Percival had hours to prepare for his rendezvous with Father Foom. And he wasn't a careless man. Percival wasn't. Foom might have been. He let all those monsters wander around his church after all. Left refugees unattended? Didn't notice a particularly obvious solitaire play?

Not relevant.

Percival was not careless. Had time. Some scholars believe he might have used that time to reach out to an old friend.

A friend who is, as might previously been mentioned, an expert on demons.

Go to **184**.

282.

Percival glanced back to Madrigal, who seemed to be following their conversation as intently as one could from the far side of the room. With curiosity, he thought, and perhaps amusement.

"Tell me this," said Percival to the little girl. "Has anyone made you a better offer today?"

The little girl wiped a last tear from behind her glasses as she considered. "Well," she said finally, "the shop lady did offer me free cheese if I go home or shut up already."

"Excellent," Percival concluded. "That means free cheese for everyone."

Go to **304.**

283.

It was an old school chum of Percival's, Footface maybe, who'd once suggested that he lose himself in a good book. At the time, Percival could think of no fate so appalling.

But now the more appalling alternative seemed obvious: To lose himself in a *baaad* book.

Was this now his fate? Certainly, the parchment sky suggested it. Those inky runes. Yes, thought Percival, I am definitely inside that book, in a hole, in an undercroft, in a condemned church.

"And I thought today was going to be boring," Percival mumbled to himself.

YOU ARE NOT BORED! came a booming-soft voice from all around him or possibly nowhere. YOU ARE NOTHING, AS I AM NOTHING!

A harsh critique, thought Percival. It was like being back at university, except for all of it.

He thought perhaps it was the absence overhead that was speaking to him, so he directed his next question there. "Who are you?" But that didn't sound quite right, so he tried again. "Or… what are you?" And again and again. "Why are you? *How* even are you?"

I AM FINE, THANK YOU. I AM NOT. I AM NOTHING. I AM THE FATHER VOID.

Percival nodded along as the nothing spoke, but he could parse precisely none of it. Except the name at the end. "If you're nothing, why do you have a name? How does nothing have a name?"

I AM AS I AM NOT, AS I HAVE ALWAYS NOT BEEN. MY ABSENCE IS AS ETERNAL AS REALITY IS NOT.

Yes, Footface. A very bad book.

Go to **102**.

284.

The girl explained, eventually, that the church had taken in a refugee family from worn-torn Sekaty'r Prime, telepaths, and put them up in the church basement. It was they who discovered the monsters.

The refugees were there illegally. Father Foom kept them hidden in the basement "for their own protection." His words. But the monsters were given the full run of the church.

They seemed harmless enough.

Until they ate the refugees.

After that, Father Foom locked down the church. Just for a little while, he said at the time. But now the flyer.

Go to **24**.

285.

Percival held up the priest's prized purple pen, quite oblivious to the alliteration.

It was an antique. An ink pen. Ballpoint.

He let his eyes focus on it. Then past it into the paper void. Then back to the pen.

"Are you...?" Father Foom could see that Percival was deep in thought. Intent on... something. But what, he couldn't say. His pen, possibly?

Percival clicked the pen absently. Once. Twice. Three times.

"Percival," said Father Foom. "Use your words to say words to me."

Percival started. Apologized. Handed Foom his pen back. "Sorry, it's just..." He hadn't quite formed the thought yet. "It's a pen, yeah?"

"Yes."

"And we're in a book?"

"Or Hell."

"Or Paper Hell?"

"And?"

"Father, maybe we can write our way out of this mess?"

"Mess" seems harsh to me.

"Or draw," said Father Foom. And he smiled, remembering a favorite story from his childhood.

Go to **4**.

286.

Percival saw his allies falling all around him and decided he only had one choice left to him: To fight.

He fumbled for his torch. Instinctively, Father Foom stepped back-to-back with him and raised his fists. "They're going to kill us," he whispered. "*You* have killed us."

He spoke these words to Percival Gynt, but he may as well have been speaking directly to you.

Percival had no skill as a fighter. I suppose I could've mentioned that to you before you chose this option? He lunged forward at the creatures, swung his torch like a cudgel, missed and fell into a pile of them, all writhing and cackling and thirsty for blood.

Ahead of him, the creatures overtook Maaba, mounted her, and began to chew through her human parts. Behind him, Foom's screams were swallowed by the dark.

The monsters gnawed at Percival, and he considered it a fitting end. Except this definitely isn't the end, because Percival Gynt didn't die on this day. In this corridor, at least.

If I might offer you a piece of advice that you can carry with you to other branching narratives and perhaps into your own life as well:

If someone offers you the choice to fight or talk, *always choose talk*.

Now go back to **311** and choose better.

287.

"What do you want?" asked Percival, more than a little exasperated. "You've murdered the innocent. Overtaken this church. Why?"

"Set me down," said the creature, "and I'll answer your question."

"Answer our question," suggested Foom, "and perhaps we'll set you down."

"Answer our question," said Percival, "and I swear that no harm will come to you."

"The fool's promise," scoffed the little thing, even as it dangled by its scruff. Averted its gaze. "But I'll answer your question."

But then it didn't, so after a moment, Percival said, "Please do."

"Some of what you say is true, and some is false. All of what I say is true, and some is false. What do I want? To live in shadow and go on living. To run. To be loved. And not to die at the hands of Percival Gynt."

Percival set the creature down on the tile before him. Slowly, gently. And the creature scrambled to its feet. It's two-and-a-half-ish feet.

"I wouldn't," said Percival.

"Some false," said the creature, and it loped to the doorway.

Foom followed after it with the torchlight, lost it between the flickers.

Go to **251**.

288.

Percival shook his head and turned his torch and his attention to the floor beneath them, inspecting a single tile at a time. "And they were murdered down here?"

"If I fought a little harder, I might have—"

"Where's the furniture?"

"Sorry?"

"You gave them furniture, yeah?"

"Oh. Yeah. Even Pete couldn't object to that. Cots. A folding table over there and some chairs. Some kitchenware. A mini-fridge from the Finches' and a couple of tablets for the children."

"Is any of it still here somewhere? Could I see it?"

Foom shook his head. "It's gone now. Taken out with the bodies. It was…" Foom wiped a tear from his eye and stifled an ugly snort. "It was unusable."

Go to **47**.

289.

Firefighters came, but by the time they'd extinguished the blaze, the church was in cinders and all evidence of the monsters incinerated.

Percival and Foom were rushed to the hospital, along with a few bystanders injured by falling debris.

Foom was in and out of the hospital in a day, thanks to certain genetic augmentations he'd received during his soldiering years.

Percival was not so lucky.

His heart stopped three times on the way to the hospital. Four more times on the operating table. After eleven hours, the doctors agreed that his injuries were too severe. They let him die.

Go to **312**.

290.

Percival's body folded inside out and back again as he fell through sixteen dimensions. In one, a tiny green man in a red cape buzzed around his face and told him to believe in himself. In another, a two-headed ogre staggered down a corridor, howling in pain. In a third, an evil spirit animated an army of the shambling dead.

Better than the little green man, thought Percival.

And then he landed, half-materialized, half-immaterial, on a cold and agreeably extant hardwood floor. There were voices speaking. A thin-voiced man in a bed beside him, and a young woman opposite.

Go to **32**.

291.

What happened next was both what Percival should have expected and also so much worse than he could have imagined. The nothingness that was Father Void reared overhead, roared with a quietly deafening fury, and lashed out with not one but a hundred tendrils of pure, unimaginable absence.

Percival dodged and dived, ducked, stumbled, lost his hat, caught his breath, and went back for it. With each strike, the not-tendrils slashed apart parchment void, revealing ink-black portals in the tatters.

Any one of them might be the way home. Or a gateway to some new nightmare.

Percival used the portals as cover, now hiding behind one, now dashing from one to the next. All as the not-tendrils continued to strike, as unrelenting as they were more generally un.

And Percival was unsure. Unsure of which portal to choose. Of if it even mattered.

But then a sign, perhaps. A single portal, amidst the inky-black that shone a perfect white.

This now was the moment of choosing. Would he take one of the many black portals? Or the single perfect white?

Percival recalled from his school days that black was the absence of light, but white was the absence of all pigment.

Honestly, in that moment, all he wanted was the absence of Father Void's not-tendrils. So he chose.

Black. Go to **43**.

White. Go to **252**.

Or, if you're thrown off by the fact that Percival has been wearing a hat this whole time and you weren't picturing that in your head, you can go all the way back to **15** and begin again, imagining Percival in a hat. Or go to **43** or **252**.

292.

"All right," said Percival, who would have rather been the hero of this story. "I think now's the time."

Go to **59**.

293.

The bartender's hand trembled over the red five. He swore. Two words. An expletive and a preposition.

Percival hadn't been sure till then. "You're Foom."

The bartender gathered up his cards, wiped away a tear with the heel of his hand, snorted a loud, snotty snort, and nodded. "I'm Foom."

Go to **267**.

294.

Father Foom unpadlocked the chains that barred the back door of the church and, with his new allies' assistance, piled them to one side. Then he unlocked the door itself.

The lights were out inside. He flipped a wall switch once, twice. Nothing.

"Your monsters cut the power?" asked Percival.

"Not mine," Foom snapped. "Never mine."

Percival offered Foom the slightest shrug, then glanced back to the others. "Any of you bring a light?"

Maaba the Cyborg tapped her temple and one eyeball swiveled to reveal a soft blue light. Much better than the glitchy, bodega-bought, just-in-case electric torch that Percival had purchased that afternoon. He motioned for Maaba to take the lead. "Cyborgs first."

Percival followed. Then Foom. Then Hestor and the rest. Maaba's eyelight shined ahead of them. The last of the party, Fulgrimm the Short, closed the alley door behind them.

A few meters in, Maaba stopped and whispered, "I'm g-getting all k-kinds of pings on my p-proximity sensors."

Percival squinted into the darkness. His mortal eyes saw nothing, but then a bit of the darkness emerged into the light, a small shape, a creature. A cat that was surely not a cat.

Its eyes were red. Shiny. Its fur, dark as midnight. The soft blue light of Maaba's eye seemed to slide off the creature, this not-cat, like the loosest of garments.

"We know you," it said, in the soft, cloying tone of an obsequious child.

"Y-You…" Maaba was properly unnerved. "You *know* me?"

"No," said the not-cat, with convincing disdain. "Not you. The one behind. The one who came here to kill us. There's a song of him." And the creature directed its bloody gaze towards our hero. "Would you like to hear it, *Percival Gynt?*"

If you would in fact *not* like to hear the song from the talking cat because, frankly, that sounds a bit naff, go to **100**.

Or if you don't want to hear the song, because actually the idea of a creepy not-cat singing to you by torchlight is clearly and profoundly unsettling, go to **100**.

Or if you just can't... can't... This is just... What *is* this? Go to 100.

Go to **100**.

295.

Go to **62**.

296.

It's to be word play then? Wonderful! You may not have noticed this, but the story that you're reading is almost entirely comprised of words! I'm really quite fond of them and, no small coincidence, Percival was as well.

So he thought for a moment, Percival did, and he stood, and he looked around. Nothing but darkness. As expected. "Pardon me," he called out, "but does anyone have a torch? I seem to have misplaced mine."

He waited. You can't do word play by yourself. That's just yammering. But he knew he wasn't alone. As he waited, he could hear them skittering closer. He breathed in slowly. Breathed out slowly.

He'd been alone in the dark before. This would be fine. Probably fine.

"He's come back to us," said a familiar voice in the dark. It was the cat who wasn't a cat. The cat who sang.

Or a different cat maybe. Did I mention it was dark?

Good, thought Percival. This one likes words too. "Are you a cat or not a cat?"

"Certainly," it answered.

Percival scowled in the dark. A point for them. He would have to be more careful in his phrasing. "What are you?"

"Nothing more than I appear," it replied, before more slowly repeating, "Nothing. More than I appear."

Two-Nil.

"And are we enemies, you and I?"

"We are Nothing of the Kind."

Three-Nil. Really. This was embarrassing.

"Perhaps you could ask me a question?"

"Perhaps I could."

Four-Nil. Percival swore under his breath. This had really seemed like the less stupid of the two options when he, and by extension you, had chosen it. Think. Think. What had the cat said in its song?

"You said I have teeth in my belly? Do you have teeth?"

"I have young teeth. You have old teeth."

"Where do you keep your teeth?"

"In my mouth."

"And where do you lose them?"

"In the dark."

"And in the light?"

"We lose more."

"Not just teeth?"

"Unjust teeth."

"And the teeth in my belly? Are they unjust?"

"Well," answered the not-cat. "It's your belly. That's something you need to answer for."

"You mean, for me to answer?"

"If you like."

"And if I don't?"

"It might be too late for that."

"I could wait till tomorrow."

"It's nice to have that luxury."

"Why? Are you going somewhere?"

"No. Never."

"Then what is there to do but wait?"

"There is a beginning, a middle, and an end. And only the middle is a waiting place."

"You don't expect to see tomorrow. You still think I'm going to kill you all."

"Not all."

"To kill you."

"Every time, by fire."

"Every time?"

"Every choice. Every outcome. Every tomorrow, we are ash on the wind."

Percival frowned in the dark. "That's bleak," was the best response he could manage. Points for them. Sort of.

"Listen," he said, changing tacks. "My friend's been eaten by a book-tendril. What can you tell me about that?"

"There's a book that has teeth in its belly."

"Is he dead?"

"The book?"

"Is the book a he?"

"No less than anything."

"Is the book dead?"

"No more than anything."

"And my friend?"

"Somewhere nowhere anywhere nothing."

"Alive?"

"You'd have to ask him."

"Him, my friend, or him, the book?"

"Of course."

"And if my friend is dead, what's to stop the book from murdering me as well?"

"Absolutely nothing."

"Lovely."

"We think so."

Percival sighed. A long, deep sigh, befitting both the hour and his ragged state of mind. "Might you guide me to the him-book? Since it's so dark, and you're going to be ash tomorrow, and my death would be lovely?"

The not-cat chuckled. "Why, of course! Why didn't you ask sooner?"

"Because I can only ask in the present moment."

"Yes," the not-cat agreed. "A point for you."

Percival smiled a weary smile. "I knew there was a point in there somewhere."

Go to **151**.

297.

"Even now, you don't see it! Or won't." Percival shook his head. "You call them children? I call them the babbling little shits of a primordial nothing-monster that lives in your basement and is even now attempting to kill us. Curate Pete was right. He tried to tell me. But you won't accept it, will you? Those creatures? They're demons. As sure as their father."

"No," said Foom, with a snarl and a glower. "Never that. A child shall not suffer for the iniquity of a parent. *Ezekiel 18:20.*"

Go to **85.**

298.

Fire spread rapidly up and down the hall.

That can't possibly be to code, thought Percival, who was I should reiterate *not* a ten-by-ten plant mass. He was indeed a human man of ordinary proportion, save perhaps for his intellect, his ego, his sharp tongue, and his deep-set guilt.

And the other man, Father Foom, a man perhaps his equal in guilt, was paralyzed beside him, presumably reliving some past trauma they had no time to dissect. Percival shouted, "WE HAVE TO GO!" and tugged on the priest's arm, and that was thankfully enough to rouse him and force him back into his wits.

"Y-Yes," Foom agreed. His voice had thinned, was older than his years. The weapon fell from his hand and landed on the ink-stained carpet with a sort of thurnk. He stepped haltingly, deliberately out into the hall, out into the fire, turned left, and was gone.

Percival bent down and took Foom's gun. It was heavier than he'd anticipated. Hotter. Percival didn't dwell. There would be time for questioning building codes, ink stains, and treating second degree burns later.

Percival ran into the fire.

Go to **117.**

299.

"Slow day?" asked Percival. Pleasantly, he thought. And he took a seat.

"We don't open till three," the bartender muttered without looking up from his cards.

"Ah. Because the door was unlocked." Percival gestured vaguely in that direction. "I just assumed—"

"Yeah. Usually, people check the posted hours outside or notice that the bar's empty and the lights are off, and they don't come in." The bartender glanced up at Percival, frowned, turned his attention back to his cards, double-frowned, scratched his beard. "I got a ShockGun behind the bar, if you're here to nap or sell me something."

"No," said Percival. "Sorry. No naps. No sales." And no pleasantries, as it turned out.

Best to get straight to it then.

Go to **83**.

300.

"Nevermind," said Percival. "Ignore most of what I just said. We should go out. Should we go out?"

"No?" said Madrigal, who was fairly certain that that was the right answer, but also slightly dazed.

"Oh. Would it help if I asked you again? Perhaps differently? Perhaps with singing?"

"No," said Madrigal. "Definitely not with singing."

Percival considered whether he should sing anyway.

If you think Percival singing sounds like a good idea, go to **7**.

If you're neither an idiot nor having a go, skip ahead to **125**.

301.

...and he said to the fishmonger, "Why don't I call some people first?"

A week after, he returned to the fishmonger's, joined by old friends and new, some enemies even, a lying robot and a rat chef, a magician and the Celestial Governor herself, a professor, a puppet, his business partner—Percival's, not the puppet's—a three-armed frog, two old thieves, a sort-of-detective, and a friend from his academy days.

They were quite cramped.

"Sure you don't wanna do this somewhere else?" asked the

fishmonger, less concerned about the space available than about the space provided.

Percival clapped a hand on their shoulder. "No, this is fine, thank you." And he flung open the book to a middle page.

Immediately, a dark tendril geysered up out of the book, whipped and struck the ceiling. Shots were fired. Spells slung. Expletives flung, less helpfully. The tendril exploded into a mess of black goo that gakked them all.

"THIS-IS-PLEASANT," one of them observed.

Next came a hand, then another, as Father Foom pulled himself up out of the book, a rather staggering display of willfully non-Euclidean physics if ever there was. He was older, to Percival's eye, though he hadn't known Foom well.

The years that had passed for Percival had passed for Foom as well. Inside that damned book.

"It's over," Percival told Foom.

"It's not," Foom answered. "You have to go back."

Percival didn't understand. He looked to the others, friends and foes, for advice.

"This isn't right," said the rat chef. "Even I can see it, and I'm famously unobservant."

"Try again," said the magician.

"Try again," said his business partner.

"DO-NOT TRY-A-GAIN," said the lying robot.

Percival nodded. Closed his eyes. "What time is it?" he asked the fishmonger.

"It's twelve past nine."

Go to **15**.

302.

Honestly, falling out of a something-story window isn't all that bad if you don't mind breaking several bones, all the mind-shattering pain and the bleeding and the sobbing into the broken pavement, the glass sticking out of your hands and your face, the lingering smell of alley poops, the weird bend at your elbow, all the unhoused people gawking at you, the facedown priest, maybe dead, or the ink-black tendril smashing its way out of a house of worship up above.

Things look bleak, thought Percival. I probably should have bought two flashlights.

After that, various other things happened. Percival defeated the monster. And its children. With fire, probably. And don't act so shocked! It's right there in the title of the story.

If I'm being honest, the whole duck thing's thrown me for a loop. I apologize. I'm genuinely not sure how to connect it to any plausible ending.

But I strive for historical accuracy, and when I interviewed her, one of Foom's exes insisted that he had a "surprisingly large duck." Per my hand-written notes. She wouldn't shut up about it.

Hence, a duck.

But I feel bad. I do. It's a letdown of an ending. So here's how I'm going to make it up to you:

Go to any section you want. Anywhere at all. Pick a random number, if you're feeling lucky. I hear **167** is particularly random. Or maybe go all the way back to **3**. Also, I'm quite proud of **308**, if you haven't seen it yet.

Just promise me you won't go to **2**. Anywhere else. Definitely don't go to **2**.

Good luck!

303.

In the beginning, I spoke of certainties. Those few events of this worst-of-days that are truly known. That are beyond dispute. Some quite grim, others trivial. This next passage certainly falls into the latter category.

But it definitely happened. So.

Shortly after 3pm, Percival Gynt ran out of toilet paper.

Auspicious! Or, um… Well, let's see where this goes?

213. 213 is where this goes.

Or, fine, we can skip ahead. Because you hate certainty. Apparently. Go to **92**.

304.

Percival Gynt had only been living in Slidetown Province for a few months by this point and had in that time taken no effort to surveil its various churches, mosques, temples, septs, or shrines. And one might be forgiven for overlooking Our Lady of Sorrows in particular, with its narrow, unremarkable façade, wedged as it was between two disused fishmongers.

"Find us at our new location, two doors down," read the sign on the first fishmonger. "We've made a terrible mistake!" read the sign on the second.

One *might* be forgiven for overlooking Our Lady of Sorrows, except that the church was itself only seven doors down Traveler's Way from Percival's own apartment building. Surely, he'd passed its doors a hundred times to and from the train station.

A killer in his own building. Monsters down the street.

What he could not see, Fate would make plain to him.

Anyway, the church. Go to **65**.

Or…? There's something awfully fishy about those two closed shops, isn't there? Let's go to **256** to investigate.

305.

The book was never found. Perhaps it burned. Perhaps it was still there, buried in the fishmonger's foundations. Percival never found out.

But he did see Father Foom again. Many times.

First, out the window of his train, as the express passed Sorrow Point Station. But that could have been his imagination. Next, a few weeks later, as part of a flash mob in a viral video Midge MySpaced to him. But perhaps that was just a breakdancer who only looked like Foom.

A guilty mind plays tricks.

One Tuesday, Percival thought he saw Foom through the cheese shop window buying cheese from Edgar. Or Gary. He couldn't be sure.

The following Thursday, he was certain it was Foom he saw jetpacking outside the dome of Lunar Colony, gasping for air.

That Easter, Percival saw Father Foom atop a float in the Easter

Parade.

That Summer, Percival watched Foom compete in *The Great British-Equivalent Bake-Off*, though for some reason everyone called him Charlie.

The following Spring, Percival dreamed that Father Foom was trapped in a microscopic Hell dimension. As it would later turn out, he *was* trapped in a microscopic Hell dimension, and all those other sighting were just people who only looked like him.

It was Percival's friend Professor Grieg who helped rescue Foom. It took some time and ingenuity and also a number of Kickstarters, not all of them successful. At one point, Foom just had a foot out and later an elbow. At one point, things looked grim, and Foom asked Percival to seek out his ex-wife and his daughter so that he could apologize to them for various old wrongs. He popped his elbow in and a few fingers out and he awkwardly signed the whole thing.

It was quite bewildering for all involved.

You might imagine that Father Foom would be rather cross with Percival when he was finally freed from micro-Hell, as owing to Percival's own culpability in Foom's abduction. But Foom was simply happy to be free and to have reconciled with his ex-wife, and also he was fairly hazy as to the events preceding.

When reading an early draft of this story, Foom ex=wife opined, "You've gotten it all wrong, Lemuel. This isn't what happened at all!"

Perhaps if you go back to **15**, you might make better choices?

306.

Percival slipped on the stairs, fell backwards, cracked his skull open and died.

I trust that was abrupt enough for you.

This doesn't seem like a very good ending though. In particular because Percival is, mild spoilers ahead, still alive in the next story in this volume.

So.

Um.

This is awkward.

Go to **204**.

307.

"Gynt," answered Percival. "Percival Gynt. And no. Not Catholic."

The curate frowned. "Thought not," he said. "You wouldn't understand. Probably think the doctrinal differences between Catholics and Anglicans are the squabbles of madmen and fools."

Percival didn't care for the Curate's tone. Go to **128**.

But maybe he didn't need to make a big thing of it? Go to **240** to not make a big thing of it.

308.

She was a ghost. We're both agreed, yes? And in that moment, in that cheese shop, she turned to Percival Gynt and she ate him. Are you happy now? Are you very, very proud of yourself?

Good. Because in seven days that little girl is going to climb out of this book or tablet or whatever and she's going to murder you unless you give this book a really great review on Amazon or Goodreads or Oppo Gldonkk.

Do it. For the love of all that's holy, do it now!

And when you come back, start this story over from **1**,

309.

Sometime later, Percival awoke. Black ash had settled into a thick coat over the alley. Over Percival. But the outline of the devastation was clear.

The church was in rubble. Ridiculously, the buildings on either side still stood, protected by their regulation adamantine firewalls. The rising sun shone through the gap.

Father Foom was sat up not so far away, staring blankly onto what remained.

"It's them," he said. "It's not ash. All of this. It's what's left of them."

Out of the corner of his eye, just for an instant, Percival thought he saw a bit of the not-ash move. Or maybe it was just a shadow. When he turned his gaze in that direction, whatever he saw was gone.

He stood, with some moderate discomfort, and he staggered over to Father Foom. Offered him a hand up.

"I've lost your gun," he told him. "It's here…" Percival gestured vaguely. "Somewhere. I was maybe asleep for a while."

Foom approached the rubble that was once his church. Muttered something Percival couldn't hear.

"What's that?" asked Percival.

Foom didn't answer.

"All right," said Percival. "I think I should go to the hospital now."

Foom didn't answer.

"All right," said Percival.

Foom didn't answer.

"We won, didn't we?" Percival asked.

Foom didn't answer.

In his heart, Percival knew they had not.

You can go on to the next story now. If you like. "The View from the 10th Story."

Or you can try again. Go to **15**.

310.

"I'm so sorry."

Percival sat next to Foom, looked out the back of a Province ambulance on the smoldering ruin of the church. A kindly firefighter, a *proper* firefighter, had placed silver shock blankets over their shoulders and given them each a cup of hot cocoa.

There were marshmallows. It all felt wildly inappropriate.

"It's not your fault," said Foom. "The curate was right. I invited those demons up out of the abyss. I'm to blame."

"You don't believe that, or you wouldn't be weeping for them now."

It was true. It had been nearly an hour, and Foom couldn't stop crying. "I just wanted to be kind. Why won't God let me be kind?"

"You were, Father. You will be." Percival rested a hand on Foom's shoulder. "Let this be me."

"I don't—"

"The authorities. Your flock." Percival took the cold cocoa from Foom's hand. "Tell them I did this. Let this be my cross to bear."

Foom shook his head. "I can't do that."

"There's no other way."

"There were witnesses, Gynt. All those people from the soup kitchen…"

"I don't mean to be cruel, Father, but the poor, the forgotten… Who'll believe them?"

"I-I can't lie."

"Your whole life is a lie. What's once more?"

"There must be another way," Foom protested.

"There's no other way."

"There must be another way," he repeated.

There was another way.

Go to **15**.

311.

Behind him, Percival's companions were being torn apart. And he and Foom were having no luck controlling Maaba, who stalked forward into the midst of the advancing creatures, spoiling for a fight. "C-C-C'mon," she stuttered, whisks-a-whirling. Her blue eyelight was cast forward, leaving Percival and Foom in darkness, save for the odd spark from her servomotors.

And more of the creatures were closing from behind.

If you believe Percival would have tried to talk his way out of this, go to **156**.

Or if you think he would have fought, go to **286**.

312.

Sometime later, Percival's brain awoke in a new, cloned body.

He didn't realize anything was amiss until the nurse told him. Didn't believe her at first, but then came the legal documents. Thousands and thousands of pages of legal documents, most of which offered some variation on "But seriously, do you really, really, really,

really promise not to sue us?"

Clone-of-Percival-with-Percival's-Brain signed eagerly, impatient to put the matter behind him, intent on never speaking of any of this ever again.

He dictated an email to his employers. To let them know that he'd be several weeks late to work. And he dictated another to Father Foom at The Wronged Vagrant dot biz:

Dear Father Foom,

I'm sorry I blew up your church. Or we. You helped. I'm not sorry that you partly blew up your church. That's on you. But I'm sorry for my help.

I'm on painkillers.

There's a little girl somewhere. I don't know her name. She was very sad that the church was closed, and I'm sure she'll be inconsolable now that it's kindling. She likes cheese maybe. Please find her and tell her I'm sorry. For my part. You can apologize for you at your discretion.

I wanted to think I had a destiny. Maybe I don't. Maybe I'm just a man who survived a terrible childhood, caught a serial killer, and burned down a church. I mean, I thought I had more of a destiny.

But I've been wrong before. If you ever need me, I'll be here. Probably still in this hospital bed. PT is going to take a while.

And when you're ready, build again. This sad backwater world needs you. This town needs you. When others fail us, when we fail ourselves, when everything around us is shadow and fire, please believe that hope too is inevitable.

I think. I'm very high right now. Also, maybe I one time ate a cat.

Your Friend, (Basically)
Percival Gynt (Basically)
Accountant (Basically)

As he listened to the playback, Percival drifted off to sleep. He was in that moment as content as he'd ever been. Probably because of the painkillers. And also because he was only three hours old.

But as he slept, he could hear them sing. The demon's children. *O, he who's got teeth in his belly, will never know peace in his heart.*

Fate was not finished with Percival Gynt.

And there are more stories in this volume.

313.

IN THE YEAR 20013

PERCIVAL GYNT
AND THE VIEW FROM THE TENTH STORY

When Percival Gynt first met Graiden Grieg, he was dead. Graiden Grieg was. Percival Gynt was a junior accountant attending his coworker's Tuesday night bridge game for the first time, which is evidence of life by at least one very, very strict definition of the word.

Percival gestured to the old man, who was in that moment slumped over the card table, head turned to one side, eyes rolled back, marinating in a pool of his own drool. In a drool-pool, if you will. Or even if you won't!

The drool-pool has happened. The story continues:

"Should we, um, I don't know, call somebody about that?" Percival gestured meekly.

"I wouldn't worry," said Midge Jha, Percival's co-worker, the evening's host, and one-time object of Percival's affection. "I think he's just stepped out for a minute."

As if on cue, a burst of electricity surged from the ZapBack™ box surgically grafted to the dead man's pelvis, jolting him back to life. "And that," said Grieg, as his head jerked suddenly upwards, "is why I have never been to Jupiter." He glanced around the room suspiciously. "You've moved places again, haven't you?"

Midge's roommate and Percival's also-co-worker Paul entered from the kitchen with a jug of margaritas. "Is he back? Midge, you told me you'd tell me when he was back."

"Do you do this often?" Percival asked the old man.

"Bridge?"

"No. Die."

"At least as often as I come back," said Grieg, with a game smirk. "Now, did you all come to gawk at the old man or are we going to play some cards?"

Paul frowned, which is to say that he resumed his default expression. It was his blank glare coming back from the kitchen that was the outlier. "*We* didn't come anywhere, Graiden. We live here. If you want to come into our home and die repeatedly, we're going to gawk. And probably take posed pictures with your corpse."

"I shall enjoy beating you and taking your money."

"Are we playing for money?" asked Percival. He'd never played bridge before, but he hadn't thought it was a betting game. He'd rather hoped that Midge's invitation meant she was coming around on him. He'd hate to think he was merely there for a shakedown.

Midge shook her head. "He means afterwards."

"With a crowbar," Grieg clarified. "In the alley."

"Brilliant," said Paul. "If you're a good guest, I promise to be caught entirely unawares."

"So, um…" Percival picked through his hand of thirteen cards, sorted them by suit, second-guessed himself, sorted by number, then back to suit again. "So, I'm partners with Mister Grieg?"

"Yes," said Midge.

"Professor," said Grieg.

"And Midge and I are partners," said Paul. "Have a drink, Percival."

Percival offered his cup, and Paul poured him a margarita. "What sort of professor?"

"One club," said Paul. "To you, Gynt."

"Professor Grieg specializes in holes," said Midge.

"To you, Gynt."

"Holes?"

"Holes in reality," said the Professor. "Dimensional breaches, connecting one reality to another."

"What? Like, alternate realities?"

"The bid's to you, Gynt."

"Easy, Paul. This is a friendly game."

"Games require participation."

"Other planes of existence. Some like ours. Some very different. Heavens and Hells and everything in between."

"Heavens? Multiple?"

"Good grief. I'm in all the Hells at once."

"Paul!"

"These holes, you can look through them?"

"Not literally. I use math, mostly. And particle detectors. Infrared. Sonar. Void faeries. That sort of thing." Grieg hacked blood and phlegm into his handkerchief.

"Percival, you should probably bid soon," Midge recommended, "so Paul doesn't eat your face."

"Is that what happened to Raoul, Paul?" asked Grieg. "Did you eat his face?"

"Who's Raoul?"

"Graiden's usual partner."

"I didn't eat his face."

"He got hit by a bus."

"A large bus?"

"I don't think they make small buses."

"Is he all right?"

"He's not great."

"But he's not dead?"

"No. It would be weird if he was dead and I said he was 'not great.'"

"Um. Agreed."

Across the table, Professor Grieg had collapsed again. His cards lay scattered face up by his limp left hand. "Great," muttered Paul.

"No," Midge scolded. "Not great."

While they waited for Professor Grieg's pelvis to resuscitate him, Midge pulled Percival aside. "Did you read the email I sent you?" she asked.

Percival didn't remember any email.

"No," he said, hopeful. "Was it about tonight?"

"It had the rules attached. I was hoping you'd read them."

"Oh. No. Sorry. But I'm a fast learner! I'm sure it'll be fine."

"Paul's going to re-deal as soon as the Professor is alive again. Just remember to count your cards. Aces are four, kings are three, queens two, and jacks one."

"If aces are fours, what are fours?"

"Fours are nothing. Please, try to be serious. If you have at least eleven points across the four suits, open with the fourth highest in your longest and strongest suit. If you have a powerhouse, jump to two. If you have seven, pass, but raise your partner if they bid. Don't be a hero. Don't double. Don't redouble. Stop at game. Got it?"

"I understood the part about counting."

"Good enough. If all else fails, pass and then rebid whatever your partner bids. You'll be the dummy all night, and you won't have to play a hand."

"The dummy?"

"It's… You'll see. It's fine. No one thinks you're dumb."

"Paul thinks I'm dumb."

"Also, the Professor thinks you're dumb. Half of the people in the apartment think you're dumb."

"You're including me."

"Excluding you, mostly we think you're dumb. Sorry. It's statistics."

"He really uses math to see Heaven through tears in reality?"

"Supposedly."

"I feel very dumb. You don't feel dumb?"

"That's the beauty of bridge, Gynt! Only one dummy at a time."

Paul began the bidding again. "One heart."

Professor Grieg was alive again, so Percival passed.

"Pass," said Midge.

"One spade," said the Professor.

"Two hearts."

"Two spades!" said Percival.

"Pass."

"Three spades."

"Pass."

Percival glanced at his cards, then back to his partner, then to Midge. "Um. Four spades, right?"

Midge shrugged. "Pass."

Grieg studied his partner for any hint of competence and, finding none, passed.

Paul smirked. "Pass."

"That makes me the dummy?" asked Percival

"Yes," said Paul. With conviction.

"That means the Professor'll play your hand for you."

"Good," said Percival. He set his cards face down in front of him and stood. "I need to excuse myself for a moment."

Midge placed a hand on Percival's elbow. "Wait till the reveal."

Paul placed the Ace of Hearts down in front of him. "Now you turn all of your cards face up."

Percival eyed Midge for confirmation. When she nodded, he turned his cards over one at a time and arranged them by suit, left to right in front of his partner. "Hope this helps," he offered.

He had no spades in his hand.

"It does not," Grieg confirmed.

In the bathroom, over the toilet, hung a framed photograph of Midge and Paul on a beach wearing matching sunhats. They were drinking from comically oversized wine goblets and laughing. Percival couldn't remember a time he'd seen Paul laugh. When he'd gotten the muffin girl fired, maybe.

Percival couldn't place the beach. The sand was purple. The sky, gold. There were three suns in the sky, two mommies and a baby. It looked like a recent vacation, but he didn't remember either of them taking time off. And surely there would have been office gossip if they'd gone together.

He supposed he was glad that Midge could make Paul smile. She was one of the few people who could make Percival smile. And Midge and Paul wouldn't be roommates if they hated each other. No, Percival decided. It was good they got along and went on secret, exotic, strictly platonic holidays together.

Percival finished his business, stepped over to the sink, washed his hands. Either it was a fake vacation or they'd faked time at work or… What, time travel?

A few spots of water splashed Percival's crotch. He sighed.

Percival walked out of the bathroom. Everything from the tip of his tie down to the knees of his trousers was soaked. "Sorry," he said. "Quite surprised by the water pressure, I suppose!"

"Weird," mumbled Paul.

"Happens to me all the time," offered Grieg.

"Be nice," said Midge. "That's not what it looks like when someone pees themself."

"That's what it looks like when I pee myself," Grieg mumbled.

Paul got up to go find a towel for Percival. Percival sat down next to Midge.

"Did you and Paul go on a vacation together recently?"

"You saw the photo? It's from last quarter's corporate conference. Remember everyone in the office went but you and Compubot."

"Of course, of course! I was sure there'd be some innocent explanation!"

"Sorry?"

"You looked very… coupley there."

"Good, yeah?"

"Sorry?"

"We're a couple. We do coupley things. Coupley-not-innocent things."

"Since when?"

"Since when? Since always. Since before I met you. Paul is my partner. This is our apartment."

"He's *your* partner?"

"You didn't think he was the Professor's partner, did you?"

"All this time, I thought you were telling me he was *a* partner."

"At Henderson, Glorp & 110100? Which partner did you think he was?"

"Um. One of them's a robot and one of them's a sort of goo monster, so… the other one?"

Paul tossed a towel at Percival's head. "You girls talking about me?" he asked.

An hour in, Percival won his first hand. He suspected someone had cheated in his favor. A sort of reverse/pity cheat. But also he understood the statistics, that even a poor player was due an undeniably powerful hand now and again. A good metaphor for life, perhaps. On your darkest day, always remember: You might win one time randomly and then immediately go back to losing.

No, thought Percival. Probably not worth printing on a coffee mug.

"So, how did you two meet?" asked Percival.

"Midge took a class with me at University."

"Not you, Professor."

"We met at work, Gynt. I asked her out, and we started dating."

"Oh," said Percival. "That was a short story."

But not in this volume.

Percival sorted his hand, weighed how best to change the subject. "Midge, were you taking physics classes at University?"

"Technically. It was a cross-disciplinary course called 'The Logistics of Temporal Paradoxes: There's No Accounting for Space-Time.' Three spades."

Professor Grief tossed his cards down in disgust. "Pass!" he groused.

Paul and Percival passed too.

Fourteen seconds later, the game and something else called a rubber were both abruptly over, as Midge Jha laid out her cards in front of her and declared absolute, indisputable victory.

"What's death like?" asked Percival, as he downed the last of his margarita. His seventh, maybe. He was usually so good with numbers. He speculated that there might be an inverse square law relating alcohol consumption to doing sums, considered grabbing a paper and stylus, lost his train of thought, considered drinking more.

"Don't know," said Grieg. "I've always been dead when it happens. Oh, I hallucinate like mad. Going in, going out. Even practiced Lucid Dying for a while when I got my first ZapBack! But I've never seen Heaven or Hell or anyplace else in that instant between death and resuscitation."

"But you study other dimensions. 'Heavens' and 'Hells,' you said. I assumed you believed in all that."

"I do not. Honestly, I've never put much stake in spirits. Souls. I say Heavens and Hells, 'cause I get more grant money that way. I just mean places that are nicer or worse than this, and that's just math. The odds of any place being exactly as terrible as the here-and-now are—" The Professor coughed through the end of his answer, apologized with a hand gesture, but needn't have.

The thought was clear enough, and Percival nodded in agreement. Even at his current state of inebriation, it was easy math.

It was approaching midnight when Percival realized that Midge and Paul had disappeared off somewhere. Probably to do something platonic, he thought. To put up shelves, maybe.

Professor Grieg had made his way out to the balcony. Percival had… well, he couldn't quite remember. Probably fallen asleep looking at his watch.

The apartment seemed to flicker in and out of existence as Percival stood, and each time it reappeared at a slightly different angle. This made walking a challenge, as did his headache and whatever was happening with sound in the entire universe at that precise moment. Percival wondered if perhaps he'd been poisoned.

Again.

When the Professor saw Percival struggling in his direction, the old man came over and put an arm around his shoulder and helped him to the balcony, where Percival promptly vomited over the side.

Ten stories below, pedestrians shouted and spat curses.

Percival wiped sick from his mouth, glared down to the tiny, angry people below, considered shouting down an apology, but thought better of it.

Grieg offered him a glass of water. "You ever been drunk before?" he asked.

Percival took the glass. Sipped slowly. Between the vomiting and the water and the night air, he was beginning to feel himself again. "Drunk?" he replied, once he remembered he'd been asked a question. "Not as such. But many other terrible things have happened to me. This doesn't seem so bad, except for the… bad parts."

Grieg chuckled. "Why are you an accountant, Percival Gynt? You seem to me like another sort of person entirely, pretending not to be yourself."

Percival looked out across the street, into the night. Into the long ago or too recent past, perhaps. He didn't answer the Professor's question, which the Professor took as possibly the best and most succinct of answers.

"You ever been in love?" asked Percival.

"Ah," said Grieg. "A new topic. Yes. I'm very old. I've been in love many times."

"And they loved you back?" Percival glanced back to the interior of the apartment. The Professor immediately understood.

"It's not love, if they don't love you back. The other thing, call it what you like. Love is the thing between two people. At least two. Three can be nice. Seven is definitely too many. What was I…? Right. Love. Love is the thing you work on. The thing that grows and changes and dies or dies with you."

"And the other thing?"

"Attraction? It can be powerful. But if it's just one-sided?" Grieg shrugged. "I've had my share of both. One is better than the other."

"How old are you, Professor?" Percival took a sip from his water glass—

"Three hundred and eight."

—and promptly spat it out over the balcony's edge and onto the tiny, angry people below.

"I know, I know," Grieg said with a grin. "Most people mistake me for a spry two hundred."

Percival laughed.

"What do you really want, Percival Gynt? Do you want to be a senior partner at your accounting firm? To have a wife and an apartment and a regular bridge game? Do you want to get drunk with old men and talk about the meaning of life?"

Percival thought. No. Yes. *No.*

The Professor put a hand on the accountant's shoulder. "Or would you rather gaze into the Eye of Hell?"

Percival's eyes lit up with a child's wonderment. "Can we?"

Grieg nodded. "I have the keys to the lab in my coat. Too drunk to drive, but we can call an UberMech™. I'm resolved to dying frequently, but I'm not suicidal."

On his third fumble with his keys, Professor Grieg was able to make the lock turn. He pushed his way into the lab and flicked on the lights. It was a small space, cluttered with dusty bookcases and work benches and half-assembled machinery. Some sort of civil war seemed to be playing out with post-it notes across the communal bulletin board.

"I share the space with my graduate students," said Grieg, as he liberated a bottle of Kentucy-style bourbon from a desk drawer. "It's torture."

Percival, still stood in the doorway, held up his hands to signal surrender. "I think I've had enough already," he said. Probably, that's what he said. He'd had two swigs from Grieg's flask on the back of the UberMech, and the starts and ends of his words were beginning to lose their clip.

Grieg drew two glasses from the same drawer and held one out to Percival anyway. "You may only live once, Percival Gynt."

Percival acquiesced, nodded, slouched into the room, and took a glass. Grieg poured, and they sat, and together they drank.

"Thought you were gonna show me Hell," Percival said eventually, essentially, full of existential ennui.

The Professor leaned past him to a squat metal box with two large antennae out the top. The front of it was covered in all manner of dials and switches and blinking lights. He fiddled with the controls until a crackle of electricity arced from one antenna to the other. He continued to make micro-adjustments until the electrical arc coursed and surged in the rhythm of a sine wave.

"That's, um, pretty," said Percival, "but I don't know is I'd call it Hell. If, I mean."

"Wait for it," said Grieg, and he slowly raised the volume until the inaudible, background hum became a high-pitched, discordant chorus of humanoid voices. All crying out at once. Such long, agonizing screams.

Percival began to weep. "What're they saying?" he asked.

"They're dying. All of them. We named their universe Abraxas-2020a, and it's dying."

"And they're crying out in-in torment? A lamentation?"

Grieg shook his head. "We've had linguists working on this sound for the better part of a decade. They're not mourning. They're singing her to sleep."

Percival wiped away tears, lifted his glass to Abraxas-2020a. "May there be someone left to sing a song for us one day."

Grieg clinked his glass to Percival's. "Speak for yourself, Percival Gynt. I intend to outlive the universe."

"I think you might."

Professor Grieg placed one brown and wizened hand on Percival's cheek, leaned in, and kissed him gently on the lips. Unexpected. The Professor's lips were cracked and dry, but he had a certain technique that he'd cultivated over the past three hundred years, plus or minus, that many found quite pleasant. Also, a light surge of electricity passed between the two of them as the Professor ever so briefly died mid-embrace. Percival took a moment to seriously consider this turn of events before deciding that he was either too drunk or not quite drunk enough to reciprocate. He pulled away, patted the Professor on the shoulder.

"You're an interesting man, Graiden Grieg, Professor of Holes."

Grieg stood and shrugged and checked the time.

"And you're a much more interesting partner than Raoul."

"Well." Percival shrugged. "I've never been hit by a bus."

Grieg smiled and showed Percival out. "Give it time, my friend. You're young."

PERCIVAL GYNT
AND THE CHRISTMAS MACHINE

"Typical," Percival Gynt muttered as the red block letters scrolled across the matte-black face of his Christmas Machine. He swiped ahead to the next screen to see how much he was out.

He'd gotten zero from his mother, per usual. And he always gave her 500 credits. Zero from Midge at work, and she was usually good for at least a tenner. In fact, zero from everyone at work, from Ms. Henderson right down to Compubot, and he and Compubot had always had an explicit give-a-hundred-get-a-hundred pact. Zero too from Father Foom. From Professor Grieg. Zero from the last of his academy friends. Zero. Zero. Zero. Last year he'd only been down a few credits. But this year, he'd gotten absolutely nothing back. He was wiped out.

No. It had to be a glitch.

Percival tried turning the Christmas Machine off and on again. The values did not change. He considered smacking the side of the Christmas Machine with his open hand as he'd seen on the occasional Original Earth program, but he didn't see how that could possibly help. Finally, he reached for his broadsheet edition of *The Daily Internet* and swiped down to refresh.

The banner headline read:

THE GLITCH WHO STOLE CHRISTMAS!
BILLIONS RAGE AGAINST THE MACHINE AS CREDITS GO POOF

Well, thought Percival. I imagine I might be called into work today.

A few seconds later, his watch chimed to signal an incoming notification. And then another. And then another. And then another and another and another, until the sound was simply one long unbroken tone.

Right then, thought Percival. Happy Christmas to me. Time to put on pants.

In the year 19989, it was proven, scientifically and unequivocally, that the best possible gift is cash.

Up until that point, many had speculated that the best possible gift was actually "three more wishes." But, as it turns out, there is nothing three wishes can grant you that's as satisfying as having the equivalent cash value of those wishes in hand. Unless you just wished for cash-in-hand, in which case it's an obvious wash.

Science also tells us that when *exchanging* gifts, the best possible gift that one can receive is "slightly more cash than I just gave you."

Now, the corporate universe is normally very good about taking these kinds of discoveries and immediately productizing them. Here, though, they were at a loss. The very revelation that people preferred cash to products upended their entire worldsview. Several multi-system conglomerates put themselves out of business trying to market buy-in cash alternatives, like Cash-U-Buy, SmartCash, Cash+1, and BitCoin.

Ultimately, it was freelance developer and stay-at-home aunt Mallory Grumb-Q'gorath of Sanctuary-8 who figured it out. The product isn't cash. The product is envy. The product is greed. The product is pettiness.

The product is the Christmas Machine.

The trains weren't running and the network was jammed up, so Percival had to hail a rocket ship. From the street. Like a poor person. And, of course, the rocket ship captain wasn't accepting credits until the current crisis was resolved, so Percival had to barter with him. Percival offered a year of free tax advice, but the captain countered with "your nice shoes." Reluctantly, Percival accepted his bargain.

Percival arrived at the offices of Henderson, Glorp & 11010 at 9:23 am on Christmas morning. He was the last to arrive and the only one sans shoes, excepting Compubot, of course, and Mister 11010, whose base was equipped with an electrostatic hover field in lieu of feet. Every landline in the office was ringing, but the staff were huddled in Conference 1 talking strategy. On his way back, Percival answered his own landline reflexively.

"Henderson, Glorp & 11010. We make your dreams reality with math. This is Percival Gynt. How may I help you?"

"WHERE IS MY MONEY?" bellowed the voice at the other end of the call. "DIE! DIE!"

Percival frowned. "Please hold," he said, "while I transfer you to someone who can help." And then he hung up the phone.

"PERCIVAL GYNT!" shouted/gurgled Mister Glorp from the conference room. "You got us into BIGLY mess. Now is time clean up!"

The first Christmas Machines were sold in the year 19994. Just a few hundred models were purchased that first year, only on Sanctuary-8, and most from a single Wal-Mart at Planet's Core. But by the year following, every single human, alien, robot, and necroblob on the planet owned one. By the year 20000, half the galaxy was using the Christmas Machine.

Here's how it works:

On Christmas morning, your Christmas Machine boots up. It presents you with a list of all of your social media contacts. Friends, family, current and potential romantic partners, co-workers, favorite celebrities, influencers, and miscellaneous acquaintances. And it allows you to assign a cash gift for each of them. You might give your wife 500 credits. Perhaps you don't give your co-workers anything. Once you've assigned, or opted not to assign, cash gifts for each of your contacts, you swipe left and wait.

Once every participant has locked in their assignment, the central network reconciles these gifts and transfers the appropriate amount of cash to each participant's account. For instance, if you gave your sister 150 credits but she gave you 200, the network would take 50 credits from her account and move it into yours.

If you come out ahead in the final accounting, if you receive more in gifts than you gave out, you get the green message. "Congratulations! You won Christmas!" But if you gave more than you got back, you get the red. "I'm sorry!" your Christmas Machine tells you. "You lost Christmas."

The product is pettiness.

Conference 1 was that morning more than usually overpacked with accountants, with senior managers and junior assistants and all manner of math nerds between. Poor Percival Gynt was forced to shoulder his way through to reach the front of the room, enduring glares and quiet insults and the occasional elbow in riposte as he did.

Halfway, his eyes met his friend Midge Jha's. She'd managed a seat at the conference table. The blessings of punctuality. She shook her head at Percival and laughed to herself, which Percival took to mean, "Everything's going to be fine, Percival. You are an all-around, excellent accountant, it's super cool to arrive late, and shoes are really for losers anyway."

That is not what Midge meant.

Mister 11010 and Mister Glorp flanked the teleconference screen at the front of the room. The snarling face of senior partner Agatha Henderson was projected in extreme, starkly-lit close-up between them. Ms. Henderson lived three galaxies away and rarely made an appearance at the office, even virtually. Under other circumstances, the staff might have felt honored by her appearance. But no one at Henderson, Glorp, and 11010 felt any sense of honor that day.

"Mister Gynt," said Ms. Henderson. She spoke quietly, but her voice blasted through the room's THX-360 speakers. A choice. "How kind of you and most of your clothes to join us."

There was scattered, nervous laughter. Percival smirked. Even under the worst of circumstances, he could appreciate a good jape.

"By your tone," he answered, "am I to take it that this is somehow my fault?"

Mister 11010 gestured with his plunger of an arm towards a person that Percival did not recognize, an impeccably dressed individual with delicate features that were just a shade lighter than Percival's, close-cropped purple hair, and a look of such exquisite disinterest that it could only belong to a civil servant. They sat across from Percival and just to Mister Glorp's left, and they held their stylus poised over a pad of yellow A4 legal paper like the soon-to-be-proverbial Stylus of Damocles™.

"Do you have a client named Velma Skoon?" they asked.

"Oh," said Percival. Then, "Yes. This is definitely all my fault."

Percival's co-workers grumbled and groaned.

"And did you devise a method with Ms. Skoon of expeditiously transferring large sums of money off-world, in such a manner that they could not later be tracked by local authorities?"

"I, um…" Percival paused to properly evaluate the situation (*bad*, he thought) and his place in it (towards the center). "Might have done? Might not. I believe I'm bound by the rules of evidentiary privilege to stay silent on that point."

"IT WAS ALL OF OUR MONEY TOO, YOU SANCTIMONIOUS NITWIT!" shouted one of his co-workers, Paul, who Percival had never particularly liked, but who was typically less shouty.

Of course, it was the sanctimonious nitwit's money as well. And his mother's! And Percival was no more thrilled to be caught out than the rest of them. Except, that is, for that small part of him that actually *was* quite thrilled. That such calamity could be down to his deft accountmanship? How all of this might burnish his reputation!

No, no. This was awful, he thought. Be sadder, he thought. Think of the orphans, he thought. He frowned. No, too sad. Fewer orphans.

Percival realized then that all of them were staring at him, waiting. That they expected him to speak. "Do you have her in custody?" he asked the civil servant.

"Yes," they answered.

"And you have some proof of her crimes?"

"Yes. She's confessed to everything."

"Oh! Well done!" said Percival, now bursting with a sense of relief. "You know I was quite concerned for a moment there. Case closed! Don't see that you need me then. I'll just pop home. Take the rest of the week off, perhaps? Feet were getting cold anyway."

"She won't give the money back," the civil servant explained. "And because of your… clever scheme, we have no idea where it all went."

"Oh," said Percival. Then again, "Oh. I see."

"WHERE IS OUR MONEY?" Ms. Henderson demanded through every speaker in the room.

"The rules of evi—"

"You may find," the civil servant interceded, "that the rules of evidentiary privilege are quite beside the point if everyone this side of the Cinnamon Galaxy has been robbed blind and holds you personally responsible. Indeed, you might find it difficult to ever work again, seeing that no one will want you for their accountant, seeing that you are the reason they have no money to account for."

"The rules of—"

"THEY-HAVE-OFF-ERED-YOU-IM-MUN-I-TY!" Mr. 11010 trilled mechanically.

"The rules of—"

The as-yet-unnamed civil servant threw their stylus down in frustration. "Clear the room," they said with a quiet, practiced, but unmistakable fury.

Mister Glorp and Mister 11010 looked to Ms. Henderson's stark projection. She nodded. That was enough for the rank and file to file rancorously out of the room. "But don't leave building!" Mister Glorp called after them. "Is still BIGLY tax emergency day for us all!"

On her way out, Midge grinned at Percival and called after him, "Don't get fired, maybe!"

"50/50," answered Percival.

When it was just Glorp and 11010 and the projection of Agatha Henderson and Percival and the civil servant left in the room, Percival unbuttoned his suit jacket and took a seat.

"Mister Gynt," the civil servant resumed, "I want you to understand that I have no patience for principles. You know where the money went, and you will tell us."

"Or else?" asked Percival.

"Or else?" repeated the civil servant, not properly understanding the question.

"What enforcement mechanism do you have, um… I'm sorry, I don't know your name."

"Fawn," they said. "Q Fawn."

"Mx. Fawn—"

"Agent Fawn…"

"Agent Fawn, I'm complying with the law as written. You may find accountant-client privilege inconvenient at this particular moment. Honestly, so do I. But you're not just asking me to betray my client's trust. You're asking me to break the law. And there can be no legal authority that compels a man to violate the very law which grants said authority."

"No legal authority," Agent Fawn agreed. "Yes, yes. But let me offer you this: There is a woman in my department who has taken great interest in your activities *outside* this office. They've become a source of fascination and occasional amusement to us, these stories she tells us. Catching killers. Fighting monsters. But we could easily bring those stories to a close."

"You're not threatening to—"

"Consider this: These people you help, would they still turn to you if they knew you'd robbed them of their life's savings? We have the capacity to make you a pariah on a galactic scale."

Percival had no witty rejoinder to this point.

"By contrast, if you were to help us, we might find the reason to push certain… opportunities your way."

Nor this.

"Mister Gynt?"

"I need to…" He wasn't sure what he needed to do. Stall, apparently. "I need to *caffeinate.*"

The galaxies-wide adoption of the Christmas Machines forever changed the holiday in large and small ways:

Santa Claus, for instance, was no longer strictly necessary. He continued on as a Coca-Cola pitchman, but his days of making toys on planets' magnetic north poles and sneaking them down children's chimneys were done.

Rudolph and the other reindeer fared… less well. Propriety propends me to obscure their fate, but suffice it to say that they were delicious.

Black Friday, meanwhile, became a day when retailers were just a little sadder than usual.

Many holiday songs needed to be rewritten. One beloved classic became *All I Want for Christmas is ~~You~~ However Much You Would be Worth on a Planet that Permitted Slavery, Not That Slavery is OK! Absolutely It is NOT! BLECH! And, Hey, What Planet is That Anyway? Because Let's Put an End to That Pronto! (But Also, SERIOUSLY, That's How Much Money I Want from You).*

The new version was, you may be surprised to hear, less popular.

Percival selected a K-Pod from the break room spinner rack, "Dutch Midnight," and he popped it into his mouth. It was very midnighty. Not so Dutch.

"You're really in it this time, Gynt," said Midge, by way of an entrance.

"Thank you, Midge," said Percival. He offered her the carton of half-and-half-and-half, and she took a swig. You could really taste the extra half.

"Did it ever occur to you to say no?" Midge asked, as she placed the carton back in the refrigerator.

"I thought that's what I did."

"To the client, Gynt. No one forced you to help her."

"I like…" Percival always chose his words carefully. Here, more so. "…interesting problems."

"I know you do. That's why you're *in it*."

"Sorry?"

Midge explained, "If you don't tell them where the money is, no one will ever want to work with you again. True. But if you do tell them, all of those *interesting* clients will know they can't trust you with their *interesting* problems anymore, and then where would you be?"

Percival smirked. "I've always said that you're smarter than I am, Midge."

"Can you tell *me* where the money is?"

Percival eyed the black dome of the security camera mounted in the corner over the water cooler, and he shook his head. "I think they're probably listening in."

Midge flashed a devilish grin. "How about I make you my accountant, and then they'd have to switch the cameras off."

"So much smarter than I am."

There were objectors. Those who felt that the Christmas Machine betrayed the true spirit of Christmas. Christmas, they said, wasn't about winning or losing. It was about guessing what your friends and family wanted most in the world, and then disappointing them with something you'd probably rather keep for yourself.

One group that was surprisingly all right with the Christmas Machine was Evangelical Christianity. According to them, no one had properly appreciated the true meaning of Christmas in centuries. In that way, the Christmas Machine was no worse than Secret Santa or Elf-on-a-Shelf or Naughty-or-Nice Purge Night.

And at least, the Evangelicals felt, it wasn't a *Holiday* Machine.

Interrogation Room 3 at Central Precinct was cramped and dirty and smelled like urine and civil rights violations. The chairs were uncomfortable. The table wobbled. The lights were programmed to flicker like they were about to burn out. A single fly buzzed about the room at all times.

Velma Skoon was half-asleep and handcuffed to the wobbly table. She had been shaved bald and dressed in prison orange and, from the look of her, been beaten by somewhere between five and all of the officers on duty. "I'm sure I didn't request an accountant," she said.

Percival stood in the doorway, smiling. "I haven't told them where the money is."

Velma Skoon nodded sleepily. "Because of evidentiary privilege."

"But they're threatening to destroy my life anyway, you'll be pleased to know." Percival walked across to the table and took a seat. The hallway door slid shut behind him. "What is the world coming to?"

"Why did they take your shoes?"

"They didn't," Percival said sharply, firmly. "Long story."

"Why are you here?" asked Velma Skoon.

"I offered to talk to you," Percival explained, "as a show of good faith, to see if I could convince you to tell them where the money is."

"And why would I do that?"

"I have no earthly idea." Percival searched his pockets, eventually pulling out a stylus and his folded-over copy of the *The Daily Internet.* "But I thought it would make *me* look better." He unfolded *The Internet* and scrolled to the puzzles. "Do you mind if I do the Sudoku?"

Velma Skoon leaned across the table, and she cocked an eyebrow. "You don't think they'll notice that you're doing the Sudoku," she whispered, "when you're meant to be convincing me to give up the money?"

Percival pointed his stylus at the black-domed security camera mounted to the ceiling. "Cameras are off," he said.

"Because of evidentiary privilege."

Percival nodded and turned his attention to the Sudoku. "They gave me one hour," he explained as he began to fill in the ones, "but I think this Sudoku should only take me fifteen minutes."

Velma Skoon chuckled at his chutzpah. "You're really just going to sit there and do the Sudoku?"

Percival glanced up from his paper. "Yes. Sorry, are you bored?"

"Somewhat."

He set down his stylus. "Well, okay. Hm. I *was* curious how you knew I wouldn't give you away?"

"Good question," said Velma, happy for the distraction. "It was no accident. I picked you specifically. Had a wizard make me something. A stone that senses…"

Percival could tell that Velma Skoon was struggling for the exact words, so he proffered a guess. "Adherence to evidentiary privilege?"

Velma smiled through broken teeth. "Spot on."

"They make stones for that?"

"They'll make stones for anything, apparently. If the price is right."

"How much does a Stone of Adherence to Evidentiary Privilege cost?"

"Not much. The demand is… not high."

"Hmph." Percival knew he shouldn't be offended, but he was offended. He returned to his Sudoku. He was working on the threes now.

"Any other questions?"

"No." Percival didn't look up. He was at a tricky point in the Sudoku where he either needed to project several steps ahead, start making detailed notes, or guess. All terrible options. He sensed Velma Skoon was glaring at him. He glanced up, just for a moment. Yes, she was definitely glaring. He looked back at the puzzle. Tried to ignore her. But he could still feel her eyes on him, all glary. He set down his stylus again. "All right. Okay. More questions, more questions. *Why*, I suppose? Did you have an interesting motivation for stealing all the money?"

"Greed."

"Oh. Right." Made sense. He shrugged and returned to his puzzle.

"Anything else?" Velma Skoon asked, expectant, desperate for any kind of human reaction that didn't involve kicking.

Percival sighed and set down his stylus for a third time. "This is not… It's not that easy, Velma. Please don't be offended, but I'm just not that interested in you as a person. But I'll, um…" Percival paused, as if a thought was just then occurring to him. As if he was quite pleased with himself. "Ah! I've got one: Did you have a plan for getting to the money, now that you're caught?"

"I figure I'll just bribe someone to help me escape. Everyone's poor now, so it shouldn't take much."

"Right," said Percival. "Right. Sorry these aren't more interesting questions."

"I appreciate the effort. How is the Sudoku coming?"

Percival glanced down at his puzzle. "I'm struggling with the 5s."

"Okay. I don't really know how Sudokus work."

He turned *The Internet* around to show her. "Do you want me to explain?"

"Definitely no. Hard pass. Any more questions?"

Percival scratched his chin so as to suggest deep thought. "Well. Um. Um. Right! I *do* have one genuine question, as I think about it! And if it's not too personal. The account on Trynadeane, the one where all the money is. You were very specific when we set up the password. I assumed maybe it had some sentimental value?"

"How old are you?" asked Velma Skoon. "Twenty-five? Do you remember what Christmas was like before the Christmas Machines?"

"I… No. My childhood was not…" Percival shook his head. "My mother got me a hat once. I don't think it was Christmas, though."

"There was this one Christmas," said Velma Skoon. She was looking past Percival now, smiling wistfully. "Back before the Machines. My son, he kept asking me for a toy fire truck. Day after day. There wasn't really a question of what I was going to get him. There was one in particular, it transformed into a robot dog and did backflips. It cost me a year-and-a-half's salary and an eye. Not mine. Anyway. My ex-husband, he got him a rock from one of their weekend camping trips. Billy loved that rock. And do you know what my midden-fire of an ex-husband says to me?"

"Capital-N-3-X-T-underscore-capital-Y-3-A-R."

"The next year we were on to Christmas Machines. Turns out there was no next year."

"Where are they now?"

"My ex? No clue. Don't care."

"And your son?"

Velma smiled as she answered. "Trynadeane."

Percival filled in the last three missing numbers from his puzzle. "Well, that's all my fives," he told her, and he folded *The Internet* back up and tucked it into his pocket.

"Hour's not up yet."

Percival shrugged. "Do you want to tell me more about your son?"

"I do."

Percival Gynt stepped out of Interrogation Room 3 at Central Precinct at precisely 3:14 pm that Christmas afternoon, precisely one hour after he entered. And he said to Agent Fawn, "I trust you got all that?"

They nodded. "The account was in her son's name. I suppose we would have found it eventually, but the password helped."

"Funny how an emergency session of the Planetary Congress overturns the laws governing evidentiary privilege at the precise moment I step into that interrogation room with Skoon."

They nodded a second time. "It turns out that politicians like their money too."

"And I trust they'll be reinstituting those laws shortly?"

"In three months, I'm told. When Congress is officially back in session. Politicians also like their vacations."

"Of course, they do."

"You've made a lot of friends today," said Agent Fawn, and they flashed a smile nearly as exquisite as their earlier disinterest.

"Is that an offer?" asked Percival.

"Friends, Gynt. Perhaps we can kick some work your way."

"Accounting work?"

"And other… problems. I have some ideas already."

"And were you able to get my money back?"

"Specific assignments were all lost in the hack," Agent Fawn explained, "so there was no way to complete the transfers. Everyone's accounts are back to where they started this morning."

"I'm very good at math," said Percival, "and that sounds like I broke even for once."

"More than broke even, I'd say." Agent Fawn offered their hand to Percival, and he took it. "Congratulations, Mister Gynt. You just won Christmas."

IN THE YEAR
20014

AND THE QUIET BARGAIN

"After Gynt Colony came boarding school, which was its own kind of disaster. I had friends for the first time, with nicknames like Mugwamma and Smalls and Footface and Gree. We would have died for each other.

"In a way, one of us did.

"Footface was the smallest of us, smaller even than me, weaker and sick. She was from a planet of warriors. Her father was rich, influential, and deeply ashamed of her. He sent her away to hide his disgrace. And every time she came home, she was subjected to the most severe beatings and abuse.

"One winter, when we knew her father was coming for her, the rest of us hatched a plan. We ambushed him on his way from the hangar bay, dragged him to a disused section of campus, beat him half-to-death with croquet mallets, and threatened to finish the job if he ever laid a finger on Footface again.

"In the moment, I actually said 'Footface.' We so rarely used each other's real names, I blanked.

"Her father never touched her again. I know this because he left without her, and four months later she was dead from leukemia.

"So in a way it worked.

"There's a little bit more to that story, but I should probably pause to clarify: This is NOT one of my famously funny-haha stories."

Percival Gynt was in that moment sitting in the dark, in a broom closet, next to a young woman named Kyma or maybe Kayma. He wasn't sure if he'd heard her name correctly. They were hiding from soldiers, or perhaps police officers. Men and women with guns and both the authority and the inclination to use them. Percival Gynt had only been on this planet for thirty minutes, and already he'd decided he didn't like it.

"Do you have a lot of those?" asked Kyma or Kayma.

"Sorry?"

"Funny-haha stories? I could maybe use one of those right now."

Percival smiled in the darkness. "I once saved Christmas," he told her.

"Who's that?" asked Kyma. No, probably Kayma.

"Nevermind," said Percival, and he stood. "Stay here. I'll lead them off."

"How are you going to do that?" asked Kayma. Keema? No, that didn't sound right either.

"Brilliantly," said Percival. A favorite joke.

He opened the closet door and stepped out into the light. And he raised his hands up as high above his head as they would go. "I am a brown-skinned man, but I am unarmed, it's the 201st century, and anyway you're all faintly purple!" he shouted. "So please don't shoot me!"

Down the corridor, from behind the barricades, the officers opened fire.

Thankfully, medical treatment on this planet was exemplary, particularly for individuals that the government hoped to execute publicly. Percival awoke in a hospital bed, cuffed to the side rails.

"Chima," he muttered to himself. "Or... Charma?"

The Doctor, a blue-skinned alien with spikes for eyes, checked Percival's blood pressure. "You're lucky to be alive," she told Percival.

"That's what I always say!" said Percival. "But you're probably talking about now specifically."

"The Most High has taken an interest in you," said the Doctor. "You're to have a Royal Audience within the hour."

"Oh good," said Percival, who was still in a great deal of pain. "Will I be able to stand by then?"

"Yes, yes," said the Doctor. "The Most High doesn't believe in killing anyone who's at less than perfect health."

"Ah. Well then, as an unrelated request, perhaps you'd be good enough to cough all over me and also stab me once or twice in the thigh?"

The Doctor's eye spikes quivered, which Percival speculated might have been her kind's equivalent to an eyeroll. "You're an off-worlder like me," she said. "You shouldn't have come here."

"Well, that's my lot, I'm afraid," said Percival with a shrug. "Someone asks for my help, I come."

"Who asked?"

Percival tried to remember. He closed his eyes, but he only saw darkness. "A friend," he said finally and without much conviction.

"And what help did you think you could be on this godsforsaken world?"

"Don't know, but I thought perhaps I'd take down the government while I'm here."

The Doctor chuckled. "Thank you," she said. "There are so few opportunities to laugh on this planet."

"Not a joke. I spent an afternoon reading your law books. You people are barbaric. You still practice trial by combat."

"Oh, the Contests are for more than just trials," said the Doctor, as she swabbed the inside of Percival's cheek. "The Contests are everything. They use them to resolve civil disputes and private disagreements, to decide which team receives in sportsball. They're how every position of authority on this mudball is claimed, all the way up to, and including, the Most High himself."

"Hah mah bah—" The Doctor removed the swab. Percival started again. "He must be quite the fighter."

"Indeed," replied the Doctor. "And every Contest fought to the death. Or worse."

"Worse? What's worse than death?" asked Percival, thinking aloud. "I mean, I've seen some things, but… on your world, specifically."

"The shame of eternal banishment."

"*Shame* is worse than death?"

The Doctor shrugged.

"Your people really don't like to lose."

"Not my people," said the Doctor. "I'm a Kaldorian. And a pacifist."

Both Percival and the Doctor laughed at that and for some time.

In the hospital, Percival wore an unflattering lime green gown that flapped open at the back. When it was time for his release to the planetary authorities, the Doctor brought him a shirt and pants of coarse gray wool called Stizzafax™, with a matching pair of slippers.

And she gave Percival twelve blue pills and six grays. It was the least and most she could do.

Percival dressed behind a screen. "You know, back home I'm quite the clothes horse."

The Doctor nodded to herself. She didn't know the phrase and wondered whether the man she'd just treated was secretly a horse.

Before he left, Percival asked the Doctor about the woman he'd shared the broom closet with. "I think her name was Sharma?" It was not.

"I wish I could tell you. If they took her," said the Doctor, "they must not have needed her alive."

Percival's Royal Audience was broadcast live to every streaming-enabled device on the planet and across the galaxy on MTV3 as part of a new show called *Snuff'd*. At the appointed hour, he was brought into a throne room by two of the same officers who'd shot him earlier. They snickered and shoved and prodded Percival past crowds of onlookers and their recording devices to stand before the throne of the Most High.

"Footface's father," said Percival, for he knew the man by no other name.

"And you are Percival Gynt," answered the Most High. He was, as years ago, a broad-shouldered man, square-jawed, faintly purple, now hunched forward, squinting down from his throne and scowling, wild-haired and bearded and dressed in robes of black and gold.

"It's a wonder I recognized you," said Percival, "without all that blood spilling out the back of your head."

"Why. Are. You. Here. Gynt?" the Most High asked, with a voice as sharp and steely as a Doctor's eyes.

Percival glanced back at his armed escorts. "Your people were *quite* insistent."

"WHY ARE YOU ON MY PLANET!"

"Ah," said Percival, "well, you see I wanted to go to the library, but all the ones on Sanctuary-8 are closed on Mondays, because, um… Well, I think that's just one of life's great mysteries."

"Our public archives are always closed to the public. I assume you know that, given that you cut a hole through a skylight to gain entry."

"Oh, I see! Yes! I'd thought that perhaps all of the library's doors and signs and most of the lights had all broken simultaneously, so the staff had gone home, but your thing makes more sense. That's my fault. I can, of course, pay for the pane of glass."

"The punishment for trespassing is death."

"I can pay for… two panes of glass?"

"Death, I said!"

Percival smirked. "You are a wily negotiator."

"DEATH!!!" called the Most High once more, now rising from his throne.

"There was a woman with me," said Percival. He spoke more quickly now and took a hesitant step backwards as the Most High advanced. "When I was arrested. Her name was… um… well, it's not important. Do you know what happened to her?"

True to his title, the Most High towered over Percival Gynt. "The criminal will kneel and accept punishment."

"The accused, surely," said Percival, in a faltering tone. "There hasn't even been a trial."

"You are an off-worlder. There will be no trial." The Most High raised his hands and tightened them into fists.

"The Contest!" shouted Percival, even as he shrank backwards, raised his arms defensively. "I've read your laws. There is no rule prohibiting an off-worlder from invoking the Contest!"

The Most High stopped. Thought. Smiled. Laughed. And his laughter carried through the crowd. "You want to fight me? Alone?"

Percival nodded slowly. "Yes," he whispered. "I invoke the Cont—"

Without an instant of hesitation, the Most High swung his fist into Percival's face, connected, and sent him flying backwards, bloody and slumping to the floor. The Most High squatted down over him and poked him in one limp shoulder. "Are you dead yet, Percival Gynt?"

"Yes," answered Percival, wheezing between coughs and spitting blood. "Yes, this is probably what death feels like."

"I can't hear you, Gynt. Perhaps I should break off your jaw and hold it to my ear?"

"I want them to see," said Percival. "Want them to see what death looks like."

The Most High snickered. "You think they will be repulsed, Percival Gynt? That they will look at your broken sack of flesh and feel regret? They want this, Gynt. THEY DEMAND THIS!"

The audience cheered. Percival forced a half-smile. He had him talking now. He'd already won. "You're a caveman, Most High. A zoo animal. MTV has put you on display for the galaxy to watch as spectacle. Help me up, and you can mock me before I die."

The Most High rose, stepped back, nodded to the two officers. They hoisted Percival up, each by an arm, so he could stare their lord and master in the eye. "What do you want to say to me, Gynt? I've thought about killing you for nearly a decade. I can wait a few minutes longer."

"I concede," said Percival, "that you're a better fighter than me. Stronger, faster, better trained. *Trained.* There's no way I could beat you in a fight. But being a better fighter doesn't make you a better king. A wiser king. A kinder king. You're a curse on this planet. A cancer that scars the galaxy. A stunted man child whose rule poisons everything you touch. And all because you're better at punching.

"You and your ancient rites are an embarrassment. A disgrace. You are a nothing, you beget nothing, and the universe is done with you."

The crowd was quiet now. Fascinated. Who was this man who spoke to their Most High in such tones? And was not immediately struck dead for the saying?

"Don't be sanctimonious, Gynt. There is a quiet bargain that all men enter into. When you accept the armed forces that patrol your streets, that guard your borders, that defend your interests across an ocean or a gulf of stars, you've accepted that the greater force will prevail. Not the wiser force. Not the kinder force. On this world, we are simply more honest with each other. He who can take, takes. He who cannot, serves or dies. *That* is the bargain. And you agreed to it."

"Did I?"

"The day you and your friends decided to solve a problem not with words, not with reason, but with the blunt end of a mallet. That was the bargain you offered to me. Concede to the superior show of force or die. That was my moment of epiphany, Gynt. You should have read our history when you broke into the archives. The Contests are no 'ancient rite.' I invented them." The Most High grinned. "It was you and your friends who gave me the idea."

"We..." Percival felt as if the room was turning sideways and upside down beneath him, and not entirely because the drugs were finally kicking in.

"Your enemy will never be convinced that he is wrong, that you are right. Your enemy can only ever be cowed or beaten into submission or killed. That is the bargain. Those are the terms! And every battle you win establishes the terms for the next and the next and the next."

"I reject that bargain!" cried Percival Gynt. "I reject those terms!"

"Too late!" snarled the Most High.

"I REJECT!"

"Everything that happens now. Everything that continues. Everything that ends. It's all your fault. I want you to know that. Before you die."

The Most High swung his fist faster than Percival's eyes could register. He heard the crack. A sting of pain. A flash of red. Then black.

In her final days, Footface endured multiple rounds of OPB Therapy, which is short for Omnidirectional Photon Bombardment Therapy, which was one of the few treatments available in the early 201st century to combat stage 23 cancer.

OPB Therapy is exactly what it sounds like. The Doctors shoot the patient with lasers. Many, many lasers. It's also exactly as painful as you'd imagine, and it leaves the patients with an extreme, incurable light sensitivity.

It wasn't enough. Footface died in the dark.

Before that, Percival would come to visit her in the hospital's blackout wing. They would sit together. He would hold her hand. She would tell him that it would be okay.

"And promise me," she said once, near the end, "that you won't let him hurt anyone else."

Percival nodded. She squeezed his hand.

"I'll do whatever I can," he said.

"Promise me," she repeated.

"I promise, Karma."

"Good," she said. And she kissed him on the cheek. "Now tell me one of those famous funny-haha stories of yours. I could maybe use one of those right now."

Percival Gynt was well-practiced in the art of forgetting. For a long time after her death, he forgot Karma, he had to, and so he forgot his promise to her. But then one night, years later, he got into an argument with his smart television, and the only channel it would let him watch was MTV3, which was on that evening midway through a 13-hour marathon of their newest series, *Snuff'd*.

It was there and then that Percival Gynt first saw the so-called Most High simulcasted from the far side of the galaxy in glorious maximum-definition, beating his citizens to death with his faintly purple fists.

And Percival Gynt remembered.

"I won't let you hurt anyone else," Percival whispered as he pulled himself up off the floor of the Most High's throne room. It had taken some time, but he was finally feeling all those uppers and pain pills the Doctor had gifted him.

Which is to say, he felt nothing.

"He's still alive!" cried the Most High, genuinely amazed. Some in the crowd cheered, not because Percival had more fight left in him, but because that meant there was more fight to go.

"I surrender," said Percival. "I forfeit."

That shut the crowd up for a half-second. Then came the boos. The Most High's mouth settled into a self-satisfied smirk. "A wise choice," he told Percival. "I will be quick."

Percival raised a hand to stay the Most High. His pinky finger dangled disconcertingly. He pretended confidence. "I do not choose death," he proclaimed to the crowd and to the billions watching across the planet and out into the stars. "Instead, I choose the eternal shame of banishment!"

A second silence. This had never happened before. Was this even possible? How could someone *choose* shame?

"You are an off-worlder, Gynt," the Most High growled. "You can't choose banishment."

"Can't I?" asked Percival. "Because I've read *The Most Officious Laws of Contestation*, and Clause 17, Sub-Clause B, Paragraph 3 clearly states—"

"I don't care what the law states! The only laws that matter on this planet are my right fist and my left."

Percival looked to the crowd. Looked to their cameras. Looked *through* them. And he spoke to the billions beyond. "Is this the world you want, citizens? No law, but a madman's fists? Ask yourselves, 'Is this justice?' You don't have to accept the Most High's *quiet bargain*. You can walk away from violence. You can choose another path. Leave this world and join me in a galaxy that isn't ruled by the strongest or the meanest but by those elected democratically for their insight, their experience, their wisdom and compassion. Come with me now. Surrender and walk away."

"What nonsense is this?" said the Most High. "These people are not criminals. They are not part of our Contest."

"Anyone may invoke the Contest!" Percival told the crowd. "Simply say the words."

They were stunned, silent, paralyzed with possibility and dread.

"You want an entire planet's population to just LEAVE?" asked the Most High. "Even if they were all cowards, how—"

The crowd was startled from its reverie by a chorus of rings and beeps, 8-bit pop tunes and bass vibrations. One by one, they began to answer their devices.

"WHAT IS HAPPENING?" the Most High demanded.

"The 17th Fleet of the Most Benevolent Armada of the Mugwam just decloaked in your orbit under the command of Queen-Consort Greezelotta, and they've robodialed every device on this planet to tell your people that they will happily relocate any or all of them to whatever destination planet they choose."

"HOW—?"

A trembling young woman stepped out of the crowd. She cradled a newborn to her chest. "I… I invoke the Contest," she said, with a voice both terrified and resolute. "For myself and my son, I choose exile!"

And hers was not the only voice. "I invoke the Contest!" someone shouted. "I choose the shame of exile!" cried another. "I invoke!" "Shame!" "Exile!" "Shame!"

"NO!" shouted the Most High. "I choose death for all who oppose me! OFFICERS!"

One of the two officers who'd escorted Percival into the throne room raised her weapon. But the other dropped his to the ground. "I invoke the Contest," the second officer told the first. "I don't want this." And he backed into the crowd.

The citizens were raising their hands above them now, their show of surrender. The remaining officer looked down at her gun. "SHOOT THEM ALL!" ordered the Most High. All this officer had ever wanted was to serve her community. To put away bad men. To protect her family and her neighbors. Maybe she hadn't been perfect. Maybe she'd bent rules. Gotten angry. She wasn't always the kindest g—

The Most High snapped her neck and snatched the gun from her loosening grip. The crowd screamed with one terrified voice. "SHAME!" it shouted. "I SURRENDER!"

The officer's body collapsed to the floor.

The Most High aimed the gun at Percival Gynt. Percival smiled a broken smile.

"And what about you, Most High? Will you stay? Will you remain here, the king of an empty planet?"

The Most High seethed, said nothing.

"When you're the only one left, the Most High is also the lowest."

The Most High seethed, said nothing.

Thirteen hours and half-a-galaxy later, a worlds-weary Percival Gynt was home. Sanctuary-8. Slidetown Province. 1636 Traveler's Way. Apartment 4D.

He walked slowly, eased the apartment door shut behind him, left the lights off, winced when a floorboard creaked underfoot. The Doctor might have healed his physical injuries, but other scars remained.

He was not whole.

From his bedroom, he heard movement. He'd woken his partner Fawn. Theirs was a new relationship, untried and untested. Perhaps Fawn would say untrusted. There was a level of intimacy that Percival had yet denied them. There were words Fawn longed to hear.

"Where have you been?" they asked sleepily as Percival lingered in the doorway.

It was a question that Percival would never answer. Not that night. Not ever.

"I need you," is all he said to them, "to teach me to fight."

PERCIVAL GYNT
AND THE LOCKED PLANET MYSTERY

"I hope you'll reconsider," implored Executive Director Shing. "The rains of Jagrahr-4 are both sentient and malevolent, and they show no sign of stopping."

"We won't," Percival Gynt replied firmly. He and Fawn had been stranded shipside for two weeks now, and they'd had more than their fill of bottomless buffets, of ping-pong tournaments and late-night karaoke, of shuffleboard and increasingly half-hearted conga lines. To say nothing of the mounting tension between the two of them. Percival's introversion, the secrets he would not tell. Fawn finding the charming man they met last Christmas turning silent and irritable and small. And the fights. The physical fights. Percival's idea. Training. Except he wasn't learning fast enough, and he was getting his ass handed to him nightly.

With a satisfied smirk.

"If you insist on going down to the planet," argued the Executive Director, "so will others. It'll start a passenger insurrection, and I simply can't ensure everyone's safety!" He had seemed a pleasant man when Percival and Fawn first met him at the ship's send-off, gregarious even, but the continued bad weather reports, the repeated cancellation of scheduled events, and the growing ill-will between passengers and crew seemed to eat away at him, even as the rains themselves ate away at the flora and fauna of the planet below.

"If you're worried about a mutiny," suggested Percival, "don't tell anyone. We'll head down to the planet in one of your lifepods and be back before anyone notices we're gone."

The Executive Director considered this, and he considered his guests. This Percival Gynt and his companion were clearly troublemakers. Better they made their trouble on the planet than here aboard the ship. "Very well," he relented. "We'll send you down, but we won't pick you up till we're ready to leave, and you'll make your own arrangements with the locals. I cannot vouch for your safety!"

Percival saluted. "Aye aye, Captain."

"He's not the Captain," whispered Fawn.

Percival shrugged. "It was a sarcastic salute. Does it really matter if I got his title right?"

Executive Director Shing, who was still standing right there, rolled his eyes and turned and left to make arrangements for the couple's impossible-to-be-too-soon departure.

It was July. Percival had purchased the tickets for the cruise in February when their relationship was still thrilling and passionate and new. He'd seriously considered breaking up with Fawn several times in April. And May. And then again in July. Except for those tickets. They were expensive. Non-refundable. And, honestly, he was excited to go. He'd never been on an intergalactic cruise before. Never been in a relationship that had lasted more than a month either. It was an endurance test with an exciting reward at the end of it. And perhaps all couples had such bumpy periods.

Jagrahr-4 was said to be a planet of rare and exotic beauty, marred only by the occasional months-long deluge of carnivorous cancer rain. The weather reports leading up to the cruise suggested that the current rainy season would continue well-past the scheduled end of their vacation, but the cruise company themselves had insisted otherwise. The rains would end before the ship reached orbit. Or, anyway, soon after. Or tomorrow. Or, well, eventually. Just be patient, and here's another free drink voucher.

The intelligent humanoid species on the planet, the descendants of Original Earth colonists, all lived in one massive structure, a converted generation ship angled downward into the swamps of Equatorial Zone B42. This structure was called T'Laa, a corruption of its original ship designation: The Lexington Avenue Apartment.

When the rains subsided, the locals and their guests enjoyed a wide variety of outdoor activities, including surfing, scuba diving, parasailing, and giant sea monster watching. Jagrahr-4 was said to have the best giant sea monsters in the Seven Galaxies, most civilized planets having long ago hunted theirs to extinction and/or nuked them from orbit. All of which might have been terrific fun for Percival and Fawn were it not for the murder rain.

No one knows how or when the precipitation on Jagrahr-4 became sentient, but it did, and the rain as much as anyone seemed aggressively angry about that fact. At every opportunity, the Jagrahr rains sought out and consumed humanoids who ventured beyond the walls of T'Laa during rainy season. The rains were known to turn sideways, veer around corners, and even bounce upwards in pursuit of their prey. Humanoids struck by the rains would face debilitating, rapidly-metastasizing tumors before being consumed and expelled as ball lightning.

Or, as the locals described them, "the flashing rain farts."

Percival and Fawn's lifepod tumbled through the upper atmosphere, plummeted through black, cackling clouds and down into the storm below before gravity stabilizers finally engaged. "Under and up," instructed a voice over radio link. It was a statement that meant nothing to either Fawn or Percival until they caught sight of T'Laa through the rain. The back end of the decommissioned ship, angled up towards the storm, was an open cargo bay, shielded from the elements by what one might charitably call a massive, domed canopy, but what any reasonably succinct personality would call a biiiiig black umbrella.

"Under then," said Fawn, as they steered their pod towards the umbrella.

"And then up," said Percival, in a failed effort to contribute anything at all of value to their landing.

As the lifepod flew underneath the umbrella's edge and into the cargo bay, gravity went sideways. Fawn re-oriented the pod to land on the new down of the cargo bay floor. The pair collected their bags and cautiously disembarked.

However ridiculous, the giant umbrella was doing its job. The cargo bay was as dry as, well, as your typical cargo bay. From everything that Percival had been told, there was nothing to stop the rain from following their trajectory in, but it *chose* not to. Curious. Perhaps, thought Percival, a living rain sees an umbrella as its primal enemy, the apex precipitation-related-predator.

Or perhaps they sprayed the canvas with something?

Indeed, he thought he recognized an odd-if-familiar odor in the air.

A man was there to meet them, handsome, young, slim and smiling. Sincere, thought Percival, though he'd been wrong before. Darker-skinned than either Percival or Fawn. Dressed in a red all-weather jumpsuit, expertly-tailored and well-cared-for. He carried a black umbrella under one arm, an umbrella of usual size. "Welcome," said the man. "I'm Emissary Khemie Hoult, and it's my great honor to receive you."

He offered the umbrella to Percival. "This is a gift for you," he said, "made from the same triple-reinforced microweave as our Great Canopy. A memento of your stay here."

Percival regarded the umbrella politely if cursorily and passed it to Fawn. "Thank you," said Fawn, with the inflection of an apology.

"It's quite all right," said the Emissary. "Our own citizens have as little use for the things. We'll hardly be offended if it finds its way into our rubbish bins."

Percival and Fawn both smiled appreciatively at this informality. "May we call you Khemie?" asked Fawn.

"Indeed you may," said Khemie, "and now that we're on first-name terms, guests Percival and Fawn, I hope you won't feel uncomfortable if I help you with your bags. We regret that the current weather will prevent you from partaking in our planet's most popular leisure activities, but we will do our best to entertain. I'm told that the Senior Administrator Himself has set aside a time to meet with you, once you're settled in."

Fawn nodded approvingly to Percival as Khemie carried they're bags to the main doors.

"You see, darling," said Percival. "I got you a senior administrator. And you said the best we'd do was regional oversight commissioner."

Fawn gave a grudging smirk. "I should never have doubted you, Gynt. You're like catnip for technocrats."

During a normal tourist season, T'Laa received tens of thousands of visitors. This year, only two. Not two thousand. Two. Which is why Percival and Fawn were given the largest, most luxurious guest suite on the ship. Three decks high, connected by no less than six spiral staircases and one rock climbing wall. There was a greenhouse. A bowling alley. A waterfall shower. A chair just for reading. And a choice of three kingier-than-king-sized beds with varying levels of artificial gravity.

When Khemie left them to settle in, he promised he'd be back in two hours to escort them to the Senior Administrator.

It was a promise he wouldn't keep.

It took Percival and Fawn thirty-seven minutes to take in the entire suite and to settle on the floatiest bed. Another twelve minutes to unpack. Four minutes for idle chit-chat which dipped briefly into sniping over their sartorial choices. Nineteen minutes to undress and have sex. Then a minute-thirty of awkward panting. Then four more sex minutes. Forty-six minutes to get showered/waterfalled, groomed, and dressed. Fawn finished first, choosing a tartan tux-and-kilt combo with mecha power boots. They flipped through pay per view channels on the three-story Sony ViewWall™, while Percival buttoned the jacket of his three-piece holographic ArtSuit, currently streaming Van Gogh's *Starry Night*.

By the time their suite doorbell finally chimed, Percival and Fawn had been sitting in icy silence for eleven minutes. He, occasionally checking the time on his pocket watch. They, watching reruns of

Snuff'd on the ViewWall. "I'll get it," mumbled Percival, and he climbed down the rock wall and answered the door.

It was not Khemie, but another less memorable member of the staff. "The Senior Administrator will see you now," said whoever-this-was.

The Senior Administrator of T'Laa was said to have been born on Original Earth over 18,000 years ago. If true, he'd achieved the least-best version of immortality. He was alive, yes, but looked and felt precisely as one would imagine an 18,034 year old to look and feel. His frail frame was splayed limply across a zero-gravity bed which drifted through the Receiving Hall quite of its own accord, occasionally right side up, but as frequently upside down or on its side or rotating ever so slowly in one direction or another. His body was draped with black-and-purple silk sheets. Among other purposes, these sheets concealed an undulating mass upon his chest, presumably either a machine that kept his lungs and heart pumping or else a particularly impressive, aggressive tumor. His head was, by this point, mostly skull and sunscreen. His eyes, having long ago failed him, stared off uselessly towards some imagined horizon. His mouth and nose were covered by a sleek black device, trimmed with purple and lit with green lights that flashed as he spoke. Or as *it* spoke. For his voice was crisp and sonorous and most assuredly computer-generated.

"Come closer," said the mask, "so that my sensors might properly scan you and itemize your characteristics."

Percival and Fawn advanced cautiously. "It's an honor to meet you, Senior Administrator," said Fawn. Percival was uncertain.

"And I you, children. You are quite brave to come to our planet at the height of the storms. If I may—SHUT UP, GHOST! Will you haunt me no longer? I said I was sorry about that!" Though the Senior Administrator's words were quite animated now, his physical body hardly moved. It was unsettling. "You'll have to excuse my ghost," the voice continued. "He's quite cross that it's 18,000 years later, and he still hasn't passed over. But it was his idea to haunt me till I die! He deserves every second of it."

"Your ghost, sir?" asked Fawn.

"He's, um, Baxter-Something, I think. He insists I knew him when he was alive, but that was so long ago, and most men's lives are short enough to be a rounding erro—Wait! He's trying to say something again. He's angry that I—that I... locked him out of his apartment? That doesn't sound like something I'd do."

Percival glanced about the room. All but empty. Beige carpets worn in a familiar pattern. A wall of windows looking out sideways onto the storm. A disused ViewWall, taped over with children's drawings of robots and superheroes and monsters. But no ghosts that he could see.

Percival speculated that this had once been a conference room for senior staff, the table and chairs having long ago been cleared away to make room for the Senior Administrator's ever-drifting bed.

"Why wasn't Emissary Khemie able to escort us here?" asked Percival, quite unsure of where they were in the conversation, or if he was interrupting anyone.

"Pardon?" said the Senior Administrator's voice.

"He said he'd be the one to bring us here, but he wasn't," said Percival plainly. "We quite liked him is all."

"As do I," said the voice. "A charming and dutiful young man. It is unlike him to shirk an obligation. My external data banks do not have a record of his whereabouts for the last hour."

Percival smiled. "A mystery."

"No," Fawn whispered curtly. "No mysteries."

"O Greatest and Most Senior of All Administrators," said Percival, forgetting whether that was an appropriate form of address or not, "we'll find Emissary Khemie for you and make certain he's come to no harm."

"No," said the voice. "I would not trouble you. You are our guests, and besides... What? Why?" Percival glanced at Fawn, and they shared a shrug. Perhaps the Senior Administrator was speaking to his ghost again? "No, ghost, I am not an idiot." So, definitely the ghost. "What do you mean, 'And all will come to a proper end?' Don't speak in riddles to me! You barely graduated high school! A man dies and suddenly 18,000 years later, he thinks he's Hamlet's ghost? Nonsense.

Nonsense. What? Yes! Of course, I remember you!"

"We should go," Fawn said to the Senior Administrator, unsure if he would hear them, and they took Percival by the arm to leave.

"Wait," said the voice. The bed had drifted all the way around by now. Percival and Fawn were staring at the gravitonic pulse jets that lined its base. "Perhaps you might speak to Emissary Hoult's wife, Iole."

Fawn glared at Percival. "We'd be happy to help, of course," they said coolly.

"Yes," said Percival, feeling alive and awake and alert for the first time in months. "We'll get to the bottom of this."

"The bottom of this?" cried Fawn, once they were out the door and well down the corridor. "THE BOTTOM? We don't even know that there is a *this* yet, let alone whether the *this* has a bottom."

"Trust me," said Percival. "There's always a bottom." He found Fawn's and gave it a swift pat. Fawn glared disapprovingly, but also this was the most turned on they'd been by Percival in months. But also-also, "the most" only meant somewhat. But also-also-also, "somewhat" was a lightyear better than not.

Percival pressed the doorbell beside Khemie and Iole's door. It played a song by an Original Earth band. The Black-Eyed Pears, thought Percival. It was catchy.

The door slid half-open as a bleary-eyed woman tied a robe closed before them. Iole was tall and tan and had the most marvelously massive fanned mohawk. It nearly scraped the ceiling. "Can I help you?" she asked sleepily.

"We were wondering—" asked Percival, before Fawn cut him off.

"We were wondering if you know when Khemie will be home. We're guests from off-world, *the* guests, and he said he might show us around later."

Iole nodded and turned, pulled her watch off a table near the door, checked the time and placed a call. "It's ringing," she told Fawn. After a moment she hung up and glanced again at the watch.

"He's not answering?" asked Percival.

"I'm sure it's nothing," said Fawn. "Any idea where he might be right now?"

Iole shook her head. "Usually, he answers when I call. Unless he's with a guest, but you're both here."

"Does Khemie smoke cigarettes?" asked Percival.

Iole frowned. "He used to, but he was meant to have quit. Why?"

"It's probably nothing," said Percival. "I am reassuring you now."

Despite this instruction, Iole was not reassured.

"Smoking?" asked Fawn as they kept pace beside Percival.

"There was an odor when we landed," said Percival. "At the time I thought it might have been a chemical to keep out the rain. A rainicide. A precipicide?"

"But now you think it was tobacco smoke."

"He was smoking in the cargo bay before we touched down. I'm sure of it. The perfect place to hide your habit, particularly during the rainy season. No one in or out."

"There's us."

"And we're not going anywhere! So now that we've arrived, he's free-and-clear to smoke as much as he wants."

"So what? You think he's been out there smoking for hours?"

Percival stopped. "No," he said. He looked at Fawn. Frowned.

He'd really liked Khemie.

As a precaution, one needed an ultra-secret four-digit security code to open the double doors that led into the cargo bay. "1-2-3-4?" suggested Fawn.

Percival typed four numbers and the doors slowly grinded open to reveal another barrier, smooth white metal etched in gold with arcane symbols. It took a split second for the couple to recognize it as the underside of their lifepod. Somehow the pod had become wedged against the doors.

"Do you hear it?" asked Fawn.

On the far side of the pod, pelting the cargo bay floor.

Rain.

"Perhaps," said Percival, "it's time we retrieved our umbrella."

"What did you find?" demanded the Senior Administrator's simulated voice, adding a stern "Not now, Baxter-Something!" before anyone in the room had a chance to respond.

Percival and Fawn and the Senior Administrator were joined in the Receiving Hall by a clearly shaken Iole, now dressed in her staff uniform, a blue jumpsuit, and by a woman in green, shorter, stern, extremely bald.

And possibly a ghost.

"I'm afraid it's bad news," explained the woman-in-green. "After our men cleared the lifepod out of the way, we confirmed that a large hole was torn in the Great Canopy. The rain came through and… I'm sorry, Iole, but it ate him."

"And the cargo bay?" asked Percival, with customary concern.

"The hole has been patched," said the woman-in-green. "The rains driven back."

"And how does one do that?"

"We can raise the temperature in the cargo bay to two hundred degrees for short periods of time."

Twice the boiling point of water. "And we're sure the rain ate Khemie?"

"The state of the remains leaves little down as to the cause of death."

"Our guests suggested that Emissary Hoult might have been smoking in the cargo bay when the rains came," said the Senior Administrator's voice. "But what opened the hole? Who moved the lifepod?"

"The canopy was made of triple-reinforced microweave," said Percival. "Difficult to penetrate. Perhaps—"

The Woman-in-Green interrupted, "We believe the lifepod may have been used as a, well… as a sort of *missile* to break through the canopy, before returning to the cargo bay."

"You're suggesting that Khemie took a joyride?"

"We found no genetic evidence that anyone else has been in or out of that cargo bay for weeks," said the Woman-in-Green, "except for the two of you."

"Well, that's hardly a likely scenario, is it?" said Fawn.

"No," said the Senior Administrator's voice, with an authority and a finality that invited no further debate. "Which leads us to the quite distressing conclusion that Emissary Hoult was, for reasons unknown, the instigator of his own death."

Isole had been crying quietly for some time, but the Senior Administrator's words triggered a distinct uptick in the volume and animation of her lament. She sobbed. She wailed. She punched a wall which was, at this point, not suspected of any wrongdoing in the matter.

"My husband would never have killed himself! Not on purpose. Not as part of some… some… *hapless joyride.*"

Percival considered consoling Isole. He wasn't a monster. "You don't have any kind of security footage of the cargo bay? Sensor logs perhaps? This used to be a starship, after all."

"No," said the Woman-in-Green. "The old sensors haven't worked in centuries, and we've never had cause to place security equipment on the outer structure."

"Your ship doesn't have sensors—" began Fawn.

Percival cut them off in a burst of enthusiasm, "but there's another ship parked in orbit that probably has gobs of data to share with us!"

"I'm sorry," Executive Director Shing apologized over radio link, "but the sensor logs contain no relevant data to share with you. Our scanners were trained outward, on the orbit path ahead of us, and on the cloud layer directly below us."

Fawn nudged Percival. Twice.

"Well, thank you for checking, Captain Shing." Nudge. "Executive Director Shing."

"You're welcome," said Shing. "Please tell me if you need anything else."

Percival assured him that he would. "I really don't like that man," he told Fawn.

"We haven't hung up yet."

Percival smiled. "I may know that, and you may know that…"

"Captain Shing is also an example of someone who knows that."

"Executive Director," corrected Percival.

"I'm hanging up now," said the Executive Director. "Please know that I really am terribly sorry about Hoult."

Percival and Fawn were alone in their suite. Each more alone, perhaps, for the other's presence. Percival was energized, pacing, considering scenarios. Fawn sat in the designated reading chair and closed their eyes. Two simultaneous acts of quiet protest.

"I thought," said Fawn, "that the point of this vacation was to get away from our work. To get away from the world, literally, and to focus on each other. But you'd rather run around pretending to be a detective, wouldn't you?"

"Pretending? Do you…" Percival could hardly contain himself. "Do you not understand me at all? This is who I am, Q Fawn. To the core of my being. A righter of wrongs. A solver of mysteries! A chance to gather clues? To pursue suspects? To solve a case? Maybe," he told her, "you can't see that. You—"

"You've forgotten," said Fawn. They weren't hurt. They weren't saddened. They were past that.

"Of course not," snapped Percival. "Forgot what?"

Fawn opened their eyes. Glared at Percival. "What do I do, Gynt? What's my job?"

Percival knew this. Probably. They'd met when Fawn was on the job. They were a, um… "Are you a bureaucrat, maybe?"

Fawn stood, slowly, deliberately. They were tired. That's the truth of it. "I'm the ranking Detective Inspector of Sanctuary-8's Interprovincial Policing Agency."

"You're, um… I…" Percival offered a smirk, disarming in other circumstances. "All right, but you're not a real detective, are you?"

Fawn threw up their arms. "I'm going!"

Percival followed Fawn out the door, sputtering and stammering. "I just meant that… that…" Percival stopped at the doorway, tried to gather his thoughts, then shouted after Fawn as they disappeared around a corner, "SHERLOCK HOLMES WASN'T A... A... WHATEVER YOU JUST SAID!"

A boy walking his dog down the corridor stopped to stare at Percival.

"It's not..." Percival tried to explain. "We're fine. Fine! Everybody knows police detectives aren't really detectives."

Sometime later, Iole met Percival in Observation Lounge 34. Plush sofas looked out sideways into the murder rain. She'd cried so many rage-filled tears. It felt like the whole planet was crying with her. Like the planet Jaghrar-4 had always known, had always been crying for Khemie.

Percival, for his part, was also very sad, but this didn't seem like the time or place or audience for his grief. "This is going to sound stupid," he warned Iole, "but did your husband have any enemies?"

The very question made Iole smile. "No," she said honestly. "He was a lovely man. How could anyone hate him?"

"Family?"

Iole shook her head. "A father somewhere. I don't know much about him. Khemie called him a 'vulture capitalist' once. Not a... He said it was a metaphor. He'd be pretty old by now. They had a falling out years ago. Before Khemie moved here."

"Oh," said Percival. "I'd assume that Khemie was a descendant of the original crew."

"No. I am. I met Khemie at University. He moved here because of me. Said that's why he liked the job of emissary so much."

Percival completed her thought. "Because he felt like a guest here, too."

Percival stepped out into the cargo bay. The lifepod, still on its side, had been shoved off to one corner, and the umbrella patched with an enormous plaid square. Percival stifled a laugh. The bay floor had been wiped clean of human remains, but a dark stain of him remained.

"Did you take your own life?" Percival asked the stain. "Did you climb into our lifepod, fly it up through the canopy, around and back, land it precisely to block the door, then climb out to die in the rain?"

Percival measured the distance from the door to the stain. Fifteen paces. "And if you wanted to die, why walk to this spot? The rain would have come to you." No. It didn't make any sense.

"An accident?" Could the lifepod have taken off on its own, precisely punctured the canopy above and then come back to so precisely block the doorway? "No."

"Someone killed you," Percival concluded. "Someone used our lifepod to puncture the canopy, then landed it precisely to block the door…" Percival turned toward the entryway. He placed his hands together in front of him, and then slowly pulled them apart. "…so that when the doors opened, the rain wouldn't get into the station."

Whoever it was, thought Percival, they cared enough about the people inside the structure to block the only way back in. But then, where did they go? Who could have survived out here?

Someone in a special suit? The Senior Administrator's ghost? A giant sea monster with a grudge?

"Of course," said Percival to no one but himself. "There's a ship parked in orbit that probably has gobs of data to share with us!"

"I'm sorry," apologized Executive Director Shing over radio link, "but the sensor logs contain no relevant data to share with you. We've directed our scanners to the surface, but have found no evidence of intelligent lifeforms in the zone outside T'Laa."

"And no ghosts or giant sea monsters?"

"Not that our sensors could detect, no, although they don't seem like likely suspects either. Haven't the local authorities designated this a suicide?"

"Not yet," said Percival. He thought for a moment, then added, "I mean, not that anyone has told me. I suppose it's been a while since I checked in."

"Perhaps you should do that, Mister Gynt."

Percival nodded, then remembered it was an audio channel and said, "Of course. Although…"

"Yes?"

"Are all the other lifepods accounted for?"

"Yes."

"And you'd know if one was taken out."

"Yes."

"Can you double check for me?"

"Yes."

But Percival already knew what the Executive Director would find.

As it turned out, the Senior Administrator *had* ruled Khemie's death a suicide. "It makes little sense," his artificial voice agreed, "but nothing else makes more sense."

"I was hoping," said Percival, "that I might speak to your ghost. Before you close the door entirely."

The Senior Administrator's mask simulated a tut. "Very well," it said. "Baxter-something! Please attend to me! The brown dandy would have words with you." Percival was offended-but-resigned-to such casual racism, particularly when dealing with the mega-mega-mega-elderly.

"The ghost is here," insisted the Senior Administrator's voice. Percival wasn't sure if this ghost was real or a delusion, but he wasn't one to ignore a potential lead. "Baxter-something will answer your questions now."

However unlikely. "Do you know if Khemie was murdered?" Percival asked the room.

"He does," the Senior Administrator's voice confirmed. "Extraordinary!"

"Was he?"

"Was he what?"

"Murdered."

"Who? Emissary Hoult?"

Percival frowned. "Can the ghost hear me?"

"Yes."

"Which way is he?"

"Back towards the door," said the voice. The Senior Administrator was in that moment slowly spinning in the opposite direction. Percival turned his back on him and towards the supposed ghost.

"Who killed him?" asked Percival.

"He says he sees the letter J or K."

"Is that the murderer's name?"

"Or the victims."

"We know the victim's name!"

"So the ghost is correct!"

"Can you tell us anything useful?"

"He says the victim died near water."

"He died *from* water."

"So he's right again!" exclaimed the voice. "Quite remarkable. In life, I always thought him quite the dullard."

Percival took a deep, slow breath. "The man who died," he told the space before him, "he wasn't like us. He was a decent fellow. He was loved. Is there anything else you can tell me?"

Percival stared at the blank wall. He could hear the Senior Administrator's bed bounce against the wall behind him. *Give me something,* he thought. *Please.*

"He says that there are elevated levels of gravitonic particles in the cargo bay. Quite beyond what one would expect from one or even two small lifepods."

Gravitonic particles. "Thank you," said Percival. And he turned to the Senior Administrator, who was just then drifting towards the ceiling. "And thank you."

When Percival returned to the suite, Fawn was waiting for him. "Can we talk?" they asked.

The two of them sat together on the least floaty bed. Fawn held his hand. Percival thought of a quip, something funny to defuse the tension, but he kept it to himself. Realized he'd been quiet too long. Fidgeted awkwardly.

"People haven't always accepted me for who I am, Percival. For every society that embraces non-binary people like me, there are a thousand more that still treat us like liars or freaks or like we're ill."

"You know I don't care about that."

Fawn smiled faintly. "Not caring is one of your great enduring qualities, Percival Gynt."

Percival smirked. "That's a quip. I thought we weren't quipping."

"My own father threw me out of the house when I came out to him. He wanted a son, and I—"

Percival's eyes went wide. He raised a hand to silence his partner.

"No," said Fawn.

"What did you just say?"

"Don't you dare."

"Pardon?"

"Don't you dare turn my childhood trauma into one of those cliché detective eureka moments!"

Percival let out a short laugh despite himself. "I'm sorry, Fawn. I really am, probably." He stood. "But I know who killed Khemie. I've known for a while. And I know how. And I'm pretty sure I can figure out why."

Percival and Fawn radioed ahead to let Executive Director Shing know they were returning, and they asked for access to the computer logs so they could verify his previous findings.

"Of course," said the Executive Director. "Anything to help bring some closure to these poor people."

When the couple landed, Executive Director Shing met them and they went straight to the central computer. The Executive Director reviewed the data with them, showed them where he logged and followed through on each of Percival's data requests. All the while Percival and Fawn hmmed and nodded and patted him on the back. And when he was done, Fawn punched him in the jaw and pulled their Smith & Wesson disintegrator pistol on him.

"Executive Director Shing, you're under arrest for the murder of Khemie Hoult. You have rights, which you may bing or google later. If you don't have an internet-capable device, one will be provided for you."

The Executive Director wiped blood from his lip, wavered in his footing, and pronounced a single syllable. "What?"

"Before we contacted you," Percival explained, "we contacted the Captain. Who is not you. He provided us with a complete copy of the logs thirty-five minutes ago. Which, as you know, don't match the version of the logs you just sent us."

"Someone… tampered with them?"

"Yes."

"I… I… I thought you were an idiot. I didn't take you seriously, so I never ran the checks."

"And you altered the data just now to avoid suspicion?"

"Yes."

"Then why did you delete the tractor beam data?"

"Sorry?"

"If we check the logs now, will they show that the tractor beam was engaged at the precise moment of Khemie Hoult's death?"

"Um…"

"Because we have the old logs, and they say that someone used the tractor beam to pierce T'Laa's canopy and reposition our lifepod."

"Why would I—?"

"Khemie lost track of his father a long time ago. Had no idea he'd bought an interstellar cruise line or that he's dying now or that, with Khemie gone, the entire company goes to you, *Executive* Director."

"I-I…" Executive Director Shing stammered with an equivocal shrug, "I've been framed?"

Percival sneered. "You can't fool the dead, J. K. Shing."

"The next train to arrive on Track 3 will be the 12:47 Local to Planet's Core." Percival and Fawn stood side-by-side on the crowded train platform at Lunar Colony. Percival carried most of the baggage.

"I think I'm going to leave," said Fawn. "When we get back, I'm going to move out."

"Okay," said Percival. He understood. He didn't want to feel this way anymore either. "But it was fun for a little while?"

"Parts of it? I liked hitting you in the face."

Percival smiled.

"I mean, for training purposes."

"I feel like people are always going to want to punch me in the face. I need to be ready."

"I know sometimes this is hard for you."

"Being punched?"

Fawn gestured between the two of them. "This."

"Oh."

"That's okay. You don't need to be good at this. No one's good at this."

"You seem okay at this."

"I cheat. We all cheat."

"We do?"

"Like, I'm sad right now. You're sad right now. What do we do?"

Percival glanced up and down the platform. "In public?"

"Give me a hug, stupid."

He did. He held Fawn for a minute, maybe. Thought of other people he'd lost. Thought of all the tears he'd spent, so many years before. Wondered if they were gone forever.

Fawn straightened Percival's tie. "If someone looks like they need a hug," they told him, "just give them a hug. You don't need to know why."

"Thank you," said Percival. "Thank you." Then, perhaps forgetting where they were in the conversation, he added, "Oh, hey! How did Shing know when Khemie was in the cargo bay?"

"Meredith told him. Did we not go over this? I got her to confess to everything while you were still investigating Shing."

"Meredith?"

"Are you joking right now?"

"Do I know her? Did we meet?"

"The Chief of Security?"

"Nope."

"You met her several times."

"Iole?"

"No, Iole is Iole."

"Oh. I thought maybe she had two names."

"She does. Her last name is Hoult."

"Oh. Um. So Meredith?"

"She… wore green?"

"Ohhhhhhhh! She had a name?"

"She had everyone's work schedules and access to station security. She was the one who told Shing when to strike."

"For money?"

"For money."

After that, Percival and Fawn stood awkwardly, side-by-side, until their train pulled into the station.

"Do you want the complimentary umbrella?" Percival asked as he boarded.

"No, you keep it," said Fawn. "When it rains, maybe we'll be even."

(*And a little bit in the year 20029.)

AND THE FORKING OF TIME

Morgus Grumb was, by his own estimation, a proper supervillain. Certainly he owned enough deathtraps, and his lair was inarguably subterranean. From time to time he donned a purple and gold costume of his own design and demanded that others call him "Lord Morgus." He was, to any objective observer, a lunatic and an idiot, but he was a fabulously wealthy, influential and powerful lunatic-idiot, and for that reason no one ever discouraged him from his pastimes.

The source of Morgus' wealth is an interesting digression. For generations, the Grumb family owned close to half the material wealth on Sanctuary-8, but it had long been divided (and divided and divided) between brothers and sisters, spouses and ex-spouses, first cousins and second cousins and clones-twice-removed. That was until an epically improbable but-by-all-contemporaneous-accounts completely coincidental and in no way nefarious series of deaths, disappearances, disownments, iron clad prenups and annulments, incarcerations, institutionalizations, comas, and alien abductions that consolidated the entirety of the Grumb family fortune into the hands of young Morgus, age 8.

The poor boy, who had recently lost his parents in a tragic piano accident, had no idea what to do with his newfound riches, and after a week spent gorging on every flavor of ice cream to be found in the Seven Galaxies, young Morgus abruptly went insane in the way that only an absurdly rich child can.

Monkey butler insane.

Now imagine thirty years of that.

In his wildest dreams, Morgus saw himself conquering the world or perhaps ransoming a moon or two. It was at times difficult to take such flights of fancy seriously, but planetary government and law enforcement nonetheless put contingencies in place should "Lord Morgus" ever take things too far. Or rather *contingency*, singular. And the name of that contingency was Percival Gynt.

Percival was still an accountant then, mostly, but he had a burgeoning reputation in certain elite circles as a solver-of-odd-problems and, as importantly, a charger-of-no-fees. Several ranking members of the planetary police force were particularly well-disposed towards Percival, because he'd figured out a way to make their pension reallocation scheme legal, if not precisely moral. And so it was that Percival Gynt was chosen to play the hero to Morgus' would-be supervillain.

The two were introduced by one Councilwoman Meeks at a charity ball to benefit wealthy politicians. Percival was there, ostensibly, to make sure nothing happened to invalidate the charity's tax-exempt status. And Morgus? Well, he was there to buy politicians and scheme schemes. In that first conversation, Percival taught Morgus about thought experiments. "Before you launch into some plot to poison the planet's water supply," Percival offered, "let's talk it through, and see if there are any flaws in your plan."

There were.

First, though neither Percival nor Morgus were experts on poison, the two men agreed that it must be enormously expensive to purchase a whole planet's worth and enormously dangerous to synthesize it for oneself. Second, even if such a volume of poison could be obtained or created, Morgus hadn't the facilities to store it or any appropriate method to disperse it. Finally, and most discouragingly, Morgus already owned most of the planet's water supply. He would in effect be poisoning himself. And the government would likely respond to this threat by cutting a deal with a third-party off-world water supplier. Morgus stood to lose trillions.

"Curse you!" spat Morgus. "You'll rue the day you crossed Morgus Grumb!"

Such invective did not discourage Morgus from arranging more meetings with the accountant to further discuss these thought experiments.

That was the start of it, the start of what Morgus called "The Great Rivalry" and what Percival, less prosaically, called "lunch, once a month, usually on the second Tuesday or third Wednesday, I'll have to check my schedule, and never for more than an hour, because I can't, I just can't, either at THE ACTUAL MOON, if you remembered to call ahead, or at the P.F. Chang's on Second Avenue next to DjinnShoppe, and obviously you're paying."

For Percival, the commitment was slim. Some months he forgot about their lunches all together and would thereafter endure weeks of angry-sad phone messages from Morgus till their next scheduled meet came 'round.

For Morgus, their relationship was all-consuming. Every waking hour of his day and every second of his dreams were directed to crafting new and terrifying plans to vex his rival and break his world. Femme fatales. Mercenary armies. Orbital lasers. Ninja monkey butlers.

One by one, month by month, lunch by lunch, Percival took apart Morgus' plans with an eye roll and a head shake and a cool smirk. "Not really my type." "Couldn't someone simply pay them more?" "Orbital *mirrors*, I suppose." "Are you quite sure? Then… bananas?"

And lunch by lunch, Morgus Grumb's hatred for Percival Gynt deepened and festered.

On the day of their last lunch, Percival arrived late. His presentation at AccountantCon had run over and then the Crosstown Express was rerouted to avoid the Necroblob Day Parade and also the Death to Necroblobs Day Parade. When Percival finally walked in at seventeen past the hour, Morgus was already sat at a table, sipping a glass of sparkling water, snickering quietly to himself. And he was dressed in his purple and gold supersuit.

As Percival approached, Morgus' quiet laughter exploded into a maniacal guffaw and knee slaps. Percival normally limited himself to three eye rolls per encounter with Morgus Grumb, so he fought against the impulse here. Instead, he smiled politely and said simply, "Morgus."

This did nothing to quell Morgus' mania, so Percival tried again after he sat. "*Lord Morgus*, I should say."

With great effort, Morgus bunched his mouth shut and pinned his hands under opposing arm pits. "This is the end," he said with such barely suppressed glee. "I've finally done it! I've finally found the true and proper method… of your *doom*."

And Percival might have believed him had this been the first time that Morgus had spoken those words. Instead, he took a sip of water, picked up the menu and, without looking up, said simply, "All right then. Out with it."

"Tiiime traavel," said Morgus, drawing out each syllable with an exquisite pleasure.

"I'm sorry?" Percival set down his menu. This was new.

"Time travel. A time machine. I have one."

"You have a time machine? *You* built a time machine?"

"Acquired," said Morgus. "How is not important. What is important is that it's real and it works, and in a few hours' time I will use it to travel backwards in time and strangle you in your crib."

For a brief moment, Percival was genuinely appalled, if ever so slightly proud, that Morgus had managed to construct a genuinely plausible evil scheme. Then he remembered who he was dealing with. "Yes," said Percival. "You should definitely do that."

"What?"

"You should definitely go back in time and strangle me in my crib."

"What?"

"You do understand the forking nature of time, don't you?"

"The…" Morgus scratched at his chin in the way that one does when one distinctly does *not* understand the forking nature of time.

"Of course I do, Gynt. But, um… Perhaps you might explain what that is for the… benefit of anyone who might be eavesdropping on our conversation for posterity?"

"The forking nature of time," Percival repeated. A brief and necessary stall while he struggled to recall that one article he'd read in that one dentist's office that one time. "It means that while you could theoretically travel back in time to strangle me in my crib, doing so would create an entirely new timeline, a second timeline, and I would survive unstrangled and in all other ways oblivious in this one."

"Oblivious, you say. Well, hm. Yes, of course. But what if I were to… take a picture of your strangled baby corpse and show it to you! That would at least be… somewhat traumatizing?"

"Show it to me how? You're in a separate timeline. In. The. Past."

"You simple child. Do you think I would acquire a time machine that only works once! Of course, I would return here as soon as I strangled you, so that I might mock you with my photographs of your dead baby self."

"Ah. Yes, sorry. Perhaps I wasn't clear. Traveling in time forks the timeline. *Forks.* So when you leave the second timeline and return to the present, you'll create another new timeline, a third timeline. One where I'm long dead and as such immune to mockery."

Morgus considered Percival's words carefully, even mouthing them over again quietly to himself. At first, he seemed properly downcast, and Percival felt a sense of relief. Whatever the actual rules, Percival was quite certain that Morgus-plus-time-travel equaled real danger. But then Morgus' expression brightened. "Oh, yes, I see! If you're dead in that timeline, you, my archenemy, then my plans for universal conquest shall go unimpeded there!"

"No!" said Percival, and if he'd had a rolled-up piece of newspaper just then he might have thwacked Morgus sharply on the nose. "In the third timeline, I died as a baby. That means there's another Lord Morgus who never had to deal with me, and surely he's already conquered the universe. And what do you think he'll do when an identical duplicate appears to challenge him?"

"Then I… Um… I'll go back in time and strangle *him* in the crib!"

"Fourth timeline!"

"And then return to the present—"

"Fifth timeline!"

"—and take over!"

"Except this timeline forked off the original well before you killed me, so I'm alive again and you've been dead for decades. That means no fortune, no subterranean lair, no deathtraps. In this fifth timeline you've created for yourself, I'm back and you're *poor*, Lord Morgus."

Morgus was rendered dumb. Dumber' than usual. His jaw was slack. His eyes teared. He'd been so sure of himself. That he finally had the upper hand. That this was his moment. He'd acquired a time machine. *A time machine*. And still. All the riches in the world and Morgus could never shake that feeling of helplessness. Looking up. Seeing the piano coming. Trying to shout, but no words came. Daddy. *Mommy*.

"Maybe," he whispered. "Maybe I could take the time machine back just the once and tell myself not to… acquire it."

Percival felt a strange pang in his gut, what he believed ordinary people called sympathy or pity. He rested a hand on his foe's shoulder. And he said the only words that came to mind. "Not unless you want to be trapped in an alternate timeline with another you who thinks you're a bit of a nag."

When a man is stripped of his last shred of dignity, all that's left to him is indignity. Morgus knew his role in this universe. He gathered himself with one deep breath, then stood abruptly, angrily, knocking his chair to the floor as he did. He hurled his water glass across the room and as the glass shattered and startled patrons shrieked, he practically growled his final words to Percival Gynt.

"I shall go now," Lord Morgus proclaimed, his lip drawn into a churlish snarl. "But know that you have not heard the last from—"

That lunch was the last that Percival Gynt heard from Morgus Grumb. A week later, in apparent disregard for Percival's counsel, Morgus stepped into his machine and vanished from the timeline. And that would have been the end of the story, if ours was the first and only timeline.

But it isn't, so it's not.

Fourteen years and some months passed before Percival Gynt had cause to think of Morgus Grumb again. There was a vagrant panhandling outside of DjinnShoppe, and Percival felt compelled to stop and offer him a small credit transfer. It was not until he'd drawn the Apple Watch from his left jacket pocket that Percival recognized, or thought he recognized, the man.

"Oh, it's you," said Percival.

"No. No, it's not," said the other, eyes downcast, with a bit of a twitchy headshake.

"You're not you?"

"No," said the other. "I'm someone else."

"You're someone who's not you?"

"Um…"

"Oh yes," said Percival. "I'd recognize that confusion anywhere. You're Morgus Grunge, all right."

"Grumb!"

Percival laughed. "He admits it!"

"Blast! Yes, all right then. I'm a Grumb," the other at last admitted, "whoever he might be to you. But not *that* Grumb. I'm another, different Grumb."

"Nonsense," said Percival. "All the other Grumbs are dead. Famously dead."

"Not another member of the Grumb family. I'm another Morgus Grumb. An earlier Morgus Grumb, from a previous timeline."

"You're—?"

The other Morgus' eyes darted up and down the street and seeing that the two of them were in that moment alone, he smirked. "Are you familiar with the forking theory of time travel?"

Percival slowly nodded his head to indicate that he was.

"This timeline is but one fork in a vast design. And it exists only because of my actions."

This was easily the most interesting thing that anyone had said to Percival that week, and it was already Friday. Percival quickly negotiated to pay this other Morgus seventy-four-point-nil-two credits for his story. That was enough for a pterodactyl with broccoli and a ginger beer at P.F. Chang's plus a three-hour Efreet rental from DjinnShoppe. Once the transfer cleared, Other Morgus told Percival his story eagerly. Of how he grew up poor. Of how his titanic genius was never appreciated in his own time. Of how he had to scrape and scrounge for decades to build his greatest invention.

"A time machine," said Percival. To which Other Morgus frowned. Of course he was talking about the time machine.

If untold riches were all he sought, Other Morgus could have sold his invention to an interplanetary conglomerate. But he didn't simply want to change his life. He wanted to change his past. He wanted to erase and overwrite a lifetime of struggles and setbacks and desperation. So he travelled back in time and he—

"It was you! *You* were responsible for all of those deaths and comas and, and, annulments and alien abductions and such!"

Other Morgus reminded Percival that he'd paid good money to hear this story and that he should stop interrupting.

"Sorry."

Other Morgus accepted Percival's apology and—

"Sorry, one quick question and then I promise I'll let you finish. Did you drop a piano on your parents?"

Other Morgus nodded solemnly. It was the only way for the money to be truly his.

"But when you returned to the present, or should I say, arrived in this timeline…"

Other Morgus explained his mistake. He needn't have bothered. Percival had already guessed what happened next. Other Morgus arrived in this timeline not realizing that he would have a counterpart here. A version who had lived through all of Other Morgus' manipulations and inherited all that wealth. A lunatic-idiot who could not be reasoned with. Percival's Lord Morgus set his monkey butler on the time traveler, chased him off and claimed his invention as his own.

"But a week later he was gone. And you, plotting from the shadows. You're identical down to your DNA. Why didn't you simply take his place?"

But the Other Morgus had looked his counterpart in the eyes. Had seen the madness that afflicted him. "*I* did that," said Other Morgus. "I made him what he was. Poisoned him with riches, as assuredly as I poisoned my great aunt Margaret or Cousin Flergol."

"I suppose it might have been the riches," Percival conceded with a frown, "or it might have been the fact that you killed or hospitalized or institutionalized or disappeared or ruined nearly everyone he ever knew or cared about."

For a time, Other Morgus thought on Percival's words. Perhaps he was right. Perhaps it wasn't the riches that destroyed his counterpart after all. Perhaps he'd eschewed money and influence these past fourteen years for nothing. Perhaps he'd reduced himself to poverty, lived rough on these streets for nothing. Perhaps it was enough to leave someone without friend or family to drive them to madness.

"But there's you, isn't there?" asked Other Grumb. "What were you to him, then? A friend?"

"A friend?" Percival repeated. He thought back to those long-ago lunches. To Grumb's scheming and posturing. To his own headshakes and eye rolls. To the laughter, not all of it derisive. To a hand placed gently on a shoulder. "No," said Percival finally, sadly. "Never his friend. Nor yours. You'll hear the sirens, if you listen for them. The Province Police are coming for you. I think you'll find that murdering your parents is a crime in any timeline."

"You… how?"

Percival pulled his watch from his pocket and showed Other Morgus the face of it. The words "CALL TO POLICE" displayed across the screen. He'd placed the call immediately after their credit transfer. They'd heard all of it.

"I should go," said Percival as he pocketed his watch. "Some of the older officers are still quite cross about what happened to their pensions."

"You set me up? ME?" cried this Morgus Grumb like a proper supervillain. "I'm not some common killer! I FORKED THIS ENTIRE TIMELINE!"

Percival shook his head as he walked away. "No, Lord Morgus. You only forked yourself."

(*Or 14000020019, by some calendars.)

PERCIVAL GYNT
AND THE LAST PALADIN

Percival Gynt stepped out of his Individual Isolation Sphere™ a scant fourteen billion and some odd years after he stepped into it. In that time, the clock on his living room wall had advanced nearly two minutes.

He scowled. The Paladins had promised that no time would pass at all. Also, in those two minutes, someone had knocked over his tea table.

"And this," Percival observed ruefully, "is why no one trusts cosmic zealots from parallel universes."

When the Paladins first entered our reality and explained to everyone, everywhere simultaneously that they were here to protect us from demonic invasion, they were met with an intense, reflexive pan-galactic skepticism. But not from Percival Gynt. No, Percival believed the Paladins immediately. Implicitly. They had those sorts of faces, he thought. And *still* he spent the better part of that afternoon mulling whether to ignore them, in all their ineffable grace, and save the universe himself.

It was a feat he'd yet to attempt, though he had once stood on the head of an Elder God and mocked it and later burned off one of its tentacles as it tried to escape from its cosmic prison.

Unless he didn't?

But then the Haagr'thii Blood Demons arrived, just after tea, and they ate four planets. That settled Percival's internal debate right quick.

"Sometimes," he'd had to remind himself, "the story isn't about you."

He was wrong, of course, but we should all take a moment to appreciate this rare and uncharacteristic moment of humility from our so often self-satisfied protagonist.

The fact that Percival's clock, his living room, his entire apartment and all its contents save that one tea table, were still precisely where he left them suggested to Percival that the Paladins must have done as they'd promised. Mostly. Probably.

Percival parted his blinds with two fingers and peered out across Traveler's Way. Yes, yes, it was all still there. The crowded buildings. The neon lights. The over-aggressive signage. That one brick wall that a robot accountant had once thrown a puppet cop into.

Only the usual devastation.

And though the streets themselves were for that one blessed moment empty, Percival Gynt knew it couldn't last.

Percival knelt down beside his tea table. The decorative bowl that once sat on it now lay in pieces on the hardwood. The wax apples that filled the bowl lay scattered across the floor.

There was some Chinese left out on the window sill. Probably Percival's. Probably not a Paladin's or a demon's. He sniffed it, shrugged, picked out the chopsticks and took a tentative bite.

Passable.

"That's the problem with Chinese food," Percival told no one in particular. "Tastes great, but fourteen billion years later, you're hungry again."

After he'd finished the box and threw it down the kitchen disintegrator, Percival went back to the living room, stood up his tea table, and swept up the broken bowl fragments. He picked up each of the wax apples and stacked them into a neat little pyramid on the table.

"You don't know," he told no one. "Maybe apple pyramids will be the new thing."

Distantly, he could hear traffic. Life resuming. He'd check the news eventually. Not yet.

The fourteen billion years of isolation confirmed for Percival what he'd long suspected. That he didn't mind being alone. That he didn't really need other people.

There were the Zoom calls, of course. For some reason, even though the universe had shut down for fourteen billion years, the accounting firm of Henderson, Glorp & 110100 stayed open. It was nice to still have a job, Percival supposed, but also faintly ridiculous.

And there was social media. Percival wasn't one for tooting or tweeting or blooting or what have you, but every few hundred years he'd have a stray thought he wanted to share, so he'd DM his co-worker Tom. And sometimes Tom would send Percival DMs with silly made-up recipe ideas. "What about a tomato bisque," he'd muse, "but with an ostrich egg in it?" Or "How about a bread bowl, with another, smaller, different kind of bread bowl inside?" Or "What about a sandwich that's also a hat?" That sort of thing.

Tom and he hadn't really been friends before the spheres. They certainly couldn't be after. It was just a strange thing that had happened because everyone was so bored.

Time didn't really make sense inside the spheres. It was fourteen billion years-ish, officially-ish, but also they didn't age, didn't sleep in any regular pattern, and everyone's perception of time was very... *specific*.

For some, the fourteen billion years seemed like only a few days. For others, it seemed to fill lifetimes. Eventually, most brains lose the capacity to process that much time, and it just becomes a blur.

Percival was simply grateful that he remembered his own name, who he was, where he lived, his Netflix password. The longer he was out of the sphere, the clearer all of that was, and the more his time inside seemed to recede.

"That's good," he said. A lie.

He wondered if it was a Haagr'thii Blood Demon that knocked over his tea table. Had the war for all of time and space extended all the way to his living room? "And why not," he mumbled. "S'a nice enough living room."

But would a Paladin really have come here, have slain a demon, and not thought to pick up Percival's wax apples on the way out?

As it would turn out, no. Well, yes. Yes, the Paladin had come. Yes, a demon had been slain. N'koo, Scourer of Worlds. One of the worst. And, yes, the apples had been left.

But the Paladin had not. Had not left, that is.

Because the Paladin, as Percival would presently learn, was still there, still struggling to stand, shivering, bleeding, staring absently, remembering, singing softly to herself, a half-forgotten tune, thinking, thirsting, waiting, wishing, living and also dying on the floor of his shower.

"Come back to me," she sang. "Come back."

Paladins did not bleed. Well, some Paladins bled. Many Paladins bled quite a lot in the very recent past, give or take fourteen billion years. But not all. Not her. Not Doreen the Pure. When she reached twentieth level, Doreen the Pure selected a capstone ability that turned her blood into rainbows and unicorn tears.

Mostly rainbows.

And now those rainbows were spilling out of her gut, where the demon N'koo had, yes, gutted her. She was dying. Fourteen billion years spent fighting a war, fourteen billion years spent *winning* a war, and now this. She'd sensed when the others had left. That they were now gone. Even Larcroix, who was her friend and sometimes her lover, had departed this universe without checking to see if she'd made it out first.

Perhaps, Doreen the Pure thought charitably, they'd simply forgotten her. Perhaps they'd thought she'd left ahead of them. Perhaps they'd looked and looked and couldn't find her and assumed her dead. Perhaps they wept.

Or perhaps they'd found her. Broken. Imperfect. Spilling rainbows onto porcelain. And deemed her lost to this lesser world.

Perhaps.

"Excuse me," said Percival, who'd been observing Doreen the Pure for some minutes before settling on this, the least-worst moment to interject. "Excuse me," he repeated, "you seem to be having a rough go of it just now, and, sure, fair enough! You've saved the universe, and that's a bit of all right, but also this is my bathroom that you're, um, irradiating? And, well, I need to go to the loo, if you don't mind, so perhaps you could…?"

"This is your domicile?" asked Doreen the Pure. Despite her wounds, despite her tears and her disorientation and her quivering agony, her voice still sounded to a mortal's ear like cloudless sky and freshly laundered blankets. Warm. Comforting. Boundless.

Percival forgot to talk.

"Is this—?" she began again, and Percival remembered.

"Yes!" he said, and he edged forward into her violet corona. "Yes, I just came out of my sphere. Well, came out and then ate some pork fried rice. It seems to have worked. Whatever you did, not the… Not the pork fried… I mean the spheres and the fighting and the, well… The demons are gone, looks like. That's good. Mind you, my wax apples—"

"Not too close," Doreen the Pure whispered through a stabbing pain. "The violet light will drive you mad. Indigo will vanish you."

Percival took a step back. "I won't ask about the blue. Can I do something for you? I have a first aid kit in the hall. Do you need bandages? A cold compress? Or, I don't know… holy water?"

"Do you *have* holy water?"

"I have a guy. Would it help?"

"No."

"Well, then."

Doreen the Pure thought for a moment. "Bandages, I suppose. Maybe some alcohol wipes?"

Percival nodded, went, and came back with a roll of bandages, tape, and the alcohol wipes from the first aid kit and also a pair of scissors. He set all that on the floor, right at the rainbows' edge, and he backed away.

"I'm Percival, by the way," said Percival.

"I'm Doreen the Pure," said Doreen the Pure as she removed her tattered chain shirt. Then she set to disinfecting the blackened flesh around her stomach wound. Blood demon claws carry 2d4 fatal diseases. You can never be too careful.

"Did you knock over my apples?" asked Percival.

"Probably. By accident. Or the Scourge of Worlds did it. He hates apples."

"Scourge of—"

"Don't worry. I dusted him."

"Thank you for that."

"You don't need to thank me. It's my job. Or was. I'm not sure if—"

Percival grimaced as he cut the Paladin off. "I'm sorry, I really do need to use the loo. It's been a mo. Do you think you could..." Percival mimed closing the shower curtain.

"THERE'S NOT MUCH TIME!" Azagorn the Great shouted, holographically, at every sentient being in the universe.

Including babies. Not helpful.

Also, deaf people couldn't hear him.

It was a tricky thing, trying to talk to everyone, everywhere simultaneously. Azagorn's tech support monkey Clive was just relieved his universal translator app was up and running. It had crashed three times during smoke testing. And, yes, they'd hoped to have an accessibility option for the hearing impaired in time for go live, but it got descoped by senior management after a third quarter cost overrun.

Also, Azagorn the Great was in that moment being eaten by a Blood Demon, which is why the next thing he said to every sentient being in the universe was "STOP EATING ME!"

Which, without an accompanying visual, was confusing.

Between grunts and cries and his eventual death, Azagorn the Great managed to shout out the instructions for how to use the Individual Isolation Spheres that Epheris the Fleet had distributed. "STEP...

INSIDE... CLOSE... DOOR... ARGH! WHEN... LIGHT... TURNS... AAAH!!! GREEN... OPEN... DOOR!"

The Paladins had promised to freeze time while they fought the Blood Demons and the rest of the universe hid. And it basically worked. Over the course of fourteen billion years, the Paladins only lost ninety-nine seconds, and those only because Stuart the Sentinel developed a brief finger cramp twelve billion years in.

"Did everyone get in?" asked Percival, half to himself, halfway through urinating. "You couldn't have gotten everyone."

"No," said Doreen the Pure. "No, every reality where we've fought the Blood Demons, there are always a few billion who refuse to go into the spheres. They assume we're lying or wrong or that they can defeat the demons themselves because they once stood on the head of an Elder God."

"Idiots. What happens to them?"

"A lot of them get et. Some are inevitably lucky, and that makes them insufferable after. Assume the whole thing was a sham, because the war never made it to their backwater world." Doreen the Pure smoothed the tape along the edges of her bandage. "It's fine," she noted absently. "Healthy, even."

Perhaps, thought Percival. "You're a better person that I am."

"That's kind of you to say," said Doreen the Pure as she staggered to her feet, "but I'm barely a person at all anymore."

Percival wiped and flushed. "I'm not sure about that," he challenged as he washed his hands. "You seem more or less human to me. I mean, now that the entire visible spectrum isn't leaking out of your gut."

"Maybe," Doreen conceded, and she winced, felt her wound. "I'm dying. That's very human."

"Are you?" asked Percival. "I was hoping the bandage..."

"I've been cut off from my people. My power. It's fading." Doreen forced her lips into a polite smile. "I don't have much time left."

Percival frowned. "How much time?"

Doreen considered her surroundings. "Well," she said after, "I'd rather not die in the loo."

Seventy-nine zillion and some odd years earlier, when Doreen was first young and not yet a Paladin, just a girl on a world you've never heard of, in a universe you've never heard of, singing songs you've never heard of as she danced through her village and lightly disparaging the hygiene of her fellow townsfolk, she dreamed of something else. Of somewhere else. Of new realms of possibility! Of true love! Of adventure!

And then the Haagr'thii Blood Demons came and ate her world. Well, most of her world. Little bits of it survived, lightly chewed, perhaps briefly swallowed and belched out into space. Little islands of ruination and despair and indigestion.

Doreen clung to one such island, and she sang a low, lonely lament into the void. It was the Paladin Kariah who first heard her. Kariah was a warrior. Her job was to fight. To kill. Not to save. But she had excellent hearing and a love of song, and she found Doreen on her island, weeping, and she drew the singer to her breast, and she wept with her.

Once the Blood Demons were routed, the Paladin King Marja offered Doreen a place by her side. It was, in some respects, the very thing that Doreen had always wished for. The new realms of her dreams. But also her planet was dead, most of her universe was dead, and Doreen was drifting in and out of long stretches of catatonia.

It would take lifetimes for Doreen to recover, to relearn herself, to sing again. But as she looked back, eons later, that time passed with the speed of a musical montage. In the end she was a Paladin. Like Kariah. Like King Marja. Doreen was tasked to save, though forced too often to fight and kill. Which was not, as Doreen would quickly learn, at all the thing she'd wished for.

She rose in level rapidly at first, gaining new powers as she gained experience. The others loved her. She had her choice of partners. Lacroix was kind. Patient. Deaf. "I'm sure you have a lovely voice," he would say to her in signs, "but you'll just have to accept that I love different things about you."

"What then?" she would ask him.

"That you don't hesitate," he would answer, "when it's time to kill. To destroy evil. Your clarity is pure."

Doreen the Pure did not always like Lacroix. But she loved him. And she was sad, now, to think that she would never hold him again. Would never leave this new and disappointing realm, this universe of ours.

It made her want to sing again. A showstopper.

Come back to me.

Percival and Doreen sat together on his couch and watched an episode of *Stranger Things*. It was from one of the later all-CGI seasons. 942, maybe? A lot happened in the 1980s.

Percival was trying to pay attention to the plot. Something about Ronald Reagan and a talking car that was also an obscure *Dungeons & Dragons* reference. But he couldn't quite get his mind off the interdimensional war that had nearly destroyed his entire universe and also upset his tea table.

He paused the TV and turned to Doreen and asked her, "Where did they come from?"

Doreen was still weak, exhausted, and hadn't seen much sci-fi. "Indiana?" she answered tentatively.

"I mean the Blood Demons."

"Oh. Hell."

"Do you mean, um…" Percival wasn't sure if Doreen was answering him or swearing at him. "…a Hell *dimension?*"

"No, Percival. From Actual Hell."

Percival frowned. "Hell is real? My friend Grieg says there's no such thing."

"And if you'd asked me yesterday," Doreen smiled, "I'd have told you there was no such thing as a Grieg. We learn, Percival."

Percival wasn't sure what any of that meant. *If* it meant anything. But he couldn't deny that she had come from somewhere. That her demons had come from somewhere.

"Also," she asked, "can you hit play? I want to know if Eleven and

George Bush find the Apparatus of Kwalish before the Russians."

At the back of his wardrobe, Percival found an old Henderson, Glorp & 11010 Summer Picnic t-shirt. He'd only worn it once, at the picnic, and only because it was required. He'd looked ridiculous, he thought. Felt ridiculous.

And, of course, all his co-workers found his discomfort hilarious.

The Monday following, he wore a three-piece suit with cufflinks and a diamond tie-pin. They also thought that was funny. Percival didn't care.

He wasn't sure why he'd kept the t-shirt. Maybe he'd be made to wear it again someday? Maybe.

There was a moment during the three-legged sack race, when he tripped over a tree root and brought down Paul with him, and he laughed. Percival, not Paul. Never Paul. It was a good laugh. Paul swore at him, and that made him laugh more. And he felt normal. Just for that moment. Normal.

And then he closed his eyes, and the wind shifted, and he remembered that when he was a boy a monster had tortured him and murdered everyone he knew and loved.

But the sack race.

Doreen the Pure wasn't modest, but she was feeling cold for the first time in lifetimes, and she pulled Percival's t-shirt on without a second thought to its backstory.

In that shirt, thought Percival, she looks normal. One costume change, and all she is is sack races. Effortless. "What was the worst of it," he asked, "for you?"

And then the wind shifted for Doreen. "All the death," she answered. "The torture. The betrayal of our principles." In her mind's eye, Doreen the Pure could still see them all. In her mind's ear, less often consulted, she could still hear them. And in her gut? "The stabbing," she conceded. "Mostly, it was the stabbing. And you?"

Percival thought back through his soup of memory. Fourteen billion years of tedium and trivialities and glib gab. But not only that. "Oh god," said Percival. He felt sick to his stomach, to his soul. How had he forgotten?

"Are you all right?" she asked him, though she knew already that he was not. She needed no special power for that.

Percival shook his head, or perhaps nodded, perhaps waved her off, then stumbled into the living room and sat. In that moment, he could only manage one word across his lips: "Tom."

Doreen the Pure got Percival a glass of water. Well, got him a glass. Then she summoned the water from... somewhere else. Heaven, maybe. And to think he offered *her* holy water. And he drank the water, and it tasted like truth and decency and also slightly like vodka. He nearly asked her if it *was* vodka, but then he remembered Tom again.

"We were on a call," said Percival, partly to Doreen the Pure but mostly to himself. The words helped him to conjure the memory, now nine billion years old. "We were days into a meeting. Weeks, maybe. Ms. Henderson wouldn't let us go until we'd each of us suggested some new operational efficiency. Fewer Zoom calls, I'd said, and fair enough, but that left one less good suggestion for the others.

"The silences were interminable. For hours at a time, none of us would even dare eye contact. Once, Paul thought to mute himself and play *Angry Birds*, except he was already on mute, unmuted himself, and for ninety-seven years he was fired. Only got his job back because of how indisputably efficient his suggestion, 'let the birds mute themselves,' was. Anyway, somewhere in the middle of all that Tom died.

"I think Mister Glorp had been talking, but then Tom's image took over the screen. He was coughing, sputtering, gasping for air, eyes red, skin pale, and his fingers. It looked like he was trying to crawl through the screen to me. Nobody knew what was happening. Maybe he'd gotten sick before isolation, and it was finally kicking in. Or he had some condition he took medication for, and the drugs were just then wearing off. For that one horrible moment, he was dying, and then he was dead. He slumped back in his seat, still perfectly framed by the sphere's meeting cam.

"And what were we supposed to do? End the call, and he was gone. We couldn't get him back. But he was dead, and we were where we were. No one could help him. So we sat, and we watched him. Too sad, too confused, too delirious to speak. For years, I think. And he, there, not aging, not decomposing. Just dead. Just *just* dead. Perpetually just dead.

"And we weren't friends. Not really. He and Mister Glorp had maybe been something more for a while. He and Midge had gone out once, I'd heard. And he and I had our DMs. But we weren't his family. Weren't the people closest to him. Didn't have a way to find those people. And there he was, just staring at us with his dead eyes.

"In the end, Ms. Henderson wouldn't let us off the call until we'd each shared one kind memory of him, bless her. All of us but Paul, indelicate Paul, who could barely say a kind word about his own mother, literally, though that's a separate story, but mercifully he was still midway through his *Angry Birds* sabbatical. Ms. Henderson offered up a knock-knock joke he'd once told her. Midge reminded us all of the time he got very angry at a haiku. Mister Glorp just cried and dripped until Ms. Henderson agreed that was enough. Compubot said filthy, filthy things. The absolute worst things you could say about a person, and we all knew they weren't true. Mister 11010 thought and processed and thought some more, but all he could think to do was underline the rest of us.

"Years later, once he was reinstated, once he'd heard the news, and had the chance to cry and swear and get himself fired and rehired a few more times, Paul told us the story of the time he'd punched Tom in the face, and Tom had laughed. 'Paul,' he said. 'You've either got to get less drunk or less angry or much, much better at punching.' And then Tom called him an Uber. Hadn't gotten a ride for him. Just called him an Uber. 'You're an Uber,' said Tom, and he laughed and laughed. And Paul tried to punch him again, but slipped and fell head first into a urinal. 'I suppose now you want me to call you an ambulance!' Tom laughed. Paul did not.

"I didn't tell them about Tom's recipes. Maybe I should have. But it felt private. They were *direct* messages, after all. For a little while, before, I'd thought maybe we were going to be friends after. Maybe we already were, and I didn't know it. When it was my turn, all I had to say was 'I underline the thing Mister 11010 said about underlining the rest of you.'

"And that was that. Ms. Henderson assigned someone to send out the meeting notes, and she booted us all from the call. We had fewer meetings after that. Shorter meetings. Sometimes they'd glitch, and Tom's screen would reconnect. It was awful. But Paul was right. Playing *Angry Birds* helped a lot. When I close my eyes sometimes, I can still see Tom's dead body. But mostly I see cartoon birds and pigs."

Percival realized he'd been talking for a long time. He half-expected the Paladin to be gone when he looked up, but there she was, standing over him, a sad smile on her lips, tears glistening down her cheeks.

"I'm sorry about your friend," she told him. Maybe she hadn't heard the part where Percival said they weren't friends. Percival had thought that was a key detail, but maybe he hadn't emphasized it properly. He thought to correct her, but then she spoke again.

"All the heartbreaking moments of our lives, all the setbacks, all the losses, all the humiliations and betrayals. Sometimes, it feels like the End of the World, yeah?"

Percival nodded. "But the world's still here."

"Not for everyone, Percival Gynt. Every day is the End of the World for someone. That day, that impossible endless day, that was Tom's End of the World. Someday, it'll be yours. Someday, it'll be mine."

"Someday?" asked Percival. "I thought you said you were dying?"

"Oh yes. I am definitely dying. So are you. So is everyone, give or take. Isn't that glorious?"

Percival wasn't sure, and he said as much.

"Maybe you're right! Maybe not. I'm quite fond of fallibility too."

Percival excused himself to make a phone call. Midge answered sleepily, said she'd already spoken to Tom's mom and arrangements were being made. "How did she take it?" asked Percival.

Midge thought before she answered. "She underlined many of our feelings about the situation."

Percival found Doreen in the kitchen. She was eating a cold can of Spaghetti-o's over the sink, giggling to herself between each bite.

"You're feeling all right now?"

She smiled a full-mouthed smile. A tiny o clung to her lip.

"What will you do next?"

Honestly, she didn't know. She gulped down the last of the pasta to buy herself a few seconds' consideration. "Enjoy life for a while, I suppose?" was the best that she could do. "Mortality, I mean? Maybe I'll dual class into bard?"

Percival didn't know what that meant, but nodded anyway. "Of course, of course."

"And you?"

Percival closed his eyes. Tried to focus on his old life. Where he'd left off. Chinese food, probably. But other thoughts, half-memories crowded his mind's eye. Of monsters and sack races. Of endless Zoom calls and disappointing apple pyramids. And this:

"I thought I might make a tomato bisque with an ostrich egg."

PERCIVAL GYNT
AND THE OTHER PERCIVAL GYNT

Percival Gynt never advertised his services. Certainly not his accounting work for Henderson, Glorp & 11010. They, of course, had their own people for that. Nor for his nascent side career as a, for lack of a proper title, volunteer-solver-of-mysteries-and-protector-of-the-innocent-and-occasional-human-punching-bag.

Perhaps it was the width of business card required that dissuaded him.

Given this fact, one can imagine Percival Gynt's surprise on opening his broadsheet edition of *The Daily Internet* one autumn morning to find the following full-page advertisement:

WHENEVER THERE'S TROUBLE,
I'M THERE ON THE DOUBLE

NO CASE TOO BIG,
NO CASE TOO SMALL

IF YOU HAVE A PROBLEM
AND NO ONE ELSE CAN HELP,
WHO YOU GONNA CALL?

PERCIVAL GYNT

CONSULTING DETECTIVE
FINDER OF LOST CHILDREN
GUARDIAN OF THE GALAXY

RATES REASONABLE

PLEASE INQUIRE AT
14 HILDEGARDE DRIVE,
APARTMENT X14

"Rates," Percival muttered with as much scorn as he could muster between sips of his Jack-O'-Lantern Latte. As if to mock him, the word danced about the page trailed by digital pink sparkles. Percival had never once charged for his services, largely on principle, but also slightly because he kept forgetting to ask. And that address? Neither his home, nor office.

No, some blackguard was doubtlessly swindling those who might turn to him for help. Trading on Percival's burgeoning good name to line their own pockets. Foolishly assuming that Percival himself would never find out, or that he would lack the steel to respond. Either way, a grave insult and one for which Percival would demand the ultimate satisfaction.

Unless…?

Percival struggled to remember whether "the ultimate satisfaction" meant being really, really satisfied or if it was always explicitly death.

"Well, perhaps just the *penultimate* satisfaction," he told himself.

Once he'd finished his latte, Percival gathered his hat and his jacket and his umbrella and his pocket watch and, from the top drawer of his dresser, his dedicated slapping glove. Before leaving his apartment, he took a long look at himself in the hallway mirror. "Yes," he said as he adjusted his tie. "You look exactly like Percival Gynt."

A better description I could not write.

Percival slipped into the apartment building at 14 Hildegarde Drive behind a pizza delivery woman. To be precise, she was delivering a package and she was made of pizza. It was five-past-eight in the morning when he knocked on the apartment door marked X14. As he waited for a response, his right hand slipped instinctively into his jacket pocket and closed around his slapping glove.

A man answered the door. Or at least that's what he seemed to be. He was easily two meters tall and broad-shouldered, but soft, rounded, smooth. He was bald. Old, maybe. There was definitely something wrong with him visually that Percival could not immediately work out. He wore bifocals on a brass chain and a pink terrycloth bathrobe. He was smiling broadly. Too broadly. And his skin. The pink of it. Too pink. Too flat. Too…?

"You're a…" Percival began, genuinely flabbergasted and now drawing from a heretofore unexpected, unexplored reservoir of prejudice. "Are you a *cartoon*?"

The other man shrugged. "On my mother's side," he admitted, still grinning. "My grandmother was a cartoon pig."

Percival wasn't sure what that meant or, if it simply meant what he said, how such a thing would be possible. I'm a racist, he thought. That's odd. But he didn't let this realization distract him from the matter at hand.

"Are you," he asked, "the man who's just today run an advert in *The Daily Internet* claiming to be Percival Gynt?"

And now the other man laughed. It was a deep, rich, joyous laughter which Percival did not appreciate in the slightest. "Not just today," said this laughing man. "I have been running adverts for a week at least! And as to claiming to be Percival Gynt? Well, that has been going on for quite a bit longer."

Percival frowned and drew his slapping glove from his pocket, and he said to the other, larger, smiling, laughing, cartoonish man, "You have wronged me, sir, and I demand the appropriate degree of satisfaction!"

But before Percival could raise his glove and slap, his enemy did something surprising. He held out his arms and he hugged Percival tight to his chest. "Did I?" he said. "Then I am deeply sorry." And he patted Percival on the back several times. "Now tell me, who are you?"

Within the larger man's arms, Percival fairly fumed. If he could have raised his striking arm just then, he would have certainly slapped this man, but both his arms were quite firmly pinned to his sides. "Who am I?" Percival shouted directly into the pink of the other man's terrycloth. "WHO AM I? 'Who are you?' is more the question! *I* am Percival Gynt! Accountant! Detective! Sort of! And you, sir, are a pretender!"

Though Percival's words were quite muffled, the other man thought perhaps he'd gotten the gist of them. He laughed again. "YOU are Percival Gynt? YOU ARE?" He released the accountant from their hug and gave him one final pat. "Do you like the tea? I shall make you the tea."

A few minutes later, Percival Gynt was sat at this man's kitchen table, sipping tea from a purple cat mug. Percival Gynt did not like tea. Or cats, you'll be sorry to hear, of any color. Or uninvited hugs. Or the other man's flat, ink-black eyes. "So, who *are* you?" Percival asked, between slow, suspicious sips.

The other man stood over him, positively gulping his tea from an oversized thermos. "Well, of course that is the root of it," he said. "I am Percival Gynt too."

"You're Percival *Gyntoo?*"

"Percival Gynt also."

Ridiculous, thought Percival, and he made a dismissive gesture to that effect.

In response, quite matter-of-factly and without any outward sign of offense, the other man took his wallet from the countertop and withdrew an identification card. Among other information, it specified "NAME: Percival Ignatius Gynt" and "SPECIES: Human (Mostly)" and "Organ Donor," the last of which is not relevant to the story at hand, but a timely reminder that we should all of us be organ donors.

The other man, the other Percival Gynt if he was to be believed, handed his identification to our Percival for inspection. Percival gave the card at best a cursory glance before slipping it into his own inside jacket pocket. "A fake," said Percival. "Clearly."

The other Percival Gynt sighed. "Long ago," he explained, "back before my family came to this planet, we were the Clan Gyntkhyb'rln'h5'w&fn****BOING!-woopwoop-fr'thng. Such a surname was considered… *unwieldy*, so it was shortened when we arrived at the induction center at Slidetown Station. I was named Percival after my grandfather, whose own father had a great love for Arthurian literature."

Percival Gynt, our Percival Gynt, considered this. Considered the possibility, however remote, that two Percival Gynts might have found their way to Sanctuary-8 in the same lifetime, lived a mere three-point-one kilometers apart in Slidetown Province, perhaps for years, and never heard as much, never encountered each other before, never been accidentally sent the other's mail or been harassed for the other's debts.

"And you're starting up some sort of detective agency?" asked Percival. It was that point of all of them that most stung his ego. That this man had set out to make a living doing what, for Percival, had never been much more than an idle hobby.

The other Percival Gynt smiled the most at this. "You know, it has been such a strange thing. Certainly, I never thought of myself as a detective. But people kept seeking me out, asking me for help. They would come straight to my door and knock. 'Are you Percival Gynt?' they would ask, and I would say, 'Indeed, I am.' And they would ask, 'Can you help me?' and I would say, 'I do not see why not.'"

"You do not see why not? YOU DO NOT SEE WHY NOT?"

"You will excuse me for saying so, but I think you are becoming ruffled."

"Ruffled? Ruffled! They were looking for ME, you idiot! You painted pile of pork! They'd heard of me, by reputation, and sought you out by accident!"

"Oh, really?" said the other Percival Gynt, genuinely amused by the prospect. "You are a professional detective?"

"Well," said our Percival. "No. But that's hardly the point. And now you're advertising your services? Charging for your services?"

"Yes, well, so many of the people who came to me offered compensation for my time. It seemed rude to decline! And I have been making a good living at it this past year, but I thought, 'Percival, if you *really* want to—'"

"YOU'VE BEEN MAKING A LIVING AT IT???"

"I quit my job at the fish market just before Christm—"

"YOU'RE A FISHMONGER???"

"Well, ex-fishmonger. I solve crimes now. Oh, and I feed the homeless on Thursdays. They do not pay me for that. But it is nice to give back."

"TO GIVE BACK?" Percival sputtered. "TO GIVE BACK? WHY DON'T YOU GIVE ME BACK MY LIFE, YOU ANIMATED BAG OF BACON?!?"

"You see? Ruffled!"

The larger Percival Gynt waited patiently for his littler counterpart to compose himself, to set down his mug and slow his breathing.

"Might I…" the larger Percival Gynt began tentatively. When he saw that he would not be challenged or otherwise interrupted, he continued, "Might I suggest that you accompany me on one of my cases. So that you might see how I operate. So you might see that I do no damage to your name. If you do not have to work?"

"IF I DO NOT HAVE TO WORK???" Of course, he had to work! It was a Tuesday. "I'll… call in sick or something," he muttered.

"Excellent," said the other Percival Gynt. "Just give me one moment to get dressed. You will be cheered to know that I do not work in terrycloth."

In retrospect, our Percival might have preferred for the other to stay in his robe, for when he returned the other Percival Gynt was wearing one of the ugliest sweaters our Percival had ever seen. It was checkered in red and purple with the words "YOU'RE A WINNER!" stitched across it in orange. And he wore brown cargo shorts. CARGO SHORTS! And a pair of black loafers with white sox. And a black bum bag around the waist.

Because of course, thought Percival, and together the two of them journeyed out into the world.

They met with Other Percival's client at a sad little corner bistro called Hooters. It might have been owl-themed? The client was sitting when they arrived. As they approached, he stood and did a quite literal double-take. "Percival," he said sheepishly. "*Percivals* Gynt?"

"FATHER FOOM!" our Percival bellowed. Father Foom was HIS client. His friend! He'd once babysat Foom's daughter when the father was trapped in a microscopic Hell dimension. And this was how he was repaid? Or, more explicitly, how someone else who was not him was paid?

"I, um," Father Foom struggled. "There are two of you?" He pointed at Other Percival. "I thought perhaps you'd just… changed your suit?"

Percival's thoughts turned briefly to his slapping glove, then back to Foom. "You thought he was *me* in a different suit? A different suit? You thought I'd bought a suit that made me look a full head taller, three times wider, and ever so faintly like Porky Pig fathered a child with an overblown balloon?"

Father Foom grimaced at the thought. "That's rather racist, Gynt. Did the suit make you racist, too?"

"THERE. IS. NO. SUIT."

Other Percival apologized to Father Foom and calmly explained, though it really wasn't necessary by this point, that he was not our Percival Gynt in a magic suit. Furthermore, it would now be the two Percival Gynts who would take on Father Foom's case.

"Will I have to pay double then?" asked Father Foom.

"Not at all," Other Percival assured him. "The other me does not charge for his services."

After they'd sat and ate and talked for some time, our Percival was finally able to relax. He asked after Foom's daughter, who was just beginning her fourth year of schooling and learning all about partial derivatives. And Foom asked after Percival's mother. "She died horribly in a fire," Other Percival answered, quite shaken. "Some nights I still hear her squeals." By the time they were done consoling him, it seemed beside the point that he'd spoken out of turn.

As to the case, Father Foom explained that one of the youngest members of his congregation, a girl named Fizz Finch, had recently gone missing and that he suspected the girl's estranged father was responsible as he'd just escaped from space-prison.

"Any idea where we might find the father, Father?" our Percival asked.

"His old partner lives a few blocks from here. Name of Fitch. You might start there."

"Finch and Fitch…?"

"Fitch and Finch, Fetch or Filch, Fingers-for-Hire," said Foom. "There might have been a jingle? They had quite the reputation in their day."

"Well, I've never heard of them!" our Percival protested. Other Percival nodded in agreement.

Foom shrugged. "Their day was… not recent."

The two Percivals got an address for Mister Fitch from Father Foom along with pictures of both Mister Finch and his daughter Fizz. "I can see the resemblance," said Other Percival on comparing the two photographs. Finch was tall and lean and pale and wizened with wispy white hair and a mean glare, while his daughter was a gleeful, dark-skinned, curly-haired cherub of a girl.

"What resemblance?" asked our Percival.

"They both have faces to begin with!"

Mister Fitch lived over a pet supply store. Not a store that sells supplies for pets I'm sad to report, but a store for those who need a steady supply of pets for… various reasons. There was no security to speak of. You could simply walk in the front and take a staircase up to Mister Fitch's second floor apartment, which is precisely what Other Percival did. At the same time, our Percival was around back, using the hook of his umbrella to pull down the fire escape ladder.

Other Percival knocked on Mister Fitch's door, and Mister Fitch answered promptly. He was a small man, or perhaps a large gnome, with a round face and a long gray beard and a few teeth left, although not the ones you'd most want. "Can I help ye?" he asked.

Other Percival grinned and Mister Fitch grinned back at him, a properly gruesome sight. "Oh yes," the Other Percival boomed. "I am looking for a Mister Finch!"

"That ain't me," said Mister Fitch. "I'm Fitch, not Finch, not an inch but an itch that'll do in a stitch! Now if ye don't mind—"

Mister Fitch attempted to shut the door, but Other Percival stopped it with a foot. "I know who you are, Mister Fitch. It is your friend for whom I am looking."

At that exact moment, Mister Finch was scrambling out the back window. Our Percival was waiting for him on the fire escape, dedicated slapping glove in hand. By the time Mister Finch caught sight of Percival, he was already half-out the window, awkwardly straddling the sill. He froze, thought to speak, to perhaps get his hands up in front of him, but the old man was well past his prime, and Percival was fast with a slap. A palpable thwack! Mister Finch's head turned. His dentures rattled. It was by no means the ultimate satisfaction, but it was still, for Percival, a deep and profound one.

Our Percival dragged the fugitive Finch back in through the window just as Other Percival was pushing his way in the front door. Mister Fitch followed, swearing-and-occasionally-rhyming in protest. The two Percivals met in the living room.

"Well done, Percival," said our Percival to the other, and he used his fugitive-free hand to pull his watch from his pocket and place a call.

The police arrived "province promptly," which is to say sometime after their coffee break but thankfully before lunch. They knew Percival Gynt by reputation. Or rather, they knew *a* Percival Gynt. They were hazy on which one. They grudgingly gave the two of them a few minutes to question Finch, before taking him and his partner away.

"I didn't know!" was Mister Finch's rejoinder once they explained his daughter was missing. "And now I'm just as worried as you are! I broke outta prison so I could provide for little Fizzy, but I wouldn't never kidnap her. Melanie and 0101011B, they're good parents."

"Then where is she?" asked our Percival.

"There's an old dumping ground on the southern outskirts.

Changes Midden. Ya know it?"

"You mean Chang's Midden," said our Percival. "Yes, I know it."

"When she was little-little, before I got sent up, she'd sneak out there sometimes to play with Paw-Paw-Paw."

"Her… great-grandfather?" asked our Percival.

"Her imaginary three-legged dog."

Both Percivals thanked Mister Finch for his help and shook his hand and promised that they'd find his daughter and return her home safely, and then they led him out to the two province police officer who were waiting for him in the hall. They already had Mister Fitch in wrist and ankle shackles, plus something called a mouth shackle to keep him from telling them any more riddles.

"I know you two!" the senior officer exclaimed on seeing the two criminals standing side-by-side for the first time. And he sang:

If ya want whatcha want,
But it ain't for sale,
Call Fitch 'n' Finch!
They never fail!

Chang's Midden was named after the poet and activist Esmerelda Chang, who died protesting its construction. "Died," as used here, is the polite way to say that she was murdered. And "murdered," as used here, is the polite way to say that she was quite deliberately buried alive. And "buried alive," as used here, is the polite way to say that she was paved over by a 14-ton artificially intelligent mechanical behemoth called a B-24C Multi-Use Ground Roller and Surface Paver, owned and operated by one Alonzo Plantagenet Oxbridge, Esq. himself the founder, owner, and chief operating officer of A.P. Oxbridge Intergalactic Developments, whose motto was "You give us 60 seconds, we'll put a mall on it," but which might more accurately have been formulated as "You have one minute to unhandcuff yourself from that rusted-over radiator befo—Just kidding! CRUNCH!"

To properly understand the whys and wherefores of the midden's construction and Esmerelda Chang's death/murder/burial/enpavement, we must consider first the colonization of Sanctuary-8 some two generations earlier. The planet that both Percivals called home was first established as a refugee world during the Last Great Intergalactic War. Its earliest peoples were outcasts from their home planets who hoped to build a new, better, freer and more inclusive society there. They knew hatred and cruelty as they knew themselves. It was a shadow burnt onto their hearts. But when they raised their children, they raised them to forget. To know only kindness and wonderment and love and psychedelic pharmaceuticals.

And for this reason, this second generation of Eighters were altogether unprepared for the stonehearted scheming of one Alonzo Plantagenet Oxbridge. He arrived at Slidetown Province's bi-monthly community zoning board meeting without ostentation or fanfare, but with a fifteen-part PowerPoint deck that painstakingly laid out his plan to build an artisanal midden in the province's to-date unused southern outstretch. To that moment, Sanctuary-8 had no concept of money, so the Oxbridge plan proposed compensating the peoples of Slidetown with an equitable split of 142 million Hope Credits, which were individually worth precisely as much as you might surmise.

Along with money, bigotry, and Hawaiian Pizza, the founders of Sanctuary-8 had also done away with thesauruses. For this reason, and also due to the overwhelming and entirely intentional impenetrability of Oxbridge's aforementioned fifteen-part PowerPoint deck, the people of Slidetown Province did not realize until it was far, far too late that "artisanal midden" was a prosaic euphemism for "miles of space-trash."

It was Oxbridge's plan to make Sanctuary-8 the galaxy's premiere destination for waste disposal. Before setting foot on the planet, he had already signed provisional contracts with a dozen off-world corporations. His fleet of robot construction vehicles was idling in orbit. He owned the land. He had his license to begin construction. All that stood between him and a lifetime of infinite riches was a woman he'd brushed off at the zoning board hearing. An activist, like her mother before her. The one woman on Sanctuary-8 who would never forget.

Esmerelda Chang, hand-cuffed to a rusted-over radiator, singing, "*Imagine no possessions.*"

Incensed, Oxbridge took manual control of the B-24C and drove.

Oxbridge got his dumping ground, but one-by-one his corporate partners backed out of their deals. Questioning both his moral judgment and his business acumen, his board of directors forced him from the company that bore his name. And the midden for which he'd lost everything was given the name of the woman who destroyed him. Chang's Midden. The folly of a man at once great and terrible and small and, finally, forgotten.

Percival and Percival arrived at the midden on foot a few minutes before noon. The welcome sign was long ago graffitied over with the words "DEATH IS NOT ARTISINAL." Ahead of them the sun beat down on mountains and canyons of discarded trash. The smells, mercifully, were too awful, too complex, too overwhelming to even process.

Our Percival bent down to examine a broken children's toy. "I had one of these as a boy," he told Other Percival. He slipped on his slapping glove so he might touch the thing without risking an infection or a parasite.

"What is it?" Other Percival asked.

Our Percival held the thing up to the sunlight. A series of multi-colored plastic blocks, faded now and crusted in dirt, strung together along a fraying thread. "I honestly can't remember."

"This place is large," said Other Percival, "and we have much ground to cover. Should we split up?"

"No," answered our Percival. "You wanted me to observe your methods. So methodize."

As our Percival soon learned, Other Percival's method was simply to wander through the Midden in no discernible pattern and with no discernible urgency and to occasionally bellow "FIZZ!" at such volume that it could only have driven the girl further from them had she heard him. At regular intervals, our Percival attempted to suggest alternative courses of actions, but each time he was shushed by Other Percival.

"You wanted to see how I do things," he reminded him. "This is how I do."

As the last glimmers of sunlight slipped behind the trash peaks, our Percival drew out his pocket watch and swiped on its flashlight. "This isn't working," he muttered, as he peered through the gloaming.

"No?" asked Other Percival. "We have been here many hours, and I have been very loud. If the girl is here, she surely knows where to find us. She knows that we are persistent, so we must care a great deal, but we are also clumsy in our search, so likely not dangerous. Now, I will further pique her curiosity."

Before our Percival could so much as parse this logic, Other Percival let loose a prodigious three-syllable shout. "PAW! PAW! PAW!" The syllable echoed through the garbage canyons. "PAW! PAW! PAW!"

And from the distance the echo was met with a mighty howl.

Our Percival grimaced and shook his head and popped open his umbrella hastily to use as a shield. "I am *not* fighting a three-legged imaginary wolf-monster," he told Other Percival. "I'm just not."

"Of course not," Other Percival replied. "For if we fight it, it is surely not imaginary!"

Before they could see the beast, they could hear her approach. Fast. Arrhythmic. Loping ever closer. Heavy and wild, footfalls into garbage, crashing through mounds of detritus. Snarling, panting, growling, howling, spitting subhuman curses into the wind. Even before she emerged, pouncing from over the hill, our Percival judged her three times a man's size.

Or two times whatever Other Percival was.

She was a thing of primeval blackness, enormous, lupine, with blood-red eyes and gnashing teeth the color of moonlight, and she was baring down on them from overhead. There was no time to count her feet, but the two Percivals were certain there were three.

In an instant she was on top of Percival, our Percival, his umbrella halfway up her throat and buckling, spittle dripping down onto Percival's suit sleeve, breath bearing down on Percival like the Devil's own. She was every monster Percival had ever faced. She was Death.

She was Fate. The past repeating.

"PERCIVAL," shouted Percival, "DO SOMETHING!!!"

And he did. Other Percival barreled into the side of the giant wolf, if that's what she was, hoping that the beast's fundamental asymmetry might render her more-than-usually vulnerable to toppling. But her frame was dense with muscle and sinew, and Other Percival was… not that. He bounced and fell back into the dirt.

Sensing he would have to save himself, our Percival let go of his umbrella and scrambled backwards as the beast's teeth snapped shut around it. He stared into the beast's eyes and she stared back, and he thought perhaps he recognized her.

She gnawed at the umbrella and then spit it out onto the ground. The stick was bent but the triple-reinforced microweave of the canopy had held. "As I recall," the beast growled, "you are made of softer stuff."

"The Stray," whispered Percival with equal parts reverence and regret. And he aimed the beam of his watchlight into the Armageddon red of the beast's right eye. The beast recoiled, let out a high-pitched whine, turned and loped away into the night.

"Three paws," said Other Percival as he pushed himself to his feet. "I definitely counted three."

From his bum bag, Other Percival produced two protein bars. One he kept for himself, and the other he presented to our Percival. Though the label on the wrapper clearly said "lembas-flavored," a closer inspection of the ingredients confirmed that the bars contained no actual lembas.

The Percivals sat in the dirt in a circle of five green-burning flares also obtained from Other Percival's bum bag, the revelation of which had prompted our Percival to exclaim, "Perhaps I need a bag like that!" To which Other Percival had responded, "I have a spare which I would happily—" Percival was able to bring that exchange to an abrupt end with a particularly judgmental glare.

It was night now. Both men were exhausted and privately, properly terrified. "Light," our Percival had explained, "is the only thing that will keep the creature at bay." At the time, Other Percival had thought it prudent not to ask questions. But now they had the time.

"You called it *The Stray*," said Other Percival. "You recognized it, and it recognized you."

Our Percival nodded. He was not eager to share the details or the shame of his previous encounter with the Stray and her kin. "It was the night I first met Father Foom. Those things had infested his church. I'd thought we'd… *gotten* all of them, but Foom was certain one of them escaped. It's been a topic of discussion over the years."

"And how long ago was this? Long enough to be this girl's imaginary friend?"

Again, Percival nodded. "They were smaller then. More mischievous than evil. Cute, in their way."

"Do you suppose," Other Percival wondered, "that it lured you here? If it knew Fizz knew Foom. If it knew Foom knew you?"

Again, reluctantly, Percival nodded. He was clever, this other him. "It would appear," he said, "that this creature has been stalking me for some time. I apologize for involving you."

"No," corrected Other Percival. "I am sorry that I blundered into these strange matters that are so clearly beyond my agency. And I am glad that I am here for you in your hour of need."

"*Hours* of need."

"Yes, certainly."

"And I'm sorry too, by the way. I felt threatened by you. And put off by your… heritage. I can see that you're a good man."

"Well, let us be glad for that! Imagine if I were awful? It would only have fed your prejudices!"

Percival frowned. Percival was right, of course. He wondered at the root of his racism. His conviction that the other him was somehow wrong. To be so close to human, but so precisely not. It terrified Percival as much and as deeply as any three-legged hellhound ever could. And perhaps for the same reason.

The past hungers.

"How much do you know about the original Percival?" asked Other Percival, interrupting our Percival's reverie.

"You mean, how much do I know about myself?"

"From literature, the knight."

"He sought the Holy Grail, yes? But he didn't find it."

"Yes," said Other Percival. "The original Percival poem was left unfinished. In later tales, his role was usurped by Lancelot's son Galahad. He is the questing knight whose quest is passed on to others. I think about that some nights. Who will finish my quest for me? Do you ever have this thought?"

"I'm not a questing knight, Percival. I'm the opposite of that."

"Perhaps you are, and you simply do not know it yet. Tell me, how did you defeat the other creatures. The Stray's kin? You used light against them? Surrounded them and—"

"We burnt down the church."

"You… Oh."

"Yes."

"*Oh*." The other Percival Gynt couldn't help but think back to a different night. To a different fire. And her final screams, when there was nothing left of her but pain.

Our Percival averted his gaze. "Not a knight," he whispered.

If the girl was still alive, then the Stray had her. *If.* Perhaps there was some affection between the two that might compel the Stray to spare her, or perhaps the beast might deem a living child the better bait. These were dim hopes. In truth neither Percival expected to ever see Fizz Finch with his own eyes, but they would neither of them surrender the possibility.

And so they walked along the midnight path ever in the direction that they first heard the beast's howl, a lit flare in each hand. "How long will they burn?" our Percival had asked when they were still sat swapping stories. "Long enough," the other had answered. But now, hours later, neither man could help but notice a flickering.

"We could call the authorities," Other Percival suggested. "Even now. It does not have to be us alone."

Our Percival shook his head. "This is Fate. Penance."

Other Percival grinned. "For you, perhaps."

Our Percival glanced at the other and smirked. "When you steal a man's identity, you steal his debts too."

Ahead of them, a stream of waste and filth cut across the path. It was slow moving and did not appear deep, but was as foul to the eye and to the nose, and one imagined to the touch, as anything that they'd encountered in their hours of exploration. Though it was only a few short strides from bank to bank, they dared not ford it. Dared not attempt to clear it with a jump. "Left or right then?" asked our Percival, his nose and mouth pressed firmly into the elbow of his jacket sleeve.

"It makes no difference," the Stray threatened. Only as it spoke those words could the two Percivals finally distinguish the outline of the beast crouched upon the far bank. "What's meat is meat," it growled, "no matter where it goes, whether it fights or flees or glows."

Earlier that day, Other Percival had found the gnome's rhymes grating. How he wished he was dealing with that little man now.

Our Percival raised a flare in front of him and squinted through its light. "I killed your kin, and you've nursed a hatred for me ever since. I understand that. But the girl you've taken isn't a part of this. She loved you, and you should let her go."

"She will be found," said the Stray, "where this stream ends. She's locked herself in a crate on my demand, safe enough for now."

Our Percival eyed the other and offered in a low voice, "There's only one of her, and this is my mess. If you go left and I go right, the Stray will follow me and perhaps you can rescue the girl."

The Stray paced along the far bank, eager, confident, but with a hunter's patience.

"And if the girl is right and I go left?" asked Other Percival.

"We're straight to that, then? No 'Don't do it, Percival! We'll slay this beast together?'"

"If you please."

"Well, perhaps the beast will leave you alone after I'm dead. Because it senses that I don't like you very much."

"Because of the racism?"

"Yes."

Other Percival placed a hand on our Percival's shoulder and smiled.

"If your racism saves my life, I will let everyone know." And he laughed.

Across the bank, the Stray crouched and lunged and within a second she was upon them. Percival ran left. Percival ran right. His foot caught on a jut of lumber, and he tumbled forward into the dirt. Cried out in pain. His ankle was surely shattered, and he'd lost his grip on the flares. One flew into the stream and sunk straightaway beneath its putrid surface. The other fell forward, bounced, and rolled a meter, maybe two, out of his reach.

Percival cursed and scraped and dragged himself along the ground towards the green flare's light.

"You called us demons," said the Stray, her breath hot on Percival's back, "but we were only children."

"The children of demons," Percival grunted as he inched himself forward, "are demons too, Stray. Just as evil, just with a shorter reach and they run a bit slower. Best—" Percival grimaced through a spike of pain. Kept pulling himself towards the light. "Best time to kill them, if you think about it."

Nearly there. Nearly into the flare's emerald halo. But nearly isn't there.

The Stray reached out her front paw and batted Percival onto his back so that the accountant could look her in the eyes a final time before dying. "Last words, meat thing."

Percival smiled. He was as calm as he'd ever been. The pain in his ankle faded to nothingness. "Just five," he said.

"Five what?"

"Percival Gynt will save me."

"You will... save you?"

Other Percival Gynt was a large and ungainly man not known to exercise, not known for his feats of strength or agility, but in that moment he positively bolted down the path, a trail of cartoon dust following in his wake. He lunged through the air, and he fell upon the Stray with twin flares driving into her pitch-black coat like daggers. The beast rose up onto her back legs and howled in pain, thinking perhaps to shake this other, larger, leaping Percival Gynt off of her, but the Fishmonger dug in, drove the two flares further into the beast's unholy hide and he bellowed, "I DO NOT SEE WHY NOT!"

Our Percival fumbled for his pocket watch and aimed its flashlight beam as well as he could at the beast's head. But the creature's eyes were turned towards another. "Look at me!" Percival shouted. "NOT HIM! LOOK AT ME!"

The Stray threw herself backwards, bringing her full weight down onto the interloping Percival Gynt. What might have crushed and killed another man, a man of less interesting lineage, merely knocked this Percival Gynt flat. Figuratively flat and just a *little* literally flat. It was enough to leave him breathless. Stunned. But this was no victory for the beast. The force of impact drove Other Percival's two flares deeper into the Stray's back, a forearm's length at least. She could feel herself liquifying from the inside out. Incensed, she rolled off Other Percival, turned, and chomped the mostly-man clean in half.

His bum-bag slid off into the dirt.

Hollowed out and still deteriorating, the Stray collapsed on top of her victim and his flares as she slowly melted away into a black mist.

What was left of the other Percival Gynt let out a low moan.

"How—?" asked our Percival before discarding the sentence as unimportant. He crawled to the other's side, to what was left of his side. Top half, mostly. Blood and organs spilled out his waist. His eyes were narrowed to inky black slits. And a halo of cartoon stars circled over his head. Percival stifled a laugh, held back tears.

He took his hands in his. "You're a winner," he whispered. "It says so on your sweater."

The other nodded. "I was fortunate, I think… that I could be you… even for a little while." His voice, once bold and booming, was thin as the veil now parting before him.

"No," said Percival, our Percival. "You were better."

"You will look after my… clients?" asked the other. "No need to… seek them out. Just list your name and… address… and they will come to you. They will ask, 'Can you help me?' You will say—"

"I do not see why not."

"You could even charge them. If you like."

"If I remember."

"And the… soup kitchen?"

"On Thursdays, yes. I was going to challenge you to a duel you know."

"There is still time."

"Yes, but it'd be awfully one-sided."

"I shall consider this… your surrender."

One last joke. And with it, one last impossibly wide grin.

Percival took off his slapping glove and closed Percival's hands tight around it. One by one, the stars that circled Percival's head flickered and flitted off into the night. When the last of them was gone, Percival placed a hand over Percival's eyes. When he lifted it again, those eyes were replaced by a perfect pair of ink-black X's.

"Oh, you have *got* to be—" Percival bit his tongue and swallowed his petulance. Still racist, apparently. A little less, he hoped. He found his watch in the dirt and called the police. He called for an ambulance. Called Father Foom and asked him to call Fizz Finch's parents. All her parents.

He wrote his mother an email, apologizing for some old argument.

And he waited for death.

Sometime later, as paramedics wrapped his sprained ankle, Percival was approached by a province police officer. "The other fellow," she said, "he didn't have identification on him. You know who he was?"

"No," said Percival, with a sad, slow headshake. "Not really. But he looked exactly like Percival Gynt."

A better description I could not write.

IN THE YEAR 20017

AND THE LACK OF CLOCKS

"It began with a clock," Councilwoman Meeks explained, before pausing to reconsider her words. "Or? No. Sorry. It would be more accurate to say that it began with *no clocks*."

"No clocks," repeated Percival Gynt with the sort of bone-tired, perfunctory smile that says, "I'm starting to suspect, despite what you said on the phone, that this is not a tax emergency, that you didn't really need me to print out a blank copy of the updated 20017 Proceeds from Broker and Barter Exchange Transactions form or for me to deliver it personally, immediately, at 3:14 in the morning no less, to the Lazy Sod, that awful dive bar down the street from my apartment, and that I didn't need to rush out into the rain in my pajamas and slippers without my umbrella or even my favorite hat, twisting my bad ankle in the rush, and that absolutely, without question, I now know that, yes, yes, *yes*, I should have ordered that drink when you offered it, and probably I should have made it a double, a triple, or some other, greater multiplier." It was that sort of smile.

Councilwoman Meeks, who considered herself *but-was-in-fact-not* a keen observer of facial expressions, returned Percival's smile and continued. "One of my wealthier constituents owns an apartment building not far from here and has asked for my help with a most troubling matter. And it has come to my attention that you have a side business dealing with such things."

"Things that… don't involve clocks?"

"If you like," answered the councilwoman, who did not care for banter or late nights at dive bars or Percival Gynt or being interrupted. "Now I will tell you about one of the apartment building's tenants, one Paul Zakadian, who suffers from Irritable Bowel Syndrome."

Percival forced himself to nod politely.

"One day, while sitting on his toilet, Zakadian looked up and slightly to the left to check the time—"

"But there was no clock."

"Correct. That particular spot was where they hung their towels. But Zakadian had the distinct feeling that there had been and/or should have been a clock there. And it came again, that instinct, each time he was on the toilet. Which was often."

"Because of the IBS."

"The what?"

"Go on."

"Weeks passed. Months, perhaps. Always the same instinct. Chronic, recurring déjà vu. And finally he decided to do something about it."

"He went to see a doctor?"

"He went to a hardware store. And then to a clock store. He took down the hooks, patched the wall, put up the new clock, the one that had 'felt right' to him in the store, and the next time he had the instinct to check the time, the clock was right there, exactly where it was always supposed to be."

"That's good then?"

The councilwoman went on to explain how satisfied Paul Zakadian was with his new clock ("very") and how the same instinct drove him to make other changes to his apartment. He moved his laundry hamper a few centimeters to the left. Exchanged two paintings in the front hall. Replaced all of his red coffee mugs for blue. With each change Paul felt better. More whole.

One night, Paul's husband came home from work to find him breaking down the wall between the dining room and the kitchen with a sledgehammer. Paul explained that the kitchen was always meant to be slightly larger. His husband was furious. He didn't understand what was happening, but what could he do? When Paul put the wall back up, his husband couldn't tell the difference. Paul could.

"And that brings us to last Tuesday. Zakadian was back on the toilet, reading *The Daily Internet*, when his hand began to itch. He held it up, and he could plainly see that he had too many fingers. So he got up, flushed, and went into the kitchen to find a steak knife. He'd already cut off six of his fingers when his daughter walked in on him.

"She screamed. He looked up, startled, embarrassed, horrified, and absolutely certain he wasn't meant to have a daughter."

"Did he…?"

"Kill her?" the councilwoman clucked. "No. By all accounts he tried, but he didn't have enough fingers left to use the knife. His husband came running, wrestled him to the ground, and the daughter called Province Police. He's sitting in a jail cell at Central Precinct as we speak."

"All right," said Percival, now straightening in his seat. "You have my attention. Now tell me why we're really here."

The councilwoman leaned forward and whispered, "It's not just Zakadian." His was the most dramatic and troubling story, to be sure. But as the councilwoman told it, many of the building's other tenants had felt similar déjà vu-inspired compulsions. Now, after Paul's arrest, many tenants were threatening to break lease and move out or, worse, to involve the authorities.

"But *you're* the authorities," Percival pointed out when the councilwoman explained that part.

"Yes," said Councilwoman Meeks with the pained expression of a politician forced to tell the truth, "but I'm coming to you now as someone else. As the friend of a wealthy donor. Please, Mister Gynt, make this go away before anyone is *truly* inconvenienced."

"You mean anyone rich and influential."

"Yes," said the councilwoman. "Obviously that."

Part of Percival Gynt was rightly disgusted by the councilwoman, but that part was small and cowering behind the part of him that grinned and quipped and loved mysteries. "Can we speak to Paul Zakadian?" he asked.

"Not tonight," she said. "And we'd like this done tonight. We've gathered a cross-section of the tenants at the apartment building to talk to you. And, of course, we can wake more people up if that would be helpful."

Percival nodded. "A couple of my associates might prove useful." Then he remembered his ankle, so he added, "Also, this case can't involve jumping."

The Hartford Apartment Building was seventeen blocks from the Lazy Sod. Percival Gynt and Councilwoman Meeks took an UberMech™. They arrived at 4:07 in the morning. Percival was still wearing his pajamas.

Graiden Grieg was waiting for them at the front door. Grieg was an adjunct professor at the University of Phoenix-Cornell-Potatoes and an old friend of Percival's. They had not known each other very long. Grieg was 312 and sustained by a cocktail of exotic chemicals and regular shocks deployed by a small device grafted to his pelvis. He was considered particularly spry for a hentriacontagenarian, which is to say that he was breathing intermittently and cranky. For some reason he was wearing a lime green tuxedo, which prompted the question from Percival, "Why are you wearing a lime green tuxedo?"

"When I ring you up at 4 in the morning," Grieg croaked between coughs and shocks, "I'll ask you about your choices in fashion and lifestyle."

A fair response, thought Percival, who turned to the councilwoman and asked, "Where's the other one from my list?"

"Father Foom wasn't available. He said it was a Catholic holiday. Somewhere."

Percival frowned. Father Foom was not Catholic.

"Well," he said, "hopefully the apartment building isn't haunted. Let's go in!"

Together Percival and the councilwoman and Professor Grieg entered the apartment building. As they did Grieg whispered to Percival, "I've heard the whole story. What do *you* think is going on here? Sorcery? Prank show?"

"I think the apartment building is probably haunted."

According to the Wikipedia page that Percival pulled up on his pocket watch, the Hartford was built in 19952 by artisans displaced from Planet's Core to make way for its third Walmart. It was not, per Wikipedia, constructed atop an indigenous burial ground or hellmouth. There had not been a single reported mass-murder or mass-suicide in the building's 65-year history. The only unnaturally cold spots in the building were directly under vents, and the only cabinet drawers that opened and closed on their own were artificially intelligent SmartCabinets™. Yet everything about the events that councilwoman described screamed "haunting" to Percival.

Though he listened patiently to Percival's thoughts on the matter, Professor Grieg had another explanation, one in keeping with his particular area of academic interest. "A dimensional breach," he suggested, "may explain these different versions of reality that the tenants are perceiving."

"But would it explain the compulsion?" asked Percival.

"No."

Still the professor was not prepared to give up on his theory. He'd brought a piece of hardware from his lab that could, if calibrated properly, detect breaches and the universes that lay beyond, a large smoke-belching contraption that his UberMech pilot had helpfully wheeled into the lobby for him. Five stars. While he began the calculations necessary to run the machine, Councilwoman Meeks led Percival up to the third-floor common room to meet with the tenants.

The pair were greeted by seven anxious, miserable, sleep-deprived mostly humans. Three men, three women, and what could have only been a necroblob congealing on the futon. Councilwoman Meeks took Percival around to shake hands-or-tendrils and make introductions. As she went, she reminded each tenant that the next month's elections were absolutely optional. "And this is Percival Gynt," she added. "He's an accountant. He's going to save you."

The tenants, for the most part, appeared skeptical. The necroblob did not, but it bubbled slightly, which might have meant something similar. When introductions were done, everyone sat. Except for Councilwoman Meeks, who disliked gatherings and voters. She stood by the door, forced her most convincing smile (not very), and discretely booted up a game of *Frogger* on her left contact lens. By contrast Percival Gynt, who normally wore a suit and tie on the job, decided to embrace the pajamas-and-slippers-ness of the night's proceedings and gamely sat down next to, perhaps slightly in, the necroblob.

Percival thanked the tenants for coming and expressed sympathy for the strange phenomena that they were currently living through. "I've heard a good deal about Mister Zakadian's difficulties," he admitted, "and only a little of your own. I hope to remedy that imbalance now."

One by one the tenants told their stories. The first of these were very similar to Paul Zakadian's, in kind if not severity, tales of unshakeable instinct slowly giving way to inexplicable compulsion. The necroblob's story stood out as particularly disturbing, from what little Percival could understand of it, but like the others before it, it offered no new insight into what was happening at the Hartford. Not so the story of Thomas Ur-Pasca.

The man that Percival Gynt would later know as Geoffrey Ur-Pasca had not given his name when Percival and the councilwoman had done the rounds those few minutes earlier. Of all the tenants gathered that night, Ur-Pasca had seemed the most hostile to Percival and the most reluctant to talk. Percival hoped that it was not merely Ur-Pasca's appearance that he found off-putting. The man's skin was scarred and bruised, and there was something suggestive to Percival in the angles of the cuts.

Once the necroblob had finished its story and all listening had had a moment to recover their wits, Percival turned to Ur-Pasca and asked, "Those wounds on your face, were they self-inflicted?"

"They're not wounds," Ur-Pasca explained through thin scratched lips. "They're surgeries. When the doctors refused me, I taught myself, watched TikToks. Some trial and error was unavoidable. I know what I look like now, what you all must think, but the scars will heal. The swelling will go down."

"Why would you do that to yourself?"

Ur-Pasca shook his head. "You're so sure you see me, but I am not the person that you're talking to. He has a different name, a different life. I'm just trying to get back to who I was."

"And who is that?"

"Everyone here calls me Geoffrey or Geoff," answered Geoffrey Ur-Pasca, "but that's not who I am. My name is Eoman Braag. I've lived here all my life, but not one of you can see me for the man I really am."

Percival nodded, thanked Ur-Pasca politely and asked the tenants for a short break, stood, and crossed the room to Councilwoman Meeks. "What?" was the only pertinent question he could muster.

Councilwoman Meeks paused her game of *Frogger*. "I thought you might have questions about that one," Meeks whispered. "His name *is* Geoffrey Ur-Pasca. He's lived in apartment 3F for the last 14 years. Before that a man named Eoman Braag did in fact live—"

"So *this* could be our haunting then." Percival held back a grin. "The ghost of Eoman Braag…"

Councilwoman Meeks corrected him. "I said that Eoman Braag used to lived here. I didn't say he was dead."

"Pardon?"

"Eoman Braag lives in a retirement community at Planet's Core. Has for over a decade. I'm told that some of the tenants even tried to take Mister Ur-Pasca to go meet him, but he refused. Insisted it was a trick."

"Ah." Point for Grieg, thought Percival, and he called the group back together.

The next to tell her story was an older woman who had previously introduced herself to Percival as Mabel. She was quiet, small, and rather unmemorable but for the twitch of her eye and the palsy in her hands. Beyond those hands, whatever existed of her below the neck was hidden under layer after layer of gray, shapeless clothing.

"Beggin' your pardon, Mister Gynt," said Mabel. "My story's a little different than the others. Whatever's happenin' to me, it ain't so bad as all that.

"To begin with, you should know I haven't had the greatest life up till now. I got in an accident when I was pretty young. Younger than you even. Nerve damage. Went on forced disability. Had to move back in with my mum. Never made much of myself after that.

"And my mum. She was my best friend. More days that not, the walls of our apartment were the walls of our whole world. We'd play cards. Watch TV together. *Murder She Wrote* was on for an hour every night, right after dinner. We knew all the episodes so well we used to recite the characters' lines right alongside 'em.

"Anyway, she died about ten years back. No tears. It was just her time. And I went on livin' in between them four walls. Except a month ago I start seein' her again. An hour a day, right after dinner. She walks in from the back, sits down in her favorite chair, and stays there, right there, and watches *Murder She Wrote* with me. And when the hour's up, she smiles at me real pretty like she used to and gets up and walks back into the back.

"And I followed her, I did. Or tried. Every day I tried, but when I got back there, she weren't there no more. And you don't have to tell me. I know she's dead. I know it. Which makes the thing I seen a ghost or a dream or my brain goin' wrong. But I miss her so much. Even if it's just a trick, you know? It's such a nice trick. Such a lovely trick. I don't want it to go away."

By the end of Mabel's story, nearly everyone in the room was in tears or a necroblob-tear equivalent. Even Councilwoman Meeks, who had had a long fractious relationship with her own mum, was seen to shed a single, solitary tear right at the end. A car ran over her frog, and that was fine. Percival reached out a hand and patted Mabel on the shoulder. A few of the other tenants offered her hugs, which she accepted awkwardly.

After that, the last of the tenants, a young man named Dennis, was quite hesitant to follow. "Yeah, um, I guess my story's not that bad either. It's not exactly, um, sad like Mabel's. Sorry, Mabel. But it's…

complicated, I guess you'd say? I've only had the one flash in all this time, but it's just about wrecked me.

"It was almost three months ago. Just finished loading the dishwasher after breakfast when I looked up, out across the counter and into the living room, and there's a woman standing by the coffee table. The most beautiful... Not... Not...

"How do I...? When you're in love, I think maybe objective beauty goes away a little bit, and what's beautiful about your partner are just the things that make her *her*. The curve of her hip. The subtle upturn of her nose. The exact color of her eyes in sunlight. All those little specificities of her, the woman you love and who loves you.

"And this woman by the coffee table, gods she was just there for a second, but I *knew* her. Knew every inch of her, and I don't mean to be prurient. I knew other things too. Her favorite book. Her ambitions. A tune she always hummed. And laughter over burnt toast. I knew she was supposed to be with me. That she was supposed to be my wife. Supposed to already be...

"And then she was gone. From the room, she was gone. But all of it, all of her, was scorched permanently onto my brain. A figment of my imagination that I would never, never get over.

"I did try. Went to bars. Asked friends to set me up. But weeks later, that brief moment still consumed me. I barely ate. Barley slept without dreaming of that second. One lunch hour, I find myself wandering the streets like I do now, and I see her. And it's really her, and she's really real, ordering falafel from a cart. Real falafel. And I don't mean to, I don't, but I follow her seventeen blocks to an office building on the other side of town, and now I know where she works.

"And still I'm thinking maybe I've gone crazy. Every day I go back to that falafel cart, hoping to see her again, and I get that this is almost certainly not okay. But seven days later, she's back. And the Tuesday after that and then the Tuesday after that.

"She's real. The falafel's real. And I understand that I'm stalking her, but I don't know what else to do. I can't talk to her, can I? How could I explain my vision without sounding like a lunatic? Or thinking that I'm some creepy creep? Without ruining any possibility of ever being with her?

"She's supposed to be my wife. I know it. And I know exactly where to find her. But I can't... I just can't..." Dennis threw up his hands in frustration and then let out a little "argh" sound.

Percival thought for a moment. "Have you considered bumping into her while carrying a large stack of books?"

Dennis had indeed considered that, but before he had the opportunity to respond, Professor Grieg entered the room, his ancient wrinkles drawn into a particularly effecting frown. "Percival, if I might have a word."

Out in the hallway, Professor Grieg shared his findings with Percival and the councilwoman. "I found evidence of a breach," he said, but without any of the superiority or gloating that Percival had anticipated.

"But," Percival prompted.

"A breach is, as I'm sure you understand, a tear in reality that opens up a sort of portal between one universe and another. My machine detects those tears, and it's located one... Well..." Grieg pointed towards the ceiling. "...somewhere upstairs. As expected. However, what my machine was not able to detect was anything on the far side of the portal."

"The other universe?" asked Percival.

"It's not there. Or if it is, I can't detect it. As far as my machine is concerned, we're dealing with a portal to nowhere."

"And why would a portal to nowhere make you move your laundry basket slightly to the left?"

Grieg shrugged. "Boredom?"

The councilwoman, who was still thinking about her mum and had not followed much of what Professor Grieg had just said, turned to Percival and asked, "So what does this mean? Are you any closer to solving this?"

Percival thought. He narrowed his eyes and bunched up his mouth. He stretched his arms and then his back. He scratched the back of his head vigorously. At moments, he seemed poised to speak but then stopped himself. Both the professor and the councilwoman admired the transparency and authenticity of his process. Finally, after a period that seemed properly interminable, Percival strung together two words: "What if...?"

Professor Grieg and Councilwoman Meeks leaned closer.

"From the beginning, I was so certain that this was a haunting. A ghost trying to recreate the way things were when it was alive. Or the way it wished things were. But the details are too specific. Why would a ghost work so hard to convince a man that he's a retiree who lives half a world away? And also care about a woman spending family time with her dead mother? *And* also be so determined to set a man up with a woman he's never met? *And* want Zakadian to kill his daughter and chop off his own fingers? *And* that's before we get to all of those little incremental changes the tenants were making."

"That's why I suggested the breach," Professor Grieg reminded him. "Because it seemed like they were attempting to conform to some other version of reality."

"Yes. But we didn't have a theory for why one universe would attempt to impose itself on another and when we looked, we couldn't find the other universe."

"But we did find the breach itself!"

"The portal to nowhere, yes. And that certainly seems to be evidence of... something. So... So... What if we're both right?"

Grieg didn't follow.

"What if it's a dimensional breach and a haunting?"

Grieg still didn't follow.

"What if," offered Councilwoman Meeks, "it's a ghost... from a dead universe?" She paused to consider what she just said and felt quite proud of the deduction. Yes, she thought. That's surely it. Which, in that moment, made accountants and university professors seem quite beside the point.

"No," said Percival, quickly deflating the councilwoman's burgeoning satisfaction. "Not a ghost *from* a dead universe. The ghost *of* a dead universe."

"That's... That's..." Grieg sputtered. "Is that even possible?"

"Are you asking if a universe has a soul? Probably not. But I've read some theories that suggest hauntings are the result of traumatic events releasing massive amounts of psychic energy that permeate the haunted location. Now imagine that a whole universe is murdered. Imagine a release of psychic energy so massive that it—"

Grieg finished the thought for him: "That it tears a hole from one universe to another."

"What could murder a universe?" asked Councilwoman Meeks, rightly horrified by the concept that Percival and Grieg had so casually breezed by.

Percival silenced her with a gesture. "Psychic energy floods into this universe, gives people visions of the dead universe. A wife who isn't. A mother who isn't. A face in the mirror that's not your own. And the compulsion. The compulsion to remake our universe to be like it. Why?"

"It..." Grieg tried to think as hard as Percival Gynt thought. "It wants to live again?"

"But not literally. It can't literally live again. Only figuratively. And what does it mean to live again figuratively?"

Grieg threw up his hands. "I don't..."

Percival smiled. "Graiden, you're really, really old. What do you want to happen after you're gone?"

Grieg teared up and nodded, then coughed, then shook as his body was hit with a seven second electric shock, then nodded again.

"What?" asked Councilwoman Meeks. "What does he want?"

Percival Gynt hugged his old friend. "Take me to the breach," Percival whispered. "I'm going to give it what it wants."

The breach was located, as Professor Grieg's math predicted and as Percival Gynt had assumed, at the point of first contact. "Paul Zakadian's bathroom," Percival muttered. "It began with *no clocks*." He entered the room with Professor Grieg behind him. Councilwoman Meeks, despite her curiosity about what the dead universe wanted, or perhaps because of it, chose not to enter Zakadian's apartment with them.

"How do you think I make contact?" Percival asked.

"Physically, I would imagine."

Gingerly Percival Gynt removed the clock that hung from the wall beside the toilet and set it aside, and he placed the flat of his hand on the circle of plaster behind.

And he waited.

"So, um, I don't want to challenge you on your area of expertise, Professor, but…"

Grieg shrugged apologetically. "Based on my calculations, I think the breach is actually about a meter above where the clock was hanged."

Percival sighed. "I was promised there would be no jumping."

"By who?"

"A… It's not…" Percival shook his head. "Shut up. Might have… Doesn't matter. Might have been a politician."

Percival took a stiff breath, crouched, sprang into the air, and slapped the wall about a meter above where the clock had hung, then fell back down, bouncing off Professor Grieg, then the toilet, and landing on his bad foot. He cried out in pain.

"Sorry," said Grieg. "That was actually slightly too high."

Percival lay on the tile floor, writhing in pain, massaging his bad ankle, and swearing many vile things in many obscure languages including Sound-Braille and Pig-Esperanto.

"*Ifekfay*," he grumbled as he pulled himself up off the ground. Without asking permission, he scrambled up on top of his old friend, despite his cough and protests and electrical shocks. Grieg's legs faltered as Percival climbed up onto his shoulders, causing him to shift back and forth unsteadily. "I'm not sure this is—" he wheezed. But Percival was beyond caring.

As another jolt of electicity shot through both their bodies, Percival slapped the wall, just below the spot that Grieg has insisted was too high. Show me everything, he thought. And as he did, his brain unfolded into colored chimes.

And in that moment, he saw everything. If not our everything, then *an* everything. An entire universe, from birth to death. Billions of years. So much darkness. The stars, so bright and raging hot and powerful, and so pitifully small. Life. By sheer chance. Microscopic bugs in the code of reality multiply and divide themselves in increasingly complex combinations. Across a trillion, trillion worlds. The same glitches emerge. Pattern. Order. Intelligence. Science. Hopes and dreams. Poetry. Magic. Love. Jealousy and War. Disease. Despair. A dark thing, cruel and ancient, advancing through the void. Moody teenagers. Hard work. Cities. Roads. Empires. More wars. Starships. The final frontier. Walmarts. Apartment buildings. Mothers and their children. Husbands and wives. A face. A clock. The past repeats. What began in darkness ends in darkness. A final glimmer. Remember. Remember. Remember.

Percival fell. Professor Grieg lay beneath him, dead. Then another shock. Alive. Alive and laughing. Percival laughed too, for a little while.

After that the déjà vus stopped. Whatever power had been behind the compulsions was satisfied. Out of respect, Percival fought to hold on to the memories he was granted for as long as possible, but the human mind was not built to sustain such multitudes. Most of the memories, good and bad, were gone within a few hours. A few he held onto for a few days. By weeks' end, all that was left of that dead universe in Percival was the profound and abiding sense that it was once a place worth living in.

Life at the Hartford soon returned to normal. If not the old normal, then at least *a* normal. Paul Zakadian returned home, all charges dropped and most of his fingers reattached. His husband bought him a new wedding ring for a new finger that they picked out together at Walmart. His daughter wrote a song about it.

They kept the clock.

Every morning Geoffrey Ur-Pasca looked into the mirror and wept over what he had become. The wounds would heal, but into a face he did not recognize.

After weeks of tortuous internal debate, Dennis decided to buy falafel. While carrying many books. It was a story he would tell his children and his grandchildren and his greatgrandchildren, until his wife Louisa finally asked him to "Shut up already!" on the occasion of their 75th wedding anniversary.

Every weeknight after dinner, Mabel received a visitor. Her local councilwoman sat in her mum's favorite chair, and they watched *Murder She Wrote* together until they could both recite the lines from memory.

When Professor Graiden Grieg finally finally died, his young friend Percival was by his side. As the doctors switched off the last of his many, many machines, Grieg managed these final words: "It's comforting to know, isn't it? That somehow... somewhere... someone... always remembers."

Percival Gynt was unsure.

PERCIVAL GYNT WILL RETURN IN

PERCIVAL GYNT AND THE CONSPIRACY OF DAYS

IN THE YEAR
20018

PERCIVAL GYNT
AND THE VOID FAERIE EXCERPT

The officers dragged Percival out of the cruiser and into the fog. He did not protest. Torture it was then, but not to be televised. Percival did not know this place, but its purpose was plain enough to him.

This was the place that you don't come back from.

The officers led Percival through a narrow break between two of the buildings and into heavy shadow. They marched him back to the cavern wall where, after Percival's eyes adjusted to the low light, he could discern a steel door built into the stone and tagged by some vandal with the words "Vargoth Gor is not dead." Percival did not know who Gor was, but at that moment he envied him.

The owner of the outsized gun removed a gauntlet and pushed the flesh of his palm flat against the steel door. Percival heard an audible thunk from within, and the door slid open. Inside, he saw only black.

"Gimme yer hands," the fat one said, and Percival complied. The officer used a tool from his belt to unlock and remove Percival's shackles.

"Thank you," Percival muttered as he massaged his wrists, though he understood that the officer was less interested in Percival's welfare than with the safety of those shackles. They intended to leave him there, but the shackles were getting a reprieve.

"Inside," the owner of the outsized gun commanded.

Percival stepped into the black. Behind him the door slid shut. "Thunk," he whispered in time with the door's locking mechanism.

Percival closed his eyes and took a slow breath. He chose to think of this place not as a trap, but a puzzle. It was the Thursday Sudoku. Difficult, but not *very* difficult.

The air around him was cool, perhaps air-conditioned? He tapped his foot twice. The floor was hard, probably metal like the door.

He opened his eyes and turned back to the sealed door. He felt on either side for a light switch. No good. But he wasn't without light.

He reached into his jacket pocket and withdrew his Apple Watch. There was no signal, and the battery was nearly dead, but if he was lucky… Percival thought of loose change between his sofa cushions, and he smiled.

He thumbed through the menu and selected the pocket light feature. A weak beam issued from the face. It would have to do.

The wall and floor were clean and white. The ceiling was high, further than he could make out in the flickering watchlight.

He turned and ventured forward into the room, which proved to be large and essentially featureless. A dozen paces in, his eyes locked on a point in the distance. A blue glimmer in the endless dark. He approached with caution.

Nearly a hundred meters from the structure's entrance, someone had hung an old-fashioned birdcage. The cage was round and domed and made of brass, and it was covered with a hood of thin gauze that could not entirely conceal the blue glow that issued from within. With his free hand, Percival removed the hood.

Though it had wings of a sort, the creature inside the cage was no bird. It was a wretched thing, not quite a half meter tall, with a twisted spine and crooked legs that barely held its weight. Its "wings" were tattered flaps of flesh, hanging limp from its distended arms. Its face was monstrous, a great wrinkle where its eyes should be and a mouth full of thorns. The blue light shined like a sea of neon from beneath its flesh.

Percival was fascinated.

Up close and uncovered, the creature's glow was bright enough that Percival barely noticed when his own light source flickered out. He slipped the useless device back into his pocket absently without taking his eyes off the creature.

"What are you, then?" he asked, not anticipating an answer. He had a suspicion though. The thrill of life and possibility was slowly returning to him.

Percival leaned in closer to the creature and he whispered, "Percival Gynt is an accountant."

The creature did not react.

Percival leaned in still closer, and again he whispered. "Percival Gynt lives in apartment 4D at 1636 Traveler's Way in Slidetown Province on the exterior surface of a planet called Sanctuary-8."

No response.

Percival studied the sad creature. Did it even know he was there? This would be the test. He leaned as close as he possibly could to the cage, his lips nearly kissing the bars, and he whispered these seven words with solemn determination:

"Percival Gynt has never known true horror."

The creature quivered and let out a helpless wheeze. The sea beneath its skin began to churn, and the blue was swiftly blotted out by inky phosphorescent white. Percival shielded his eyes, for the light was even brighter than before. Even as he turned away, the image of the ghoulish creature was still burned into his retinas.

Thunk.

As Percival wiped the spots from his eyes, the door at the end of the room slid open. A small man entered, he of dwarven proportion, wearing a dapper suit and a sour expression. He stopped just inside the door to adjust the knot of his red power tie.

"You have a void faerie!" Percival shouted across to the small man with more than a hint of admiration.

Behind Percival the white light was fading. Behind the small man the entry door slid shut and locked.

"You know, I've never seen a void faerie before. They're a bit miraculous, aren't they?" Percival allowed his thoughts to unspool out loud in the encroaching dark. "Didn't think you could get one if you weren't a smuggler or a space pirate or a, um… I don't know… smuggler of space pirates?"

Darkness swallowed the small man as the bright white beneath the creature's skin gave way again to soft blue.

"How does the rhyme go?" Percival called into the dark. "Blue in the darkness, white when you lie, red if there's danger…"

Percival's voice trailed off. He feigned to forget the rhyme's conclusion. What sort of man was he up against? He wanted to hear the stranger say the words, to hear his tone. To glean his character. Somewhere, some distance away in the dark, the small man took his bait, finishing Percival's rhyme with grim flatness:

"…and black before you die."

Lovely, thought Percival. Bureaucrat.

The small man clapped his hands twice, and the room was full of light. From a hundred meters above, massive banks of florescent bulbs bathed the room, and finally Percival could see where he was.

He stood in the middle of an enormous underground hangar. The space was octagonal, and at every obtuse corner sat a hulking rusted machine, a relic of the planet's centuries-old tunneling fleet, each drill pointed upwards towards an open shaft.

Behind him all light was gone from the void faerie's skin, leaving it a sickly gray. It made a pathetic half-choking, half-hissing sound in Percival's general direction.

The small man approached, pulling a folded sheet of paper from his pocket as he walked. Percival slipped his hands into his trouser pockets and waited.

By the time the small man had reached Percival, he had unfolded the sheet of paper to a full A1. The small man tapped the page, then held it out at arm's length, widthwise, for Percival to see.

Percival was looking at the image of two Province Police forcing their way into an apartment in Slidetown. No, "looking" wasn't the word. He was watching them, watching them break down the door and storm inside with weapons drawn.

The flat has been upturned. Drawers have been emptied. Mirrors have been broken. Tables have been overturned. A couch has been torn apart.

The lead officer points to one door near the entrance, while he continues wordlessly towards the back. He climbs over the remains of the couch, surprisingly stealthy in his bulky red armor, and reaches a door ajar at the far end of the room.

He pushes the door open with the tip of his gun. It won't go all the way, so he slides in, gun ready.

He gasps. At the foot of the bed, blocking the door, lie the bloody remains of a human being, a woman. His head jerks up. He nearly fires. Parts of the husband lie in a pool of blood on the bed. Blood is smeared on the floor, on the walls, on the ceiling.

Across the room, the window is open wide. The officer steps cautiously over the dead and takes position by the side of the window. He counts backwards from three to calm himself. Then in one swift movement he steps out in front of the window, jerks his head and gun outside, looks down the fire escape, looks up, looks side-to-side.

The officer begins to climb outside as his partner calls out to him.

"Sir, we have a problem."

The officer climbs back in, glares at his partner.

The partner fumbles with his helmet, revealing the face of a frightened rookie. "I mean an even bigger problem." He holds up a picture in front of him, glass frame smashed:

A man and a woman and a hollow-eyed ten-year-old boy.

Percival recalled reading something about this in the morning download. He repeated the headline quietly to himself. "Man and Wife Slain, Child Abducted in Slidetown Province."

With his video complete, the small man lowered the paper.

"Did…" Percival knew what he had to ask, but he didn't want to say it, didn't even want the thought in his head. But, however reluctantly, he forced himself to form the words: "Did the woman on the platform have something to do with this?"

The small man frowned. "My name is Fred," he told Percival without answering his question. "I work for the government."

"Oh. Um." Percival thought for a moment. "Did the woman on the platform have something to do with this… Fred?"

This amused Fred mildly. He allowed the faintest twitch of a smile to half-form at the very corner of his mouth before suppressing it entirely.

"The woman on the platform was Millicent Lamb. At least, that's the name she gave to her employers. She arrived on Sanctuary-8 three weeks ago, looking for a position as an *au pair*. She had an excellent resume but passed over several enviable opportunities with wealthier families at Planet's Core to accept an opening with Martin and Joanne Cooper of 17 Fisherman's Court, Apartment 31S in Slidetown Province. The Coopers required someone to help them care for their son Kevin, a boy with special needs. Martin and Joanne Cooper, who are now dead. And Kevin, who is now missing."

"Millicent Lamb." Percival said the name to himself. It didn't sound right. "You said the boy had special needs? What sort of special needs?"

"That's classified."

Percival started to chuckle, then realized that Fred was not making a joke. "Oh, sorry."

Fred continued. "This woman who calls herself Millicent Lamb, have you ever met her before today?"

"No," Percival answered.

"And did she tell you anything about herself? About where she was headed?"

"No."

"About the boy?"

"No."

"Just stopped for a quick snog and went about her way, then?"

Percival chose to ignore Fred's cheap taunts, his whole line of questioning, and to instead test a theory of his own. "The boy in the photograph, he looked sick. Was he?"

Fred didn't answer.

"Province Police working hand-in-hand with mysterious government agents? Witness interrogations conducted in forgotten, out-of-the-way locales? Exotic supernatural creatures procured to ensure my veracity? He was more than sick, wasn't he?"

Fred didn't answer.

"I don't think you're trying to catch a killer, Agent Fred. I don't even think you're worried about the boy. You're just trying to cover up whatever it is you did to him."

Fred didn't answer.

"What did you have incubating inside of him? A new drug? A new curse or poison? What weapon did our government see fit to secret in that scared little boy?"

Fred struggled to maintain his cool. "You're off-base, Gynt," he spat. "This *isn't* about the boy."

Percival smirked. "You're lying."

And in that moment the white light of truth ignited behind Percival with all the fury of an angry god. The tiny man threw his arms up to shield his eyes. He fell to his knees, cowering from our silhouetted hero.

"All right. All right!" Fred confessed as the faelight began to fade. "We have a special interest in the boy, yes. That much is true. But it's not what you think. We were *protecting* him."

"Protecting him from what?" Percival demanded.

Fred shook his head as he pulled himself from the floor. "I don't know. It really *is* classified. But whatever the threat, it endangers us all."

"So what now?"

"We need your help," Fred muttered glumly.

Percival checked his ear for wax. "Sorry?"

"We need your help," Fred repeated with the same defeated tone.

Percival glanced behind him to the void faerie. Still gray. Maybe it was broken?

"We're running out of leads, we're running out of time, and we need your help, Percival Gynt. Will you help us?"

Percival grinned. "All you had to do was ask."

"Good. We don't have a great deal of time left to us, so I will attempt to be both thorough and succinct.

"There is a woman in my office who collects stories about you.

Some tell of the wunderkind accountant, yes. But there are *other stories* of Percival Gynt. Of how you survived the Gynt Massacre. Of the crimes of Alexander Eeps, the Christmas Machine heist, the haunting of the Hartford, and more. In short, Mister Gynt, I know who you are. I know what you're capable of. And today I need your help."

Percival nodded for Fred to continue.

"The woman who called herself Millicent Lamb is gone. She departed Lunar Colony approximately twelve minutes ago, stowed away aboard a cargo freighter headed for the Lower Rim."

"If you know where she is, why don't you—?"

"She doesn't have the boy. She may not even know where the boy is, but she's our only lead. We could capture her, interrogate her, but we can't be sure that she'll cooperate.

"But there's you. She reached out to you. By design or by coincidence, the two of you seem to have made a connection. Perhaps we can use that connection to our advantage.

"All we want to do is to make sure that the boy is safe. Our intentions are essentially honorable." Fred eyed the void faerie, perhaps afraid he might be challenged on this point. He continued, "If you can convince the girl of that, of our good intentions, then we may still be able to save the boy."

"So you want me to chase this woman down for you, and—"

"Talk to her. Convince her to turn herself in. Convince her to help us. Convince her to do the right thing."

"And if I can't?" Percival asked.

"Then an innocent boy will die. And perhaps others."

Percival thought carefully. "I have terms."

"Terms?" Fred was not prepared for a negotiation. "What terms?"

"If I do this, I do this alone." Percival was firm. "You give me a fast ship, and you send me on my way. I'll intercept the freighter and talk to the girl, and depending on what she says, I'll decide what to do next. If I sense for a moment that you're up to something underhanded, I'm done."

"No."

"Sorry?"

"No," Fred repeated. "No, we can't just give you a ship. We'll partner you with one of our men. He'll be there to assist, and to…"

"I don't need a minder," Percival insisted.

"Maybe yes, maybe no. But you're getting one nonetheless."

"Fine, but I need someone… subtle."

Fred smiled. "We have someone in mind."

"Someone subtle?"

Fred's smile broadened. He wisely refused to answer that question in the presence of the void faerie.

AND THE ABOUT THESE STORIES

For those who find such things interesting, here are some notes on the various stories in this volume and how I conceived of them.

AND THE CAUSAL FRIDAY

I nearly didn't include this story in this volume. It is, as noted upfront, a light reworking of the chapter "Casual Fridays" from my novel *Percival Gynt and the Conspiracy of Days*. In the context of *Conspiracy*, "Fridays" was always a bit of an odd duck, a digression that never deigned to justify its form or presence in the novel, the precise sort of nonsense that a better or worse writer would've cut without a second thought.

I wrote "Fridays" in Hawaii. I'd reached the point where I had too many vacation days saved up, too many hotel points accrued, and a soon-to-expire voucher from an airline that had left me sitting on the tarmac too long one Friday afternoon. Also, my passport had expired. So I flew as far away as anyone would take me and stayed as long as anyone would have me and wrote this story at least in part over breakfast at the Waikiki IHOP.

Because I'm fancy.

For those who read this story in its original context and thought,

"Seriously, what?" it's my hope that the new edition and its new placement within the larger narrative is similarly perplexing.

AND THE QUESTION OF HORSES

Early on, before I decided to include "Fridays" in this volume, "Question of Horses" was going to be the lead-off story and, as such, would have had to address the whole of the Gynt-Eeps case. It would've been called something else. I hadn't settled on a title yet. "The Fourteenth Clue" maybe? Don't count them!

Once I made the decision to include "Fridays," this story became the tale of the before and after of that first story's climactic confrontation. When looking for another element to tie everything together, I seized on the character of Compubot, who's been one of my favorite background characters in *Conspiracy of Days*, despite only managing a few brief mentions in that volume. Here, he basically took over, all but turning Percival's pursuit of Eeps into a subplot.

As Compubot would say, "I-AM-GREAT-LY-SADD-ENED-BY-THIS."

AND THE INEVITABILITY OF FIRE

Which brings us to "the Beast." I'm not sure what possessed me to create a *Choose Your Own Adventure*-style novella at the heart of this collection. Masochism, maybe?

When I began work on this collection, I'd thought I'd have it done in a few months, a year perhaps, and into the hands of readers in mid-2019. Ah, the folly of slightly more youthful middle age! In fact, this single story (if you can call it a single story) took longer to write than all the other pieces combined.

About halfway through writing it, I was diagnosed with inattentive-type ADHD, a condition I've dealt with since childhood but never had the words for. It's the reason *Conspiracy of Days* took me ten years to write. The reason writing has always been a struggle.

When I sit down at the keyboard my mind fractures. My focus shatters. I chase after half-formed thoughts. Scramble after ever diverging paths. Desperate to make sense of the disparate. To cohere sense from nonsense. In part, this story took so long to pull together because its structure is my structure, with all its faults and virtues.

Not that I'm complaining! It provided a grand canvas for all of my worst impulses: Epic silliness. Maudlin self-recriminations. Too-clever Easter eggs. And the chance to write a reader directly into the story in the most literal way possible.

Writers tell writers that to be truly successful they need to "kill their darlings." To excise their most beloved ideas, if they don't all fit together. Just once, just this one time, I was happy to be able to include it all. Every mad, contradictory impulse.

But it was a beast.

Worth mentioning, this story is the first time you get the series narrator's name along with a few other personal details. I'll leave them to you to find, but suffice it to say: This may not be the last you hear of whatever-his-name-is.

Oh! And as a pro-tip: if you'd like to read the least-apocryphal version of this story, whenever you get the chance, pick the option that ends with a 3.

AND THE VIEW FROM THE TENTH STORY

The title of this story is an in-joke. Except I'm now going to explain it to you, so I suppose that'll make it a sort of an… out-joke???

There were originally meant to be ten stories in this volume (more on that below), and this was both the tenth conceived of and, because "Inevitability" took so long, the tenth completed.

If you've read "View" already, you'll have noticed that very little happens in it. I knew that I wanted to introduce Grieg. To begin the pivot away from the accounting firm characters. To give some clarity, if not quite closure, to Percival's relationship with Midge Jha.

And I wanted to write a story with some bridge in it. This volume is dedicated to my grandmother, who died as I was finishing up *Conspiracy* and beginning to write these stories. She loved bridge and taught me how to play back when I was in high school.

I think she would have enjoyed this one.

AND THE CHRISTMAS MACHINE

Of course "Christmas Machine" is just my sad, shameless pitch to venture capitalists. For the right price, the ~~Torment Nexus~~ Christmas Machine could be a reality!

AND THE QUIET BARGAIN

I really enjoyed the movie *Black Panther*, but was disappointed that the ending devolved into a knife-fight for the crown. The structure of the movie so clearly demonstrates the absurdity of "the strongest will rule" and then it completely undoes itself for the sake of a rousing third act fight scene. I get it. I like rousing third act fight scenes too. But what I really wanted was a King who would denounce antiquated tradition and win over his people by dint of his wisdom and compassion to defeat an otherwise superior foe.

And obviously the scenario in "Quiet Bargain" isn't quite that. Percival Gynt is no T'Challa. But I wanted to explore that idea, and our own culpability.

Also, it was a chance to dig into a heretofore unexplored moment in Percival Gynt's backstory. If I ever write a Percival Gynt YA novel (say, *Percival Gynt and the Academy of Death*), you'll know it started here.

AND THE LOCKED PLANET MYSTERY

I have three things to say about this story. First, I wanted to do at least one proper mystery in a volume that was at one point intended to be an entire collection of detective stories. Second, I wanted to figure out a way to tie the Percival books together with the world of *ArchEnemies*, the graphic novel I wrote as a 20-something New Yorker. Third, I wanted to wrap up the Percival-Fawn arc.

When I was a young, single guy, I found that I was forever making plans with girlfriends that projected out well beyond the length of those relationships. "Yes, we've broken up, but also isn't it wonderful that we have tickets to this romantic couples retreat!"

In my own experience, we all have foibles that are relatively harmless when we're single that become awful and unstomachable once we're subjecting others to them daily. And either those things break you apart or the relationship helps you fix them.

Or, in Percival's case, a little bit of both.

AND THE FORKING OF TIME

"Forking" was one of the first stories I wrote for this volume. It began life as a comic strip, or the idea of one, just the central back and forth between hero and villain that forms the pivot to that final scene.

Once I decided it was going to be a Percival Gynt story, I had to figure out who the villain was going to be, and that brought me to Morgus Grumb. Who was he? *Why* was he?

Once I had the two of them together, the larger story emerged. Percival denies that it's a friendship, but I don't know. Theirs reminds me very much of my most nerdy friendships. Friendships maintained almost exclusively through hobby. Someone you play D&D with, but would never call up to go shopping. Someone you talk TV shows with at work, but would never grab a beer with. Someone you'd provide a third example to, even though you don't have a third example.

Look over there!

AND THE LAST PALADIN

As mentioned above, for the longest time I'd only intended to include ten stories in this volume. And at times even that seemed inconceivable! But then 2020 happened, an entire year of the inconceivable, and this eleventh story simply happened to me.

I was struck how so many of us have had such completely bizarre, completely traumatizing, often diametrically different experiences that year. And I wondered whether it would ever be possible to reconcile all of those experiences.

I'm still not quite sure.

AND THE OTHER PERCIVAL GYNT

As a matter of metaphor, this is the story where Percival Gynt dies so that he can finally become the hero he was always meant to be.

Also, literally that's what happens.

AND THE LACK OF CLOCKS

The final story in this volume is also the first story I wrote for it. (Excepting "Causal Friday," of course, which already existed in its original form.) And yes, the seed of it came to me while I was sitting on the toilet, pooping maybe, and thinking that there should be a clock on the wall right above the towel rack: the idea that déjà vu could become a compulsion to reclaim a reality that never was.

I didn't immediately know that this was a Percival Gynt story. At the time, I didn't even know there'd be any more Percival Gynt stories. But he wormed his way into the narrative. And then I thought, all right, maybe I'll release this one short story to promote the novel. And then the next story came to me and then the next and then the next.

A whole volume stories, as if recalled from some other universe.

AND THE ACKNOWLEDGEMENTS

Shortly after my grandmother died, I was told an unlikely story. At some point in her childhood, so goes the story, my grandmother was struck in the ear with a blackjack. Or, um, maybe she just fell over near a blackjack? I don't quite remember that part, but it's not the interesting part of the story, so I'm not going to dwell on the details.

What's interesting is that, again according to the story, forever after that my grandmother supposedly gained the ability to hear strange sounds, tonal beeps, that no one else could hear. Sounds she would go on to transcribe in a series of notebooks. Sounds that were often nonsense, but sometimes cohered into Morse code and, I swear this is the story I was told, predicted future events. The 1980s stock market crash. The death of President Kennedy, maybe.

Even now, part of you wants me to produce evidence to prove my story is true. I can't, obviously. It's not true. People don't hear weird sounds that predict the future. Probably.

My grandmother died at 97. She held on long enough to fly an airplane and ride on an elephant, to program computers with punch cards, to travel to all seven continents, to play a lot of ping pong, and to meet her great grandkid, our best kiddo Sam.

She might not have heard actual signals from, y'know, outer space or the 25ᵗʰ century or wherever, but my grandmother was definitely tuned into the future. She was and remains an inspiration. She died a few weeks before my first novel was published. I brought a pre-release copy to her hospital room that last time, but it hardly seemed important.

Thank you, Grandma, for showing me the future.

And thanks as well to my brother John, to my sister Sarah, to my mother and my late father. You'll have to buy another book to find out more about them.

Thank you again to my wife Laura, who continues to be my first and best reader. And thank you to best kiddo Sam who, since even before learning to read, has never stopped asking me when I'm going to finish "the fire book."

Now, Sam. Now is when.

And thanks to Victoria, my intrepid editor-and-mother-in-law. As always, all typos and curious grammatical choices that make it into the final, published book are my fault; not hers.

Thank you to the collective wit and wisdom and occasional rancor of the old #writingcommunity on Twitter. I'm on Bluesky now and it's never going to be quite the same, but I'm enjoying building something new.

Thanks also to my current writing group, the Inkwells, who provided absolutely zero feedback on this book, but who've helped me tremendously on other projects and who continue to inspire me and motivate me to keep writing.

And finally, big thanks to Edward Packard, the creator of the _Choose Your Own Adventure_ format, and to all the authors who've continued to work in and develop that format over the years. I've taken particular inspiration from the work of Ryan North, Jason Shiga, Dan Slott, and of course whoever wrote that one story where the guy throws a pie in a dragon's face and gets burnt to a crisp.

I swear it happened probably!

AND THE ABOUT THE AUTHOR

Drew Melbourne is the neurodivergent geek author of *ArchEnemies* (2007), *Percival Gynt and the Conspiracy of Days* (2018), this book (now), and probably other things (future).

Drew was born and raised in the Philadelphia suburbs, where he read a lot, played a lot of *Dungeons & Dragons*, and watched a lot of *Star Trek* and *Doctor Who*.

He graduated *magna cum laude* from the University of Pennsylvania with a degree in Creative Writing. If not for his ADHD, he presumably would've either majored in something more practical or written many, many more books by now.

After a couple of decades spent New Yorkering, Drew is now back in the Philly suburbs with his wife Laura, best kiddo Sam, and cats Elsa, Dancer, and (omg why am I not done listing cats?) Kitten McTalkerson.

You can find Drew online at **www.drewmelbourne.com**.

9 780999 874820